The Emperor's Bone Palace

INFERNAL WAR SAGA II

HAILEY TURNER

Cover design by James T. Egan, www.bookflydesign.com
Map by Daniels Maps: www.danielsmaps.com

Professional Beta Reading by Leslie Copeland of LesCourt Author Services.
Developmental editing by Mackenzie Walton.
Edited by One Love Editing.
Proofing by Lori Parks: lp.nerdproblems@gmail.com
Proofing by M.A. Hinkle at LesCourt Author Services

To Katia Tsvetkova.

For always being there when it mattered most.

Pray for a star to burn as a guide
Never to live, always to die
A road is a future and it carries a past
For what is burned is only ever ash

~ Guidance hymn from a Star Order prayer book

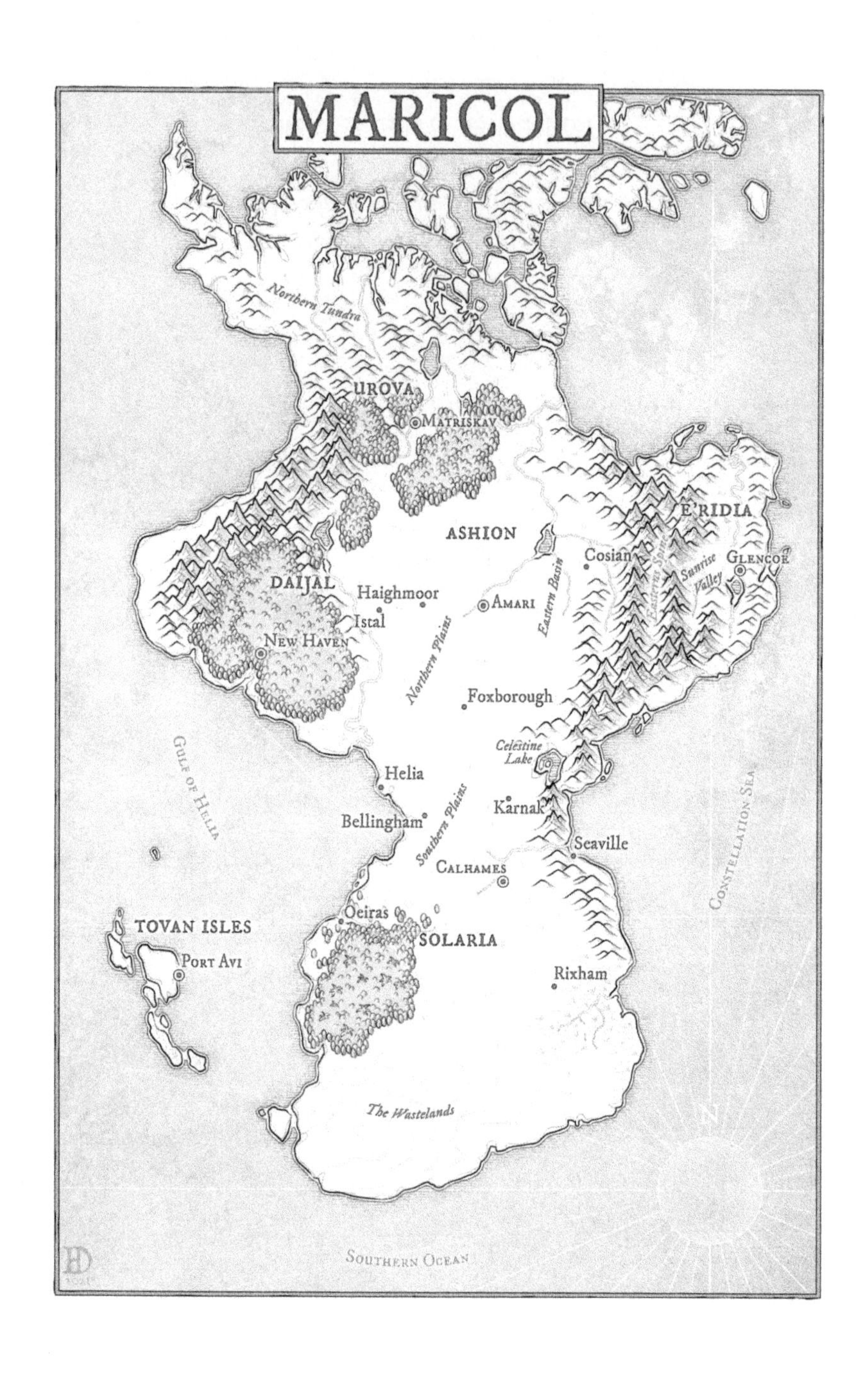
MARICOL
Northern Tundra
UROVA
MATRISKAV
ASHION
E'RIDIA
Cosian
Eastern Spine
Sunrise Valley
GLENCOE
DAIJAL
Haighmoor
AMARI
Eastern Basin
Istal
NEW HAVEN
Northern Plains
Foxborough
GULF OF HELIA
Celestine Lake
Helia
Karnak
CONSTELLATION SEA
Bellingham
Southern Plains
Seaville
CALHAMES
Oeiras
TOVAN ISLES
SOLARIA
PORT AVI
Rixham
The Wastelands
N
SOUTHERN OCEAN

Divergence

936 A.O.P.

One

VANYA

Some roads would always be lonelier than others, but they all had to be walked beneath the stars.

Emperor Vanya Sa'Liandel, of the House of Sa'Liandel, holder of the Imperial throne and ruler of Solaria, arrived back in the capital city of Calhames in the early hours before dawn three days after the *rionetka* attack in Oeiras. The trade talks with the Tovan Isles ambassador had been hastily concluded, and he'd returned by way of airship to a city he couldn't assume was safe and a palace that didn't feel like home—not without Raiah and Soren by his side.

Stalking through the low-lit corridors of the Imperial palace, Vanya made his way toward his private office in the family wing. The *praetoria* legionnaires guarding the antechamber to it made Vanya want to flinch, but an emperor never took a step back. Besides, the ones guarding *him* were at least trustworthy.

Captain Javier Molina, in charge of the *praetoria* legionnaires who'd escorted Vanya to Oeiras, planted his feet before the antechamber doors, fists on his hips. "Step forward."

The *praetoria* legionnaires standing at attention on either side of the entrance obeyed immediately, saluting the captain before bowing to the Imperial degree at Vanya's presence. The ones surrounding

Vanya kept their hands on their pistols, eyeing their fellow soldiers. If the pair on guard duty were uneasy at the distrust being shown them, they didn't acknowledge it.

"Strip off your shirts and jackets," Javier ordered.

One of the *praetoria* legionnaires seemed taken aback by the order. She hesitated a couple of seconds before obeying. In that time, Vanya noticed the way the *praetoria* legionnaires around him tightened their grips on their pistols. No weapon was unholstered, but the sentiment of being willing to shoot was there.

The pair stripped, baring their chests to Javier's critical eye. Their skin was unmarked, carrying no vivisection scars, and the *praetoria* legionnaires around Vanya relaxed ever so slightly at the proof they weren't facing off against *rionetkas*.

Javier nodded sharply. "You may dress."

While the two hastily redonned their uniforms, Vanya swept past everyone into the antechamber and headed for his private office. "Work with Alida to clear my household, the *praetoria* legionnaires on duty, and the staff."

"Yes, Your Imperial Majesty."

Such an undertaking could not be done quietly. Whatever spies from other Houses might be in the palace would be put on notice, but it couldn't be helped. Everyone who stayed within the palace walls would be required to prove they weren't a *rionetka* before sunrise. All the rest would arrive at a security check Javier would oversee until the higher-ranking *praetoria* legionnaire officers could be cleared.

If any *rionetkas* were within the palace's employ, Vanya hoped to ensnare them. It was why he hadn't formally announced his return to Calhames. The flag indicating he was in residence would not be flown over the palace until after the sun broke the horizon.

Vanya turned on the gas lamps once he entered his office, illuminating the space. The windows overlooking a narrow arcade and private inner courtyard were closed against the heat the flagstones hadn't yet given up during the night. Vanya went to crank them open, the panes folding outward to settle flat against the exterior wall.

He drew in a breath, smelling the blooming flowers spilling over the edges of the pots scattered across the tiled floor outside in the courtyard. The riot of plants had been picked out by his mother, Empress Zakariya Sa'Liandel, and Vanya's staff carefully tended the flowers she no longer got to enjoy. Oeiras had smelled of the sea, but here, in the private wing of the Imperial palace, it smelled like home.

The sound of raised voices in the antechamber caught his attention. Vanya stepped away from the window, moving to seat himself behind his wide wooden desk. Everything was exactly how he'd left it before departing for Oeiras weeks ago. His records of the newly signed treaty with the Tovan Isles would be presented to the Senate at some point, but for now, it would be delivered to the care of his chief minister.

Vanya reached for the framed tintype photograph of Raiah, her laughing face smiling up at him. He wondered where she was, if she and Soren had made it safely to Karnak yet. His televox hadn't rung since Soren had driven out of Oeiras with Raiah in his care. The worry had not and would not leave him, not until he held his daughter in his arms again and Soren was back by his side.

"I find it insulting to strip in public when not in a bathhouse, Your Imperial Majesty," Imperial General Chu Hua said irritably as she appeared in the doorway to his office.

Vanya set the tintype photograph aside. "There is a reason for that precaution."

Chu Hua bowed to the Imperial degree, her uniform back in place after being required to prove she wasn't a *rionetka* before allowed into his presence. Vanya eyed her, wondering about her loyalty after all that had happened in the last few days.

The crimson and white *effiyeh* she wore was edged in three gold lines, the mark of her high rank as the Imperial general. She'd spent the majority of her career rising through the ranks of the *praetoria*, the personal guard of the Imperial throne. She held no allegiance to any major or minor House. Her loyalty was to the Imperial throne and whoever sat upon it. The issue of the *rionetkas* was one she would find most distressing.

"You did not announce your return," Chu Hua said as she straightened up.

Vanya waved her inside. "For good reason. The assassination attempt while I was in Oeiras wasn't typical."

Chu Hua raised an eyebrow, the faint wrinkles at the corners of her eyes deepening a little. Her hair was still nearly all black, but her age could be seen in the weathered lines gracing her face and the scattered strands of silver in her hair. "I heard they breached your sleeping chambers."

"They would have killed me if Soren was not with me at the time."

Chu Hua made a soft, considering sound as she closed the door behind her before sitting. She was armed, with both a pistol and a wand, and while she was a magician, her skill with the aether did not lend itself to magic other than shielding. Vanya's attention lingered on the weapons for a second before he pushed aside his unease. If she'd had vivisection scars, the *praetoria* legionnaires would not have let her pass.

"Who were the perpetrators?"

Vanya never looked away from her face. "*Praetoria* legionnaires."

Chu Hua stiffened in her seat, something like anger flashing across her brown eyes. "That goes against the duty to the Imperial throne the *praetoria* legionnaires are expected to adhere to."

"Duty can be overridden."

"If it were bribes—"

"It wasn't." Vanya stood. "Come with me. I will show you."

Chu Hua silently followed him out of the office and through the halls of the Imperial palace. More and more people were coming awake as Javier and Alida worked to confirm the absence—or presence—of *rionetkas*.

The *praetoria* legionnaires guarding him remained those who had been with him in Oeiras. They followed Vanya and Chu Hua from the low-lit hallways of the Imperial palace to the coolness of a summer night, dawn closing in from the east.

The pathways to the private star temple on the palace grounds used by the Imperial family were lit by gas lamps. Typically guarded year-round, every hour of the day, the number of *praetoria* legionnaires on duty at the star temple had doubled since his arrival home. With them were spiderlike automatons patrolling in nonstop circles.

The reason for the heightened security lay within its walls, watched over not by a star priest but by a Legion magician, whose clarion crystal–tipped wand never left their hand.

"Your Imperial Majesty," the *praetoria* legionnaire said, coming to attention at their arrival. "Imperial General."

The trio of metal coffins taking up space near the star temple's altar were locked, though not welded shut. Each coffin carried the corpse of a *rionetka,* the rest of the bodies having been burned in Oeiras. A much smaller box sat on top of the center coffin, carrying the remains of the clockwork metal hearts that had given corrupted life to the men and women who had once served Vanya and ultimately found a different master.

Vanya gestured at the coffin on the left. "Open it."

The legionnaire kept her wand pointed at the coffin as she stepped forward, tracing the spell lines wrapped around the locks with her wand. Vanya could sense the flow of the aether through the clarion crystal, the element transmuted into magic. Her control was perfect, and the magical ties keeping the metal locks in place went dormant. The keys she carried on her hip undid the locks themselves, the sound of gears turning loud in the star temple.

It reminded Vanya of what lay below the tiled mosaic floor and the mechanism that kept the crypt sealed away from prying eyes. Tonight, they weren't there to bury the dead, merely to bear witness.

Two other *praetoria* legionnaires on duty inside the star temple stepped forward to lift the lid off the coffin. A faint hint of decay drifted up from it. Vanya didn't react, for he'd smelled worse things in his twenty-eight years of life.

Because of the way the Houses vied for power—through marriage, murder, and skirmishes along *vasilyet* borders—death was a way of life in Solaria and sanctioned by their guiding star. The Imperial family always traveled with a royal embalmer to ensure their bodies could be brought back to Calhames for proper mourning and, eventually, secret burial.

Vanya had instructed the embalmers to preserve the bodies of the *rionetkas*. They'd been stored in a massive ice box in Oeiras under heavy guard before being loaded onto the airship. They could not be stored anywhere else on the palace grounds. The dead had to be handled with care, and while Vanya doubted the *rionetkas* would rise as revenants, one could never be too careful.

Chu Hua stepped up to the coffin, nostrils flaring at the rancid smell. She gazed down at the mutilated body inside, expression unchanging. "Are these the kinds of scars you're searching for? No one has been forthcoming on that bit."

"Yes." Vanya joined her by the coffin, peering down at the body with its sunken-in chest, vivisection lines cut through cold flesh. "We found clockwork metal hearts inside each of their chest cavities."

She turned her head fractionally to look at him. "Similar to the one found in the assassin who attacked during your coronation a few years ago?"

Vanya nodded slowly. "I did not know what it meant then. I do now."

He'd allowed Soren to carry that heart back to the Warden's Island for further examination. The wardens hadn't been able to decipher the spellwork on the metal clockwork heart back then. The self-destruct spell embedded in the metal meant the devices broke apart after a certain period of time once the host was dead, whether or not magic was involved. Vanya had hoped to retain them whole, but the pieces were in the box on top of the center coffin.

What Soren had uncovered back then in that assassin's chest had been known by very few people in Solaria. Chu Hua was one of them, which was why Vanya was meeting with her here, at this hour, keeping secrets for just a little longer.

"Javier used mind magic to interrogate them before they died. Part of their memory was missing, and who they were was no longer a truth they lived. They called themselves *rionetkas*," Vanya said.

Chu Hua made a moue of distaste. "Puppets."

"Ones who were sent to kill me and take Raiah from Oeiras."

"Did they succeed?"

For all that the broadsheets had reported on his survival, Raiah's absence had been noted as well. Vanya stepped back from the coffin, nodding at the magician to close the lid and lock the dead away again. "My daughter is safe."

"But she is not with you." Chu Hua tipped her head to the side. "Neither is your warden."

Chu Hua had no vivisection scars on her chest. She belonged to no House. Her loyalty was to the throne, but that meant her loyalty could change with whoever claimed that seat of power. Vanya trusted her with Solaria's Imperial throne and his country's security, but he did not trust her with his daughter.

They were not one and the same—yet.

"Any news from Bellingham?" Vanya asked, redirecting the conversation. He'd ordered her to send a platoon of *praetoria* legionnaires to the *vasilyet* governed by the House of Kimathi under the guise of field training. He hadn't been informed of the results, too busy finalizing the trade talks and then trying to guard against the threat of *rionetkas*.

Chu Hua moved away from the coffins, clasping her hands behind her back as she turned to face him. "The House of Kimathi arrived in Calhames several days ago. As for the rest of it, do you wish to speak of such things here?"

Vanya had spent a lifetime learning how not to react to terrible news. He kept his displeasure about the House of Kimathi off his face out of habit. "Let us return to my office."

They left the star temple behind, taking the path back to the palace proper, *praetoria* legionnaires always within arm's reach. The palace was far more active now than it had been at his early arrival. He'd yet to receive an update from Javier or Alida, which made Vanya hope they would come up empty with their task of searching for *rionetkas*.

When they reached his office again, he discovered Alida waiting there, carrying a tray with a small plate of finger food and drinks. She inclined her head at his arrival. "I thought you might like some chai, Your Imperial Majesty. I oversaw the making of it myself."

"Thank you," Vanya said.

Alida set the tray on his desk and deftly poured two cups of chai before setting the teapot down and leaving, closing the door behind her. Vanya retook his seat and picked up the cup, breathing in deep the scent of spices. The drink would give him some energy for the long day ahead. What little sleep he'd had on the flight to Calhames would have to be enough when he faced the Senate and the Houses.

"What of the quarry?" he asked.

Chu Hua picked up her glass and sipped at the piping hot chai. "Burned, with nothing left except the remnants of foundations. Everything was ash. If there were survivors, which I highly doubt, they were no longer there. Odds favor the House of Kimathi taking custody of them if that were the case. I have tintype photographs for you. I will have an aide courier them over once the sun rises."

Vanya frowned, thinking of what Soren had told him days ago in Oeiras. "The entire quarry was burned?"

"According to the report flown back to me, some areas of the ground appeared melted, like a lightning strike. We've no record of a weapon that can slag land like that save starfire."

"The warden who stumbled across the quarry escaped being put into a death-defying machine by use of a bomb."

Chu Hua tapped her fingers in a slow, steady rhythm against the armrest of her chair. "I know my weapons, Your Imperial Majesty. The pictures do not show the wreckage from a bombing, but perhaps the wardens have a weapon that could scar the land so. Their alchemy is far more advanced than any country's on Maricol."

Vanya was doubtful starfire was the cause of whatever had been done at the quarry. Soren was a warden, and the wardens took in no one whose name was written down in the royal genealogies. But no evidence meant a weaker argument. The bodies in the star temple would have to be enough, along with the tintype photographs. His mother had done enough with less information than he currently had. He could only hope to emulate her.

"Recall the platoon you sent into the House of Kimathi *vasilyet*. I want them checked over for vivisection scars, but do so quietly."

Chu Hua inclined her head. "Identifying these *rionetkas* in the Legion ranks will take weeks. It will be impossible to keep secret why we are inspecting everyone, and the targets may slip away. We'll make note of any defectors and investigate accordingly."

"I plan to meet with the Senate about this threat. I need the reason behind our search to stay quiet until then. If we find any *rionetkas*, I want them taken alive if possible. The ones who attacked me had no choice in doing so. Finding out who is targeting our people for this depravity is a top priority."

Vanya had his suspicions, and judging by the look Chu Hua leveled him from across the desk, she had the same. "Do you know what magic binds them? Is the spell traceable?"

He shook his head. "No. We're still researching it."

"Then it may be prudent to install some spell-detecting security devices here in the palace. They could prove useful in specific areas." She glanced up at the ceiling before shrugging. "Here would be a good location, though I would counsel you not to inform anyone in your House or household that it is present if you agree to its placement. The less people know, the less chance of tampering."

"How would it work?"

"The device's range can be adjusted. The clarion crystals are cut in such a way so as to detect most types of spellwork. We typically set them for military spells, but we can adjust the parameters for a broader range."

"If you think it's worth doing, then make it happen. I'll block out a time to meet with you tomorrow to set everything up in here."

"At your will, Your Imperial Majesty."

They finished their chai in silence before Chu Hua left, bowing her way out of the office. In her wake, Vanya sent a prayer to the Dawn Star, hoping she would hear him. "I cannot walk this road alone, Callisto. For the good of Solaria, guide me true."

VANYA

Vanya took no meetings or audiences on the day of his return to Calhames save for one. The midmorning meal at the palace was a quiet affair, held in the private courtyard located within the family wing of the palace, and Vanya did not dine alone.

Such spaces were the center of every home in Solaria, an area where families gathered for meals and company. They could be small and intimate, or vast and elaborate, depending on the household. The courtyard where Vanya and *vezir* Amir Vikandir, of the House of Vikandir, met brimmed with well-tended ferns and small trees in various-sized ceramic pots. The fountain was a soft burble of white noise easily tuned out.

Flowering vines hanging from the balconies overlooking the courtyard provided a living curtain. When Vanya looked up, he could see the clear blue sky past five stories of the palace. Part of the courtyard was still in shade due to the position of the sun, but they could not escape the heat. It was a near-oppressive blanket that not even the mechanical fans set up nearby could fully blow away.

The spread of food on the table was heavier than the light dishes Alida had served Vanya and Chu Hua well before dawn. The lack of sleep made Vanya's eyes burn, or perhaps it was the scent of spices used in the tomato sauce and egg dish still bubbling away in the shallow iron pan that sat between himself and Amir.

The much older man's elaborate robes were at odds with the white-and-gold robes and trousers that Vanya wore. The gray and dark blues favored by the House of Vikandir were offset by silver embroidery that picked out the constellations of the star gods across his shoulders. The House of Vikandir's gold ranking medallion was pressed with the depiction of the callia wildflowers that grew in the hill country to the east. The mark of Amir's rank glittered against his chest, denoting a position he'd held for nearly half his life.

As *vezir*, one was expected to uphold their House's worth, make alliances, and evade enemies, all in pursuit of a throne and a crown and the blessing of their star god. Houses, both major and minor, sought rulership, and few would have walked away from such a private meeting with the emperor everyone hoped to one day replace.

To that end, Amir's entourage had been relegated to the public wings of the palace. The legionnaires he'd traveled with had taken up posts in the hallways beyond the courtyard, overseen by *praetoria* legionnaires. None of them had initially been granted entrance to the palace until after they'd been ordered to strip and bare their torsos for inspection.

Amir had been incensed by Vanya's demand. He seemed less disgruntled now after Vanya's explanation. The food on his plate had remained untouched since Vanya finished speaking of the assassination attempt in Oeiras. Vanya had no compunctions about serving himself another poached egg drenched in spiced tomato sauce. He tore off a piece of flatbread from the platter and dipped it into the yolk, breaking it to mix it all together.

"Do you have proof?" Amir finally asked into the silence that had settled between them in the courtyard.

"Of the *rionetkas*? I have bodies and shattered clockwork metal hearts. Javier will swear to what he found in their minds, and the high priestess can confirm his truthfulness. As to who is behind their orders?" Vanya shook his head. "That I have no proof of."

Amir's mustache twitched as his lips twisted in a grimace. "But you have your suspicions."

Vanya reached for his glass of cold red wine. "Yes."

He didn't speak Joelle's name, but there was enough bitter history tying their Houses together that he didn't need to. Amir's loyalty and that of his House was to Vanya through a past marriage and other political deals. That support was the strongest Vanya had, for he'd lost much after his mother's death. She'd held the debts owed to their House, and many had been granted to her personally. Which meant not all had transferred to Vanya after she was buried.

The lack of support from critical Houses was a weakness he'd worked hard to offset. His efforts to date had come up hard against Joelle's political pressure, a roadblock he'd not had to face head-on since Nicca's death four years ago. That had very recently changed.

"If you accuse the House of Kimathi of such atrocities against Solarian citizens without proof, you will lose the support of every House you've managed to claw back to your side," Amir warned.

Vanya arched an eyebrow. "Do you include yours in that assessment?"

"I would not be able to turn a blind eye to such an accusation."

Vanya would take that as a *yes*, which was not unexpected. Every House did what was best for their House in the fight to take control of the Imperial throne. Alliances were easily made and just as easily broken, bought and sold like how Daijal treated their debt slaves. "I hope it will not come to that."

Amir finally reached for the flatbread, tearing off a piece to dip into the food on his plate. "You are aware *vezir* Joelle and her House have returned to Calhames?"

"I am."

"And are you aware of her outreach to the Houses under the guise of opposition to your right to sit upon the Imperial throne? She still mourns her granddaughter."

Vanya nodded, the gold crown he wore not shifting with the motion. "She has always sought to turn the Houses against mine ever since Nicca's name was added to their House's memory walls. She's always blamed me for my wife's death and will not hear that I had no part in it."

At the time, he'd hoped to build a relationship with Nicca, to mirror the one his parents once had. His efforts had been futile in the face of maternal tragedy. While Nicca had died, Raiah lived, and Vanya had refused all other offers of marriage since. He would not put a target on his daughter's back and see her die before him.

"I would say it is grief that guides her, but that would be a lie. She removed Karima as her heir two years ago and tapped Artyom to inherit the House and rank of *vezir*. As far as I know, Karima still grieves the loss of her daughter," Amir said.

"And Joelle resents the loss of access to the Imperial throne."

Amir leaned back against the cushioned bench, his robe pulling tight over the bulk of his frame. "Have you thought this could have all been averted if you had granted them the right to see the Imperial princess?"

Vanya had learned young how to control his temper, but the cold anger that rose in him at Amir's words left him momentarily speechless. He swallowed a sip of wine in order to unclench his teeth. "If I had ever allowed Raiah to visit Bellingham without me, Joelle never would have given her up. I'd have been forced to set the Legion against that city to get my daughter back."

In doing so, he would have risked losing the Imperial throne and his life. The Houses had not taken kindly to the eradication of the House of Laxsom by his mother all those years ago. Neither had Zakariya been pleased to be faced with an attempt at secession. In the end, the two choices could not be reconciled, and the effects of that choice and that loss still lingered.

To follow in the footsteps of Ashion and Daijal—to allow a *vasilyet* to cleave itself into a new country—would weaken Solaria. Vanya had known that even at the age of eight, when he'd left with his mother to lay siege to a city and a House that refused to acknowledge the Imperial throne. They'd won with the backing of the other Houses, but that support from some had been reluctant.

Losing a House how they had, along with a city, was crippling in a way. Vanya still ruled in the shadow of his mother's decision, and the wardens still guarded that border, ever watchful over the hundreds of thousands of revenants that wandered that city of the dead. But his mother's way was not a road he could walk down during this fraught time.

Daijal moved on Ashion up north, intent on breaching the long border between the two countries and shattering the armistice that had been cracked from the Inferno. Vanya's spies had reported back over telegraph wires that Crown Princess Eimarille Rourke had murdered King Bernard and her husband, Crown Prince Wesley. She'd taken over the Daijal throne and had stricken her son's Iverson bloodline in the royal genealogies, replacing it with Rourke.

As the last living member of that ancient bloodline, she carried starfire in her soul the same way Vanya did—deep and powerful, the aether like a living thing at his fingertips. But Eimarille wasn't the only one up north in those two countries who could cast it. The broadsheets out of Ashion hadn't given up on reporting about Miss Caris Dhemlan, daughter of a baron and heir to an engineering company, who'd cast starfire in the midst of a revenant incursion in Amari and was now impossible to locate.

Vanya wasn't blind to the fractures up north. When their civil war had happened several centuries ago, Solaria had sent its Legion to its northern border, refusing to engage in the fighting within Ashion at the time. Somehow, Vanya didn't think staying neutral would be possible this time if war truly broke out again between Daijal and Ashion.

The northern border was already weakened in the northwest, courtesy of Joelle's governing decisions in her *vasilyet*. The poison fields had only grown in that part of the country, with revenants wandering where they shouldn't, seen in numbers that even had wardens worried about their origins. If the death-defying machine could truly raise the dead faster than spores, as Soren had suspected in his oral report to Vanya, then that was a threat every country needed to be aware of.

Who had invented the death-defying machine and who had

created the *rionetkas* were most likely one and the same. Uncovering the truth amidst political upheaval would take time—time Vanya did not have.

"Joelle is determined to meet her great-granddaughter. She will not stand down, not about this," Amir said after a moment.

Vanya dragged a piece of flatbread through the spiced tomato sauce and ate it, chasing it with a sip of wine. "I have given Joelle many opportunities over the years to let Raiah know her mother's House. Joelle has refused to set foot in Calhames or any city I visit."

"She is here now while your daughter is not."

The delicate statement was one Vanya didn't acknowledge, not right away. He tipped his head back, squinting at the blue sky overhead, listening to the servants bustling about the serving table on the other side of the courtyard. When he spoke, he kept his voice low so it wouldn't carry. "I sent her to Karnak, to your House, in the safety of someone I trust."

Amir sighed as if the answer aggrieved him, reaching for his wineglass. "Your warden."

"He's not my warden."

Amir snorted indelicately and gestured with his wineglass, nearly sloshing the drink over the rim. "You've not let a courtesan warm your bed since you buried your wife. You've had him, when you've had anyone at all."

If it were anyone else speaking so bluntly, Vanya would have them banished from his presence. But in some ways, Amir had come to inhabit the space his parents used to stand in, when Vanya came to them, wanting advice. "Does it matter who I fuck?"

"It does when people talk." Amir took a sip of wine, gaze steady. "There are rumors, you must know that. You favor your warden over anyone else, when wardens aren't meant to stand where he does beside you."

"He brings the border reports."

"He brings you pleasure, do not lie."

Vanya tipped his head fractionally in acknowledgment of that statement. "Then I won't. But Soren will not stab me in the back or poison me how some might."

"A commendable stance in anyone, but he moves outside the boundaries that wardens have kept for generations. People have noticed, and people are talking. Joelle is loudest of them all."

"And what does she say?"

Amir set his wineglass down and leaned forward, resting his elbows on the edge of the table. "She is questioning what you owe him for you to allow him into your household and grant him access to your time that no other has. And her words are finding a home in ears primed to listen."

Memory flashed across Vanya's mind, a moment in time of tumbling through a derailed train, barely able to breathe with quiet killer on his tongue. He'd lived only because Soren had done his duty, and Vanya ever owed him for that. The vow still hung around Soren's throat, a promise of unrestricted aid that a warden might find himself in need of one day.

Only he'd never asked Vanya for what he wanted, never came to request payment. Six years they'd been in each other's lives, and Soren had not once asked for what was owed when any other House would use such a vow to cripple Vanya's.

His mother had warned him of offering such a thing, but he'd offered the vow anyway. Wardens were nameless and stateless and owed no loyalty to any government. Vanya had simply done his best to keep Soren by his side the only way he knew how.

"She knows you took him to the crypts," Amir said in a voice so low Vanya could barely hear the words. "All the Houses who have ever held the throne and were present that day remember the unspoken law you broke. The rest who did not attend found out after the fact. It is but one of many reasons why you have found it difficult to cultivate loyalty."

"There is no law about the dead except what we make of it."

Amir shook his head. "If it is known that the wardens are aware of how we handle the dead who once sat upon the Imperial throne, then you have damned the country to sanctions through the Poison Accords. The Houses will never forgive you and yours for that."

"It is my duty to rule with an eye to Solaria's future. I have done so. I don't trust what Joelle has allowed to happen within her *vasilyet*. The border with Daijal she oversees is porous, and the number of revenants there is incompatible with the historical border reports."

"I understand your concern. I share them as well, but Vanya, there were other roads for you to take. Ones that did not allow the wardens to know about the crypt."

Vanya smiled thinly. "Were there? If I move against the House of Kimathi in an official capacity without evidence and without support, the Houses and the Senate will protest. I will lose what little loyalty I have gained and become the target of assassination from all corners of the country. Believe me when I say Joelle would not pass up such an opportunity, and she would find a way to take the Imperial throne."

"That is a game we all play."

"Perhaps, but I don't trust that she is loyal to *Solaria*. I made a choice to allow the wardens to know of our misdeeds that have occurred since the founding of our country to ensure someone knew the truth and could stand against her power if I am dead. I did so to keep our country *safe*."

"Sanctions are a punishment, not safety."

Vanya pushed his plate away from the edge of the table, finished with his meal, if not his drink. Beside his plate was a small stack of tintype photographs lying face down. He picked one up and passed it across to Amir.

"There was a quarry in the House of Kimathi's *vasilyet* that once housed a factory. Inside that factory was a death-defying machine that a warden assures me can raise the dead faster than spores. There were thousands of revenants in that pit before he bombed the place." Vanya caught Amir's gaze and held it. "Tell me, *vezir*. What would you do in the face of a House who allowed such depravity on its lands and upon its citizens?"

Amir stared at the tintype photograph for a long moment before carefully setting it aside. "Spores create revenants. No one will believe such a fantastical machine exists without *proof*. Your word and these photographs will not be enough to sway a House's opinion. Anything your warden says will be viewed through his loyalty to you. This isn't proof, and Joelle will fight you on it."

Vanya tapped a finger against the stem of his wineglass, slow and methodical. "Let her."

He'd find his proof—somehow. Until then, he would sow enough doubt about the House of Kimathi amongst all the rest that Joelle would not be able to escape it.

JOELLE

The innermost city walls of Calhames contained the majority of the estates belonging to the major and some minor Houses. The estates weren't typically occupied year-round, and the House of Kimathi's estate had been near empty beyond a small number of legionnaires assigned to protect it since Nicca's death.

Which meant the return of that vaunted House and its *vezir* sent the rumor mill spinning once a flurry of activity was detected there. All manner of servants and aides from other Houses were dispatched to its grand pillared gates with letters that first day, to be received by the majordomo of the household and brought to the attention of *vezir* Joelle herself. She played favorites with no one, setting her staff to reply with sufficiently pleased and coyly thankful responses on her House's embossed stationary and having the missives returned that same evening.

While Joelle didn't commit to showing up at another House's estate just yet, she did take care to be seen in public. Which was why, on the day of the emperor's return to Calhames, the exclusive Eclipse Society Association found itself graced with Joelle's presence.

Her motor carriage pulled up to the guarded entrance of the discreetly decorated building, only a small copper sign bolted to the black-painted door denoting its name. One of the doormen stepped out from beneath the overhang that provided scant shade from the sun to open the door to Joelle's motor carriage and offer her his hand.

She set her elaborately decorated cane with its carved clarion crystal handle to the ground first, then moved until her feet came in contact with the pavement. The doorman let her hand go once she stood, then bowed to the precise rank due her station. Joelle's lips twitched, pleased that the staff's training was still as rigorous as ever.

Artyom came around the motor carriage and deftly offered Joelle his arm, the more fitted style of his robe recently ordered for this occasion and matching their House colors. The gold ranking medallion he wore was smaller than hers but still noticeable for what it meant. Her son and heir smiled down at her before escorting her into the cool interior of a place Joelle hadn't stepped foot inside in years.

Lightly burning incense hit her nose just inside the door, the black mosaic floor beneath her feet sparkling with flecks of gold like the night sky. A magician stood from their stool in the corner, clarion crystal–tipped wand in hand, and bowed to her.

"*Vezir* Joelle, of the House of Kimathi. The Association has missed your presence and welcomes you," the older woman said.

This place was neutral ground amidst the games the Houses played. Murder might have been a sanctioned way of prayer for their goddess of death, but the owners refused to allow anything untoward to happen to members within the Eclipse Society Association's walls. Which meant both Joelle and Artyom stood still as the magician flicked her wand in their direction.

Aether-powered magic rose up like a fog from the floor, twining briefly around both their bodies. Joelle didn't shiver at its touch, knowing that it searched for weapons and poison, not thoughts. She knew the feel of mind magic and its subtleties, courtesy of Innes' teaching.

Joelle prayed to the god of fire and had for a good portion of her life. Callisto had never heard her prayers, and Joelle had found guidance down a new road, following a different star. He'd taught her many things over the years, but patience was something she'd learned on her own.

The spell dissipated to nothing, finding no threat on their bodies, as Joelle knew it would. The magician stepped back with a shallow bow, retaking her seat on the stool. "The Association bids you enjoy what is on offer."

Joelle nodded at the formal phrase granting admittance to the decadence found farther inside. Artyom escorted Joelle through the interior archway and down a hallway that opened up to a courtyard overlooked by three stories of balconies on all four sides.

A garden was spread out before them, blooming with desert plants and wildflowers. Low tables and cushioned chairs or chaises for lounging were scattered beneath tree branches or umbrellas for shade or set up against the balcony railings. Mechanical fans attached high up on the pillars gently blew cool misted air over those gathered, magic keeping the small water tanks attached to the machines cool in the heat.

No one announced their arrival, which was typical of the establishment's rules. Still, those taking the midday meal in the courtyard knew Joelle by sight and greeted her as due her station of *vezir* of a major House.

A blonde woman in elegant green robes stood from the center table and made her way toward them. She was tall and lithe, younger than Artyom, younger even than Karima had been when she received the ranking medallion as Joelle's heir. But the young woman who straightened up from a precise, formal bow knew her place, if Joelle was to go by the sharp intelligence in those deep brown eyes.

"*Vezir* Joelle Kimathi, of the House of Kimathi, it would be my House's pleasure to have you and your heir sit with us," the woman said.

She was tanned, with dark freckles scattered over her nose, her blonde hair swept back away from her face in several thick braids that pulled together at the base of her neck in a long, loose queue. The ranking medallion she wore was a delicate thing, burnished gold and pressed with the imprint of a curling wave.

"Lady Vesper Aetos, of the House of Aetos, I would be delighted to join you." She withdrew her hand from Artyom, giving him a brief nod. "The card tables in the study will be more to your liking, I think."

"Of course, Mother," Artyom said with a quick smile.

He bowed to her as an heir would and left her to the wealth of gossip to be found amongst their contemporaries. He'd report back later with what information he gleaned from the men and women who preferred tabac and brandy and a decently dealt hand of cards over a formal tea. Artyom knew his place here and what was required of him.

Vesper led Joelle to the shaded table servants had swiftly added one more place setting to while they spoke. By the time they reached it, Joelle's seat was ready for her, and she sank down into it carefully. The potion she'd taken that morning to ease the ache in her bones was wearing off, and she couldn't take another until she returned to the estate.

Joelle was well used to living up to a lie, and it was easy enough to smile a greeting at those seated around her. She knew their faces and their Houses, most of them loyal to her own through shared goals, bribery, or debts. Vesper's House governed the *vasilyet* surrounding Seaville on the east coast, in the hill country. That trade city was almost as integral as Bellingham when it came to contact with another country.

"How fares your father?" Joelle asked Vesper as a servant poured her a glass of cold red wine, fruit floating at the top.

Vesper passed her a small dish of sweets, the layered, honeyed pieces sticky-looking. Joelle placed two onto her plate. "He's in Seaville, overseeing the summer season."

"Are you here with your mother?"

Vesper's smile was slight but proud. "No, *vezir*. I am the voice of my House here in Calhames."

Which meant she'd rightly held the pinnacle of social status in those present in the courtyard until Joelle arrived. That she deftly stepped aside without a fight spoke well of her training—or perhaps she remembered what her House owed Joelle's.

"It has been years since you've last graced Calhames with your presence," *vezir* Suresh Gevorgyan, of the House of Gevorgyan, said from the side of the round table. "What changed your mind?"

His hair was going gray at the temples, brown curls trimmed neatly in deference to the humid climate he came from. The House of Gevorgyan was a major House in what once had been the House of Laxsom's *vasilyet*. When that House had fallen, the *vasilyet* had been cut up administratively and given over to other Houses, both major and minor, to govern over. Joelle knew his area encompassed a good chunk of the swampy wetland in the southeast before it hit the edge of the Wastelands.

The wardens could only cleanse the land against the climate so much. Rixham had been a city that stood against the encroachment of revenants in the shape of humans or wild beasts, the dead poisoned by spores in the swamps or the red desert dunes of the Wastelands. The smaller towns didn't have the capacity a city did to fight back against a horde of revenants. Wardens did what they could, but the southern border had always been in flux.

The House of Gevorgyan had little love for the House that sat upon the Imperial throne. No debts were owed by that House to hers, but loyalty could perhaps be found in a shared goal.

What Suresh's House lacked in livable land was more than made up for by the number of magicians born into their bloodline. Several members of his House could even cast starfire, though not to the depth of the current emperor. It spoke well of the management of their ancestry, of keeping poison at bay through numerous generations. Any marriage between his House and another would result in children who could have the capability of casting starfire or, at the very least, passing it on to the next generation.

"I could stand no longer the road our country is being led down," Joelle said, affecting a concerned frown. "Since the emperor refuses my blood right to see my great-granddaughter in my own *vasilyet*, I thought it only prudent to finally demand a visit with her. Raiah deserves to know her mother's House."

A soft murmur of agreement rose from the table, with more than a few nodding in support. Joelle took another sip of her wine, ignoring the faint ache in her finger joints as she gripped the glass.

"The broadsheets have only reported about an assassin, but I heard the attack on the emperor a few days ago was perpetuated by someone within the *praetoria* legionnaires," a young man to her left said.

"If the *praetoria* legionnaires are against the emperor, that is a statement on the status of the throne we should not ignore," another woman said.

Vesper kept her attention on Joelle. "What say you, *vezir*?"

Joelle slipped through the opening the way a blade slipped between ribs. "Empress Zakariya ruled with a ruthlessness her son lacks and which Solaria is in need of. It's a pity the assassins failed."

Everyone at her table relaxed minutely when it became clear that Joelle was of the same mindset they were—that Emperor Vanya did not deserve the Imperial throne.

"The House of Sa'Liandel has ruled for so long, I think most people have forgotten what other Houses can do if they sat upon the Imperial throne."

Vesper's words brought a faint smile to Joelle's mouth as everyone at the table nodded in agreement, no artifice that she could see in their faces. That didn't mean much, but Joelle knew the history of the Houses who broke bread with her at the moment. None held easy alliance—if they had any—with the House of Sa'Liandel.

"Empress Zakariya never allowed a Conclave of Houses to form during her reign. She was too deft at working the back channels and holding on to debts for any House to call one to order. Her son lacks such skill and promises owed." Joelle met the gaze of every person seated around her. "I think it's past time we called for one."

Vesper said nothing to that statement, merely lifted her wineglass in a toast of agreement that was mimicked by everyone else at the table. Joelle was the last to lift her wineglass, acknowledging their support for the secret road she planned to lead them down.

Four

CARIS

The first day of Ninth Month saw the rise of the Eclipse Star over the Dusk Star, with the Leviathan constellation dominating the night sky. Miss Caris Dhemlan, heir to her bloodline's Six Point Mechanics Company and a landless barony title, watched the constellations fade amidst the onslaught of dawn.

The sun rising in the east would bring with it the heat of summer, but all Caris felt was cold as the E'ridian airship flew swiftly through the sky. Her ears popped as they began to descend, the majority of the crew having been up for well over an hour already on their captain's orders.

Caris leaned her elbows against the railing, the fur-lined leather flight jacket she wore borrowed from someone on the airship's crew. The plaid curving over the shoulders indicated ownership by someone associated with Clan Storm. She didn't know who had offered it up, only that Blaine had placed it around her shoulders within minutes of her arrival on the airship. That had been two days ago, and no one had yet asked for it back.

The open front deck of the airship was cast in shadow from the balloon above. The chill in the air made her breath fog, and the wind from their passage made her eyes water without goggles to protect them. Caris preferred to blame outside factors for the tears that left her lashes spiked, not quite done grieving over what she'd been forced to leave behind.

She lifted a hand to touch the lump hidden beneath her work blouse that was the signet ring Nathaniel Clementine had given her in the quiet of her lab back in Amari.

After a moment, she drew the chain free, staring at the gold ring resting in her palm, watching the way sunlight glinted off the flat top of it. His family's Clementine Trading Company's crest was etched into it the way a bloodline's might be. He wasn't noble in blood, only deed, and Caris missed having him by her side.

But Nathaniel had been arrested by debt collectors on a warrant for treason she knew was false. He'd gone without a fight to protect her, and the chain of cogs he was tied to was in danger of being shattered.

None of that could be fixed—not here in their desperate escape through the sky or even when they reached the earth again—and it left Caris frustrated and furious. She considered herself an engineer before anything else, capable of carving clarion crystal better than anyone she knew. All her professors at Amari's Aether School of Engineering had been impressed with the shapes she could cut. But she could not carve a way out of this mess, and there was no one to soothe away her anxiety.

They'd left her parents behind in the civic center of Amari, Portia and Emmitt Dhemlan lost amidst a protest and revenant incursion perpetuated by people masquerading as cogs in the Clockwork Brigade. Caris still didn't know the status of her parents, and despite Blaine having access to a televox, she couldn't call them. It was too risky, according to Lady Lore Auclair, and none of Caris' arguments had swayed her.

Grimacing, Caris tucked the signet ring and the promise it represented back beneath her blouse. She drew the edges of her leather flight jacket together, ducking her head a little against the wind.

Below, the summer-dry prairie was coming into sharp relief, clusters of trees becoming more defined as the airship's altitude decreased. At the edge of her hearing, she could just make out the hum of the clarion crystals in the engine, the aether tugging at her awareness.

"We'll be home soon," Lore said from behind Caris, startling her.

Caris scowled, refusing to look back. "It's not my home you're taking us to."

Lore came to stand beside Caris at the railing. "True, but my bloodline's ancestral estate in our province was the only safe place we could conceivably retreat to."

Caris bit the inside of her bottom lip and said nothing to that. She'd have preferred returning to Cosian in the Eastern Basin, but her wishes had been ignored during their initial frantic escape from Amari airspace.

She looked askance at Lore, taking in the other woman's pinned-back blonde hair, stray wisps fluttering in the wind. Like Caris, she was in the same clothes from two days ago, a borrowed leather flight jacket her only addition. Unlike Caris, she carried herself with a calm sureness that spoke of knowing her place, even amidst chaos.

Caris no longer had that luxury. She thought she'd known who she was. She'd thought the road that stretched before her was set in stone, the name she'd been born with the only one she'd ever carry, even in marriage if she didn't marry up. She knew differently now, and it felt as if her entire worldview had shifted on its axis, like she was a clarion crystal cut wrong and one pressure point away from shattering. The discordant notes of her life made no sense anymore.

"You know it was the right course of action, not turning back, don't you?" Lore asked.

Caris crossed her arms over her chest and didn't answer right away. When she did, she had to pry her teeth apart. "That's your opinion."

"You're a cog, Caris. You must know that to shed some gears in the chain is to protect everyone else. I don't mean that unfeelingly," Lore cautioned when Cari's head snapped around. "Only that we have a duty. Not just as cogs but as nobles. Do you think I don't also worry about my mother and siblings left behind in Amari?"

Meleri Auclair, Duchess of Auclair, and her oldest and youngest children, Lady Brielle and Lord Dureau, hadn't been with them in their mad dash through the country's capital. Caris didn't know what the aftermath was like—none of them did at the moment—and wouldn't until they landed.

They'd been flying with no communication allowed, taking a roundabout flight path to the east to try to shake any Ashionen airships that might have given chase. At a certain point, they'd changed course in the night while running dark to head south to a town whose nearest city was Foxborough, in a province governed by the Auclair bloodline.

Caris swallowed tightly and shifted on her feet to account for the sway of the airship. The crew on the decking behind them were shouting in E'ridian, the language washing over her. She couldn't understand it—she had a better grasp of the trade tongue from growing up in Cosian—but the men and women had been nothing but kind since she boarded.

"We're descending. The town only has a small airfield, and all hangars are currently closed. We're being told to hold position at a marker until we're given clearance to land," Blaine said from behind them.

Caris craned her head around to look at him. He'd been her professor once, under an assumed identity, masquerading as Ashionen when he was culturally E'ridian after escaping to that country as a ten-year-old boy. He'd taken Caris with him on the night of the Inferno but left her behind in the wilds of the Eastern Basin before he found a home in Clan Storm and a life married to a *jarl*.

He looked more E'ridian now, blond hair done back in a small braid twisted through with a beaded leather ribbon, hazel eyes squinting against the early morning sunlight. The flight jacket he wore was a little too big for him, but the plaid curving over the shoulder panel carried the colors and pattern used by Clan Storm. He looked at ease like this, on the swaying deck of an airship, more so than he ever had with his feet on the ground in Ashion's capital city.

Caris wondered how she'd missed it the last four years. She'd thought she'd known the secrets of every cog she worked with. How arrogant of her to think so, she realized.

"How is the ambassador?" Lore asked, turning to face Blaine.

Blaine tipped his head to the side, shifting to plant his feet as the airship's descent picked up. He did it in a way that seemed like an afterthought—habit of a life lived in a place like this, on the deck of an airship, and not in a classroom.

"Honovi is doing better. The crew we travel with had a magician in their ranks," Blaine said.

"Interesting how the E'ridians had such an armed airship on standby to come to our rescue."

Lore said it lightly, but her tone held an accusation that Blaine steadfastly ignored. "The *Comhairle nan Cinnidhean* was enraged over the assassination attack on their ambassador and *jarl*. They opted to recall Honovi immediately. They spared no expense to have him escorted home safely."

"Yet my bloodline's ancestral province isn't your home."

Blaine's gaze strayed to Caris, impossible to read. "It's home enough for some of you. Honovi wants you in the flight deck, Lore. You've the authority we need to cut through the bureaucratic nonsense."

Lore huffed a little, allowing herself to be dismissed from the conversation without an argument. She walked away, darting nimbly between the crew. Caris remained where she was, wind whistling past her ears. Answers had eluded her from Lore, but Blaine had proven to be far more open to her questioning—when she could pin him down at all to have a conversation with.

The crew of the airship were vastly protective of him and Honovi. She supposed, since the two were married, that made a certain amount of sense. It was frustrating, though, for when she wanted to make sense of everything that had happened in the last week.

Blaine came to stand in the spot Lore had vacated, bracing his hands against the railing and staring out at the land rushing up to meet them. In the distance, colored smoke exploded in the air, and the shouts of the crew behind them grew a little louder. She could see a herd of bison heading toward the outskirts of the airfield. Perhaps that was the reason for the delay in landing.

"You should wear a veil before disembarking," Blaine said. "Just to be safe."

"I'm not the one with a warrant and a bounty on my head," Caris said.

Blaine's mouth tipped into a faint, bitterly amused smile. "Better they come for me than you, if they try to come for us at all in this town. This province is under the duchess' protection, but I'd rather err on the side of caution."

"Her bloodline governs here. It should be safe enough."

Blaine slanted her a look. "Do you really believe that?"

Caris went quiet at that question, thinking of the reach the Daijal court had these days. She scraped her fingernails against the metal railing, the sound they made lost to the wind, but she felt the shiver of it in her bones. She'd used starfire to save them all back in Amari, the strongest form of magic distilled from the aether and a mark of royalty in all six countries of Maricol.

It made her a target, but perhaps she'd always been one.

The Inferno twenty years ago had eradicated the Rourke bloodline down through the cadet bloodlines. That bloody coup had left behind only a single person capable of casting starfire, or so the history books taught. Crown Princess Eimarille Rourke had been spirited west and grown up in the Daijal court, under the eye of the distantly removed family of the Iverson bloodline. She'd married into the Iverson bloodline but kept her own name as a gift from a star god.

Eimarille was the last living Rourke, not Caris, no matter what everyone in the upper ranks of the Clockwork Brigade believed. More and more, that lie she told herself held no comfort.

"You and I seem to always meet on airships when it matters most," Blaine said after a moment.

Caris swallowed, throat dry. "I'd rather we didn't."

"Yes, well, I would have stayed in E'ridia with my husband if it weren't for my duty. But I lived because a star god willed it, as did you."

"I never asked you to follow my road."

"You didn't need to. I was Westergard, long ago, and taken as witness. I'll see my duty through to the end, whatever it might be."

Caris pressed her lips in a thin line. "I'd never ask that of you."

"You weren't the one who asked." He reached out and tapped his gloved knuckles gently against the back of her hand. "We all make choices, and I made mine. Honovi understands."

"Is he staying?"

"The *Comhairle nan Cinnidhean* wants him home to report in person about the *rionetka* attack. That's part of why they recalled him. I'm certain there will be more issues he'll have to deal with once he's back in Glencoe. He needs rest, though. I've convinced him to stay for a few days so that he can get it. Lore has promised to send for a doctor to assess his state of healing."

"He flew into restricted airspace and fired on a crowd. I'm certain people will object to his methods. It might be safer if he continues to E'ridia."

"We're alive because he came, and that crowd was revenants in the end."

If there was anything that Caris had learned at Meleri's side, it was that they'd most likely lost their chance to spin the story how they'd have liked, and the public would believe something else. Thinking about the duchess left a sour taste in her mouth, though. Caris was still angry about the lies woven around her by people she'd cared about. That betrayal of trust was like glass in her throat.

"The public won't see it that way."

Blaine sighed tiredly. "No, they most likely won't. We'll have our work cut out for us in that regard. The Clockwork Brigade has always been a group that many people in Amari and the western provinces held negative opinions about. This will only make it worse."

"Lore says there's little doubt her mother will leave Amari and return here."

"There were always contingencies in place."

"For me?" Caris couldn't help but ask, voice coming out sharp.

"For you, yes, but also the Clockwork Brigade and the country as a whole. When the Daijal court claimed Ashion, their king knew he'd lose support immediately across all provinces if Daijal invaded right away. The slow creep of propaganda he used Eimarille for was worse, in a way. Meleri worked hard to ensure enough of the surviving nobles and the army never gave their loyalty to the Daijal court."

Caris frowned, turning her head to look at him, and found Blaine staring at her rather than the rapidly approaching airfield. "The Ashion army was wound down to abysmal numbers. Everyone knows that."

"Was it? I'm sure you'll see differently once we land." Blaine nodded in the direction of the town, lit by early morning light that glinted off the spires of several star temples held within the protective walls. The bison herd was long shadows on the ground, and Caris could see movement on the town walls close to the airfield. "The army is far larger than it appears on paper, and much of that was Meleri's doing. Haighmoor is still its historical city, but the majority of its ranks can be found in towns like this and in the east."

Caris drew in a breath, letting that knowledge tumble through her mind, and could only see one road built from that decision. "You think there will be another civil war."

"I think Meleri held out hope for a very long time and wanted to ensure there was a way to fight for her country. To fight for you."

"I'm no Rourke," Caris protested, giving her head a hard shake.

"Your name was never written down in the royal genealogies, but that doesn't make you any less the daughter of a queen."

"I have a mother and a father. They raised me in Cosian. *They* are my family."

"No one will dispute that, not the way they'll dispute your true heritage."

Caris scowled, eyes narrowing. "I suppose that's what you're here for? As witness?"

"Queen Ophelia put you in my arms, and I carried you to safety because the North Star gave my father orders the night of the Inferno. The star gods present that night were meant to save Ophelia's children. My understanding is they could only save two."

"Eimarille seems to have thrived."

"I didn't mean her."

Caris jolted a little, blinking rapidly. "The prince is dead."

Blaine tipped his head in her direction. "Everyone was supposed to grieve as if he were, but I never have."

"Then where is he? Did you leave him somewhere like you left me?"

"No. All I know is the Dawn Star took him from the queen and I never saw him again. He was not who I was tasked to bear witness for."

"So for all you know, he *could* be dead."

Blaine grimaced, as if that thought pained him. "Yes, but the star gods built roads for you Rourkes that are meant to be walked. If I was a betting man, I'd bet in favor of him still being alive. Which means both you and he, wherever he is, are a threat to Eimarille's rule."

"She could sit on the starfire throne and take Ashion back. She needn't resort to subterfuge and war."

That was the only way to rule in Ashion these days. Everyone knew it. The North Star had set down that decree days after the Inferno. The broadsheets still occasionally ran stories about the people who tried to sit on it and ended up burned to ash—the occasional arrogant noble, the unfortunate drunks. The remnants of the once majestic throne room that was now a pavilion in a park were merely a reminder of loss.

"Eimarille has not attempted to test it," Blaine said.

"Does she need to? The Twilight Star showed his own favor. Eimarille is Rourke. She has the right to the throne."

"Would you see her on it and ruling both Daijal and Ashion? Would you see her encroach on Urova and Solaria? Perhaps E'ridia? The Tovan Isles would be the last, I think, to succumb to her desire to rule."

Caris hunched her shoulders, watching as the colored smoke

drifted ever closer to meet their forward momentum. "What makes you think she wants to rule the entire continent?"

"What makes you think she doesn't?"

Caris bit her lip, chewing on the soft skin there. His words left a disquiet in her, like the discordant song of a badly cut clarion crystal. "I'm not what everyone thinks I am, even with you as witness."

Blaine smiled crookedly, gaze filled with a tired, old sort of grief Caris had only ever seen in her mother's eyes. She hadn't understood it then but thought she did now. It made her ache for her mother, missing Portia like she missed a limb. She wanted her parents with her, wanted to know they were safe.

"I thought I could turn away from the road laid down before me. I tried, but it always led me back to you. I've learned not to regret that." Blaine pushed away from the railing and tipped his head to the side. "Come, let's find you a seat for landing before I get that veil for you."

Caris would argue about many things with Blaine, but airships were his territory and not hers, for all their shared history at cross-roads in their past. Caris followed Blaine past the flight deck for the covered crew staging cabin. A hard bench lined the wall there, lap belts interspersed down its length. One or two other crew members were already seated inside. They nodded a polite hello to Caris but gave a deeper, more respectful nod to Blaine.

Caris sat and buckled up. When she looked up again, Blaine had left the doorway, most likely gone to see about the engines. Caris curled her fingers over the belt, pressing the heels of her boots against the deck, listening to the shouts beyond the crew cabin. The thrum of the engine hummed with a song that pricked at her awareness, drawing her attention. It sang with a sweet, high tone that no one else seemed to hear. Whoever had carved the clarion crystals that helped power the airship had certainly excelled in the cut.

Caris closed her eyes and leaned her head back, resting it against the wall. She took in a steadying breath as the airship dropped through the air, feeling the quick change of atmosphere twist its way through her gut. Somehow, in the coming days, she would have to find the strength to refuse to be everyone's pawn.

At the moment, she found herself bracing herself on the bench as the airship juddered in an unexpected way, suddenly changing directions and rising higher in the air. Shouts outside the crew cabin had her opening her eyes again. "What's happening?"

The crew members were already undoing their safety belts, lips flattened into a determined line, and one of them said, "Revenants."

Five

BLAINE

Lore hunched her shoulders, trying to make herself small in the tight quarters of the flight deck, holding the airship's radio receiver in one hand. "Air traffic control is rescinding our landing orders. We're not to land while the horde of revenants is in the vicinity of the airfield. Even the automatons aren't allowed to shoot."

Blaine watched Honovi yank on a lever before glancing at the pressure gauge for the ballonets as the auxiliary blowers reversed themselves. The airship juddered through its entire frame at the sudden change in pressure, dropping quickly enough that Blaine needed to brace himself against the metal wall by the engine readouts. The swooping sensation in his stomach faded in moments as they leveled out, flying lower despite the order they'd been given.

"What do you *mean* the automatons can't shoot the damn things? Isn't that what your town's defenses are for?" Honovi growled.

Lore glared at him. "That horde is too close to the airfield. The town's defense team can't direct the automatons to shoot into a space filled with gaseous balloons and engines liable to explode. They risk causing an explosion and destroying property. I would think you, of all people, would recognize the precaution for what it was."

Honovi's lips curled. "That just means their automatons and wall crews have terrible aim. Blaine? We'll need to clear the way so the wall defenses have room to shoot."

"Deck master told me there's about thirty of the damned things near the outlier piers and moving toward the wall. Everyone in the airfield seems to be holed up in hangars. I don't know if anyone's been hurt by the revenants," Blaine said.

If they were, they'd be left outside the wall and given either a pistol or a potion to ease their way into death. The only people who could survive a revenant's bite were wardens, and even then, it was dangerous. Although any bite from an undead bison would lend itself toward loss of limb first, followed by a quick, painfully bloody death.

"We've picked off worse numbers in tighter space while flying through the Eastern Spine." Honovi glanced over at Lore. "Have any wardens been called?"

"I'll ask." She returned her attention to the radio, handling their contact on the ground. Typically, a crew member would be the one on communications duty, but this was Lore's bloodline's territory. If anyone could override local law and get them clearance to land in the midst of a revenant attack, it would be her.

Blaine went to stand beside Honovi, peering out the front viewport. Listening to his husband bark out orders was soothing in a way, despite the situation. It'd been years since they'd worked together like this, but old habits came back easily enough.

"Thirty bison revenants is more than is typically found together," Blaine said, pitching his voice low. The hum of the engines belowdecks helped hide his words. "I'd expect one, maybe even a handful of revenants like this, but not a horde. That's not natural."

Animals died, like everything else on Maricol. That didn't mean every corpse would become a revenant. The wardens had cleansed much of the land over the centuries, with the borders of the poison fields ever changing. Spores drifted, that was inevitable, but this was outside what anyone could expect since the civil war that cleaved Ashion into two countries.

"Nothing about the dead rising has ever been natural." Honovi flicked a couple of toggles, his attention dancing from the control panel to the sky outside where they stood. "You think it's the death-defying machine?"

"There's been more revenant sightings and incursions the last couple of years in Ashion than the decade prior. I'd wager yes before I'd wager no."

"Fantastic."

"The town is hosting only half a dozen wardens at this moment. They're on the way to the walls, but we're closer," Lore finally reported. "I've been told the wardens are restricted from using heavy ordnances because of the revenants' location."

Blaine returned to his station to check the engine gauges, finding them all within typical range. "Tell them if they do, to steer clear of our field of fire."

Lore bit her lip, too well-bred to fidget, but the tell was atypical of her. "Shouldn't you leave the revenants to the wardens? We can't risk getting close to a horde like that."

"What makes you think we're leaving the airship to deal with them?" Blaine waved a hand at her. "I left Caris in the crew cabin. Go keep her company so she doesn't fling herself into the fray like she did during the train raid."

Lore scowled at him but didn't argue his order. She'd tried in the beginning during those first few hours on the airship after they'd fled Amari. Eventually, Lore came to understand that while it might still be Ashion skies, she had no claim to the airship and its crew. She'd held her tongue when it came to orders since then. Now, she slipped out of the flight deck with nary a retort, hopefully off to find Caris and keep her from using starfire.

"We'll need to draw them away from the airfield. The engines will hold if you want the crew to play bait," Blaine said.

Honovi moved another lever up a notch before getting his hands back on the wheel. "Tell the crew we need four volunteers to strap themselves into harnesses. We're low enough without needing to worry about wind shear that I'd—"

"You won't." Blaine jerked his head around to glare at his husband. "*You* will keep your feet on the deck."

The thought of Honovi strapping into a harness to rappel over the side of the airship to hunt revenants from the air with a still healing wound in his side was enough to make Blaine want to lock him belowdecks.

Honovi tipped his head in Blaine's direction. "I'll bring us about. We'll spear one of the revenants to get the attention of the rest and get them focused on our lures."

They'd learned in the Eastern Spine, with the beasts who called the peaks and valleys home, how to kill from a distance. Even revenants couldn't rise again if they were in so many pieces. If they could draw the horde away from the airfield, they could let off the Zip gun with little risk of damage to people or property and leave the rest to the wardens.

But first, they needed to get low enough to do so.

This airship wasn't the *Skyborne*, but the *Katabatic* was more than capable of their needs. Built along specifications for E'ridia's air force rather than a commercial airship, it excelled in speed and maneuverability. It was why Honovi had chosen it for their escape out of Amari, prescient in a way Blaine was thankful for.

"Go be my eyes," Honovi grunted, adjusting the controls so the prow of the airship angled to the port side, moving away from the colored smoke being torn apart by the early morning breeze.

Blaine hurried onto the deck, breathing in air that felt thicker in his lungs than during the flight over. The sky was brighter, sunlight chasing away the stars and the dark. The crew cast long shadows over the decking as Blaine ran to the railing, leaning over to get eyes on the ground. Honovi was guiding the airship low enough they'd skim treetops if there were any to be found.

But the land below was free of trees and scrub bushes, only covered by prairie grass parched from the summer sun. It would be an enticing meal if the bison were alive, except revenants had no need to feed. The spores that drove them onward had only one driving need once they'd set roots into flesh, and that was propagation in living flesh. Revenants might be mindless, but they were always a threat.

Blaine could see automatons on top of the walls, their built-in weapons pointed at the horde of revenants, but law stayed their hands. The gates to the town hadn't opened yet, which meant the wardens hadn't made it to the wall. Their crew would have to do some of the work until the wardens could take over.

"Let's get the Zip gun ready. I want our best gunners in the turrets on the port and starboard sides. Who is going in the harnesses?" Blaine yelled.

"We already rolled dice for who gets to play bait," someone called out behind him.

"Then the lucky winners get to strap in." Blaine placed their location in the sky with a practiced eye before retreating back to the flight deck. He braced a hand against the doorway, peering at Honovi. "Got about one hundred feet to drop. We'll be kissing the dirt if you go any lower than that."

Honovi flashed him a smile that was all teeth, eyes on the horizon and hands steady on the control levers. "We'll descend hard in thirty seconds."

Blaine turned right back around to shout the warning, his words repeating through the crew on the deck. Three men and one woman were already strapped into harnesses and pitching themselves over the railings to the ball turrets built onto either side of the airship, fore and aft.

"Hold fast!" Blaine shouted, curling his fingers around a grab handle on the outside of the cabin.

A hard descent was quick and brutal and required a level of skill that not all pilots had. Blaine would always trust Honovi to fly them true. He heard the engines change pitch as air reversed in the ballonets, filling rapidly. The *Katabatic* lurched downward at a speed that made Blaine dig his heels into the decking to hold himself steady.

The airship juddered when Honovi reversed the controls, leveling them out so low to the ground they were about the height of the town wall. It was more than enough space for the crew to work with.

Blaine turned around in time to see a slim figure dart out from the crew cabin toward the railing. He swore under his breath as he realized Caris, followed by Lore, were terrible at listening to orders.

Truly, he shouldn't be so surprised about that. Lore was a noble and a high-ranked cog in the Clockwork Brigade. Caris was a noble and an engineer whose curiosity would always get the better of her.

"I told you two to stay in the crew cabin," Blaine said when he reached them.

"But I can help," Caris protested.

She had the sense to at least press up against the railing and stay out of the way of crew running between stations and rigging, but he'd much prefer if she wasn't out on the deck at all. "Your particular help isn't needed right now."

Lore touched her shoulder, and Caris jerked away almost immediately. Lore didn't seem put off by that reaction. "I told you Blaine had a plan."

"We're not allowed to shoot them, though," Caris said.

"Not this close to the airfield." Blaine peered over the railing, getting eyes on the fore gunner in the ball turret. The windowpanes had been slid open, and while the Zip guns were quiet, he could hear the clacking of gears as a crew member readied the harpoon cannon. Hanging even lower than that were the crew members acting as living bait for the dead. "We'll lure them far enough away that any active fire won't cause damage."

Even as they watched, the *Katabatic* came about broadside, and the forward-placed ball turret on the port side cranked the harpoon cannon into position. The gunner discharged the weapon a second later. The harpoon shaft was almost too quick to follow its trajectory, but it found its target with brutal efficiency.

The revenant reared up on its hind legs with a raspy sort of cry, the rotten flesh hanging off its rib cage swaying with the motion. No burst of spores erupted from the body, indicating the gunner had chosen well. When its front legs met the earth again, its hooves scrabbled against the ground as it shook its massive head from side to side.

The harpoon shaft from the aft ball turret of the airship discharged, streaking through the air. It, too, found a home in a revenant's body, tearing through dead flesh to hook deep in the body. The revenant bellowed, the sound rough and ragged, drawing attention from other revenants. It wasn't so much the predicament of the speared revenants that got the horde lurching toward the airship but the crew members hanging off the side in low-dangling harnesses, alive and kicking and far too enticing for spore-addled bodies.

Blaine shoved himself away from the railing and raced back to the flight deck, skidding inside. "Two revenants have been speared, and the rest are coming after our bait."

Honovi nodded, hands moving over the controls. "I'll turn us about."

The engines worked hard to stay aloft at their current low level, all the while hauling the dead after them. Blaine took a quick moment to check the engine readouts and found them within acceptable levels before returning to where Caris and Lore stood at the railing, still refusing to return to the crew cabin.

"You ladies risk pitching over the side, and that's a drop neither of you will survive. Please get back into the cabin," Blaine called out.

Lore tugged firmly on Caris' arm, pulling her away from the railing. "We'll take cover."

Caris scowled, reminding Blaine he still needed to find her a veil. "I've not seen how E'ridians handle a horde. I'm only curious."

"I'll draw you diagrams once we're inside the walls and safely tucked away in Lore's home. For now, *please* stay out of the way," Blaine said.

They went, and Blaine no longer had to worry about an accidental fall. He moved toward the prow, dodging around a set of chains that anchored the air balloon. Their navigator was at the secondary radio at the prow, calling back to Honovi their position and the status of the crew in the harnesses.

"How is our position?" Blaine asked.

Juni had her feet planted wide to brace against the airship's low-altitude maneuverings. "Captain has us on a steady course."

Blaine nodded, looking over at the crew members who were handling the winching machines that would haul up the crew in the harnesses at a moment's notice. Blaine gripped one of the safety handholds and leaned over the railing to get eyes on the ground.

The horde was following after the dangling bait. They were high enough off the ground that the revenants shouldn't be a risk. These weren't the sort of revenants that could jump, bound as the spores were by the structure of the bison's bodies.

That didn't mean they weren't dangerous.

With the high city wall impossible for them to breach, the revenants followed the pulse of the living, moving away from the gated entrance and the outskirts of the airfield. They gave chase, the morning breeze carrying the scent of decay in it. The revenants weren't old husks, as if they'd wandered the plains for weeks on end, searching for live bodies to transfer spores to. No, these ones were days old, and it made Blaine wonder if Ashion had a death-defying machine within its borders after all.

The airship bobbed in the air as it navigated away from the horde at a pace that would keep the revenants coming. Their interference bought the town's defenses space to maneuver. While the automatons stayed their fire, the heavy gates finally opened, just wide enough to allow several velocycles to drive away from the safety of the wall.

"Wardens on the field!" Blaine yelled, the cry being taken up by the crew.

The crew on duty at the winches got ready to haul those dangling in the air back up to the decking to get them out of the range of whatever fire the wardens were bringing. The rumble of well-kept velocycle engines grew louder, dust kicking up behind the tires as four wardens sped toward the horde.

They broke formation to drive around the farthest edge of the horde from the airship. Blaine didn't see the grenades being tossed, but the explosions that followed sent dirt and ripped-apart chunks of revenants flying into the air.

Gears clanked as the metal ropes were rapidly winched up. The crew on the deck helped haul over the railings those who'd been strapped into the harnesses, gas masks still in place. The clack of gears was soon drowned out by the heavy *rat-tat-tat* of a Zip gun discharging.

The *Katabatic* had four of the multibarrel weapons mounted to its hulls at the ball turrets, and the gunners knew their duty. They were careful to keep their fire relegated to the front of the horde while the wardens attacked the rear. None of them wanted to harm a warden, not when wardens were the ones that made Maricol safe and livable for everyone else.

Honovi's skill showed itself in the way he kept their incredibly low altitude steady as the airship maneuvered around the horde, providing aid when necessary. Between their Zip guns and the wardens' grenades, the horde of revenants was annihilated. What remained were blackened holes in the earth from explosives and enough ripped-apart flesh and shattered bone to carpet the prairie grass.

"That's a mess I'm glad we don't have to deal with," Juni said before lifting the radio receiver to relay an update back to Honovi.

Blaine leaned over the railing again and waved down the nearest warden that he could see. The warden drove their velocycle closer through the remnants of the horde, uncaring of the dead the way few could afford to be.

"Hail the airship!" the warden shouted at them, her voice carrying easily.

"Our thanks for the assist," Blaine called back. "Your orders?"

"We need to clear the airfield. Stay aloft until we signal it's safe to land."

"Shall we call for you?"

"Yes." She snapped off an easy salute. "I'm Raziel."

Blaine returned the salute before straightening up. "You heard the warden. Let's get aloft."

Juni relayed the information to Honovi via radio. Blaine crossed the decking to return to his husband, the *Katabatic* swaying as the engines changed pitch to gain altitude, away from the remnants of the dead.

Six

BLAINE

The town they eventually docked in was called Veran, a plains settlement that had never grown large enough to be called a city, and its citizens preferred it that way.

Veran's foundations were old enough that its innermost city wall was made of a smooth stone that reminded Blaine of the kind found in the catacombs beneath Amari. Its presence spoke of numerous generations who had called this town home throughout the Ages. There was history here and secrets as well. The birthplace of a family of spymasters would hold nothing less.

Veran was where the surrounding province's governing heart was located, its people taking pride in the town's history. The Auclair bloodline's ancestral estate stood behind its own set of walls in the center neighborhood of the town, well-known and well guarded. The convoy of motor carriages that had driven through the city from the airfield after the revenant attack hadn't split up, making a straight shot toward their destination, much to Blaine's displeasure.

"When an Auclair returns home, we don't hide that fact," Lore had told him tartly before ordering everyone about like the noble she was.

She hadn't tried to impress her will on Honovi or the airship crew, though. Honovi had followed Blaine's lead on the ground, and Blaine had followed Lore. Which found them driving past the iron gates and onto the estate grounds less than an hour later after they were allowed to dock in the airfield. From there, it had been a whirlwind of activity, with the estate's servants waiting to attend their lady and her guests.

"How is the view?" Honovi asked from his spot on the plush armchair in the bedroom they were going to share. It was extravagantly decorated, with a mural of a hunt spanning the long wall. The wallpaper in the rest of the room was done up in amber and greens, the color reminiscent of the Northern Plains in late spring.

Blaine turned away from the window he'd been peering out of and the gardens beyond, the flowers somewhat withered beneath the summer sun. "Nothing like the gardens in Glencoe."

Honovi arched an eyebrow. "Did you see the guards on duty?"

"You mean the soldiers? Yes, I saw them."

"You don't seem surprised they're here."

"The Auclair bloodline was the oldest bloodline left after the Inferno and wholly dedicated to Ashion over Daijal. It made sense the military would rally around the duchess."

"I thought she called Amari home?"

"The Auclairs have lived here since before their names were written in the nobility genealogies. It was always the place we were to retreat to in the event everything went to pieces." Blaine shrugged stiffly. "I suppose a revenant incursion and the framing of the Clockwork Brigade counts toward that."

Honovi waved him over, and Blaine went willingly, happily, even. His husband was still in his flight leathers, the plaid of Clan Storm curled over his shoulders on the panels there. His shirt collar was open, revealing the marriage torc settled around his throat. The glint of gold drew Blaine's eye, and he was viscerally aware of the absence of his own. He knew it was kept safe back in Glencoe, but he missed it all the same.

Honovi caught his wrist once he was close and tried to tug Blaine onto his lap, but Blaine resisted. "You're still hurt."

"I'm healed enough."

Blaine firmly shook his head before sinking to his knees between his husband's spread legs, hooking one hand around an ankle. Honovi looked down at him with hooded brown eyes, his neatly braided hair hanging over one shoulder. A beaded leather ribbon was twined through it, anchoring the metal hair adornments scattered down its length. Blaine had combed and braided Honovi's hair last night and shaved both sides of his skull in the privacy of the captain's quarters of the airship, relishing in the task.

It had been something Blaine had missed during his years spent in Amari—the habits of clan, of family, of sleeping beside his husband after so long sleeping alone. His second language, which had become his first, was always there at the back of his throat, ready to shape his tongue to the rolling sound of E'ridian than the sharpness of Ashio-nen. Shaking off the persona he had lived out of duty for a truth Honovi had kept safe for him was a little like a valley flower unfurling after a harsh winter.

"Lore said she'd send for the doctor once she got everyone settled. She's in charge until her mother gets here, and opening up the estate after a long time away requires some dedicated work," Blaine said.

"The servants seemed capable enough."

"So did Siv. Lore's being discreet, but she needs to check for signs of *rionetkas*."

Honovi grimaced, lifting a hand to brush back the shorter strands of Blaine's hair with bare fingers, his gloves tucked away in a pocket. "Everyone can't be a *rionetka*."

"I won't take that risk, and neither will Lore."

"What about Caris?"

"She's staying in the room given her. She said she wanted to be alone for a while."

"You chose not to guard her?"

"She's safe enough here. Besides, she made it clear she's still angry. The chat we had on the airship made that clear enough."

Honovi's fingers dragged down the side of Blaine's face, palm pressing flat against his cheek. "She had your veil when we disem-barked. I don't like your face being on display like this."

"Lore didn't bring extra from the stores in Amari. We left in a hurry, and Caris needs it more than I do."

"Your warrant is still active."

"We'll have to hope the Auclairs have a firm grip on the servants here, won't we? If any debt collectors come knocking, she'll run them off."

He'd made the right choice, he knew. The stack of broadsheets that had been handed to Lore upon their arrival at the estate by a cog had offered up a sobering reality. The printed picture of Caris wielding starfire against peacekeepers had been on the front page of every single one, and it'd only been a handful of days since they'd left Amari.

From what the cog had said, with Caris safely hidden behind the veil, the press was painting her as equal parts a savior and a threat. Her presence alone was a crack in Eimarille's plans to rule, and that meant she was both a prize and a target. Blaine wasn't arrogant enough to think he was in the same category as Caris, but he was the only one who could stand as witness and prove her ties to the Rourke bloodline.

Right now, the public couldn't know that either of them resided in the Auclair bloodline's ancestral estate. How long their presence would stay a secret without the interference of a magician with mind magic was anyone's guess.

"The Auclair bloodline can't keep you safe forever, not even here," Honovi said.

Honovi didn't ask Blaine to come home with him to Glencoe, though his lips thinned in displeasure. They both knew Blaine would go home if a decree by the Dusk Star didn't keep his road pointing at Caris.

He tilted his head into Honovi's hand, rubbing his chin against warm skin for a moment before pulling away. Sighing, Blaine straightened up and reached for Honovi's belt. "I want to check your wound."

Honovi curled his hands over the armrests, not protesting as Blaine deftly undid his belt buckle and the buttons of his pants, then his shirt, parting the fabric to reveal the ugly bruise that spanned his right side over his hip, all that remained of a gunshot wound.

The bullet had been a through and through, missing vital organs by a miracle. The way he'd been standing at the time he was shot had saved Blaine and saved himself from a worse fate. Blaine still felt as if he had Honovi's blood beneath his fingernails, though. He still saw the way Honovi had collapsed to the floor of the embassy's telegraph room in his dreams that were little more than screaming nightmares.

Karla, a former star priest and current member of the E'ridian diplomatic corps as well as a magician, had stabilized Honovi before he could be transferred to the hospital, where doctors had finished what healing magic had started. A different star priest assigned to the E'ridian embassy in Amari had stayed with Honovi after he left the hospital against the advice of the attending doctor. The star priest's magic had been enough, along with the potions and pills, to accelerate the wound's healing.

The mix of medicine and magic wasn't something just everyone could afford. A magician skilled in healing was expensive to employ, either on a once-off basis or full-time. Only someone with money could hope to have a magician heal them, and Blaine had never been so grateful for Honovi's rank than in that moment.

But he wasn't completely healed because magic could only do so much. Between the medicine and the spells, the star priest hadn't wanted to overload Honovi's body, and so what remained were bruises. The strain of captaining the airship in a foreign country while recovering had left lines of pain at the corners of Honovi's eyes and mouth. Blaine gently touched his fingertips to the deeply bruised skin, finding it warm, though he'd been assured it wasn't from infection.

Honovi pressed his hand over Blaine's, flattening both over the healing wound. He took a deep breath, and Blaine could feel the way his body moved with the motion. "I'm all right."

"I'd rather you never take a bullet again," Blaine said, rising up on his knees to press a soft, open-mouthed kiss against the edge of the bruise.

A warm hand settled against the nape of his neck, playing with the short braid there. Honovi had done up the plait, and the hairstyle was at once familiar and not after wearing his hair in a queue for so long.

"I can't promise you that, and I won't lie to you."

Blaine dragged his lips over Honovi's middle, nipping softly at the hard muscle there. "I know."

He'd kept secrets of his past during their friendship and later, during their marriage. Honovi had never held any of it against him when Lore had come calling to Glencoe, looking for Caris at the behest of the North Star and finding Blaine instead. Honovi had only ever loved him, and Blaine knew any road that didn't have Honovi by his side or at the end wasn't one he ever wanted to walk down.

Honovi's grip tightened imperceptibly over the back of Blaine's neck as Blaine kissed down his lower abdomen, following the narrow trail of dark hair that disappeared beneath his underwear. Blaine glanced at Honovi, seeing him staring back with a heat to his gaze that made Blaine go warm with want.

They'd never had the luxury of sharing a bed in Amari. The nights he'd met with Honovi in the E'ridian embassy had been quick moments of heated kisses and desperate touches on the floor, against the wall, over a table—anywhere they could before Blaine had to walk away. They hadn't done anything in the captain's bunk on the airship other than sleep. Blaine hadn't wanted to risk aggravating Honovi's wound, and the swaying of an airship in flight wasn't a comfortable thing to brace against when one was hurt.

"Let me make you feel good," Blaine murmured.

Honovi tangled his fingers through the base of his braid and pulled his head back. "You always do."

Blaine missed the feel of the marriage torc around his throat, but the weight of Honovi's cock on his tongue more than made up for it once he got his mouth on it. He breathed in the musky scent of his husband as he bobbed his head in a slow glide. The feel of Honovi's cock growing hard made him shiver, his own desire pooling in his gut. His own cock grew hard, and he reached down to press the heel of his palm against the growing bulge, hips hitching up into the pressure.

Honovi used the grip on his hair to guide Blaine into a rhythm they both enjoyed, allowing Blaine to catch his breath before sliding ever deeper into his throat. When Blaine's nose finally pressed against his husband's body, he swallowed around the cock in his throat, air locked in his lungs. Honovi's grip tightened on his braid, holding him there, as if he'd ever want to be anywhere else.

"I've missed your mouth on me," Honovi said, voice low, filled with a pleasure Blaine knew he was responsible for.

Pulling off just far enough so he could breathe, Blaine looked up through his lashes at his husband before swallowing Honovi back down again. He kept at it until his jaw ached, until Honovi's hips lifted off the cushion, until there was nothing left to do but eagerly swallow his husband's release. Honovi came with a groan, spilling down Blaine's throat, and his own cock throbbed in his trousers.

Honovi pulled him off with a guiding hand, and Blaine let his cock slip from his lips with an obscene pop that wouldn't be out of place in a brothel. He followed the grip on his hair, making a protesting noise when Honovi tried to pull Blaine onto his lap.

"Your wound—" he protested.

"Will be fine. Come *here*," Honovi growled.

Blaine went, incapable of defying Honovi when he spoke like that, hands firmly guiding him. Blaine settled on his lap, and Honovi made quick work of his belt and trousers, hands sliding beneath his underwear to take him in hand. Blaine swore and dug his knees into the cushion on either side of Honovi's thighs, bracing himself against the back of the armchair.

"Like this," Honovi said, pressing biting kisses to Blaine's bare throat. "I want you to come like this."

He didn't try to hold back, taken well in hand and unable to do anything but what Honovi asked. Blaine came with a cry that echoed in the bedroom, back bowed, making a mess of both their clothes. Honovi steadied him with one hand, still sucking bruises in the place where his marriage torc would be as Blaine tried to catch his breath.

"After you finish walking this road the Dusk Star sent you down, when you come home, I'll marry you all over again," Honovi said, words pressed against the pulse of Blaine's throat.

Blaine closed his eyes and dropped his hands to Honovi's shoulders, giving them a squeeze. "I love you."

"And I you."

Blaine slipped off the armchair and stood, holding up his trousers with one hand, wondering if he could beg a servant to ransack Dureau's closet for some spare clothes. "We should clean up. Lore said we could use her family's telegraph machine to contact the *Comhairle nan Cinnidhean*. They need to know where we are since we're not arriving when Karla told them we would."

Honovi didn't protest, but Blaine knew he wouldn't. He was a *jarl* and knew his duty.

They both did.

Seven

CARIS

Ninth Month arrived some days later, and with it, the Duchess Meleri Auclair.

Caris woke one morning to the sound of motor carriages rumbling down the short drive, a multitude of voices calling out, and footsteps in the hall outside her bedroom. Knuckling her eyes, Caris sat up, blinked a couple of times to clear her vision, then got out of bed.

She padded over to the window that overlooked the front of the estate, parting the curtains to peer down at the drive. It was barely dawn, but the gas lamps lining the drive illuminated the line of motor carriages easily enough. Caris' attention caught on the redheaded woman who exited the silver motor carriage, Meleri dressed in her finest travel clothes.

A tall young man hurriedly exited the motor carriage from the other door—Lord Dureau, the duchess' youngest child and only son. Caris reached for the latch on the window, winching it open to let in an early morning breeze and allowing her to get a better view of the motor carriages. She silently prayed that her parents would be next to leave one of the vehicles, but her searching gaze came up empty.

The duchess had left Amari without Caris' parents in tow.

Perhaps it had been too much to hope the nightmare of separation would end. Caris let the curtain drop down again, leaving the window open. The simmering anger that had sparked in Amari had yet to leave her, and the roots of it twined their way to the woman who had just arrived.

Caris clenched and unclenched her hands a few times before shaking them out. Her emotions were like steam caught in the pipes of a machine, pressing in tight against her skin, waiting to explode. Or perhaps it was her magic, the incandescent heat of starfire buried deep inside her soul having finally found a release and refusing to remain locked up any longer.

Little sparks flickered at her fingertips, bright white in the dimness of the bedroom, and she absently snuffed them out. She hadn't slept well since fleeing Amari, fear for her parents and Nathaniel keeping her awake during the night. Some of the blame could be placed on her magic. Most of it, she was sure, could be blamed on the duchess.

Squaring her shoulders, Caris slipped into the attached washroom to tend to her morning ablutions. Once clean, she dressed for the day in a pair of neatly tailored trousers and a slim fitted day jacket that Lore had arranged to be delivered after they'd first arrived.

Caris smoothed her hands down the front of the day jacket, eyeing the veil lying stretched across the dresser. The delicate thread magic woven into the gossamer-thin fabric gave it a faint shimmer, the metal clasp of it designed to look like a necklace. Caris left the veil where it lay and exited her bedroom as herself.

She was unsurprised to find Lore coming up the stairs, skirt hiked up to midcalf in her haste. The older woman huffed out a breath, strands of blonde hair drifting around her face. "There you are. Mother has arrived, and she has news for us that hasn't yet made its way into the broadsheets."

"Did she bring news about my parents?" Caris asked. "What about Nathaniel?"

Lore had spent her entire life keeping what she thought and what she knew off her face and out of her voice and eyes. She was a cipher to Caris' gaze, giving nothing away. "We're meeting upstairs in the library. Third floor, east wing, on the side that faces the garden. I'll wake Blaine and Honovi."

"I saw Dureau outside earlier. Did Brielle stay behind?"

"Yes, she's staying in Amari with her family. Someone had to remain behind to keep their fingers on the pulse of politics. We can ill afford to be without a voice in parliament." Caris was unsurprised by Lore's answer. Lady Brielle Auclair, known as Whisper to the Clockwork Brigade, held her mother's seat in the Ashion parliament.

Lore made a shooing gesture with her left hand, pointing at the stairs behind her leading up to the third floor. Then she swept down the hallway, intent on waking up Blaine and Honovi. Caris stuffed her anger down and climbed the stairs to the private family level above.

The walls on that floor were done up halfway in dark wainscotting, the rest of the space covered in pale ocher wallpaper. Caris walked on quiet feet over old but well-cared-for rugs that spanned the hallways of the east wing. She eventually found the library, tucked halfway down the main hall of the east wing.

Caris found Meleri and Dureau ensconced in a room twice the size of her bedroom, papers and broadsheets strewn between them on a low marble table. Caris paused in the doorway, barely seeing the bookcases filled with books and hand-cut clarion crystal figurines that sang with a high, sweet sound at the very edge of her hearing. Meleri's voice was a discordant tone to the song that only Caris could hear.

Their low conversation broke off when Meleri caught sight of Caris in the doorway. Caris stepped into the library, never taking her eyes off the duchess. Meleri looked *tired,* looked her age, in the soft glow of the gas lamps scattered around the room. Her short, pale red hair curled slightly against her skull from the encroaching heat. She wore no rouge or powder, though Caris thought nothing sold in any perfumery shop could hide the dark circles under Meleri's eyes.

"Caris," Meleri said in greeting, sounding relieved. "I'm so glad you made it here safely."

Caris said nothing to that, gave no greeting of her own as she approached the scattered armchairs and chaise that made up the conversation circle the pair had claimed. An image caught her eye, and Caris finally looked away from Meleri. She looked at the broadsheet folded open on top of other papers and ledgers on the marble table, her own face staring up at her from the front page yet again.

"Have you news of my parents?" Caris asked. The silence that settled in the room was fraught. She looked away from the broadsheet, meeting Meleri's gaze. "They didn't arrive with you, so I'm assuming you left them in Amari."

"Caris," Dureau began.

Caris made a cutting motion with her hand. "I'm not interested in excuses. I want to know where my parents are. I've read nothing of them in the broadsheets, so surely they are safe. Surely you know where your cogs are, Meleri."

"I am not a star god who hears every prayer of their children and knows where they are on the roads they walk," Meleri said.

"That isn't an answer."

Meleri clasped her hands together over her knees, spine straight, ever mindful of manners, even here. "Please, Caris. Sit with us."

"I want to know where my parents are. I want to know what's happened to Nathaniel. We're all in this position because you put us here."

"That's an unfair accusation. Everyone has a choice to join our cause or not," Dureau protested.

"Yes, and if they decline, you send a magician skilled in mind magic to take their memories of that offer," Caris bit out.

"Too many lives are at stake to not take such precautions," Meleri said.

"I'm only worried about three."

"And it's my duty as Fulcrum to be worried about all of them."

Caris took a step forward, unable to keep the desperation out of her voice. "Just tell me if you've any news on them. They're my *parents*."

"Caris—"

"I want to know where they are!"

Her voice cracked, and so did a place deep inside her. The distant song of the clarion crystals around her cut off as every crystal in the library *shattered,* sending shards flying through the air amidst sparks of starfire. Dureau and Meleri both ducked their heads as Caris staggered from the instinctive use of aether-driven magic.

She locked her knees and stared at the mess of crystal shards embedded in books and wood and scattered on the floor. The song was gone, leaving behind a quiet that did little to settle her nerves.

"Well, that's a bit of a mess you've made," Blaine said from behind her.

Caris jerked around, staring wide-eyed at where Blaine and Honovi stood in the hallway just outside the doorway, Lore peering over their shoulders. Caris swallowed thickly, trying to steady her breathing. "I didn't mean to."

Blaine gave her a faint, encouraging smile, and there was no blame in his eyes when he looked at her. "I know you didn't. But let's all sit down and hear what Meleri has to say, shall we?"

The three stepped into the library, and Lore closed the door behind her. "I've put Wyatt into a guest room under guard."

"The inventor?" Caris asked. "I thought he was to remain in the safe house?"

"There's still a warrant out for his arrest. With everything that's happened, we thought it prudent to keep him with us," Meleri said.

Blaine touched a hand to Caris' elbow and nodded toward an empty seat. Caris followed the silent order, needing to pick up a few thin shards of clarion crystal from the cushion before she sat. She tried to ignore the flush that came to her cheeks at her loss of control, but at least she was still awake, though she could feel a headache building behind her eyes.

She'd been taught better control than this in order to keep her secret, to hide what she could do because she wasn't ever meant to be a magician. Her mother and father would be so disappointed in her. These days, Caris was finding she wasn't meant to be a lot of things she'd hoped to be. That her road had so many forks in it she couldn't be sure which was the true path the star gods wanted her to follow.

At least she was no longer losing consciousness. The outbursts of magic today and during the riot in Amari hadn't been like at the pub. That eruption of starfire had been more instinctual than her use of it during the riot. The abruptness of casting it after years of not drawing from the aether had left her unconscious. Using starfire was building up a strength she hadn't known she'd been missing.

But her parents' warnings about hiding, about not ever casting starfire where people could see, still rang like temple bells in the back of her mind. As a Dhemlan, she wasn't meant to be a magician but an inventor.

A tiny voice wondered, then, what she was meant to be if she were a Rourke.

"The news out of Amari isn't good," Meleri said tiredly once everyone was seated around the table. She appeared drawn and exhausted but held herself with the rigidness of her station and a lifetime of manners that wouldn't let her wilt. "The loss of the Clementine Trading Company for safe passage of debt slaves is a devastating blow to our efforts."

"Was the entire family caught up by debt collectors?" Blaine asked.

Meleri nodded, and Caris couldn't stop the full-body flinch that ran through her.

"The Collector's Guild has given interviews to the press about their successful execution of warrants. They've finally listed the names in the broadsheets." Meleri leaned forward and picked up the broadsheet with Caris' image on it and unfolded it. She tapped her finger on an article headline that showed up on the second page. "The Clementines are currently being held by the Collector's Guild in Amari but are set to be transferred to Daijal. Their company has been confiscated by the Daijal court."

"More like it's been confiscated by Eimarille. If rumors are true, she eradicated the Iverson bloodline the same way they eradicated hers. At least, the ruling family," Lore said.

"She's consolidating power. I received a report before leaving Amari she's set to crown herself."

"In Daijal?" Blaine asked.

"She's in New Haven, according to the reports, and hasn't left yet."

"Will she come to Amari? Do you think she will try for the starfire throne?"

"She'll try for an invasion," Dureau said flatly. He reached into his inner pocket and pulled free an envelope. The piece of paper he withdrew from it was covered in code, but he could read it easily enough. "There's a worrying amount of troop buildup along the border between Istal and Haighmoor. I wouldn't be surprised if she crowns herself and taps the Daijal army for an invasion."

"The western provinces will thank her for it," Lore said bitterly.

"Not all of them. Haighmoor is a city we can ill afford to lose, but the army isn't headquartered there."

Caris blinked in surprise. "Isn't it? The military academy is there."

"The Daijal court worked hard to wind the Ashion army down and put restrictions on the number of soldiers who could be enlisted. That doesn't mean we listened," Meleri said.

Caris thought about the people she'd seen guarding the Auclair estate here and the numerous people who had come to visit Lore in the last few days. She thought, too, of the groups of gunslingers who offered their services of protection for those who traveled the roads in the Eastern Basin.

The hints had always been there, she realized. Eimarille might have pushed a policy of political propaganda, but that didn't mean Meleri and the other nobles who still held allegiance to an empty throne had sat idle. The Clockwork Brigade was only one aspect of their rebellion, she was coming to realize.

"You have an army? One large enough to withstand an invasion?" Honovi asked in a painfully neutral voice.

Meleri pursed her lips before shaking her head slowly. "Ashion's army is not the size of Daijal's, and we can't beg for help from other countries through diplomatic channels. Not officially."

"Not unless Eimarille crosses our country's borders as well," Blaine said evenly.

The look Honovi shot him was heavy, but he didn't argue against that warning. Caris supposed the existence of *rionetkas* was enough to hold his tongue, or perhaps the bullet wound he'd acquired was the reason for his silence.

"The death-defying machine has been in use for years, from what Wyatt said. Both in Solaria and in Daijal. It's not just an army of the living we have to worry about, but one of revenants," Lore said.

"I find it unlikely that Solaria's emperor has thrown his lot in with Eimarille," Honovi said.

"It's not his House who gave support to Eimarille's desire," Meleri said.

Honovi tipped his head in silent acknowledgment of that statement. "The last time the Houses attempted war against each other, a city fell."

"This time, it might be their country. If they have a House working against them and with Eimarille, then the southern border will not be neutral. Ashion will have a fight on two fronts."

"Three," Dureau piped up. "Urova has favored Daijal over Ashion the last few generations. I wouldn't trust our northern border to hold."

"We still need to ask them for aid. They might give it." Meleri turned her head to look at Honovi. "Do you think the Eastern Spine will be enough to hold Eimarille back if she follows this road at the urging of a star god?"

Honovi seemed troubled but unsurprised at her question. "The *Comhairle nan Cinnidhean* has been aware of the threat Eimarille poses for some time now."

"The Clockwork Brigade's overtures have found no solace in your country's politicians."

"You are a rebellion, and Ashion has no head of state. Your parliament is beholden to Daijal and has been since the Inferno. You cannot send a delegation that will be listened to."

He spoke with a sureness that made Caris' stomach twist, but the cold unease that swept through her came from Blaine's words.

"But Caris could. Was that not your plan all along, Meleri?" Blaine asked. "Was that not why you came for me in Glencoe?"

Caris dug her fingers into her knees, keeping her attention on

Blaine rather than everyone else looking back at her. The regret in his gaze made her want to scream.

"I'm no figurehead," Caris said. "I'm no *queen*."

"You're hope enough to bring together even those who have questioned the Clockwork Brigade's existence over the years," Meleri said.

"I won't be your pawn."

"Then what will you be, when war comes to our country?"

Caris had no answer to that question because the idea of war had seemed so abstract to her until she'd become a cog in the Clockwork Brigade. Now, she knew it was inevitable, but the role she'd thought she would play had drastically changed.

She was little more than a *rionetka,* just lacking the scars, but the strings? Oh, Caris felt those wrapped like a noose around her neck, her road no longer her own.

Eight

HONOVI

The prairie around the town's airfield was green-gold, grass bleached by the summer sun. The land was flat as far as the eye could see, the horizon broken only by scattered trees. They were too centrally located in the continent to see any mountains, and the vastness of the sky not interrupted by peaks looked different from the ground than on the deck of an airship. The view always made Honovi miss home.

"I suppose this is goodbye until our roads cross again," Blaine said. He stood next to Honovi on the dock leading into the hangar that housed the airship. Despite the Ashionen clothing he wore, he'd opted to converse in E'ridian. They were far enough away from any airfield worker to hear them.

Honovi knew better than to ask his husband to join him in the sky. "It's never a goodbye between us. You know that."

Still, Honovi had lingered in Ashion long enough. It was time to fly.

Honovi's crew had stayed on the airship to guard it, knowing that, even with the changes they'd made to the paint job—literally on the fly—it could still possibly be recognized. The broadsheets hadn't been shy about printing copious amounts of photographs of their descent into the riot to rescue Blaine, Caris, and Lore.

Given the choice, regardless of the risk, Honovi would do it all over again.

She wasn't the *Skyborne,* but the *Katabatic* was a rock-solid airship, powered by an engine that Blaine had checked over during their flight to Veran. If Honovi couldn't have his husband by his side, he'd take the fruit of Blaine's labor any day.

The *Katabatic* was properly anchored in a berth, though she'd be leaving it shortly. The stripes of colored paint close to the railing gleamed brightly against the darker shade covering the hull. Honovi could see where wind had made a hand unsteady, but the swirls helped hide the mistakes made while in altitude. Lore's bloodline ties had meant no one questioned them much when they'd landed.

The crew was busy filling up the cargo hold with supplies that would feed them on the flight over the Eastern Spine. The duchess had offered to pay for it all, but Honovi had declined, not willing to put himself in debt to her more than he already had.

He would be facing a reckoning once he landed in Glencoe; of that, he was certain. While the *Katabatic* had no identifying marks to tie it to Honovi as an owner, and its docking records had been falsified, one could always tell an E'ridian airship from others. It was in its flight capabilities and maneuverability, as much as it could be about its design. Their flight in and out of Amari had been repeatedly remarked upon in the press, with some articles stating that the Ashion parliament had reached out to E'ridia, demanding answers.

What had come of such efforts hadn't been reported on, at least not publicly. Honovi knew his father and the rest of the *cinn-chinnidh* who made up the *Comhairle nan Cinnidhean* would give no statement to foreign press. It would be handled through diplomatic channels, but since he wasn't yet within his country's borders, Honovi couldn't explain *why* he'd disregarded Ashion air space and fired on a crowd of revenants. Until he returned, E'ridia's silence on the matter would continue to fan the political flames Daijal was coaxing into burning.

Even with Karla ferrying home news of the *rionetkas,* he'd placed his country in a precarious situation. Honovi could only hope that the explanation of Siv being a *rionetka* would be enough to soothe the

Comhairle nan Cinnidhean's initial anger. Honovi wouldn't know until he stood before them, and he'd stand there alone once he finally made it to the capital after several years away.

"At least promise me you'll get some rest up in the air? Let your navigator fly until you hit the mountains," Blaine said.

Honovi turned to look at his husband, seeing not the beloved face he'd grown up with but a stranger's. The veil Blaine wore gave him brown hair and dark eyes, a nose just a shade too large for the features woven over his own. The visage was a lie, but it meant safety, and Honovi would always choose that first during this dangerous time. Meleri might believe her servants were loyal, but that loyalty could not be ascertained by the town.

So Blaine wore a veil because the warrant out for his arrest could buy a person's way into the nobility genealogies. It was enough money to change a person's life while destroying Blaine's. Despite the risk, Blaine had been insistent he'd see Honovi off. They'd kissed their goodbyes in their borrowed room that morning, and the taste of him still lingered on Honovi's lips. Home would always be wherever Blaine was, and leaving him behind cut deep as surely as it always had.

"Sitting idle is not the job of an aeronaut captain," Honovi said.

"It can be when you're still healing." Blaine frowned, the concern in his eyes familiar even if his face wasn't. "Don't push yourself. Your skin is being held together by magic at this juncture. Let it heal so you don't split the wound open."

Honovi pressed a hand to his right side, feeling the lingering heat of the bruise through his shirt. It *ached* and would for a while yet. Forced healing through spells and potion, paired with the more mechanical means of healing by way of sutures performed by a doctor, meant the bullet wound was closed up.

He'd be completely healed by now if he had stayed put in the hospital and let the magicians and doctors assigned there assess him more thoroughly. His rank would've seen them treat him with no expenses spared. As an ambassador and *jarl,* Honovi had the means to pay that fee, something few people outside the nobility genealogies could afford.

Honovi had pushed for a quick healing, despite the situation and what was owed. One that knit flesh together enough that he'd stopped bleeding and could walk. In hindsight, he was glad he'd chosen to leave because it meant he'd been there when Blaine had needed him. In the end, the pain was worth it.

"I'll be tended to when we land in Glencoe. It'll be a straight flight east now that we won't have to double back. We'll have strong winds, if the Dusk Star is benevolent," Honovi said.

"May she be benevolent." Blaine sighed, tucking his hands into the pockets of his day jacket. The outfit was new, the lightweight fabric perfect for the summer heat. "I'd go with you if I could."

"I know, but you're needed here."

That knowledge was less bitter this time than he'd thought it would be. It was either growth or acceptance, Honovi couldn't be sure which. Blaine's duty was to the Dusk Star and a young woman who would be queen, even if she didn't want the crown. He had to finish walking that road before he could return unencumbered to Honovi.

Honovi's duty was to his country and, through that road, his husband. Ensuring no one in a seat of power back in Glencoe was a *rionetka* meant there'd be a place for Blaine to come home *to*. Honovi was under no illusions that Blaine was a target just as surely as Caris was. He could stand as her witness, after all, and argue her right to have her name be written down in the royal genealogies. Without him, there would always be those who wouldn't believe in the future she represented.

Honovi knew a future with Caris ruling within her own borders was a far better one than that which Eimarille was after.

One of the crew jogged out of the wide hangar doors and made her way down the pier toward them. "Captain! We're cleared for launch."

"That's your signal," Blaine said, managing a crooked little smile.

Honovi turned to face Blaine, wanting badly to kiss him one last time, but they'd said their farewells already. "You have the televox?"

Blaine patted his pocket, drawing attention to the square shape pressed against the striped fabric. The device wasn't in widespread use yet, but Honovi found them exceedingly convenient. "Yes. Ring me after you've landed and spoken to the *Comhairle nan Cinnidhean*. I doubt they'll like what you have to say."

"I will never apologize for saving you."

"Yes, well, you may have to." Blaine held up a hand, forestalling Honovi's protest. "We both know you shouldn't have come back for me. Not at the expense of E'ridia as a whole being accused of interference in a sovereign nation. Your father and everyone else will remind you of that."

"I made a vow to my country, but I also made one to you. I aim to keep both."

"As I keep trying to teach Caris, sometimes we aren't allowed to follow our heart's desire. Say whatever you must to extricate yourself from this mess. I won't mind the insults. You know that."

Blaine held out his hand, and Honovi could only clasp it in his own, grip firm. The veneer of a casual goodbye was all they could afford out in the open. It didn't stop Honovi from stepping close and ducking his head so he could whisper in Blaine's ear. "I'll see you again."

Blaine tightened his fingers around Honovi's hand, as if he couldn't bear to let go. "My road will always lead me back to you."

They just needed to get through this deviation, but Honovi had faith the star gods would guide them true.

When Honovi left the town of Veran behind, prow of the airship pointing east, it was without Blaine by his side but in his heart.

Nine

EIMARILLE

Princess Eimarille Rourke had been born the heir to Ashion's throne before fire stole that road from her. She'd grown up on a different path, knowing that Daijal would also be hers. The star gods willed it, after all.

Or at least, the only one that mattered did.

King Bernard Iverson had thought her a tool for him to use, and she'd let him. Eimarille became what he expected her to be when she arrived in New Haven as a ten-year-old child—demure and cowed, always bending a knee to a crown everyone thought would never be hers.

Except the blood of queens ran through her veins, and starfire burned in her soul, a mark of royalty no one could take from her. She'd kept the name Rourke when she'd been allowed to keep little else over the years. The Iverson bloodline could not claim what Eimarille's ancestors had gifted her—it had guttered out in theirs long after the armistice was signed—so they had stolen it in a night of betrayal orchestrated by a star god.

Innes, the Twilight Star, had shined his light on her road that night, guiding her ever forward. It was only fitting he saw her be crowned, even if it was only the first of many Eimarille knew she would wear upon her head.

"I'd take the starfire throne if you'd let me," Eimarille said as she studied herself in her vanity mirror. The soft glow of the gas lamps lining it highlighted the rouge on her lips and cheeks and the soft shade of color blended onto her eyelids.

Strong hands settled on her shoulders, fingers splayed over the bare skin shown off by her off-the-shoulder coronation gown. The warmth of the star god's touch was like standing too close to a fire, though it didn't bother Eimarille. Innes smiled at her in the mirror, but it never reached his eyes, which held a glint of aether in them that looked like stars.

"What did I tell you when you were a child, my dear?" Innes asked.

"That you'd guide me true."

"And have I?"

Innes had taken her from Ashion during the Inferno and set her down a road she knew had not been the one the North Star had initially given her. But Eimarille had stuck to it—partly because there was no home for her to return to in Ashion, mostly because he'd promised her a future worthy of the queen she knew she still deserved to be.

She was a Rourke, after all, and the Rourke bloodline was meant to rule.

Whether by decree or by force, one way or another, Eimarille would take a throne and wear a crown.

"You have always guided me down my road. I would not be the queen I seek to be without your guidance," Eimarille said.

Innes' smile was sharp in the mirror, but the kiss he pressed to her temple was indulgent and soft. She thought she could feel the lingering heat of flames against her skin even after he pulled away. "Progress has always been hard fought for, especially in this Age. Aaralyn would see you wither like a flower in winter. I'd rather you shine like a star in the night sky."

Eimarille pursed her lips, carefully adjusting a blond curl that fell artfully from the updo Terilyn had painstakingly set her hair in. The diamond- and sapphire-tipped pins keeping her hair secured sparkled in the sunlight streaming through the nearby window of her private bedroom. They matched the heavy teardrop earrings secured to her ears and the choker wrapped around her throat. She looked at herself carefully in the vanity mirror one last time, satisfied with her appearance. Innes' hands dropped away from her shoulders, and she stood, smoothing out the skirt of her grand coronation gown.

The soft squeak of the hinges on her bedroom door had Eimarille glancing over her shoulder at the woman who entered. Terilyn curtsied deeply to Innes, head bowed, gown fluttering around her. Eimarille easily picked out the weapons Terilyn carried, the Blade having spent the majority of her life protecting the woman who owned her heart.

Eimarille loved Terilyn in all the ways that mattered, the two having grown up together amidst the politics that gave the Daijal court life. They'd stood together and schemed together, all the while finding a way to this moment with as little bloodshed as possible.

Unlike Bernard, Eimarille hadn't targeted the noble families who carried ties to the Iverson bloodline. She hadn't eradicated generations of people simply for the sake of power. She'd only killed Bernard —lit him on fire and pitched him out a window—and held no guilt for her actions, having already sent his wife to dance amongst the stars years ago via poison disguised as an illness. Bernard had brought his downfall to live in his court, expecting Eimarille to abide by his will and marry his son, to provide an heir more easily controlled.

High General Kote Akina had executed Eimarille's husband out of loyalty to her and her alone. She had married Wesley not out of love but out of need to survive. She'd given birth to Lisandro and chose to love him fiercely, as any mother would, because he was her son, and he was *hers*. He might have been born an Iverson, but Eimarille had given him her name in the end. Terilyn guarded Lisandro as much as she guarded Eimarille, and Innes' favor had lingered around all three in the face of Bernard's desire for political and actual conquest.

The civil war that had separated Daijal from Ashion several hundred years ago had ended by way of armistice. There was no peace treaty between the two countries, as each side considered the other as belonging to them. Bernard had succeeded where others had failed due to the backing of a star god. But in the fallout that came after the Inferno, the North Star had given her own decree and supported what remained of Ashion's politics in ways Eimarille was still unraveling.

There'd been no invasion back then, with Iverson forced to chip away at Ashion's power while holding Eimarille hostage. A heavy, constant propaganda push meant Ashion's western provinces looked more favorably upon Daijal now than they had in over a century. The Ashion parliament was reduced to a body of government beholden to the Daijal court's approval to pass any major law. For twenty years, Ashion had no queen other than the promise Eimarille represented that Bernard had kept for his own uses.

That was no longer the case.

Ashion would be Eimarille's, despite the threat of a girl the broadsheets kept reporting on. Eimarille had contingencies in place, courtesy of the *Klovod*, of which Terilyn had been overseeing since they'd arrived home in New Haven. The *Klovod* had his own orders when it came to making *rionetkas*, and she trusted him to do his job.

"Have you news, darling?" Eimarille asked, greeting Terilyn with a soft kiss on the mouth.

"The train with debt slaves will depart Amari tomorrow. The Collector's Guild has publicized the presence of Nathaniel Clementine on the train through the warrants section in the broadsheets. My sources say the Clockwork Brigade will attempt a raid once it leaves that country's capital," Terilyn said.

Eimarille smiled. "Good. And the Dhemlans?"

"Detained the evening of the riot. Quietly, as you requested. They're being held in a secret location under house arrest in Amari."

"Good."

She would not follow Bernard's road into eradication, for there was use to be found with Caris Dhemlan's parents. Eimarille knew the pressure points of politics, especially with the nobility. Arresting them for their involvement in the Clockwork Brigade gave her political cover when going after the nobility.

Her assumption of the Clockwork Brigade's ruling ranks had solidified with Nathaniel's stolen memories. Duchess Meleri Auclair and her family were the heart of a problem Eimarille needed to cut out like a *rionetka*'s. The duchess had her claws sunk deep into Caris, her ward a problem Eimarille would see dead before summer was over if she had her way.

Bernard had been too heavy-handed during the Inferno. Precision attacks and targeted assassinations, in conjunction with political pressure and propaganda, were far better tools for removing an obstacle.

"Shall we?" Eimarille asked, glancing over at Innes, who smiled at her.

"Your people await," he said.

Her coronation would not be conducted in a star temple the way her marriage had been. Eimarille did not need the blessing of a high priestess as a representative for the star gods when the only one that mattered had already given his. She would crown herself for all to see, as was her right.

Eimarille led the way through the palace to the grand balcony that overlooked the forecourt and the main boulevard beyond the palace gates. Even before they reached the gallery room it was connected to, she could hear the crowd beyond, with its cheers and impromptu music.

Lisandro was there waiting for her, watched over by his nanny, who curtsied deeply once Eimarille arrived. Her son scampered over to her with an excited smile on his face and a tiny gold circlet clutched in one hand.

"Mama, they said this one is mine," he exclaimed.

Eimarille crouched to his level, the heavy skirt a bulky bit of fabric between them. It wasn't enough to stop her from hugging her son. "It was made specially for you, my darling little prince."

The palace tailors had outfitted him in a matching suit with a day jacket and short pants that hit at his knee. His blond hair was turning a shade that matched her own the older he got, though the color of his eyes was closer in shade to his father's. That was the only bit of Wesley that shined through in her son's appearance. Everything else about him—from his looks to his smile to his growing intellect—was all Eimarille.

"Shall I crown you as well?" Eimarille asked with a smile, playfully tapping her son on his nose.

Lisandro giggled before nodding, holding out the small gold circlet with its cluster of sapphires and diamonds in the center. Eimarille took it and lowered it gently upon his fair head, settling it in place.

"There," she said, pleased with how it looked upon her son's head. "Now you're a proper crown prince."

Terilyn held out her hands, smiling at Lisandro with the same sort of adoration Eimarille always found directed her way. "Come, *malynshka*. You'll be with me when we step outside."

Terilyn had been in his life since he was born, and Lisandro went to her the way he only ever went to Eimarille—secure in the knowledge he was loved and would ever be kept safe. Terilyn swept him up into her arms, propping him on her hip, keeping her hand free to always reach a weapon.

Eimarille stood and turned to face the man whose loyalty to her hadn't needed mind magic to cultivate. High General Kote Akina had always favored Eimarille over the rest of the royals, and her outreach toward the Daijalan military had borne fruit since she returned to New Haven. Born of a Tovanian father and a Daijalan mother, refused the right to have his name listed in the nobility genealogies, Kote had found his own road in life. It eventually crossed hers, and Eimarille didn't see it ever deviating.

Kote bowed deeply to her, pride in his eyes when he looked at her. "Your Royal Majesty."

He stood beside a table, guarding a plain metal case that had been hidden away in the crown jeweler's vault since it was taken out of Amari during the Inferno. The tiara Eimarille had worn when she confronted Bernard—a gift from an Ashionen historical society—was now stored in the vault as well, unneeded for today's ceremony.

Kote opened the box with a flourish, revealing a crown nestled against black velvet. Golden filigree and flowers were clustered along the band, golden spikes reminiscent of sunbeams rising from it.

Diamonds of various sizes and colors were set within the filigree, the largest of which was a deep blue-green prominently set in the forefront of the crown.

She remembered her mother wearing this crown, as had all the rulers of Ashion. It was only fitting Eimarille carried on the tradition.

Innes stepped closer to the table, undoing the cravat around his throat. "I'll carry it."

Eimarille nodded and gestured at Kote and Terilyn to follow her out onto the grand balcony. As soon as the curtains were pulled aside by palace servants, a military band immediately started playing. The sound of brass horns and drums echoed through dozens of speakers set around the palace forecourt and down the boulevard.

Eimarille stepped outside to cheers that sounded like a roar in her ears. New Haven in summer bloomed with flowers and bunting hanging from gas lamps, city walls, and railings on buildings. Anything and everything that could carry a decoration was in use. She'd been told businesses had made a run on several printing presses in the last day or so, eager to put up signs of their support for her.

She liked to think their loyalty was true. The shock of Bernard's death had been alleviated by Eimarille's control over Daijal's military and the support she carried with the population whose lives were written in the public genealogies that kept the records for the majority of Maricol's children.

The nobles who might have pushed back against her claim to the throne had found themselves without the political power they'd held under Bernard's rule. They could only fall in line, and what schemes they would have attempted to cultivate were poisoned at the roots by the presence of Blades who had shown up in their homes as extended guests.

Eimarille had many pieces in play, Maricol a world of opportunity, as it had been for their distant ancestors. She intended to cement her rule of it all, and today was the grand beginnings of that effort.

She went to stand at the center of the balcony, right in front of the voice amplifier that had been set up that morning. She lifted a hand to wave at her subjects, the cameras of the press stationed below in the forecourt going off like fireworks. Terilyn stood to her right, Lisandro in her arms. He, too, followed Eimarille's lead and waved at the crowd.

"I was born in Ashion, but I stand here today as one of you," Eimarille said, the noise of the crowd dying to a hush so they could hear her. "I have been your princess, and I will be your queen, for I am of the Rourke bloodline, and we have a duty to rule. The Twilight Star has ever guided me true, and he has led me here today to fulfill a promise owed to the citizens of Daijal."

Her voice crackled through the speakers, echoing in the air, drowned out at the end by the crowd's roar of agreement. Eimarille smiled, lifting her arm to wave once more, the diamond bracelets around her wrist sparkling in the summer sunlight.

"King Bernard broke his oaths to the star gods, and he was judged accordingly. His loyalty was to himself alone, not to you, and I saw that firsthand while growing up in the Daijal court. Here and now, I swear by the stars that I will perform my duty to ensure Daijal's future and reunification with our sister country in the east.

"We two countries were once undivided, and I pledge all my efforts to guide us down a road that will see our eastern border once more meet the Eastern Spine. Daijal has always been my home, but so was Ashion once, and I promise I will live to serve you for all my days as queen of both," Eimarille said.

The crowd roared and clapped their approval, the sound rising in a tangled gasp. Eimarille didn't need to look behind her to know what had caught everyone's attention—or rather, who.

The heat of starfire kissed the nape of her neck and back, a partner of warmth to the sun that shined above. Eimarille turned so she could face Innes as the Twilight Star stepped to the edge of the balcony.

The gold Viper constellation tattoo curved over his shoulders and pectorals, the lines incandescent with starfire. Streaks of fiery gold blood dripped down his chest in slow rivulets, molten like metal, never to be found running through human veins. Starfire curled around his hands and the crown he carried like a living thing, the heat of it a comfort.

There was no denying who and what he was—a star fallen to earth, meant to guide her true.

Out of the corner of her eyes, Eimarille could see the crowd lower themselves to their knees out of respect for the Twilight Star.

"Every ruler needs a crown, my child," Innes said, his voice ringing through the air and the speakers for all to hear.

He offered the crown to her, and Eimarille took it, never flinching from the starfire that twisted around her hands and crawled up her arms. The crowd's awed response echoed in her ears as she raised the crown above her before placing it on her head.

The metal dug into her skin and hair, heavy and warm, but she was otherwise unaffected. Starfire flickered over her vision, leaving colored spots to dance in front of her eyes in the aftermath, but it didn't bother her. The faint tickle of flames cascaded down around her neck and shoulders like a veil, never burning her.

If she had been born anyone else, it would have.

The weight of the crown was negligible amidst the thunderous roar of approval from the crowd stretched out before her. Eimarille's name fell like a prayer from countless mouths, and the title they gifted her rang in her ears like a blessing. Beside her, Terilyn slipped her hand into Eimarille's, lacing their fingers together.

Queen Eimarille Rourke indeed.

Ten

EIMARILLE

High General Kote Akina came to attention in Eimarille's brand-new office the morning after the coronation. His heels clicked together and shoulders went back in a tight line as he saluted her. "Your Royal Majesty."

Eimarille inclined her head at a title still new enough that she savored the sound of it. "High General. I know we're running on a tight schedule, but I promise not to keep you for very long."

"Take as much time as you need."

She gestured at the chairs situated in front of her desk, the cushions there delicately embroidered. Kote was mindful of the belts and buckles that came with his officer's uniform and sat carefully on one of them.

Eimarille folded her hands together over the desktop, studying the man who had killed for her. His green eyes were bright against his tanned skin, wavy black hair slicked away from his face. The dark green and tan uniform he wore clashed with the soft blues of her office, but no one other than herself was present to notice.

This had been Bernard's office mere days ago. Terilyn had ruthlessly overseen the redecoration of it over the course of a single night, and the results were much more to Eimarille's liking. Terilyn had peeled apart every single piece of furniture Bernard had owned, uncovering a few secret stashes of information: a code book, a list of noble bloodlines and debts secretly owed, and a ledger of accounts for half a dozen banks for his personal use.

She'd sent messengers to those banks with a crown warrant in hand to ensure the funds were transferred to her control. The debts owed she would keep as leverage if the families in question didn't adhere to the national support Eimarille was busy cultivating.

"Will the revenants we're letting loose into the eastern provinces of Ashion be enough for you in this push?" Eimarille asked.

Kote nodded. "More than, at this juncture. We've set them to towns rather than the main cities, with the intent of making travel difficult. Haighmoor is ill-equipped to handle an incursion of that magnitude, thanks to the old king's forcible drawing down of the military."

"I suspect he wasn't as successful as he thought he was. Not with Meleri and the Clockwork Brigade working to stop him."

"We don't believe the Ashionen army will have the capacity to deal with the threat."

Eimarille hummed thoughtfully, running down her mental checklist. "And the wardens?"

"We expect towns to call for aid, but we've loyalists situated at key communication towers. Limited requests will get through, and the wardens who answer the calls should be overwhelmed. We expect the first calls for help to go out today."

"Excellent work. I'll look forward to your reports in the near future as you press our advantage."

The crisis in the east was a manufactured one that Eimarille had painstakingly planned and built over the course of years. It was merely the first feint in her inexorable march across Ashion. Letting the wardens answer their traditional call as ordained by the Poison Accords was needed, for when they failed—and she'd engineered that they would—the Daijal army would cross the border.

In a matter of days, the long border separating her two countries would be shattered in the name of humanitarian aid.

Kote had been integral in laying down the groundwork when Eimarille couldn't, and her trust in him hadn't been misplaced. She leaned back in her chair and nodded in satisfaction. "I leave our march in your capable hands, High General. Do call when you've taken Haighmoor."

"Certainly, Your Royal Majesty."

The office door swung open without a knock, allowing Terilyn to enter with a tray holding a tea service balanced on one hand. She inclined her head slightly at Eimarille as she approached and set the tray down on the side credenza.

"Your Royal Majesty," Terilyn said in greeting. "High General. Your aide-de-camp wanted me to inform you that your motor carriage is ready to take you to the airfield."

Kote nodded and got to his feet, saluting at Eimarille before following it up with a bow. "The front awaits me."

He'd land in Istal in the early evening if the airship launched on schedule, which Eimarille had no doubt it would. The Daijal army was nothing if not efficient these days. The officers she'd dined with last night in celebration of her coronation had rarely been invited to such festivities, but they'd been more comfortable than the nobles to Eimarille's discerning eye. Perhaps because they knew they had her favor.

Kote took his leave, closing the door behind him. Terilyn busied herself with pouring the flowering tea into two cups, the petals of the blossom inside the glass teapot jostling a bit with the motion. When she finished sweetening the tea with sugar to each of their own liking, she carried the delicate teacups and their matching saucers over to the desk.

"I've been reliably informed the emperor of Solaria has returned to Calhames," Terilyn said.

Eimarille reached for the violet-hued teacup edged in gold and breathed in the smell of the pale gold tea. "And his daughter?"

They'd both read the broadsheets about the assassination attempt and received telegrams in code from their spies in Oeiras. Eimarille knew Imperial Princess Raiah Sa'Liandel of the House of Sa'Liandel lived. They simply did not know where she was currently located.

Terilyn leaned a hip against the desk and crossed her arms over her chest, her own tea cooling on the wooden desktop. "There's been no word, but the emperor doesn't appear grief-stricken, according to our spies."

"I'd say one such as himself would be able to hide such a thing, but that is a grief no parent could bury easily." The mere thought of losing Lisandro was a nightmare best not entertained.

Terilyn tilted her head to the side, the waterfall of long, loose black hair falling over her shoulder. "He'll learn to, if all goes well. At least until he's been disposed of."

Eimarille lifted her teacup and chanced a sip. It was still too hot, so she set it aside before reaching for her lover. She curled her fingers around the fabric of Terilyn's skirt, the material soft beneath her grip. Terilyn had always followed Eimarille's sense of fashion, every outfit worn with an eye to its use, from making a political point or to hide the weapons of a Blade.

In this moment, it was a gown far more embellished than Terilyn typically liked. The green gown was embroidered with gold thread over her hips and breasts in the shape of falling flower petals. The collar rose to her neck and wrapped around her throat but left her shoulders bare. They were instead covered by layers of pearl necklaces, the jewels once belonging to the former queen of Daijal. For all of Aleesia's faults, she'd had glorious taste in jewelry, and Eimarille liked the idea of draping Terilyn in expensive jewels as a sign of her love, even if all anyone else would see was political favor.

Terilyn was Eimarille's voice in places that Eimarille could not be. For now, with her schedule cleared because Eimarille willed it to be, it was just the two of them, with no one to see how Eimarille tugged Terilyn to stand between her and the wide desk. She shoved the grand leather chair back with an unladylike push of her feet, the legs of the chair scraping loudly over marble.

Eimarille pressed her hand against Terilyn's hip through the layers of fabric she wore, far fewer than was typically favored by the courtiers. But it gave her room to move in defense of Eimarille when needed. She stroked her hand downward, palm gliding over the shape of a holster strapped to her lover's thigh beneath the gown.

"Do you have anywhere you need to be?" Eimarille asked, looking up at Terilyn's narrow face.

"I'm yours to command, as I always have been," Terilyn replied.

"Then lift your skirts, darling."

Terilyn sucked in a breath, a faint flush pricking across her cheeks. She moved with a grace that always fascinated Eimarille, reaching to gather her skirt in bunches and yank it up to her hips, showing off her shapely bare legs. She never wore stockings, finding them too constricting, and the only one to ever see her like this—peeled apart in layers—was Eimarille.

The knife in its flat leather sheath on her right thigh was secured by thin straps connecting to a slim, butter-soft leather belt wrapped around her waist beneath the gown. On her left was a derringer secured in a holster that always went unnoticed beneath the gowns she wore. Eimarille trailed her fingers up warm, scarred skin until she could hook her fingers over the delicately woven underwear Terilyn wore. The fabric slid free, falling down her legs and over her weapons under Eimarille's guidance.

"You'll want to brace yourself," Eimarille said.

Terilyn's lips twitched at her words. "Shall I now?"

She still hopped onto the desk without looking, rattling the teacups on their saucers, but nothing spilled. Terilyn gathered the skirt of the gown close, lifting one foot to brace her heeled boot against the armrest of Eimarille's chair. The position opened her up, and Eimarille swayed forward on her seat to kiss Terilyn's inner thigh, one hand resting on the other woman's knee.

Eimarille's shoulders pressed Terilyn's legs wider as she ducked beneath the twisted fabric of the skirt. Eimarille licked a stripe over the softness of her entrance before sucking lightly at the sensitive clit, tongue flicking over it rapidly. The sharp, indrawn breath from

Terilyn was followed by gentle callused fingers settling over the back of Eimarille's neck beneath her hair, tangling with the diamond necklace she wore.

They'd had each other like this last night, amidst silken sheets and softly glowing gaslight, the curtains drawn to block out a world Eimarille had stolen. Like then, she dipped her mouth lower, sliding her tongue into wet heat that always tasted sweet to her. She danced her fingers up Terilyn's thigh, sliding two inside her lover before angling her mouth back up to tongue at Terilyn's clit.

Eimarille licked and teased and curled her fingers deep over and over until Terilyn came with a soft cry, hand heavy now on Eimarille's neck, body pressing hard against her mouth and fingers. When Eimarille finally raised her head, her lips and chin were slick from her lover's release, the evidence of it glistening between Terilyn's legs.

Heavy-lidded eyes stared down at her, the flush to Terilyn's face beautiful. Eimarille loved her like this in the aftermath—languid and soft in a way the Blade rarely let herself be in the defense of Eimarille's life.

She braced her hands against the desk on either side of Terilyn's hips, rising to better kiss her properly. Terilyn licked into her mouth with a sureness that Eimarille had always missed when it'd been Wesley kissing her. Eimarille reluctantly pulled away, ignoring the pulsing heat between her own legs for the day's duty ahead.

Eimarille bent to retrieve Terilyn's underwear and helped put it back on, pressing a finger flat against the center once the fabric was in place, feeling it dampen at her touch. With a sigh, she pulled her hand away. "I've a meeting soon with the new prime minister."

"I'll have the servants prepare the Gold Parlor."

The Cobalt Room was still undergoing hasty renovations after Eimarille had damaged it when she removed the country's previous ruling bodies. The royal architects had assured her it would be ready for use in about a week. Eimarille had conducted meetings in far less grand surroundings over the years.

"I suppose I ought to wear my crown."

Terilyn smiled slightly as she slid off the desk and let go of her skirt, the fabric falling back down around her ankles. "The new prime minister knows who you are with or without it. They all do."

Terilyn leaned in for a kiss Eimarille always granted her before sweeping out of the office, off to do Eimarille's bidding.

Eleven

SOREN

The acrid stench of smoke still clung to Soren's field leathers and to his hair, lingering in his lungs. He thought he could still taste ash in the back of his throat. It wasn't anything he hadn't smelled before as a warden, but it made him worry about Raiah.

At the height of summer, in the expanse of the Southern Plains that stretched between Calhames and Karnak in Solaria, the ground was covered in prairie grasses where the earth wasn't cracked. It was nothing like the charred circle he'd left behind near the way station some days ago. That mess had reminded Soren vividly of the quarry he'd been forced to cleanse outside Bellingham—a burn scar deep enough that nothing would grow for seasons.

The thrum of his velocycle's engine was loud but not loud enough he couldn't hear the sniffles coming from the ride-along seat behind him where Raiah sat. Grimacing, Soren slowed to a stop, tires kicking up dust that the sluggish breeze stole away. He kicked down the stand and switched the engine off before swinging his leg over the velocycle to dismount it. He could ride for hours on end, but his passenger needed a rest break.

Soren's skin still felt too tight over his bones, the pressure in his chest from using starfire long since faded. He could feel the echo of it when he breathed sometimes. Soren flexed his gloved fingers, wincing at the feel of leather moving against still-tender skin. He shoved the discomfort aside in favor of the duty of care he owed the teary-eyed little girl he'd promised to protect.

Imperial Princess Raiah Sa'Liandel, of the House of Sa'Liandel, looked up at him through the child-sized brass goggles she wore, helmet still in place. Her cheeks were damp from tears and made muddy by dust kicked up from the velocycle.

She hadn't been harmed during their wild escape off the steam train and the time spent between then and now traversing the Southern Plains. They'd left behind the smoking remains of racing carriages and an ornithopter when they escaped from the people sent after them. Soren had driven into the back roads of Solaria because travel by way of a steam train could no longer be trusted.

People couldn't be trusted, not when their loyalty could be subsumed by mind magic and clockwork metal hearts.

Neither, really, could the Imperial princess, not with the secret of starfire Soren desperately needed to carry alone. Only, he couldn't be sure if she'd kept her eyes shut during the attack or if she hadn't. If she'd seen the starfire he'd cast—clumsily and desperately wielding the mark of royalty when he was a warden—then he'd somehow have to lie to her.

He hoped she hadn't.

Soren settled his hand on her small shoulder, and Raiah twitched hard, booted feet knocking against the framework of the velocycle. She sniffled loudly again, bottom lip trembling. Soren undid the straps, hauling the four-year-old princess into his arms.

"I want my Papa!" Raiah cried. She tucked her face against the curve of his shoulder, little arms wrapped tight around his neck, too tired and upset still to even try reaching for the hilt of his poison short sword sheathed against his back.

"Shh," Soren said, trying to soothe her. "Shh. It's all right, little one. You're safe."

The lie felt awkward on his tongue. Comfort had never come easy to him. He'd learned by watching Vanya, having never experienced such a kindness growing up. He'd seen Vanya hold Raiah like this plenty of times before, though. Soren allowed himself a moment to soothe her, even though he knew they'd run out of time back on the steam train.

The hunted never got peace in the midst of the chase, after all.

"I want"—Raiah hiccupped—"my Papa!"

"I know, but he's not here right now, and I need you to be strong for me."

If anything, that tipped Raiah over into a full-on crying jag. Soren winced, wondering if he should risk calling Vanya on the televox. Surely, Vanya was back at Calhames now, able to pick up his personal line.

Soren closed his eyes, thinking about the charred ground and half-melted remains of the enemy's vehicles they'd left behind. He winced as he realized explaining away their escape to Vanya would mean lying. Soren couldn't be sure Raiah would know how to keep a secret like this if she spoke to her father—and he would have to let her.

His stomach clenched at the thought of asking her to lie, and Soren knew he couldn't. He'd not make a child lie to her father simply because Soren didn't know how to speak a truth denied to him by the star gods. And Vanya had to be warned because the *rionetkas* chasing them had been tipped off by someone, either at a way station or on the train itself. Someone knew Soren's face, as surely as they knew Raiah's.

I should have asked for a veil, Soren thought.

But what was burned was ash, and there was nothing to be done with the past. Besides, Raiah's magic was still instinctive at this age. There was no telling how she'd have reacted to wearing a veil for hours on end. It may have provided anonymity for a time, but it wasn't a guarantee of safety, not if her magic ruined it.

And that was what Soren desperately wanted for her—safety. After what they'd survived, he couldn't be sure the city they were traveling to was safe, but that begged the question if *anywhere* was safe.

Sighing, Soren tried to put Raiah back in the ride-along seat, but she clung to him tightly, shaking her head. "I want to stay with you."

Soren rubbed his hand over her back. "I'm right here. I'm not going anywhere."

He'd not been more than an arm's length from her since they'd left the train. Traveling with a child was slow going, though, and he wasn't nearly as far along as he'd hoped they'd be by now. He had to stop far too often to scan the horizon with his double-lensed spyglass, looking for revenants and *rionetkas*. More than once, he'd seen airships in the distance and braked to a halt so he could throw the camouflage tarp over his velocycle and hide them under its shade until the possible threat had passed.

Those moments he treated as a game for Raiah, trying to lift her spirits if she didn't want to nap. Traveling the back roads like this was tiring for her, and Soren couldn't press onward as he normally would if he were alone.

It took a few minutes and a whole lot of cajoling, but Soren finally got Raiah to stop crying. She clung to him, sniffling pathetically, goggle lenses misted over from her tears. Soren knelt to set her on the ground, though she didn't want to immediately let go.

"I'm right here," he promised like he always did.

Raiah reluctantly unclenched her fingers from his clothes, scrubbing furiously at one cheek with her hand. Soren clucked his tongue at her softly before lifting her goggles off and undoing the strap of her helmet. He set both on the seat of the velocycle, smoothing his other hand over the frizz from her braided hair.

They were both filthy from travel, but he couldn't provide her the amenities she was used to. What food and filtered water he had in his travel compartments would only get them so far.

"I miss Papa," Raiah said softly, wiping at her nose.

Soren snagged one of her small hands in his, biting back a grimace as he tried to get his bearings. The problem was he couldn't tell a *rionetka* from a living person, not without confirming if they carried vivisection scars. The *praetoria* legionnaires that had attacked in Vanya's bedroom had appeared normal right up until they tried to pull the triggers on their pistols.

Using the Imperial writ Vanya had issued him could maybe aid

Soren with uncovering if a person was acting of their own free will. Except Soren had wanted to travel under what anonymity they could as a warden and a wayward tithe, and using the writ would defeat that purpose. Karnack was the closest Solarian city to the Warden's Island, well used to wardens passing through its city walls. No one would have looked askance at them.

It was still risky. Riskier was staying in the back roads.

He'd left Oeiras with no answer as to who had ordered the *rionetkas* after Vanya and Raiah, though Soren rather thought Vanya's suspicions were correct. Joelle Kimathi, *vezir* to the House of Kimathi, would risk the ruin of her House to gain the Imperial throne through her great-granddaughter.

Soren pulled out the vow hanging around his neck, the weight of it familiar. It'd been years since Vanya had bled on the metal and pressed it into Soren's hand, offering up a promise worth the life of a prince. Soren had never asked for payment because wardens weren't supposed to *want*.

But, oh, Soren wanted so many things.

And presently, he wanted Raiah *safe*. What safety he'd hoped to find behind Karnak's city walls was a pretty little lie out here in the poison fields. No House could be fully trusted, not in the wake of the ashes they'd left behind near railroad tracks and the *rionetkas* clawing at their heels. The House of Vikandir's *vezir* was tied by way of blood and past marriages to the House of Sa'Liandel, but that was no guarantee of loyalty. Not in the face of *rionetkas*. Vanya swore by the House of Vikandir, and perhaps, with use of the writ, Soren could prove their loyalty by the absence of vivisection scars.

But first, he had to *get* there.

If Soren wanted to outrun whoever pursued them, he had to take a different back road. Somewhere no one would think they'd venture. Without conscious thought, Soren's gaze strayed north.

A person's greed for power had ruined a country Soren hadn't set foot in for years, and that same greed was sinking fingers deep into Solaria. He doubted Joelle would believe Vanya would ever allow his daughter to leave the country. But that was precisely what

Soren realized he needed to do in order to get them safely to Karnak.

"Would you like a rock sugar stick?" Soren asked, needing to distract Raiah for a bit.

Raiah's eyes brightened at the offer, and she nodded furiously, some of her discomfort momentarily forgotten. Soren straightened and opened up the side travel compartment where the food supplies were kept. Alida, her household's majordomo, had slipped in a small cloth packet of rock sugar sticks, the half dozen treats sweetened with different flavors and tinted in all manner of colors. He let Raiah choose, and while she happily munched away on a red one, Soren set about working on their reroute.

He had a map, buried at the bottom of his travel compartment, that showed the northern border of Solaria in detail where it ran up against Daijal and Ashion. In all his twenty-five years, Soren had never crossed it into the north. The wardens' governor had always assigned him to borders in Solaria since he'd become an active warden.

A warden's job was to watch over the borders—those between countries and those between the living and the dead. Maps were their livelihoods, and Soren dug his out, using his compass to navigate a route north into Ashion.

Joelle could have *rionetkas* anywhere in Solaria, but he had to hope she had none in Ashion. If he could get Raiah there by way of back roads, he could try for an airship to take them to Karnak. Ashionens wouldn't know Raiah the way Solarians would. A quiet, ruthless little voice in the back of his head whispered that if the worst came to pass, at least Raiah would be safe for a time beyond Solaria's borders and Joelle's grasping schemes.

Soren pulled the oblong-shaped televox with its filigree-pressed cover from the case on his belt. The shards of clarion crystal forming the Lion constellation glinted in the sunlight. Soren undid the tiny latch and thumbed it open. Small buttons and switches surrounded the metal mesh of a speaker. He tapped out the pattern of Vanya's personal code, the soft chimes of the televox catching Raiah's attention.

She reached for his belt with sticky fingers, standing on her tiptoes. "Are you calling Papa?"

"Yes, but I'm not sure if he'll answer," Soren said.

The glow of clarion crystals flickered in time to the chimes the televox let out. The sound continued for nearly a minute before it cut off and Vanya's voice came through, a hint of desperation in his tone. "Soren?"

"Papa!" Raiah shrieked, reaching for the televox and jumping up and down.

Soren lifted his hand higher, steadying Raiah with his other one. "It's us."

Raiah's ecstatic cry wasn't loud enough to drown out the punched-out sigh of relief from Vanya. "Have you made it to Karnak?"

Soren tightened his grip on the televox. Hearing Vanya's voice was both a blessing and a curse, to know the other man was alive but not there by Soren's side. "About that."

"What happened?" Vanya demanded.

Soren grimaced, looking at the horizon while Raiah danced from one foot to the other, impatient in the way all children could be. "*Rionetkas* found us on the train we were riding. More were waiting for us at the next way station stop. I got us off the train, but we couldn't outrun them. They had racing carriages and an ornithopter at their disposal."

Vanya sucked in a heavy breath. "Are you both all right? How did you escape? Where are you now?"

"I used a bomb," Soren lied. "The same sort I used in the quarry. It stopped our pursuers, but traveling through Solaria to Karnak is no longer a safe option."

"Amir would not harm her or you. He's promised nothing but safety."

"I know, and I hope you're right. But getting there is our current problem. I have some options, one of them being I turn my velocycle back around and head to Calhames."

Vanya was quiet for a moment, long enough that Soren thought the call had somehow ended before he spoke again. "Joelle is presently in Calhames."

Soren looked up at the sky, squinting against the sunlight. "I see."

And he did, in that moment—all the dangers that Vanya faced alone in the capital without him. It made the distance between them even worse, despite knowing the separation was needed.

"Until I can sway more Houses from Joelle's circle of influence, it isn't safe for Raiah to be here with me at this time."

"Does Joelle know where you sent your daughter?"

"She must if the *rionetkas* found you and Raiah."

He could hear the banked-down fury in Vanya's voice even through the tinny, long-distance connection. The rage provided some bit of comfort, despite the situation they found themselves in.

"Traveling through Solaria isn't safe. Not with *rionetkas* hunting us," Soren said.

"Then what do you suggest?"

"Joelle's reach can't cross the border."

Vanya's refusal was near instantaneous. "No."

"I'm already in the back roads, hiding when necessary from passing airships, but it's not completely safe out here. I can't get the rest I need while guarding Raiah. There are border towns we can hunker down in once we make it north so I can get some sleep. The Ashionens there won't know who Raiah is. That close to the Warden's Island, they'll think she's a tithe."

"It's not safe."

Soren couldn't stop the frustrated noise that slipped past his lips. "*Nowhere* is safe right now, but some places are more defensible. I can take her there, and then we can buy passage on board an airship back over the border to Karnak."

"The Daijalan army is crossing the border into Ashion under the guise of aid against an incursion of revenants they say the wardens can't handle alone. Those two countries will be at war with each other before the year ends."

Soren jerked at that news, even though Vanya couldn't see him. "When did *that* happen?"

"Today."

"Wardens have handled revenants since the Poison Accords were signed. That's a flimsy excuse for King Bernard to use to break the armistice."

"The king is dead. Eimarille is queen and is the one who gave the order."

Soren's eyes widened behind his goggles. "What?"

"You didn't know?"

"I don't get access to broadsheets in the back roads, Vanya. King Bernard is dead? Truly?"

"As is the Daijalan crown prince. Eimarille rules in both their places."

Soren went quiet. Once, when he was someone else, he'd known the princess turned queen. He'd turned from that truth as a tithe at the behest of a star god, and all that remained were distant memories that could not matter.

"I'll cross the border. We're far enough east that it shouldn't matter for now," Soren said.

"Soren—"

"I promised you I'd keep Raiah safe until she could return to you. I'll take her north and bring her to Karnak a different way. We can't trust Joelle doesn't already have *rionetkas* there, but I'll do my best to keep Raiah disguised when we land in that city. But you need to trust me that I'll keep my promise."

"That was never in doubt."

"Good. Now, talk to your daughter."

Soren handed the televox to Raiah and let her chatter at Vanya for several minutes, knowing they both needed the comfort of hearing each other, even if they couldn't see each other. Folding up the map, he secured everything in the travel compartment and waited for father and daughter to finish their conversation. Vanya eventually instructed Raiah to hand Soren the televox, and he took it with a soft thank-you.

"Let me know when you reach Karnak. I don't care what the hour is," Vanya said.

"I will." The lull that stretched between them was filled with all the unsaid words trapped behind Soren's teeth. He thought Vanya could hear them anyway. "Keep yourself safe so Raiah has a father to return to."

"I'll be here waiting. I miss you both. That won't change until you're returned to me."

Vanya's words settled warmly in his chest, and Soren would blame the flush that came to his cheeks on the sun if anyone of note had been present to see it. "We'll make it back to you."

"See that you do."

The soft hum from an ended call disappeared after Soren closed the televox. He tucked it back into his belt pouch and then turned his attention to Raiah. She'd gone back to munching on the remnants of her rock sugar stick but didn't protest when he picked her up and got her settled back in the ride-along seat. Neither did she put up a fuss when he took the rock sugar stick from her and returned it to the packet for safekeeping while they traveled.

He put her helmet and goggles back on before swinging his leg back over the velocycle. He looked over his shoulder at Raiah, giving her an encouraging smile. "Ready to ride?"

Raiah nodded, small fingers curling over the sturdy leather of the straps keeping her secured. She looked far happier after speaking with Vanya. "Where are we going?"

Soren kicked the stand up and revved the engine. "On an adventure."

936 A.O.P.

One

VANYA

"You need more of a House presence if you are to sway the others," Amir said on the morning Vanya was set to appear before the Senate.

"I didn't ask for your advice," Vanya replied coolly as he adjusted the position of the crown on his head.

Amir sketched a shallow bow over the cane he always carried. "Nevertheless, I offer it out of loyalty to your House. You cannot stand alone before the Senate and the Houses. They will see that as a weakness."

Vanya pressed his lips into a hard line, trying to smooth the anger from his face. He stared at himself in the large mirror of the foyer that led to the forecourt where his motor carriage awaited. His formal white robes were tailored to perfection, showcasing the gold embroidery that spread over his shoulders and down the front like starfire, the design depicting the Lion constellation. The trousers were cut narrow, and his white leather shoes were tipped in gold.

When he was younger, he used to stand like this with his mother and father, ensuring that the last little details of their appearances were taken care of. Leaving the Imperial palace as a united front had always been politically important. Since he'd buried them, it had only ever been Vanya to walk this road alone. Raiah was still so young, and he wanted to protect her for as long as possible from the double-talk and falsely caring stares of those who would see them removed from power.

Not all Houses were against them, as proven by Amir's loyalty. Where the *vezir* of House Vikandir went, the generations around him followed. But he was one House who had not ruled on the Imperial throne for several centuries, and Vanya knew there were those in his bloodline who coveted power.

And, grating as it was, Amir was correct in his opinion. One House was not enough to hold the Imperial throne. Vanya could not stand alone, he knew that.

And yet.

Over Amir's shoulder in the mirror, he caught sight of Alida hurrying down the hallway, the majordomo's keys jangling on her belt. When she reached them, she bowed to the Imperial degree in Vanya's direction and offered a shallower form of greeting to Amir.

"Your Imperial Majesty, I've been made aware that your *valide* has arrived," Alida said.

The words didn't make sense at first. When they finally penetrated, Vanya turned away from the mirror to glare at Amir. "Is this what you mean by more of a House?"

Amir lifted his chin, meeting Vanya's gaze with an honesty that could get a man killed. "If I had called for your father's family, the Senate and the Houses would not see them as your House but mine."

"You had no right to ask for anyone on my behalf."

Amir's eyes blazed as he drew himself up to his full height, mustache quivering from the harsh breath he let out. "I asked on behalf of my *own* House and have the right of it. Taye may be dancing amongst the stars, but he was House of Vikandir before he joined with yours. Some see marriage as a debt even if it isn't. Your great-aunt is of that mind, and I used it to my advantage."

Vanya was too well taught to reel back in shock, but he wanted to. One did not offer a debt without weighing its worth, and few Houses did so lightly. Even if Amir never meant it as such, the veneer of owing someone was dangerous at their level. "Why?"

"Because I cannot offer you a marriage with a son or daughter of my House. Because I would rather people think I owe yours than another. At least in doing so, I know mine might live, but only if you do."

The main bloodline of the House of Sa'Liandel was whittled down to two, but its roots were buried in other homes and households. Zakariya had been the oldest of three children. Vanya's aunt had died in her teens, and his uncle had wanted nothing to do with House games, having stepped back years ago to command the Legion.

His uncle had taken a bullet to the back in a skirmish between two minor Houses, and Vanya could not say his mother hadn't orchestrated the trigger pull. There was risk involved, after all, in having the Legion feel loyalty to someone not seated on the Imperial throne. He saw the aftermath of that with the *vasilyet* in the northwest. Meanwhile, his handful of cousins lived in luxury, bartering their connection to the Imperial throne for wealth and inroads to other Houses.

None in his generation could cast starfire.

Past generations? Well. Of those who could, apparently Amir had summoned the only one alive and capable of such feats away from the salt air of a well-to-do seaside town overlooking the Constellation Sea. Calhames, Vanya knew, would not be to *valide* Taisiya Sa'Liandel's liking.

Angry at being outmaneuvered—whether or not it was to the betterment of his House didn't matter—Vanya stalked past Amir. Rather than step outside to the forecourt, he headed down the hall Alida had come from, the majordomo taking great pains to not overtake him as she hurried to keep pace.

"We had *valide* Taisiya checked per current protocol, Your Imperial Majesty," Alida said.

Vanya's lips curled. He rather knew how *that* must have gone. "Where is she?"

"The family library, at her request."

Vanya knew the way. It took long minutes for him to return to the family wing of the palace. Alida remained in the hallway when Vanya entered the library, closing the double doors behind him.

"You are not one for last-minute trips to the capital, *valide*," Vanya said in greeting.

"I am not one to turn down the facsimile of an offered debt. We own such things and never owe them. Your mother should have taught you that," Taisiya said in that raspy voice of hers. One would think she had carried a lifelong indulgence of tabac into her seventh decade. One would be wrong if they remembered the poison she'd drunk on her wedding day.

Not quiet killer, nothing so gentle, death a sigh on the tongue with that poison, as Vanya well knew. Fervere had scorched her throat, viciousness hidden in the wine she'd toasted her new husband with, and it very nearly stole her voice. It hadn't killed her, but it might as well have. Taisiya had once been one of the most revered theater singers in the country until the day of her wedding. These days, she watched the sea, well removed from the games the Houses played but never fully free of them. She was *valide*, the matriarch of the ruling House that held the Imperial throne of Solaria, and here because of that.

Taisiya was shorter than Vanya, with shoulders rounded from age and a face more heavily lined than most of her contemporaries, mouth dragged down at the left corner. Her visage was a mask of subtle scars she wore out of spite, untouched by shades of rouge or lip paint, never hiding behind a veil. Her brown skin was dominated by darker freckles, curly auburn hair gone gray in streaks throughout.

The gown she wore was a dark green, the light robe layered over it a shimmery gold. Heavy gold cuffs inlaid with emeralds weighed down her wrists. The jewels matched the ones in the ranking medallion she wore, the flat oval links of the chain sparkling from the gas lamp lit overhead. She was slight-looking but not forgettable. Her sheer survival over the years was, perhaps, something to aspire to.

"If I had need of you, I would have called, *valide*."

Taisiya's hazel eyes were more green than brown, but there was no warmth in her gaze, only cold calculation. "I never took you for a fool."

"I would not sit on the Imperial throne if that were the case."

"You'll lose it, and our House's right to it, with your arrogance. *That* is why I am here."

Taisiya crossed the library to stand before him, weathered hands weighed down by gold and emerald rings reaching for him. Vanya stood his ground, never flinching from the touch of her cool, dry fingers to his face.

"I do what I must," Vanya countered.

"So like your mother in that regard. She thought she had to destroy Rixham to keep it. Tell me, will you do the same to Solaria?"

Vanya finally stepped back, spine rigid. "Secession is never the answer. This is not the Age of Separation but the Age of Progress."

"One could argue the two are the same."

"I am not the one perpetuating ruin upon our citizens. That blame is laid at the threshold of another House."

Taisiya lowered her arms, clasping her hands together in front of her. "So Amir informed me. So I discovered when I arrived and was ordered to disrobe. I had hoped these stories of *rionetkas* were merely that."

Vanya's lip curled imperceptibly. "Did you now?"

"The House of Vikandir has married into ours many times throughout the centuries. It has not been officially indebted to us for generations. That House's loyalty is one of the few we can trust to a certain degree. I see no reason for *vezir* Amir to lie. The story he spun was worrisome."

"There is a death-defying machine that turns the dead into revenants quicker than spores. There are *rionetkas* masquerading as people who are no longer themselves. You would never know they were against you until the bullet pierced your back. We play games of death in honor of the Dawn Star, but I think even she would question these sorts of prayers."

"And you think to prove all this at the Senate today?"

"I am taking the bodies to the Senate today for the session. I hope the senators will see reason."

"My child, that isn't the proof you believe it to be."

Vanya ground his teeth, pacing away from his great-aunt to the credenza that held a glass case. Inside was a leather-bound book, its pages aged to yellow and opened to one listing out names. It was a certified copy of the royal genealogies held by the Star Order in Solaria. His gaze rested on his daughter's name inked onto the page. Of the names written out, there were precious few that did not have a date in the death column.

"It doesn't have to be," Vanya said. "That is not my intention with today's session. I mean it as a warning."

"What use is a warning if none will believe in the threat?"

"I'll give it a face."

"You should do that before she gives it yours."

Vanya straightened up and turned to face Taisiya. "What have you heard?"

Taisiya tipped her head to the side, hair falling across one shoulder. "I know you took a warden to the crypts. I know Joelle has ever schemed for the Imperial throne. I know she would take Raiah if she could."

He'd forgotten that Taisiya and Joelle were contemporaries. They'd have seen each other in the Imperial court growing up, on distant sides of a House divide—Taisiya never wanting to rule and Joelle aching for it.

"She tried in Oeiras."

"And do you have proof?"

Vanya grimaced, irritation making his skin prickle. "None that would grant a blood feud. None the Houses would believe. But tell me, who else would be behind my attempted murder and Raiah's attempted kidnapping?"

Taisiya sighed heavily, a rasp that sounded painful. "Every House that is not ours. You foolish boy. If you have no proof, then you must provide rumors. I can guarantee you Joelle has already started those."

"If you only came here to disparage my choices—"

"I came to ensure we still have a House at the end of this mess," Taisiya interrupted sharply. "The Imperial throne will outlive us all, but I would not see our House fall to ruin the way the House of Laxsom did. You live in the shadow of your mother's choices, and we all pay for them. Or did you wonder why so many fought to have their debts die with her?"

Vanya snapped his teeth together. "Mother did what she thought was right."

"And we've a country kept whole because of her, but ask yourself how much longer that will remain true if what you bring to the Senate today is believed?" Taisiya turned and headed for the door, stride slow due to age, but she carried herself with a regality that came from her station. "I am not your enemy, Vanya. I am of your House, and I am your *valide*. Now, come. I would see you act the emperor and not the fool."

She left, and Vanya had no choice but to follow. His mother had trusted Taisiya's counsel when she ruled, despite the distance between them. He could not say the same just yet, but she was of his House, and there were so few of them left to stand against the currents of politics that ruled his every step.

VANYA

The Senate building was a grand thing, edged in gold, with its domed roof of the central building covered in a mosaic depicting every House emblem in Solaria. Surrounded by its own set of walls well guarded by legionnaires, it was a place of power that every emperor and empress had worked to oversee.

Vezirs of major Houses governed their *vasilyets* at the grace of the Imperial throne, with the understanding that the senators they sent as their representatives to Calhames debated laws that would live or die by the stroke of the emperor's pen. Committee work was a slog, but it was where political and House alliances were made.

The Imperial throne oversaw the Senate as it had since the Dawn Star had decreed Solaria's form of rulership. Vanya had learned much from his mother, both in listening to her counsel those who sought an audience with the Imperial throne amidst the court back at the palace or here, within these hallowed halls, where even blood feuds were momentarily set aside for the sake of the country.

Vanya knew there was a risk of creating a blood feud today with the House of Kimathi with the accusation he intended to level against Joelle. But his mother had taken a risk at Rixham all those years ago, and he would do the same here. When he walked into the Senate chamber with its senator seats and the mezzanine above for the Houses, he did so leading coffins bearing the dead into a place of the living.

The gasps of surprise and, yes, even shock echoed through the air. The gas lamps burned bright around the room, allowing him to see the concern and even hints of horror on the faces of nearby senators. When Vanya glanced up at the mezzanine, he found nearly every seat there full, numerous members of Houses peering down at the Senate floor and the currently empty golden throne on the dais.

It was easy to pick out the House of Kimathi, Joelle sitting front and center in the first row, flanked by her son and heir, Artyom, both of them dressed as if for a state occasion in their finest robes and jewels. All they lacked was the crown on Vanya's head, and the juxtaposed symbolism wasn't lost on him.

The section located directly over the throne was reserved for the House of Sa'Liandel. Those seats were filled on occasions by distant relatives, seeking favor and to flaunt their ties to the Imperial throne. The august body gathered there for the latest session erupted in a surprised murmur of countless voices as Lady Taisiya Sa'Liandel of the House of Sa'Liandel was escorted to her seat by Amir.

Vanya met her gaze from the floor of the Senate, and she inclined her head toward him in acknowledgment before gracefully taking her seat, the only member of his House in attendance. Amir bowed to her before taking his leave to find his own seat amongst his House several sections down the length of the mezzanine.

"What is the meaning of this?" the sergeant at arms demanded from the front of the chambers, standing ramrod straight in his pressed uniform. Maurizio was a man who knew the rules of the Senate like the Imperial tax collector knew taxation laws. Everyone was bound by Senate rules inside these walls.

Everyone save the person who sat upon the Imperial throne.

Like his mother, Vanya rarely broke the rules of the chamber for his own needs. To rule in such a way was to invite assassins into one's life. Vanya's job as emperor was to think of Solaria as a whole, and he worked in tandem with the Senate when required to achieve that harmony. His House would not be seen as a dictator, though he knew others saw them that way, especially after what was done to Rixham.

"I am here to put to rest the rumors of what happened in Oeiras," Vanya said from the Senate floor, gaining everyone's attention.

The *praetoria* legionnaires in charge of the coffins lined them up side by side before the dais. At Vanya's nod, the magician stepped forward, wand raised as she worked to undo the spell keeping them sealed. Senators reared back in shock at her actions, voices rising in protest.

Vanya ignored the furor with a calmness he didn't fully feel, but he'd spent his entire life projecting a sense of command. This was no different.

"The dead should not be here," Maurizio snapped, recoiling as the coffin lids were raised.

"The time has passed for them to have risen as revenants. I bring the dead here for a reason." Vanya stepped closer to the coffins, taking the box that held the shattered pieces of clockwork metal heart. "It is true it was *praetoria* legionnaires who attacked me in Oeiras and sought to take my daughter. But the men and women who were once loyal to the throne did not lose their loyalty by choice."

Vanya opened up the box, the pieces of once-spellbound metal shifting inside. "A captain who was not afflicted used mind magic on the dying and discovered they called themselves *rionetkas*. They were loyal to a different master, made that way by having their hearts replaced with clockwork gears and alchemy, with mind magic to ensure control. They acted normal, right up until the moment they tried to kill me."

Vanya stalked across the open floor of chambers, slipping between two coffins, until he could stand before the sergeant at arms. He offered Maurizio the box, raising an eyebrow when he didn't immediately take it.

"It will not harm you," Vanya said with a gentleness that felt like a lie on his tongue. "Whoever was behind this atrocity set a self-destruct to the clockwork hearts. Pass it to the senators."

Maurizio was all too willing to pass the shattered metal pieces to the next person. "With all due respect, Your Imperial Majesty, the dead should not be here."

"The dead are what hunt us, and the *rionetkas* are no different, being little more than living puppets."

"Who is to say you did not carve the bodies open yourself?" Joelle called out, her voice carrying. A soft murmur of agreement drifted up from other Houses present, lending their support.

"Speaks one whose *vasilyet* is overrun with revenants and a border porous in ways that speak of deficient law," Taisiya countered almost immediately. Her rough voice didn't carry as well, but the immediate hush that settled over the Senate proved she was still someone all those present listened to.

Vanya tipped his head back, crown never shifting, as he stared up at where Joelle sat. Artyom had stood at Taisiya's accusation but said nothing, not while Joelle commanded his silence. Raiah's great-grandmother looked down at him, expression carved from stone.

"A heavy charge for a House who lets the dead be viewed when they shouldn't," Joelle said.

Her words were like a double-edged blade, designed to slice through all defenses. She didn't accuse him of bringing a warden into the crypt, but she might as well have. The buried dead was a secret for the Houses who had sat upon the Imperial throne to keep and not meant to be argued in public. Joelle skirted the unspoken law by bringing up that subject, but then, Vanya himself had broken it when he'd brought Soren to his parents' funeral rites. Here, in this chamber, Vanya would keep his teeth sealed on recognizing the bodies buried beneath the palace.

Joelle was not to be so easily deterred.

She stood, looking as if the motion pained her, and Vanya was reminded of the many assassination attempts she'd survived. "You speak of these *rionetkas* as if they are real. Who is to say you have not desecrated the living to lie with the dead? This horror you yourself could have ordered—just like your mother."

Others murmured agreement to her words, a hubbub of noise that cut off when Vanya raised his hand. "This is not about secession. I am not here to bring a *vasilyet* to heel."

"Yet," Taisiya demurred, drawing a sharp look from Joelle.

Vanya didn't allow himself the indulgence of smiling at her pointed remark. "I have witnesses from the remainder of the *praetoria* legionnaire who were with me in Oeiras and those of my household."

"That means nothing," Joelle countered.

"I suppose it means as much or as little as the quarry in your *vasilyet* full of revenants." The accusation came out sharper than he intended, but Joelle's expression didn't falter. "One must wonder if the uptick of revenants in the northwest of Solaria is manufactured. I've heard complaints from merchants about the risk of road travel in your *vasilyet*. The border reports have nothing good to say about the known attacks in land under your governance."

"I know nothing of this quarry you speak of."

Vanya allowed his voice to be like ice. "Of course you don't. But a warden saw firsthand the atrocity you allowed and Imperial General Chu Hua confirmed its existence. *Praetoria* legionnaires brought back photographs of the charred landscape."

"For all we know, they did the damage themselves during field training. As to this warden—" Joelle tilted her head, bracing herself against the mezzanine railing as she leaned forward. "—I give no credence to a warden's word if they are the same one who sleeps in your bed."

Vanya had expected such a dagger-tipped accusation, and he let it wash over him like so much water, ignoring the speculative looks in the Houses surrounding him. "Who I sleep with is not your concern."

"It is when they are around a member of *my* House. Where is my great-granddaughter? No one has seen her since Oeiras. You have made it known for years that if I am to see her, I must visit Calhames. Well, Your Imperial Majesty. I am here, and I would see one of my House."

Vanya's teeth ground together, having seen the verbal corner she'd been herding him to well before the conversation even started. He'd expected such a demand since first hearing the House of Kimathi had returned to Calhames. "Raiah is not a subject for the Senate to debate."

"But the Houses are allowed to, and so we shall." Joelle straightened up, gesturing widely with one hand. "My fellow Houses, I call for a Conclave of Houses, as is my right when a member of my House is under duress."

"One wonders why you wouldn't call for a blood feud," Vanya said sharply.

"Will *you*, Your Imperial Majesty?" Joelle asked with such sugared sweetness the insult was known by all.

Vanya didn't move. "You have nothing I want."

It went unsaid that he had everything she desired, and the fury that seeped through the cracks of her iron control was a victory Vanya knew he'd never get to savor.

"The House of Aetos is amenable to a Conclave," Lady Vesper called out, neatly cutting through the rising murmur of voices with a calm sureness that spoke of political ties already knotted together before today.

Where the House of Aetos went, others followed. Enough support was present that there was no outmaneuvering Joelle in this moment. Vanya could only tally those in favor and those reluctantly so. One could not deny a Conclave of Houses, a public judgment of peers that could not strip Vanya of the Imperial throne, but it could strip him of support, and that was a death knell in and of itself.

Debts were handled in secret, as were assassination orders and bribes. A public airing of grievances was done to give cover to the backdoor politicking that could and had realigned House ties in the past.

"The Imperial throne has never stood in the way of a Conclave of Houses, and it will not do so now. The House of Kimathi will have their grievance heard so long as the House of Sa'Liandel's grievance is given the same contemplation," Vanya said.

"And what grievance do you carry?" Joelle asked, careful to keep the scorn out of her voice, but the polite coolness of her tone was a barb nonetheless.

At this, Vanya allowed himself a smile. "As your emperor, I hold grievances for the whole of Solaria. The border reports do not lie and the wardens have taken notice of your hostility to the Poison Accords and the right of passage they are allowed through all countries. I would have the Conclave review your decisions as *vezir* to see if you are still worthy of such a title."

The uproar from the House of Kimathi was expected, with Artyom crying out, "I will not stand for this insult!"

"But you will be judged by it," Amir said loudly, banging the tip of his cane against the mezzanine floor. "The House of Vikandir supports the emperor's request."

Despite the support lost with his mother's death, there was still some shred of loyalty amongst the Houses owed to him, even if much of it was wound through the House of Vikandir at this present time. It was enough to allow for Vanya's own charge to be brought before the Houses, which was all that mattered.

Vanya retreated to the throne, taking his rightful place. "The Senate and the Houses will view the bodies of the *rionetkas* before leaving today's session. The bodies will then be burned by the Star Order, but their existence will not be denied. I would advise that all households search their family and their employees for vivisection scars."

With the dead still in the chambers and an Imperial order handed down, senators and the Houses had no choice but to obey. Doing so would remove the dead faster. No matter the embalming technique used to keep them from decaying or the magician on hand to guard them, everyone knew the dead must be burned.

It was different for those of the Houses who had sat upon the Imperial throne. They knew of the traditions carried out for the Dawn Star, of the royal dead buried in the crypt beneath the palace. They still recoiled from the bodies of the *rionetkas* when they saw the mess of their carved-up chests and burned forms, gazes flickering to where Vanya sat.

When Joelle walked between the coffins, she barely glanced at them, attention on Vanya rather than the dead. She said nothing, but the curve of her lips was prideful in a way Vanya had never trusted.

She'd orchestrated a Conclave of Houses, after all, conducting what he knew would be a terrible whisper campaign to steal support from his House and his hold on the Imperial throne. What she could not achieve through Nicca, she'd try through Raiah, and Vanya was viscerally glad that his daughter was elsewhere, safe in the only pair of hands he trusted.

Joelle bowed to the exact degree required for a sitting emperor, no more and no less, before taking her leave, Artyom by her side and leading her away. Only when star priests and priestess of the Star Order entered the chambers did Vanya stand from the throne, allowing them to take control of the dead. The bodies would be burned, ashes sent to finally dance amongst the stars.

He swept out of the chambers, finding Taisiya waiting for him in the hallway. She nodded a greeting, and Vanya kept to her pace rather than his as they made their way down the marble hall, guarded by *praetoria* legionnaires.

"I believe it is time I reacquainted myself with the social season of the Houses," Taisiya said.

Vanya offered his arm to her, and she curled her hand around the bend of his elbow with a surprisingly firm grip. "I thought you weren't one for gatherings."

"I am old, Vanya. I would have stayed in my estate with poison tasters I trust, but I suppose I will put yours to work here."

It would mean days and nights of entertaining guests at the palace and being entertained elsewhere. Even with protections in place, with everyone looking for *rionetkas,* they would need to be on guard against more mundane threats.

Poison was tradition, after all.

"My household is yours to command," Vanya said.

Taisiya tightened her grip in silent acknowledgment, a quiet force to be reckoned with, much like his mother had once been.

Three

NATHANIEL

Nathaniel Clementine's body was a battlefield, and his mind was a graveyard of who he used to be.

The cage of his bones was like iron, teeth locked tight against words that battered against his skull. But his tongue couldn't shape them, the oily feel of mind magic staining every thought he strung together and twisting the truth into a lie.

Exactly like what passed for his heartbeat now.

The metal in his chest was cold, icy in the way of magic, a weight he'd never forget was there and edged in agony. The potions he'd drunk in that underground horror cell had provided a healing that was anything but kind.

Nathaniel gasped for breath in the alleyway he had stumbled into, his body bracing itself against the filthy wall with one hand. His other clutched at his throat, skin there bare of a bank number, but he'd rather have that than the reminder of what he'd gone through carved into his chest.

He couldn't say he was alive because Nathaniel wasn't even sure he was that anymore.

A living person wouldn't carry pink and raw vivisection scars hidden beneath a veil woven large enough to lie atop the sewn-up cuts and held in place by tiny metal hooks pierced through his skin. It had been the last thing the *Klovod* had done to him before telling him to dress and then leave, the orders Nathaniel carried in his mind thick and cloying and guiding his feet ever onward through Amari.

The *Klovod* had picked apart his mind, leaving traps behind for any magician who dared go looking. Nathaniel was terrified of what would happen to whoever tried—but that was if they even knew to ask if anything was wrong.

Not that he could answer truthfully.

His hand shoved his body away from the wall, feet taking him forward without his consent. His body left the alleyway behind for the streets, the flickering orange glow of the gas lamps lighting the way to Paradis.

He tried to fight against every step his body took, but his efforts left him screaming into the void that was his mind, magic keeping his body in lockstep to the *Klovod*'s orders. It wasn't Nathaniel who jangled the locked door of Scarlette's burlesque club.

It was the *Klovod*'s puppet.

His *rionetka*.

The door wasn't spelled, but someone was watching, perhaps from the window. Whoever was on watch duty would have seen his approach. This late at night, even Paradis had chased the drunks from its beds. What remained were cogs Nathaniel had no choice but to betray.

The lock clicked from the inside, gears turning, and his hand let go of the knob, body stepping back. The door cracked open, and Nathaniel found himself staring past the barrel of a pistol into Scarlette's vivid green eyes.

He felt his mouth curve into a relieved smile, the strings of the *Klovod*'s mind magic playing them all for a fool. "Scarlette."

Her eyes widened in shock, and she immediately lowered the pistol. "Nathaniel!"

Scarlette jerked the door open and grabbed him by the dirty collar of his shirt, hauling him inside Paradis. She hip-checked the door closed, and one of the boys—pretty and big-eyed and casually holding a shotgun—reached out to lock it for her. Scarlette framed his face with both her hands, her touch warm in a distant way. Everything felt so removed to him, the haze of the *Klovod*'s orders coloring everything.

"Rumor had it the Collector's Guild took you on a warrant for treason," Scarlette said tightly, her gaze staring right through him and seeing nothing but a lie.

Nathaniel's hand reached up to gently encircle her wrist. "Rumor would be right. We got caught up in the riot, though, and the debt collectors with me were killed by revenants. I stayed hidden in the wagon and got free with the help of a protestor who returned looking for their friends. I've laid low since then in the catacombs."

The lie was a pretty one, spun up from mind magic, taking his memories and building something believable. The tension in Scarlette's shoulders flowed out of her like water. "We thought we'd lost you. That your chain had broken. I've sent as many people on out of the city as I could. Amari hasn't been safe since the riot and revenant incursion."

His gaze strayed to the blooming roses tattoo on both sides of her neck that covered the bank number tattoo she'd carried for years in Daijal. Every debt slave who stepped inside Paradis received a similar tattoo and copies of their loan discharge paperwork in triplicate before disappearing across Ashion with the help of the Clockwork Brigade. Of course she would not join them. Of course she would stay to help.

Scarlette had always had a target on her back, but Nathaniel knew it would get struck after he left her. This body had its orders, and the *Klovod* would be informed of the information he retained here tonight.

"But you'll stay?" Nathaniel prompted, unable to stop the words from leaving his lips.

Scarlette sighed and let him go, stepping back. "Someone must. Come, I'll make us some tea. Have you heard the news about the Dhemlans?"

If Nathaniel still had a heart, it would have skipped a beat. "No. As I said, I was in the catacombs."

Her lips twisted into a faint moue. "Well then. I believe it's time we had a chat."

His body went where Nathaniel didn't want it to go, following Scarlette down the hallway and into the burlesque club proper. The performing room with its curtained-off stage was empty and dark. A flick of a switch turned on the gas lamp chandeliers overhead. Nathaniel's body followed Scarlette to the bar and past it into the small, cramped kitchen that was just as empty of people.

He watched her pull a kettle, teapot, and some cups from a storage cupboard. She filled the kettle with water and placed it on the stove, lighting the burner. The tea she scrounged up wasn't from her personal store, but it was the kind offered to paying customers. When it was finally steeped and poured into his teacup, Nathaniel drank it, even if he didn't taste it.

"Your lady," Scarlette said after a moment, keeping her voice quiet the way he assumed debt slaves kept secrets.

"Miss Caris Dhemlan," Nathaniel said, screaming all the while in his mind.

"She's been in the broadsheets. She escaped the riot with aid of an airship the press is saying was captained by E'ridians."

"The airspace over Amari is restricted."

"She wouldn't have survived if they had obeyed that law." Scarlette paused long enough to take another sip of tea, knuckles white. "Or perhaps she would have. The press caught her using starfire."

He knew, of course, of Caris' secret, of the power that sparked at her fingertips and the hope she could become for so many people. He knew as well that secret had been stripped of him and handed over to Queen Eimarille Rourke, and here he stood to do her bidding.

Scarlette studied him, green eyes overly bright in her face. "Did you know?"

"I'm a cog, Scarlette."

They all were, and they all had their duties to tend to. Nathaniel wished, in that moment, he'd never known his.

"Of course you are." Scarlette tapped a finger against her teacup before setting it aside. "I've been given orders by Fulcrum to help certain cogs leave the city. You weren't on the list, but I'll send you on regardless."

"To where Caris is?"

Scarlette shook her head. "I don't know where Caris is, but I do know her parents were put under house arrest."

If Nathaniel had control of his body, he'd have needed to lock his knees. The desire to stagger back was so visceral he thought he felt it in his nerves, but his stance didn't change. All his body did was drink more tea. "I need to find her."

Scarlette smiled sadly at him. "I wish you all the best with that endeavor. I will smuggle you out of Amari tomorrow. Tonight's rendezvous for package pickup has already passed."

Nathaniel wanted to warn her that he couldn't be trusted, that the second he left was when the debt collectors would come for her. But his lips stayed sealed, and Scarlette never saw through the façade he was living. The threat of *rionetkas* must not have spilled down the chain of cogs yet, and her ignorance would cost Scarlette her life once he left her capable hands.

They finished their tea, and then she brought him to the basement below Paradis and into the secret hidden rooms there, where debt slaves were tattooed and kept out of sight. The row of cots was empty, as he was the only package at the moment when he wished he wasn't.

"You haven't asked about your family," Scarlette said as she watched the body fuss with the blanket.

"If I was taken, then so were they." His body shrugged its shoulders, and whatever expression his face showed to her had Scarlette coming to Nathaniel's side, grief etched into her own. "But I can't stay, and my parents would understand why."

It was eerie the way the *Klovod*'s orders put just the right amount of tremor into his voice—some hint of grief and guilt guaranteed to put another person at ease with the humanity of his response.

Scarlette took his hand and leaned in to kiss him softly on both cheeks, a dead woman walking, whether she knew it or not. "We'll look for them. The Clockwork Brigade is still standing."

It wouldn't be for very much longer if Eimarille had her way because Nathaniel was a piece meant to shatter it, and no one in Ashion knew of his treachery.

SOREN

Soren thought Ashion should feel different once they'd crossed that northern border, but nothing changed, only their position on the map. The same summery heat from the sun overhead followed them from Solaria into Ashion, to a border town whose walls were old but not crumbling. No town that wanted to keep citizens could ill afford damaged walls. Taxes kept the safety measure in place, but these walls were in need of an upgrade.

It was still a place that wasn't in the back roads, wasn't out in the open, and hopefully safe enough that Soren could get some much-needed *sleep*. Running for days on field stimulants meant his vision was blurring at the edges in a way he knew he couldn't afford, not if he wanted to keep Raiah safe.

He steered the velocycle off the grassy plains and onto the road, tires leaving the dirt behind. No railroad tracks passed it by, but it had a communication tower on account, which meant it would have a resupply station. Its airfield was of a decent size for a border town, with half a dozen airships anchored at its piers. There were some perks to be had for living on a road that led directly east to the Warden's Island in the Celestine Lake.

"Can we stop? I'm hungry," Raiah piped up from behind him.

"We're stopping," Soren promised.

The gates to the town were open, guarded by a pair of peacekeepers who were more interested in their card game than Soren's arrival. A rusted-looking automaton stood on the other side of the gate, its Zip gun arms pointed at the ground and not at any threat on the horizon. A sign stretching over the gates listed out the town's name as Rouilly.

Soren slowed to a stop in front of the open gate but didn't remove his helmet or brass goggles. His Ashionen was practically nonexistent, so he stuck with the trade tongue when greeting the peacekeepers. "Where can I find the resupply station?"

The peacekeeper jerked his thumb over his shoulder. "Western quadrant of the town, off Summer Square. We've only one inner wall, and it's near that."

As directions went, they were terrible, but part of being a warden was knowing where you were and navigating accordingly. Soren revved the engine and drove into Rouilly. He followed street signs on a meandering ride into the western quadrant, needing to ask directions from a traffic attendant only once before finally reaching the resupply station.

Not every town was guaranteed to have a resupply station. The building it was located in was nondescript, the roof weathered from sun and summer storms. A single velocycle was parked out front, indicating at least one other warden was taking a break from the road. He took the other parking spot, turning off the engine with a tired sigh.

"Up!" Raiah demanded from behind him.

"I'll let you up, but you need to remember rule number one while we're here," Soren reminded her as he swung his leg over the velocycle. Her accent was distinctly noticeable here in Ashion.

"I'll be quiet," she promised.

He undid Raiah's straps, curling his hands beneath her arms to haul her out of the ride-along seat. He set her on the pavement, not needing to tell her to stay close. These many days together, she knew not to leave his side.

"None of that," Soren said when she started fussing with the buckles of her helmet. "Keep it on until we're in the room."

"I want a bath."

Of course she did. Resupply stations had rooms for traveling wardens, but they most certainly never had bathhouses. If Raiah expected to find the comforts of home inside these walls, she'd be sorely disappointed, and Soren hated for her to be disappointed.

"I promise we'll get you cleaned up."

Soren hauled his main gear from the travel compartments, slinging his rucksack over one shoulder before taking Raiah's hand in his. She looked up at him through her goggles, curly hair hidden by the helmet, and dressed in nondescript trousers and a linen robe. Alida had chosen her clothing well for a road trip.

He led Raiah into the resupply station, the scent of oil and metal and a hint of chemicals hitting his nose. Wardens were alchemists by virtue of their trade, and resupply stations had on-site workshops to aid in the chemical-based supplies they used in the poison fields.

Soren looked down at Raiah. "Don't touch anything."

She wrinkled her nose at him and stuck out her tongue but didn't speak. He kept a firm grip on her small hand as he went up to the unmanned counter and pressed a finger to the mechanical call button. The chime of the bell echoed in the room, drawing the warden on duty out from the back workroom.

The woman's gray hair was shorn close to her skull, showing off the jagged scar near her temple and the missing top of one ear. Soren recognized a bite wound when he saw one, still carrying the ragged imprint of teeth on his own arm from the revenant attack in the quarry. Her brown eyes were sharp, though, and undamaged, the magnifying goggles she wore making them appear even larger than they truly were.

"Huh," the warden said in the trade tongue, eyeing Raiah. "Did you find her on the road?"

"Tithe," Soren said smoothly. "She was the sole survivor of an overrun camp near a back road."

"She'd be better off with the Star Order."

Soren shrugged. "I was told by government officials to count her as a tithe and deliver her. They've marked her as such already in their records. I'm taking her to the Warden's Island. We've been on the road for a few days now, though, and I need to sleep. Is a room open?"

The warden raised a hand to shove her magnifying goggles on top of her head. "Only one is taken. You're welcome to any of the others upstairs. I'll log you in. Name?"

The only thing wardens owned was their name, and offering it was tradition for those who guarded the borders. "Soren."

No recognition flickered across her face as she reached for the logbook beneath the counter and flipped it open. "I'm Coralie."

"Well met."

She took a pen from her pocket and wrote down the date and time of his arrival, along with his name. That done, she put the logbook away and pulled a set of brass keys off the wall behind her. "This unlocks the largest room on the premises. There's a shared washroom at the end of the hall upstairs."

Not the bath Raiah truly wanted, but it would do. Soren took the keys with a nod of thanks and guided Raiah upstairs. It was a matter of moments to dump his gear in the assigned room, dig out a set of clean clothes for Raiah, and escort her to the small washroom at the end of the hall that housed a toilet, sink, and narrow shower.

It was clean, courtesy of the warden downstairs, whose duties included caring for the property as well as keeping inventory of the resupply station below. Soren had helped Vanya bathe Raiah when she was a baby and a toddler on occasion, and this was no different. He helped Raiah get undressed and used one of the wash rags in the basket to scrub her clean. The water ran dark with all the dust and dirt they'd accumulated, and her skin was a little pink in areas despite his best efforts to protect her from the sun. He'd need to find his burn balm for that.

Raiah pouted as Soren gently rubbed at her cheek with the wash rag. "I wanted a bath."

"I know. Perhaps next time."

When they finished, he wrapped her up in a clean but scratchy towel, dried her off, and got her dressed. It took a little bit of time to detangle her hair and clumsily separate it into two braids. Vanya was far more skilled than he was at doing Raiah's hair, but Soren did his best.

"There we go," he said, patting her head.

Raiah smiled toothily up at him. "Can we eat now?"

Soren nodded and opened the door, stiffening when he caught sight of someone else in the hall. Another warden, this one tall and blond and broad-shouldered, waited in the hall, arms crossed over his chest. Gray hair edged his temples and the shadow of a beard he sported, face weathered from a life spent in the poison fields. His bushy eyebrows crept toward his hairline when he caught sight of Raiah by Soren's side.

"What are you doing with a kid?" the warden asked.

"She's a tithe," Soren said, placing a hand on her head, wishing he'd put her helmet back on. "And not your business."

The warden blinked lazily at him, decked out in full gear, which made Soren hope he'd be leaving. Perhaps this was the owner of the other velocycle parked outside. "Not saying she is. Name's Harald."

"Soren."

Another blink. "And the kid?"

"Nameless." It was tradition for a tithe, after all. Soren remembered that well enough, even if Callisto would rather he'd forget how he came to be the man he was today. "She's hungry."

Harald shoved away from the wall, turning enough that Soren got a better look at the poison scimitar the other warden carried for close-quarters combat duties when facing off with revenants. "I've been here for two days. I can show you to a good café."

"We'll be fine."

"Consider it business. I'd like to know where in the poison fields you found her. We've had a lot more revenants than usual in Ashion these last few years, and it's only polite to pass on a warning. With what's happening in the west right now, one can never be too careful."

Soren had an answer to that, even if he couldn't share it. What proof there'd been he'd destroyed with starfire no warden should ever have. And rumors of the death-defying machine weren't circulating amongst the general public in any country or amongst wardens. The wardens' governor had kept that information restricted, and Soren didn't have the authority to disclose it.

"We'll have a late meal somewhere close by. She'll need a nap afterward," Soren finally agreed. If word got around that he was reticent to share reports from the poison fields that could possibly aid other wardens and keep them safe, it would cause complications.

Harald snorted. "If she's a tithe, naps won't help her."

Training had never been easy, but the wardens tasked with teaching them how to survive had still made allowances for the care younger children needed.

He kept hold of Raiah on the way out of the resupply station and to a café three blocks over, set up against the town's inner wall. The place seemed to cater to the neighborhood as opposed to those passing through. Raiah's eyes went wide in her face when she saw the clockwork toy train that rode around a set of miniature tracks attached to the wall near the ceiling.

"Look!" she said, pointing at the toy train.

Soren fought back a wince at her excited cry in Solarian, Raiah clearly having forgotten not to chatter here. But she was four and used to getting her way, and Soren couldn't be angry at her excitement. She'd not had any of the comforts of her home since fleeing Oeiras, and if the toy distracted her, so much the better.

"Came from the south, did you?" Harald asked.

Soren didn't respond as he guided Raiah over to an empty table by the window. She climbed up onto the wooden chair, head tilted up as she watched the toy train make another circuit around the café.

The waitstaff consisted of a middle-aged woman who bustled over to their table with a notepad in hand, a smile for Raiah, and a polite nod for the wardens. She spoke in the trade tongue, her accent influenced by the country they were in. "Menu is posted on the flip cards, but what would the little one like to drink?"

"Fruit juice, if you have it. I'll take some water," Soren said, sticking to the same language.

"Iced tea for me," Harald said.

The woman left to fill their drink order. Soren picked up the small metal stand that had several cards attached to it by a ring. He flipped through it once before leaning in close to Raiah, switching over to her native Solarian. "They have a meat pie you might like."

"Yes," Raiah said, most of her attention on the train.

She'd been mostly good about not arguing with him about the food he gave her. Their supply was low in his pack, and he aimed to replenish it in the town for her. He could hunt while on the road, but he'd never feed her any wild game.

Soren opted for a meat wrap when the waitress returned, placing his orders while Harald went with half a roasted chicken and some summer vegetables.

"Your Solarian is good. Is your Ashionen that terrible you won't speak it?" Harald asked, sipping his iced tea. Several slices of citrus floated in it, the colorful rinds mixed in with the ice.

"I handle borders in the south," Soren said.

"Gone a bit out of your way by coming up here if you were meaning to head back to the Warden's Island."

"Revenants." Soren shrugged. "You know how it is. I needed a safe place to rest for her. I can't get that outside of city walls."

Raiah had twisted around in her seat, head back as she watched the clockwork toy train make another circuit around the café, passing overhead. Soren knew for a fact she had plenty of clockwork toys back in Calhames, though none had been packed for their travels. She must miss them.

"Did you deal with the revenants in Solaria or Ashion?"

"Does it matter? I dealt with them."

Harald gulped down some of his iced tea, slouching in his chair. The café was only half-full, it being well past noon, but the patrons present eyed their table with an uncomfortable wariness Soren had seen all his life.

A warden's job was to cleanse the land, and that included eradicating revenants. Most people always focused on the dead over the alchemy involved in their job, fearful of contamination from spores by being within proximity of a warden. But the Poison Accords granted them access to every town and city in every country on Maricol. There was no border or wall closed to them. That had been agreed to millennia ago.

It didn't stop people from being uncomfortable around wardens.

When their food came, Soren cut a hole in the crust of Raiah's meat pie to let the steam out. "Let it cool first."

Raiah picked up the child-sized fork that came with the plate and proceeded to dig out a bite and blow on it loudly. Soren left her to it and took a bite of his meat wrap. He was disappointed in the lack of spices, far too used to Solarian heat in all the dishes he ate with Vanya.

"How is it someone your age managed to get a job delivering border reports to the Imperial court?" Harald asked halfway through their awkward, silent meal.

Soren didn't freeze, only because he'd spent enough time around Vanya and in the Imperial court to know that was a fine way to lose the verbal high ground. "I don't know what you mean."

Harald waved his fork at Soren, gaze intent. "Not many wardens named Soren in our ranks. Even fewer jobs that handle contact with government bodies and heads of state to carry border reports back to the governor. You're not supposed to be handed that position without earning it."

An undercurrent of jealousy colored Harald's tone. Soren set down what was left of his meat wrap, abruptly not hungry anymore and completely on guard. "I did earn it."

"By lying on your back?"

The words weren't said with malice, but the tight smile on Harald's face made his opinion clear as the most expensive clarion crystal. Soren slid a hand off the table to reach for Raiah, wanting to assure himself she was within reach. If it put his hand closer to his pistol, well, so much the better. "We all follow orders from the governor."

Harald shook his head before stabbing a piece of carrot and shoving it into his mouth. "Not to the degree you do."

"How I guard the borders assigned to me isn't any of your business."

The whole of the wardens didn't know about the crypt hidden beneath the Imperial palace in Calhames. They didn't know about the royal dead and the sanctions prepared but not yet levied against Solaria for breaking the Poison Accords. They didn't know about the death-defying machine and the *rionetkas* and the mess of politics Soren had run from. They didn't know, and wouldn't, not until the wardens' governor authorized the release of such information.

"Wardens talk, and the gossip columns in the broadsheets are worse, even in other countries," Harald said.

Soren let Raiah go, resting his hand on his thigh, forearm pressed to the holster on his belt, well within easy reach of a draw. "I don't know what you've read up here in Ashion, but I can say it isn't true. The press likes to embellish things. I'm a warden, same as you. We know not to mess around with matters of state."

"You're fucking one."

Soren supposed he should be glad they were discussing this in the trade tongue, Raiah oblivious to the words and the insult and the sudden pounding of Soren's heart. He liked to think his closeness to Vanya wasn't common knowledge, but he knew that was a lie, not with the Houses aware of how much Vanya favored him, even if they didn't know about the vow he carried around his neck.

"I think you're mistaken," Soren said evenly.

Harald's gaze never wavered. "Am I?"

Soren refused to answer that. He'd known for a while now that some wardens were resentful of his assigned duties. The extenuating circumstances couldn't be explained, and Soren dealt with such judgmental opinions from his fellow wardens by not spending a lot of time around them. The less chance for questions, the better.

Soren stood and reached for Raiah, smoothing his hand over her hair. She looked up at him and smiled sweetly before yawning. She wasn't finished with her meat pie, but he'd buy her another one later. "We're leaving."

Raiah set down her fork and slid off the chair, for once not arguing, which told him more than anything about how tired she must be. She hadn't understood the conversation they'd just had, and for that, he was grateful.

Soren dug a money clip out of his pouch and tossed down several auron bills to cover the two meals. Harald watched him with a clear-eyed gaze for a moment before shrugging and turning back to his meal, ignoring their leaving.

Once outside, Soren swung Raiah up in his arms and carried her back to the resupply station. Coralie was at the counter and looked up at their arrival, giving him an absent nod hello. Soren approached her, gaze skimming over the wall behind her with all its many and varied supplies on offer.

"I need a full refill of ammunition and some chemicals, along with some safe food supplies. We're leaving tomorrow morning," Soren said.

"I'll get it packed up for you by tonight and have it ready at the counter."

Soren went upstairs, weighing the risk of staying to get some rest over leaving to retain some semblance of safety. Harald hadn't asked after Raiah, but his attention on the princess had left Soren feeling cold.

"We'll leave tomorrow morning," Soren said once they were inside the room and the door was locked behind them.

Raiah nodded against his shoulder and didn't fuss when he put her down on the narrow bed, drawing the thin blanket over her. It was summer, and even with the window cracked open, the room felt stuffy. After years spent in Solaria, neither of them was bothered by the heat, but Soren found himself missing the airiness of the Imperial palace.

Raiah dropped off to sleep rather quickly. Soren spent a little time sorting through his gear to make room for what they'd be leaving with before bedding down on the floor, using his rucksack as a pillow, weapons close at hand. It was warm enough that he didn't need a blanket or sheet, and he nodded off with the quickness of one who'd spent years in the poison fields snatching sleep in increments.

But even asleep, a warden's instincts were typically on high alert. Soren woke hours later to Raiah still sleeping in the bed and the faint click of gears and tumblers in the door's lock being undone by a lockpick.

Soren sat up and soundlessly rolled to his feet, glad he'd slept in his boots. He stayed kneeling, putting himself between whoever was breaking in and Raiah asleep in the bed behind him. He unholstered his pistol as quietly as he could.

In the dimness of the room, Soren watched the knob turn, the door creaking open on hinges that hadn't been oiled in quite some time. The sound of it must have woken Raiah, for she stirred in the bed, smacking her lips together as she came out of sleep.

"Soren?" she mumbled.

He didn't think, merely turned and yanked her out of the bed along with the sheet twisted around her little body. Soren hauled her into his arms and pitched them both away from the door as it slammed open. Harald stepped inside, pistol leading the way, and the muzzle flashed in the graying light of the room, bullets peppering the bed where Raiah had been.

She screamed, wrapping her arms around Soren's neck, while starfire he didn't cast erupted along every wall in the room.

Five

SOREN

Soren pulled the trigger, but Harald was already moving, not startled at all by the starfire burning so hot it felt as if they stood in an oven. Harald jerked back into the hallway, out of sight, Soren's bullets slamming into the door rather than a living body.

"I only want the girl! She's worth more than you!" Harald shouted.

"She was asleep in the bed you just shot up!" Soren snarled.

Harald let out a harsh little laugh. "I think the queen of Daijal could make use of a princess whether she was dead or alive."

Soren shifted on his feet, eyeing the starfire eating its way through the walls while Raiah sobbed against his shoulder. He kept his pistol pointed at the entrance to the room. "The girl is a tithe."

"You lie about her as well as you lie about your place in her father's bed."

To hell with bullets.

Soren holstered his pistol and reached out his hand to the starfire burning like molten fiery gold all around him. Flame licked at his fingertips, making him shiver. The aether churned against his awareness, a vast power distilled into the starfire Raiah had inexpertly called out of instinct and fear.

He tugged at it clumsily, guiding it how he had before, an ache blossoming in the back of his head as he did so. The starfire twisted itself around his hand and wrist, snaking up his arm like an almost living thing. It was—warm, but it didn't burn him. Soren drew in a steady breath, hiking Raiah up farther in his other arm, keeping hold of her and the starfire both.

"Keep your eyes closed," he told her.

She'd stopped screaming, but she hadn't stopped crying. Soren desperately wanted to comfort her, but he had to keep her alive first in order to do that.

Footsteps thundering up the stairs heralded the arrival of Coralie, her voice ripping through the air. "What the bloody hell is going on? The room is on *fire*!"

A pistol went off in quick succession, the heavy thud of a body hitting the floor making Soren grimace. He couldn't believe Harald would attack a fellow warden so ruthlessly—but he could believe it if Harald wasn't himself. Jealousy was one thing for a warden. They all had moments of wanting something easier, a life less fraught. Betrayal, though, that went against who they were as a people, stateless though they were.

But mind magic could twist anyone, as he'd seen in Oeiras.

"Give me the girl. I won't ask again," Harald snapped from the hall.

Soren gathered more starfire in his hand, the bright heat of it almost otherworldly. He extended his arm toward the door, flexed his fingers, and *pushed* as he had at the quarry. The aether tore through him, spinning the starfire ever outward to encase the hallway and the warden in burning heat.

Harald screamed, the same way the *praetoria* legionnaires had when Vanya set them aflame. Raiah whimpered loudly, face tucked against his neck, shaking in his arms. He wished she didn't have to keep listening to people die around her, but Vanya would be the first to say every child of a House had to face the threat of assassins whether they liked it or not.

Soren's hand shook with the effort to keep the starfire contained. Unlike at the quarry, he couldn't let it rage here in a border town people called home. Distant, hazy memories of another night, another city burning, flickered through his mind before he pushed them aside. That life he'd come from had no bearing here, for all that starfire fell from his fingers.

He curled his hand into a fist, teeth clenched tight as he sought to put the starfire out the way he'd seen Vanya do before. Soren was a novice at this, and the power of it wasn't easily controlled in such a refined way, and he had no clarion–tipped wand to help him focus the aether. But desperation aided him, and Soren managed to snuff out the starfire after a fraught few moments.

The walls of the room were blackened and charred, smoke drifting hazily through the air, making him cough. He needed to get Raiah out of there. A garbled moan drifted up from the hallway, spurring him on. Soren reached down and grabbed the strap of his rucksack and poison short sword, knowing they only had so much time before peacekeepers and the fire brigade arrived.

Raiah clung to him, keeping her eyes squeezed tightly shut. Soren stepped into the burned hallway, finding Harald sprawled on the floor, his field leathers a charred mess and the rest of him not much better. Soren couldn't recognize his face, burned as it was, skin pinked and blackened, shiny in the way of deep damage.

His clothes had all but been burned away, revealing damaged skin and the puckered scars of vivisection cutting over his chest. Despite the heat all around them, Soren felt doused in ice water at the sight of those scars.

"*Rionetka*," Soren said, staring down at Harald.

He received no response to that statement, as he knew he would. Soren wasn't a magician. He didn't have the skill or the ability to pick apart a person's thoughts with mind magic how Captain Javier had in Oeiras. Regardless of the starfire he could not acknowledge, he had no ability to pry answers out of the near dead.

Soren did not know where Harald had been assigned—whether here in Ashion or across a country's border—but he'd been a warden and now a *rionetka*. Soren knew in that moment he couldn't trust that no one else at the Warden's Island would be the same. For all that the wardens' governor knew about the mechanical clockwork hearts, he hadn't reported back to Delani yet about the *rionetkas*.

He realized he couldn't be sure she wasn't one herself.

Soren knew Harald wouldn't survive the burn wounds. If they were anywhere else, Soren would put the other warden out of his misery. But Soren had Raiah in his arms, and he wasn't going to put her through that. He stepped over the bodies in the hallway, clattering down the stairs. He paused only long enough to go behind the counter and shove boxes of ammunition into his rucksack.

Rather than leave out the front entrance of the resupply station, Soren took the rear exit, coming out into a narrow alleyway. He paused long enough to set Raiah down on the ground, secure his poison short sword to his back, and haul the straps of the rucksack over both shoulders. Then he picked her up again and squeezed past the trash bins, coming out onto the gas lamp–lit street just as a fire brigade truck came racing around the far corner, its bells ringing shrilly in the evening air. It startled Raiah badly, the little girl clamping her hands over her ears with a shriek.

"Shh, shh," Soren said. "I have you."

He needed his velocycle, which was parked outside the resupply station. Soren headed around the corner and toward the chaos unfolding there. Peacekeepers had arrived, their motor carriages with specialized horns affixed to the top blocking the road.

Soren hurried closer, affecting a worried expression on his face as he approached the resupply station. A small crowd had gathered, which Soren pushed his way through. A peacekeeper held up his hand at Soren before realizing who he was stopping.

"Warden," the peacekeeper said.

"What happened?" Soren demanded, knowing full well what they'd find inside the resupply station.

"We're not sure. There's been an attack and fire damage, but the flames appear to have been put out," the peacekeeper said.

The small crowd shifted around Soren, pulling back once they realized he was a warden. Raiah lifted her head, blinking blearily at the peacekeeper, her face streaked with tears. "Loud," she complained in Solarian.

The peacekeeper blinked at her. Soren cut off any questions with "She's a tithe. We were coming back from dinner because she needs to rest, but it doesn't look like we can rest here. Is this the only resupply station?"

"We were lucky to get this one about fifty years ago."

Soren grimaced, gaze flicking over to the forced-open front door of the building. "I'll need to inform the wardens' governor about what has happened. Is the communication tower available?"

"It's built into the mayor's office, but it's after hours right now. It'll open up in the morning."

The peacekeeper offered up an address. He promised he'd pass on word about Soren's needs, which was all he could hope for at the moment. The town was too small to have a proper set of telephones or televoxes, so it'd be telegraph machines. All of which would be fine to use if Soren was truly going to reach out to the wardens' governor.

Only he wasn't, because he didn't know if Denali could be trusted.

Ignoring the bustle of the men and women in the fire brigade, Soren strapped Raiah into her ride-along seat, put on her helmet and goggles, stored his gear, and drove away from the quiet horror left inside the resupply station.

The thing was he still needed *sleep*. The few hours of rest he'd managed wasn't enough to clear his head completely. Soren's eyes burned from days on the road and stimulants that had kept him awake. He refused to put Raiah at risk, and that meant finding a place to sleep now that the resupply station was no longer viable. Which meant an inn, and he was thankful for the aurons Vanya had supplied him with.

Soren drove to the other side of the town, closer to the gated wall entrance, paid for a room, and locked the door behind him. It was small, with only one bed, which he laid Raiah down on. She'd stopped crying, but she didn't look well, too wide-eyed and frazzled. Soren smoothed a hand over her hair, giving her a tired smile.

She blinked up at him, little hands gripping at the sheets, and said, "You have starfire like Papa."

Soren froze, breath stuttering in his lungs. "Ah, no."

Raiah frowned at him, nose scrunching up. "But—"

"The starfire burned itself out. It does that," Soren lied. She was young enough; perhaps she would believe him. "I think it's time you went to bed."

Raiah fussed at him for a bit, still keyed up from what had happened at the resupply station. Eventually, Soren shucked off his gear, leaving it on the floor by the bedside, but kept his pistol on the rickety nightstand. Then he lay down in the bed, Raiah curled up beside him, one little hand clutching at the gold chain of the vow hanging around his throat.

Raiah slept, and eventually, so did Soren.

In the morning, hours past sunrise, when a mayor's aide came calling on the inn, looking for Soren, the warden and his charge were nowhere to be found. Soren had fled the town at dawn, buying passage for both himself and Raiah on an E'ridian airship heading southeast on a route meant to cross the southern border.

Six

SOREN

When they finally landed in Karnak, the sun was in the west, afternoon sunlight casting long shadows for the airfield workers tasked with securing the airship. The anchoring caused the airship to judder as it dropped more heavily into its berth. Raiah, with her nose pressed to the viewport window of their cramped little room, exclaimed loudly.

"Are we getting off?" she asked.

Soren finally came up with her helmet, where it had somehow fallen halfway down his rucksack. "Yes, but you need to put this on first."

Raiah climbed off the bench and went to stand before him. She was dressed in a pair of dark trousers and a beige robe, her shoes covered in dust from the road that no amount of brushing could clean up. Her hair was a frizzy mess, despite Soren's attempt that morning to redo the braids.

She stood still as he settled the helmet on her head and secured the strap beneath her small pointed chin. Raiah demanded to put the brass goggles on herself, and Soren let her do as she liked. Then he shouldered his rucksack over his poison short sword's sheath, took Raiah by the hand, and made his way off the airship for the docks.

A warm wind blew across the airfield, clouds drifting along overhead. Soren kept them pressed to the railing of the dock inside the hangar, waiting for his velocycle to be offloaded. Raiah stood quietly beside him, watching everything around her with wide eyes behind her goggles, clutching Soren's hand with her own small one.

With her face and hair hidden and Soren very clearly a warden, no one paid them much attention. Karnak was the closest city to the Celestine Lake, where the Warden's Island was located, but it wasn't an easy route to take. No direct railroads linked the lake to Solaria's most northern city. Solaria typically delivered tithes via airship.

But Karnak was used to wardens traveling through its city walls. Soren's presence wasn't remarked upon as they left the airfield behind for the city gates. His status as a warden got them waved through with no issue.

He'd been to Karnak plenty of times over the years when driving through Solaria to his assigned borders. He knew where every warden resupply station was within the half dozen inner-city walls, and Soren made certain to never get within half a mile of each one on his way to the rich neighborhood the *vezir* of the House of Vikandir called home.

The estate in question was located behind the innermost city wall in Karnak. Soren slowed his velocycle to a halt in front of the main drive, staring through the wrought iron gate at the grandly pillared estate beyond, subtle mosaics lining the arches of the doors and windows in golden tile. His view was abruptly obscured by the pair of legionnaires who placed themselves between him and his objective.

"What calls you here, warden?" the legionnaire on the left said, her hand resting lightly on her pistol.

"I want to speak to the *vezir*," Soren said.

"This is no border but a House, warden. Add your name to the list of citizens requesting an audience. The *vezir*'s majordomo controls the schedule, and you are not above anyone else here."

Soren slipped two fingers beneath the leather waistcoat he wore, pulling free the Imperial writ Vanya had given him in Oeiras. He unfolded it and held it out for the two legionnaires to read, watching as they both went rigid where they stood. "You'll find that I am."

They both came to attention and snapped off a salute before bowing—not to Soren, he knew, but to the voice of their emperor he represented. "We will escort you to the House of Vikandir."

Soren carefully folded up the Imperial writ and put it away in his pocket for easier reach. "Undo your uniforms first. I'd like to ensure neither of you is compromised."

The confusion in their expressions did not disappear, but they obeyed the order without argument. Such was the power of an Imperial writ, Soren presumed. Their uniforms were unbuttoned to show off unmarked skin on their chests. Soren forestalled them from stripping any further, satisfied they weren't *rionetkas*.

The pair did up their uniforms before the taller legionnaire opened one side of the gate. Soren guided the velocycle off the street and onto the drive, the engine a dull thrum in the air. The gate clanged shut behind them, and a legionnaire jogged up the drive alongside Soren, the ends of his *effiyeh* fluttering behind him. Soren drove at a slow enough pace to enable the man to keep up. They passed through a tunnel built into the front of the estate and appeared inside a forecourt. It lacked any plants and flowers but had an abundance of motor carriages parked alongside the wall.

Soren steered his velocycle to an unused section of the wall, kicking the stand down and turning off the engine. He got off the velocycle and undid the straps securing Raiah in her ride-along seat.

"Are we going to see Papa?" she asked.

"Your Papa isn't here," Soren said, lifting her into his arms.

The legionnaire eyed them both with a sharp, knowing look in his eyes, gaze lingering on Raiah. Soren didn't remove her helmet or her goggles, hoping to keep her identity a secret just a little longer.

A servant stepped outside of the nearby entrance, her gown a dusky green and made of a lightweight fabric in deference to the heat. It swirled around her ankles as she came to meet them. Before she even made it over to them, Soren had the Imperial writ out and ready for her perusal.

She stared at the piece of paper in Soren's hand that granted him all manner of things worthy of an emperor for a long moment before her wide-eyed gaze flicked up to meet his. "Come with me. I will take you to meet with the House of Vikandir's majordomo."

"All right." Soren nodded at the servant. "Please don't think me rude, but if you would pull down the neckline of your gown enough for me to see your collarbones, I'd appreciate it."

The absolutely scandalous and affronted expression on her face wasn't enough to make Soren back down. After a brief, tense moment, the servant angrily tugged at the neckline of her gown, revealing unmarked skin. Soren nodded his approval, and the servant huffed her opinion on his request.

The legionnaire took up guard duty at the door while Soren followed the servant inside. He was taken through the halls of a working estate that reminded him of the Imperial palace in its business and wealth, though the decorations tilted in a different artistic direction.

The sand-tiled floors were a match for the pale walls and the mosaics they passed, many of which drew inspiration from the coastal hills and mountains in the east. The House of Vikandir's personal sigil held prominent placements in many of the artistic designs. Soren couldn't help but look for the Sa'Liandel lion head and kept coming up short.

Eventually, they were led into a comfortable-looking office packed with folios and other items of bureaucratic necessities. A majordomo, as he'd come to learn through his interactions with Alida, ran the equivalent of a business when it came to running a House's personal household.

A mechanical fan stood in one corner, the hum of its blades as they spun easily ignored. The servant gestured for them to take a seat on the chaise pushed up against the open window before taking her leave. Soren set Raiah down and let her scramble onto the chaise and peer out at the courtyard below.

Soren kept half his attention on Raiah and the rest on the door. The next time it was opened, a tall, graying blond-haired man entered, his robes impeccably embroidered. Blue eyes met Soren's, and the man bowed deeply.

"I am Evander. I have the pleasure of carrying the title of majordomo to the House of Vikandir's personal household. I understand you speak with the emperor's voice?" Evander said.

Soren wordlessly handed over the Imperial writ for perusal. "I need an audience with the *vezir*."

Evander's expression didn't change as he handed back the writ. "Apologies, but *vezir* Amir Vikandir is not in residence. He is presently in Calhames attending to House duties for the emperor. Lady Malia Vikandir is available to meet with you in his stead."

"Fine. Take us to her."

Evander nodded, waiting patiently while Soren coaxed Raiah back into his arms and carried her down another hallway to a parlor decorated in deep greens and bright gold. The rugs were plush underfoot, and Soren would've apologized for the dirt he left behind if he remembered his manners. But they'd traveled a long ways from Oeiras, and Amir's wife welcomed them with a smile that didn't fade, even when Soren demanded she show off a body free of scars.

"I've been warned of such *rionetkas*, and I can assure you, my mind is my own," Malia said as she parted the seam of her elegant robes and shrugged it off her shoulders, revealing unmarked skin across her shoulders and the top swell of her breasts.

"Van—the emperor has announced the threat?" Soren asked.

Malia inclined her head, the gold chains draped over her tied-back black hair shifting with the motion. "He has. The House of Vikandir has ensured that all members of our House and household carry no clockwork metal hearts in their chests."

She straightened her robes, gazing at Soren with blue eyes lined in shimmering gold color. Her pale face looked lived-in, framed by gray hair threaded through the black, hints at her age that didn't come through the youthfulness of her face. She was slender and decked out in the jewels of her office as lady of a House and wife to a *vezir*.

Despite her assurances, Soren wasn't quite ready to trust her.

"I'm hungry," Raiah announced.

Malia's smile became fond. "I'll have a dinner tray prepared, and we can take our meal here if you like."

"That would be best," Soren said, putting Raiah down.

She immediately pushed her goggles off and tried to undo the strap beneath her chin but got frustrated with the buckle. Soren gently pulled her hands away and undid it, taking off her helmet. Her braids were frizzy and messy, in need of redoing, but that would have to wait.

Malia stood and bowed to a degree worthy of the heir to the Imperial throne. "I am glad to know the Imperial princess is alive and well. The rumors have not been kind to her absence."

Soren ran a hand over Raiah's head, the silent touch enough to keep her by his side. "What do you mean?"

"The House of Kimathi has called for a Conclave, partly because Joelle has been denied the right to see her great-granddaughter." There was much Soren could say about that woman, but he kept silent instead. Malia noted his lack of response and nodded as she headed for the parlor's door. "Amir will want to know you both have arrived safely, to say nothing of the emperor."

"I'll be the one to tell Vanya we're here."

Malia inclined her head in his direction before opening the door and talking briefly with a servant waiting outside. Then she closed it again and came to where they stood, clasping her hands together in front of her. "Dinner won't take long to arrive. I've instructed a room be prepared for the both of you, as I'm quite certain you'd decline separate ones."

Soren nodded. "Raiah stays with me."

"Of that, I have no doubt."

"I want a bath," Raiah said, peering up at them both but not letting go of Soren's hand.

Malia's smile stretched wider. "We'll make sure you get one, Your Imperial Highness."

Raiah could have whatever she liked here in the questionable safety of the House of Vikandir so long as she never left Soren's side.

Seven

VANYA

Vanya had promised Taisiya he would take the evening meal with her in his private courtyard before the dance of words that was the Conclave of Houses got underway in the morning. When he walked into the courtyard dressed in a casual set of robes, he saw the table occupied and the servants gone. At first, he thought the woman sitting there was Taisiya, but his *valide* did not have so dark of skin as the woman who sat with her back to him.

Neither did she have a golden constellation tattoo wrapped around her throat, the shape of the Lion in those starbursts and lines.

Vanya's steps faltered, and he came to a stop there in the middle of the courtyard, staring at the Dawn Star breaking bread alone.

"Your prayers are loud, and I would speak of them with you," Callisto said, her voice ringing in the air.

For a moment, Vanya was frozen in place, caught in the orbit of a star god. The Dawn Star had not answered his family's prayers in at least two generations. A small voice at the back of his mind wondered why she was here now, answering his.

She turned her head to look at him over her shoulder, eyes like a field of stars, or maybe it was a trick of the light. The gown she wore was a deep blue, like the sky at twilight, and her smile looked nothing like the ones found on the carved-marble likenesses of her in the star temples.

Vanya bowed deeper than he ever had to his mother when she sat on the Imperial throne. "My lady."

Callisto raised her hand, two fingers curling in his direction like a summons. "Sit and share your meal with me."

Vanya straightened up and slowly approached the table, cognizant of the empty courtyard and the heaviness of the air above. Everything was quiet when the Imperial palace typically rang with sound. He couldn't even hear the wind.

He took his customary seat on the cushioned bench and reached for a pair of cups from the tea service. He poured the strong red tea he knew Taisiya favored into the cups, serving the Dawn Star first before himself. She took no honey from the tiny ceramic pot even as Vanya added some to his.

"A good blend," Callisto said after taking a sip.

Vanya tipped his head in silent thanks to her, fingers curled loosely around the teacup as he waited for it to cool. The glass was heating up against his skin, but it didn't bother him at all. "My lady, why now? My mother prayed to you many times when she was alive, and you never guided her."

Callisto took a sip of her tea, staring at him with unblinking eyes. "I heard her prayers, but guidance was not needed for her."

He wondered if she'd meant for Rixham to fall, then, for his brother and parents to die, for him to stand alone as head of his House. It was a lonely road she asked of him to walk, and Vanya could only swallow his bitterness. One did not argue with a star god, after all.

"What made you answer mine?"

"I'll keep my counsel on that, thank you. Suffice to say your road is one I have a particular investment in." Vanya opened his mouth, but before he could speak, his televox chimed in the pocket of his robe. Callisto's mouth quirked at the corners. "You'll want to answer that."

Vanya slipped his hand into the pocket of his robe to retrieve the televox. The clarion crystals embedded on the front were glowing, and he thumbed it open to answer, heartbeat quickening at who it might be. "Hello?"

Soren's voice came steady and clear through the tiny device. "We're fine, but we have a problem."

Vanya tightened his grip on the televox, trying not to fall apart in relief before a star god. "What happened?"

"Papa!" Raiah said gleefully, her little voice sounding distant but no less healthy. "Papa, I miss you!"

Vanya closed his eyes for a brief moment before opening them again. He had to remind himself that her absence was a form of love, but hearing her voice settled him somewhat. "I miss you, too, my sunshine. Have you been well?"

"Um."

The quiet hesitancy in her voice made Vanya grimace. "Soren?"

"We made it across the border into Ashion to a town that had a resupply station. One of the wardens passing through was a *rionetka*," Soren said.

A cold knot of fear settled heavily in Vanya's chest, catching at his lungs. "Are you and Raiah all right?"

"Neither of us is injured. Raiah did cast starfire, though, and we had to abandon the resupply station after I killed the *rionetka*. We took an airship to Karnak, where the House of Vikandir took us in."

"She's four. She isn't trained for that."

"I'm fairly certain it was instinctive, and she managed to put it out."

Vanya blew out a breath. "What of the wardens? Have you warned the wardens' governor about what occurred?"

"Delani knows about the clockwork metal hearts, but I haven't told her about the *rionetkas*. I didn't have the time in Oeiras before we left." Soren went quiet, and Vanya listened to his lover breathe for a few heartbeats. "I don't know if we can trust the wardens. Not unless we're standing in front of them and they can prove they don't carry vivisection scars."

"Your governor knows about the dead here in Calhames. If she cannot be trusted—if her loyalty does not lie with the wardens but with Joelle—Solaria is at risk more so than before."

"The engineer in the quarry implied I wasn't the first warden who had made it past their walls and died there."

"You're no revenant."

"Neither am I a *rionetka*, but Joelle is playing with both abominations." Soren sighed thickly, and Vanya wished desperately that Soren could be there by his side and not in Karnak. "This is a border issue. I think you should demand a meeting with the wardens' governor. Have her come to you in person and see if she is truly of her own mind or not."

"If she comes now, it will not reflect well on my House," Vanya said after a moment. "Joelle has called for a Conclave of Houses."

"Lady Malia mentioned that."

"Every decision I make will be watched and picked apart until it is concluded. If I called for the wardens' governor, if the Houses knew for certain Delani was aware of the crypt, judgment against my House would be passed with swift intent. Joelle questions my place and Raiah's absence already. With no heir, it is easier for her and others to take the throne."

"You have an heir."

"Raiah is safe with you, but the Houses see her absence as a weakness for me. I can't prove she lives, and they think me without a successor to lead my House much less sit upon the Imperial throne."

Soren cursed quietly in the trade tongue. "Leaving you wide open politically when you can't afford it."

Across the table, Callisto lifted her teacup to sip at the brew. She spoke soft enough that only Vanya could hear her. "You should bring them home."

Vanya eyed her sharply, most of his attention still on Soren, who echoed the star god's suggestion. The smile she graced him with lacked any sort of warmth.

"I'll bring Raiah home," Soren said.

"I knew the political risks when I let you take her out of Oeiras. I'd still make the same decision. You're the only one I trust her with. But I'd like you to keep yourself safe as well," Vanya said.

"Worried about me, princeling?"

"I'm allowed to be."

Soren cleared his throat. "I'd prefer you stay alive as well to greet your daughter."

Vanya desperately wished they were already here. "It will take more than a Conclave to unseat me. My *valide* has come to Calhames. She's skillful enough with her words to shift Houses to our cause."

"I'm glad to know your House will still be standing once Raiah and I make it back to you. Lady Malia has offered the use of her private airship to return to Calhames in two days."

"Soren—"

"Don't argue, princeling. The back roads aren't safe for a child, not long term. Everywhere else in Solaria leaves us a target for *rionetkas*. I won't risk either of you. Now, chat with Raiah for a bit."

Seconds later, his daughter's voice spilled through the televox, and Vanya bit back a pang of regret for being unable to hold her in his arms. That would change once she returned, for better or for worse, and he knew she was safe with Soren at the moment. Vanya trusted no one else the way he trusted his warden.

When it was time to say goodbye, he did so reluctantly and ended the call with Soren's words ringing in his ears. "She misses you. I miss you. Don't let Joelle win."

"Never," Vanya agreed, and then the clarion crystals went dark, the televox gone quiet. Vanya set it down on the table but didn't let it go.

Across the table, the Dawn Star stared at him with an unblinking gaze, the glow of gas lamps in the background haloing her head like a crown. "You should keep the warden close."

"Soren isn't mine to order about, as he routinely likes to remind me."

"He carries your vow."

Vanya fought the urge to curl his lip. "And he has never asked for what he wants."

Callisto set down her teacup and folded her hands together over the edge of the table. "Your roads were always meant to cross. You need to be prepared for when that happens."

His mother had always warned about the grace given by star gods, that the answers to prayers could be anything but kind. "We are already in each other's lives."

"Are you?"

Vanya opened his mouth to protest, but the sound of a door closing had him looking off to the side, movement catching his eyes as Taisiya entered the courtyard. When he jerked his gaze back to the seat across from him at the table, he found it empty.

His ears popped, sound rushing back to him, though he almost missed Taisiya's greeting, so focused was he on the empty space once inhabited by a star god.

"Is dinner that terrible?" Taisiya asked as she approached.

Vanya shook his head slowly. "No. I asked for your favorite dishes."

"How thoughtful of you."

His *valide* sat in the same place Callisto had, eyeing the tea already poured before gracing him with her full attention. It reminded him of meals spent with his mother, absorbing all that she could teach him of what it meant to rule—a country or a House, it didn't matter, for the idea of power was still the same.

"Shall we discuss which Houses we must attempt to sway at the first Conclave meeting tomorrow?" Taisiya asked.

Vanya could only nod. If he was to win this game of whispers and rumors against Joelle, then he needed to put aside the lingering disquiet of Callisto's visit and her words that echoed in his ears more as a threat than a blessing.

Eight

VANYA

"Remember, there is no bloodshed allowed during a Conclave," Taisiya said as their motor carriage rolled to a gentle stop in the front drive of the estate belonging to the House of Kimathi in Calhames. Gatherings were held in the mornings or evenings to escape the midday heat, and the drive was crowded with vehicles already.

"Only poisonous words," Vanya said as a valet swiftly opened the motor carriage door for him.

He stepped out beneath the late-morning sun, the gold crown on his head a weight Taisiya had not suggested he leave behind. The Conclave of Houses was a dance of whispers and words, of quiet promises of loyalty in exchange for promises kept. Vanya could admit, standing on the grounds of a House he knew would rather see him dead, that he had not done enough since his mother's death to sway a majority of the Houses to his side.

He would need to rectify that now.

As her right for calling the Conclave, the first political salvo was a morning gathering put on by the House of Kimathi and overseen by Joelle. She would, he knew, have the advantage. Which meant he needed to take it from her, a feat easier said than done.

"Do not lose your temper," Taisiya murmured for his ears alone as they headed for the door to the estate. The *praetoria* legionnaires who had escorted them in two other vehicles followed behind.

Vanya said nothing to that, aware of all the ways he knew Joelle would attempt to force him into a corner. They were met not by anyone of the House but the household, Joelle's majordomo bowing to the precise degree for greeting an emperor and no more.

"Your Imperial Majesty," the majordomo said. "*Valide*. The House of Kimathi bids you welcome."

"Do they?" Taisiya drawled. "I see no House present. A shame Joelle has forgotten her manners. A poor reflection on her mother's teachings."

The majordomo was too well-bred to say anything, keeping her face impassive, though Vanya knew she would repeat back to Joelle every word he and Taisiya spoke. "I'll lead you both to the garden."

The House of Kimathi was old, and their claim as a major House could be seen in the size of the estate in Calhames. They were led through half a dozen halls until they reached a courtyard that acted as the entrance to the estate's gardens at the rear of the property.

The welcome from other guests in the courtyard was rote but a far cry warmer than the one they received when Vanya and Taisiya made their entrance to the gardens—which was precisely none. The musicians serenading the Conclave of Houses did not break their performance for the pair's arrival, continuing with their music. Vanya allowed himself a smile that was all teeth as he took in the clusters of men and women dripping in gold and jewels pretending to not see them, House colors and symbols on full display.

The gas lamps lining the garden pathways in intervals were cold in the light of day. Vanya uncurled his left hand and reached for the aether far outside himself and the starfire it could provide. It came to him the same way breathing did—easy and thoughtless. He flexed his fingers and sent it skipping over the tops of every gas lamp in the garden that he could see, tiny tongues of flickering flames nearly as bright as the sun above crackling into existence.

Heads snapped around to look at them, bodies shifting on their feet. A sour note or two lingered on the air before the musicians rallied again. Vanya rubbed two fingers against his thumb, starfire twisting against his palm before he let it fade away. Taisiya offered him a dry look. "It is summer."

"One can never be too warm," Vanya replied blandly.

Taisiya let him go, holding her chin high as she left his side to do her duty to their House. Vanya strode forward, the pristine white fabric of his robe brushing against the tailored trousers as he walked. The guests nearest him bowed or curtsied deeply, greeting him with quiet murmurings of his rank and well-wishes. How true the latter were remained to be seen.

A familiar face appeared in moments, Amir bowing over his cane as far as his girth comfortably allowed. "Your Imperial Majesty."

"House of Vikandir," Vanya said, using the formal greeting as required by the rules of the Conclave.

Amir managed a smile, though it was thin beneath his mustache. "House of Sa'Liandel. Shall we help ourselves to the wine?"

"Only if it isn't poisoned."

Amir laughed, turning on his feet. "There is but one way to find out."

The flagstone path Amir took him down passed by a servant standing beneath the shade of a small tree and carrying a tray of wineglasses. Vanya picked a wineglass at random, as did Amir, glancing at the fruit floating within. He didn't hesitate to drink it because to hesitate would indicate distrust. While he did not trust Joelle *at all,* he trusted she wouldn't try to poison those she hoped to sway to her side.

Not at first, at least.

Amir sipped at his glass as they walked, attention on the people around them. Vanya took note of the space accorded them and knew nothing good could come of that.

"The odds do not favor your House," Amir said in a quiet voice.

Vanya kept his expression calm, the grip on his own wineglass easy. "Is that so?"

"By my count, you have my House, several minor ones who hail from your *vasilyet* around Calhames, and perhaps the House of Dayal."

Vanya resisted the urge to frown. That was far fewer than he had hoped for, with only a handful of minor Houses and the possibility of one other major House outside Amir's. "Joelle has been busy."

"You see now why I requested the aid of your *valide*." Amir slanted him a look, wineglass raised to his lips to hide the shape of the words that left them. "You would fare better with a spouse."

"I will not be responsible for the death of my daughter."

"Raiah is not yet here." The emphasis on the word *yet* proved Amir was aware of what transpired in his House back in Karnak. "Her absence aids you not. They think the assassination attempt successful."

"They can think what they like, but I will not remarry. If that is the price of loyalty the Houses expect from me, they will be sorely disappointed."

It would, logically, be the correct road to take. Agreeing to a marriage with someone from a major House that could bring their influence to bear upon other Houses would tilt support his way during the Conclave. But marriage contracts could take months, and Vanya knew the price of such an agreement would be Raiah losing her rightful place as heir, something Joelle would rage about.

Vanya loved Raiah too much to take her birthright away from her. He loved her too much to want to lose her. "I've buried enough of my family and my House. I will not bury my daughter."

"The Houses will dislike that, but we shall find a way forward down this road. Let us start now."

Vanya took the lead this time, guiding Amir into the swirling conversation of the Houses presiding together under the Conclave. This was the opening salvo, *vezirs* and those who spoke for them representing every House in Solaria as they politicked the accusation Joelle had levied at him and considered his own.

"Are these *rionetkas* truly mindless?" an older man asked, the ranking necklace he wore indicating he was a voice rather than *vezir* of the House of Tsui. It was a minor House, having never managed to claim the Imperial throne in its entire existence, but Vanya would never hold that against them.

"No. They act the same as they were before being changed, but their thoughts are not their own. Whatever mind magic that binds them to the magician in control, whoever that master might be, makes it so they cannot speak of their situation. They cannot disobey an order from their master. The *praetoria* legionnaires who attempted to assassinate myself and my daughter were not acting of their own free will, but they were not mindless like a revenant," Vanya said.

"And how *is* the Imperial princess? Purportedly, no one has seen her since the attack," *vezir* Suresh Gevorgyan, of the House of Gevorgyan, asked. His tone was just the right shade of curious and worried, but his gaze was cool in a way Vanya knew not to trust. The House of Gevorgyan had not favored the House of Sa'Liandel since Rixham had been walled off by Vanya's mother. Vanya knew winning Suresh to his side was a losing battle.

"I would think any parent would wish to keep their child out of sight and as safe as can be after an attempted kidnapping."

"The broadsheets state it was an assassination attempt."

Vanya offered a smile of his own, attention caught on movement in the crowd behind Suresh. "Oh, the *rionetkas* attempted to murder me, but their orders were to spare my daughter and flee Oeiras with her. One wonders why the eradication of my House wasn't the goal."

"I've sent thankful prayers to the star gods that my great-granddaughter survived. We only have your word, after all, that these *rionetkas* spared her and not you," Joelle said as the knots of people shifted to let her pass, Artyom beside her.

It was the first time in over an hour that Vanya had seen a member of the host House. Ill manners indeed, but the pointed slight was not unexpected at the start of the Conclave.

Joelle wore a light summer gown in pale gold with black accents, a match to the finely cut onyx hanging from gold links on the headdress she wore. The subtly raised spikes were meant to mimic sun rays, but all Vanya saw was an imitation of the crown he wore.

"Is my word not enough?" Vanya asked mildly.

Joelle released the hold she had on her son's arm to fold both hands over the top of her cane. "You know it is not."

"I would say the same of your own."

"I am not the one who betrayed our ways to the wardens by taking one as a lover after murdering a member of my House."

Vanya bared his teeth. "I trust the wardens to do right by *all* of us, which is more than I can say for you. Nicca died in childbirth, and Raiah nearly followed her into the stars. There was no murder to be had in that tragedy."

"Yet you deny me blood rights to see my kin."

"I have never barred you from Calhames."

"No, you merely forbid she visit her House."

"The Imperial princess has a House," came Taisiya's raspy voice as she approached with Amir by her side. "The House of Sa'Liandel, which rules yours. You were never barred, Joelle. You just chose your *vasilyet* and its ills you beget over Raiah."

Joelle's eyes narrowed as Taisiya settled herself at Vanya's side, lips pressed into a thin line. "My border is *kept*."

"Yes, you do keep it. Well enough that you bar wardens from your land and refuse them entry to your city. It begs what you hide, though I know what you burned in that quarry," Vanya said.

Joelle lifted her chin. "You speak more lies. Will you use them the same way your mother did to destroy Rixham? Your brother was not worth a city. One wonders if you think your daughter is."

Vanya stared her down, knowing how *easy* it would be to eradicate the threat to Raiah standing before him by using starfire against Joelle. Doing so would gain him nothing but enemies who could not be cajoled or bribed into loyalty. Starfire gave the right to rule in Solaria, but that didn't mean people were comfortable with such harsh displays of power. The Imperial throne was held by the House with the most power, and that did not always mean magic.

"If you think I have wronged your House, then call for a blood feud. It won't be the first levied against mine, but I will treat it with all the care as the rest that were settled in our favor over the years."

"You put Solaria at risk with the leeway you give wardens. I need call no blood feud to accuse you of betrayal to our country," Joelle shot back. Around them, those who claimed ties to the major Houses nodded faint agreement.

"Betrayal like how you allowed a death-defying machine to function in your *vasilyet*? Tell me, Joelle, how many Solarians did you feed it?"

"I know not what you speak of."

"It seems you know nothing of worth that happens in your *vasilyet*. One must wonder at your ability to rule if that is the case."

Joelle's eyes flashed with fury. "Do not question how I rule my House."

"This is the Conclave. That is precisely what we are here for."

Joelle would cry ignorance of the death-defying machine and the *rionetkas* to the stars, and there would be no prying that lie away from her. Vanya knew the only way to claw support to his side during the Conclave was to prove he spoke the truth—about the death-defying machine, about *rionetkas*, about the betrayal spreading like poison throughout the northwest.

Vanya's gaze swept over the gathered Houses, meeting eyes that held his own or looked away. "I am your emperor. The House of Sa'Liandel has ruled Solaria for centuries and will continue to rule with the Dawn Star's blessing. Would you rather the Imperial throne be held by a House who holds no loyalty to Solaria or one that has done everything to keep our country whole?"

"Eradicating a House and walling off a city favors no one," Joelle said sharply.

"My Lady Mother had her reasons for such actions. Yours, however, leave much to be desired. Betraying your country and every House in existence favors only you, Joelle. Every House wants the Imperial throne, but none of us has ever gone down the road you seem to be walking," Vanya replied coldly.

He turned his back on her before she could respond, a calculated dismissal in her own House. Vanya offered Taisiya his arm, and she took it with a faint tip of her head. Amir caught his eye and bowed, his stance easy, in no hurry to follow.

"Your Imperial Majesty," Amir said, opting for Vanya's title rather than his House to show his allegiance.

Vanya left the Conclave, knowing Amir would act in his place to lure Houses to their side. Vanya's only goal today was to plant seeds of doubt in the fields of words Joelle had already cultivated. If even one blossomed, it would be a blessing.

Nine

JOELLE

The first thing Joelle did when the Conclave gathering at her estate was over and all the unwanted guests were gone was to take time alone in her office for a private call. She dialed the number to a televox from memory, knowing the risk of communicating over borders but doing so anyway. She pressed the cold metal receiver to her ear as the line rang for some time before finally being answered.

"You know better than to call from your capital," Eimarille's Blade said in near-perfect Solarian. Even then, Joelle could hear the faint curl of the woman's Urovan accent in her words.

"I didn't call to speak to *you*," Joelle retorted. "I called for your queen."

"My queen is busy."

"Not for me."

Joelle knew it was a risk to initiate a call from the heart of Solaria's politics. But her majordomo had assured her that all precautions had been taken to secure their communication wires and the telegraph room on the premises. Every machine had been examined after the Conclave gathering had ended, for Joelle knew better than to trust any House who had wandered through her home.

Terilyn hummed in a way that gave no clue as to her opinion but which Joelle considered a sign of disrespect. "Hold."

The line echoed with the buzz of a connection paused, and Joelle's lips curled in distaste at the other woman's rudeness. If anyone in her household or under her rule had been so brusque and dismissive of her in person, she'd have taken them to task.

Joelle leaned back against the plushness of her office chair, glancing at the metal clock hanging from the wall, its hands ticking away the time. She was overdue for a session with her House's healer, the magician most likely waiting impatiently on a summons, just as she waited impatiently for the Daijal queen to answer her call.

Eventually, the line clicked, the buzz replaced with a smooth voice that held no hint of irritation. Like Joelle, Eimarille Rourke was skilled at the game of politics. "My Blade tells me you are in Calhames. We agreed to no communication while you are in your country's capital."

"We agreed if no present need arose," Joelle replied.

"Ah. Careful, *vezir* Joelle. You owe enough debts. Are you sure you wish to add another?"

Eimarille's tone was light and seemingly gentle, but Joelle knew the spine of the woman who had wrestled away one crown and greedily sought another. If Eimarille had been of the Houses, she would have been a dangerous opponent indeed. As it was, Joelle was quite aware of the danger she danced with when she had acquiesced to the Twilight Star's guidance and was more than willing to land each step perfectly.

Eimarille could have the rest of the continent so long as Joelle retained Solaria.

"I have called a Conclave of Houses, as we agreed."

"Daijal will not interfere in whatever games your Houses play. I gave you my word on that."

"Yes, but Houses are not what I worry about. It is the wardens."

The sigh on the other end of the line made Joelle want to gnash her teeth. "The wardens will not be a problem for either of our countries. They'll be too busy dealing with revenants to worry about borders or see the threat aimed at the Celestine Lake."

"During his parents' funeral, Vanya took a warden into the crypt beneath the Imperial palace. If we are to use what is there, it must remain intact. I have heard of no sanctions levied against my country since then, but that is not to say they aren't coming. I will not have us pay it, and I would prefer such a threat be dealt with while the Conclave happens."

"Your situation is not a problem for Daijal."

"Isn't it?" Joelle asked sharply. "Your country borders mine."

"And you've lost a death-defying machine as well as needed revenants." A hint of annoyance slipped into the other woman's voice, icy in a way few people ever were with Joelle. "The wardens will be dealt with, as we discussed, but I will not move up my timeline to satisfy your mistakes. Handle your Conclave, but do so knowing you owe me a debt, and your House will still owe it long after you are ash."

The tone of a dead line echoed loudly in Joelle's ear. She swore quietly before dropping the receiver on the cradle, knuckles throbbing from how tightly she'd gripped it. She chafed her hands together, scowling at nothing. "Pieces ever in motion."

The wardens as a whole would be handled—eventually. She'd have liked it to be now as opposed to whatever timetable Eimarille had drawn up. It had been a risk to call and give her demands, but she refused to be seen as subservient to someone who was not Solarian. Eimarille could not have crossed Daijal's eastern borders without the revenants created in Solaria. She could talk about debts Joelle owed all she liked, but Eimarille owed them as well.

She needed to see to one particular warden if he ever showed up during the Conclave. Considering the task Vanya had assigned him, Joelle had no doubt the warden would arrive at some point. The last she'd heard from the *rionetkas* in her control was that they'd located the warden and Raiah on a train. But that had been days ago, and the poison fields were no place for a child.

Of all the wardens, Joelle wanted the location of the one Vanya had given his daughter to, not only because she wanted Raiah back, but she wanted to see if Soren was indeed someone who could cast starfire. The quarry was ruined, but there was no alchemy or bombs involved with its destruction. The only thing to ever scorch the earth like *that* was starfire. Joelle should know, as she could cast it herself.

Eimarille did not know about the possibility of another living Rourke. Joelle wasn't sure if Vanya even knew what secrets Soren might be keeping, but whatever they were, she intended to pry them out of the warden however possible.

Sighing, Joelle reached to press the button on the machine that would summon one of her handmaidens. When the knock came on her office door, she bade them enter. The younger woman bowed deeply.

"Send for Artyom and bring a tea service," Joelle ordered.

They had much to discuss, after all.

Ten

CARIS

"The Daijal army has occupied Haighmoor."

Captain Hyacinth Votil tossed the morning broadsheet down on the table in the library the Clockwork Brigade was working out of in the Auclair estate. Caris reached for the broadsheet and slid it closer to herself.

The captain had been sent as a liaison for the Ashion army and was both a magician and a cog, currently bivouacked in the estate since her arrival the day before. If Caris listened hard enough, she could hear the faint hum of the magician's clarion crystal–tipped wand, a well-cut piece. Right now, over the clink of teacups touching plates, the rustle of paper, and the murmur of voices, the hum was impossible to hear.

Hyacinth was a woman ten years older than Caris, whose father was a general in the Ashion army. Hyacinth had followed in his footsteps by becoming not just an officer but a cog as well. Whether out of necessity or choice, her road had found its way to Ashion's old spymaster. It was easier, after all, for a lower-ranked officer to slip away when necessary, while a general found it almost impossible to leave their duty behind without their absence being noted.

That's where Hyacinth came in, a woman who was as dedicated to eradicating debt bondage as she was to pushing back against Daijal influence. Her family's name was written down in the genealogies kept by the Star Order, going back generations.

Their loyalty wasn't in question, though Caris still didn't care for the reverence Hyacinth had greeted her with yesterday upon their introduction. The uncomfortableness of being known for something she'd kept secret for so long left her feeling too seen. That hint of near-instantaneous loyalty had made Caris flee to the garage turned laboratory that had become her sanctuary since their arrival in Veran.

She didn't want to be what everyone hoped she was.

"The bulk of the army is not in Haighmoor," Meleri reminded everyone in the room. "Neither are the supplies."

Hyacinth glared down at the headline typed across the morning edition broadsheet, jaw twitching. Her brown hair was cropped short to her skull, and she carried calluses on her right hand from years of wielding a pistol. "Once the Daijal army realizes that, it'll only encourage them to make a deeper foray into Ashion."

"What was their reasoning behind the occupation?" Caris said.

Lore tipped a teaspoon of sugar into her tea and swirled it around deftly enough that the spoon never clinked against the sides of the cup. "Apparently, the wardens weren't enough to handle a revenant incursion, and the mayor claims he received no aid from Amari."

"I find it highly unlikely the wardens weren't enough to handle revenants. That job is what they were made for," Blaine muttered as he slouched lower on the sofa from his spot beside Caris, rubbing a hand over his face. His clothes, Caris noted, were of Ashionen style save for the leather flight jacket he still wore, with its plaid panels curved over the shoulders. His hair was even braided back again, the plait short and tied off with a beaded ribbon.

"Propaganda is what you make of it, and the western provinces have always been susceptible to Daijalan lies," Meleri said.

Caris unfolded the broadsheet and laid it flat on the table before opening the front page. She froze at the lead article on page two, eyes drawn to the ink-pressed pictures of her parents at the top center of the page. For a moment, everything went quiet, as if the world faded away as she stared down into the haggard lines of her parents' faces.

"*Caris*."

Blaine's hand wrapped around her wrist, his voice in her ears like a siren bringing her back. The library held no clarion crystals anymore, but when Caris jerked her gaze away from the broadsheet, she found every teacup on the table shattered, with tea splattered everywhere. Damp splotches seeped into the broadsheet, blurring some of the words.

"Oh," she said quietly, tongue numb in her mouth. She used to be better with her control. She didn't understand why her magic—carefully leashed over the years—was slipping free so badly now.

Blaine grimaced and let her hand go only long enough to move the broadsheet off the table. Caris made an aborted grab for it, but Blaine didn't toss it away, merely folded it up to better read the article, eyes flicking across the page.

"I didn't know they were printing articles about prisoners," Hyacinth said quietly, sounding apologetic, though her words were directed to Meleri rather than Caris.

Caris clenched her hand into a fist as she stared at the broadsheet that Blaine held. "What does it say?"

Her voice didn't sound like her own, low and harsh as it was. Blaine reached without looking to grip her shoulder, still reading the article. "Detained for being cogs. You're mentioned at the end as being wanted for questioning."

Caris leaned into his grip and turned her head to better see her parents' faces. "But they're alive?"

"For now."

"Who ordered their arrest?" Meleri asked.

"The article doesn't say."

"I'd wager good money the order came from Eimarille and not the Collector's Guild," Lore said with a grimness to her voice that had her reaching for her teacup automatically before remembering it was destroyed.

Caris couldn't help the flinch that assailed her body. "I put them in danger."

"No," Blaine said, looking up to meet her eyes. "They were cogs before you ever came to the Clockwork Brigade. They knew the risks, just like all of us. You had no part in what has happened to them."

"They're my *parents*."

"And they sent you on to keep you safe."

"If I hadn't been seen casting starfire—"

"We'd be dead," Lore cut in. "I'm thankful we're not."

Caris snapped her teeth together, catching the edge of her tongue. The faint hint of copper crept through her mouth, and she swallowed the taste of it. "We need to free them."

Lore gave her a pitying look. "We can't."

"I won't leave them in Eimarille's hands!"

"They are cogs, and when a cog is compromised, we have to let them go."

"Easy for you to say when your family is here and safe—"

"Do not think for a moment we don't grieve the people we lose—"

"*Enough*," Meleri cried out, cutting through their argument, causing Caris to snap her head around to stare at the duchess. "The prominence of the article about the Dhemlans' involvement in the Clockwork Brigade was not a *mistake*. This is a lure, and you know it, Caris. We cannot give in to what is a trap meant to bring you back to the capital."

Caris pushed herself to her feet, feeling flushed and overly warm. "I won't condemn my parents to whatever horror Eimarille will do to them."

Meleri stared at her with a fierceness that reminded Caris this was the woman who had held Ashion together after the old monarchy fell and would not be swayed from her road. "Would you condemn all the rest of us and the country as well for your selfishness? Eimarille wants you dead—you must know that. You are a threat to her taking the starfire throne, and she will dangle any bait she can to get you within her reach. You will not survive that encounter."

Caris stepped away from the sofa, needing to move. Tears pricked her eyes, but she blinked them back. Part of her knew Meleri was right, but most of her wanted to risk the warrant on her head to save her parents. "This is my fault for leaving them behind."

"It is no one's fault save Eimarille's and Daijal's," Blaine said.

She made a cutting motion with her hand before crossing her arms over her chest. "If they use mind magic against my parents, then none of us are safe. Eimarille will know about all of us."

"That was a risk we always knew was inevitable," Meleri said, sounding weary. "The only way to subvert that has been to offer up a different road."

Caris' lip curled upward as she turned to glare at the duchess. "Me."

"You were always meant to rule."

Caris had been trained to run a business, to create inventions that would make living on Maricol easier. What she'd learned at Meleri's side over the last few years wasn't even close to the skills Caris knew she'd need to rule a country—something she didn't want to do.

Or even knew if she could.

"I am not your queen," Caris said, clutching at her elbows.

"As you say."

Caris opened her mouth, not sure what she would have said to that—something her mother would've been disappointed in hearing, she was sure—when the piercing sound of a warning siren echoing through the walls nearly made her jump.

Lore cocked her head to the side, pursing her lips. "That tone is for revenants, not a storm. They'll be closing the gates."

"A second attack so soon is not normal. I'm on wall duty when the sirens sound, so I will take my leave," Hyacinth said brusquely.

The captain left, closing the door to the library behind her. Caris huffed out a breath before heading for the door as well.

"Where are you going?" Lore asked sharply.

"Anywhere but here," she tossed over her shoulder.

Caris walked out, the thought of her mother's ire about her manners the only thing keeping her from slamming the door shut behind her. She quickly made her way through the estate until she reached the ground floor and the door that led to the small courtyard set between the main house and the detached garage.

The garage doors—both for the motor carriages and for people—were guarded day and night by military personnel, with at least one being a magician. Though the soldiers weren't dressed in the typical military uniforms, they carried military-issued pistols and wands. Caris saw their hands twitch in aborted motions of a salute at her approach. It was yet another reminder of the position everyone had placed her in, whether she agreed to it or not.

Caris shouldered open the side door with a soft grunt, stepping inside what felt like an oven. Someone had winched open the high windows lining the garage and set up portable mechanical fans in the corners to move the heavy air about. It was still hot enough that Caris found herself shrugging out of the day jacket she wore and rolling up the sleeves of her linen blouse.

Dureau looked up from the stack of blueprints spread out over the worktable on the left, blinking at her through the dust motes dancing through the sunbeams. "Did the meeting finish already?"

"No," Caris said shortly.

Dureau arched an eyebrow but didn't say anything. She appreciated him not needling her, but mostly, she knew his silence was due to the company he kept there in the garage. Caris sidled up to the table Dureau was at rather than the worktable Wyatt had taken up. She looked at where the inventor sat hunched over shards of clarion crystal scattered around his workspace, with a crate of them situated off to the side.

Blueprints were all well and good, but they were a *plan,* not an actual machine with moving parts. They needed to see how the energy of the aether flowed through the death-defying machine if they were going to at all understand what Eimarille had created. The gaseous and spore components were purposefully missing from the build, but the energy output was something they needed records of and which Caris was determined to study.

Despite the horrific transmutation process that occurred, the underlying technology could hopefully be parlayed into something better, something that could give aid rather than do harm. Caris was a fierce proponent of technology and inventing. While she knew they wouldn't be able to undo the effects of the death-defying machine, she hoped something better could be built out of the tragedy Eimarille was overseeing.

Wyatt's knowledge of the death-defying machine was helpful, but no one trusted the Daijalan inventor. Even with mind magic to prove he'd had no choice in aiding the Fletcher bloodline with this endeavor, indebted as he was to Samuel Fletcher for his schooling, it didn't absolve him of all the deaths he'd been a party to.

Caris could see it in his eyes whenever he managed to meet her gaze, could hear it in the sick regret that came through his voice whenever he spoke about what he had done, what he had seen. She'd pity him if she didn't know that some of those revenants he'd helped create were quite possibly clawing at Veran's walls right now.

She skimmed her gaze around the space Meleri had allowed them to take over. She noted the pair of soldiers sitting at a different table near one of the fans, their attention never leaving Wyatt. Caris shifted on the stool, picking at the corner of a blueprint. "My parents have been arrested."

"I'm sorry," Dureau said.

She didn't want platitudes or sympathy—she wanted a plan to free her parents. But with the breach of the western border and the occupation of Haighmoor by Daijalan forces, Caris knew everyone's attention would be on the threat aimed at the country, not the one aimed at Caris' heart.

She flattened her hand over the blueprint, studying the precise lines marked there that delineated a layer of the death-defying machine's inner workings. "I need something to do."

Dureau nodded in Wyatt's direction. "He's got plenty of clarion crystals for you to cut."

Caris pushed away from the worktable and went to the other one, slipping onto another stool a few feet away from Wyatt. She looked at the diagrams he was using as reference, eyes tracing the patterns the clarion crystal needed to be cut into. Not a style she'd ever used, but then, she would have never dreamed up a death-defying machine.

She picked up a crystal-cutting tool, pulled a diagram sheet closer to her, and reached for a rod of clarion crystal, determined to lose herself in work. It was better than thinking about what her parents were going through.

She lost herself to the task of cutting clarion crystals, listening to the crystalline hum that she'd always been able to hear in moments like that but which no one else had ever been able to. The rod of clarion crystal in her hand was a smoky gray in color, with minimal occlusions. The design of the shape on the diagram could be cut from the rod in her hand, but every line she made into the crystal left discordant song notes in her ears.

"The crystals aren't meant to be used this way," Caris muttered as she carefully rotated her wrist to adjust the angle of the handheld cutting saw she was using. "They don't like this shape."

"Clarion crystals aren't alive. These designs were the only shapes that have worked for the transmutation process," Wyatt said offhand.

"That should have been your first clue it was a terrible idea."

Wyatt didn't respond, but his shoulders rose a little toward his ears. Caris pressed the edge of the cutter to the clarion crystal, intent on ignoring the way her hand *wanted* to move in favor of cutting it how Wyatt and that bastard Fletcher had designed when the door to the garage slammed open, making her jump in her seat.

"Caris," Blaine called out. "The duchess wants you. There's something you need to see."

She snapped her head around, carefully setting the clarion crystal and cutting tool on the table without looking. Blaine's voice was tense in a way that reminded her of when they'd been in the thick of the riot with danger all around them.

"Do we have to leave town?" Caris asked as she hurried across the space to him, Dureau a mere half step behind her.

Blaine shook his head. "No, not yet. But—well, you'll see. Follow me."

They stepped outside, the sun directly overhead, indicating hours had gone by since Caris had stormed out of the library. Her stomach growled, reminding her she was due to eat, but it could wait. Whatever had sent Blaine racing after her couldn't be good.

He led her back into the estate, their rapid footsteps against the hardwood floor echoing in the halls. Voices up ahead were indistinct until they weren't as Blaine stepped into a doorway that led into a windowless study. Caris peered over his shoulder and let out a sharp gasp, one hand coming up to clutch at the ring hanging from the necklace around her throat.

Standing in the study with a rough linen shirt unbuttoned to show off a bare, unmarked chest was—impossibly—*Nathaniel.*

He broke off mid-word, gaze finding her unerringly. The expression on his dirty, tired face twisted, disbelief stealing across his eyes before turning to wonder. "Caris? You're really here?"

The world went blurry in an instant, and Caris covered her mouth with her hand, leaning against Blaine's back for support. "You were—Nathaniel, *how?*"

"He was one of the last stragglers through the gate before the revenants reached the city wall," Raziel said from where the warden stood near the wall, out of the way. "We wardens had to clear everyone just in case after we dealt with the revenants. When he said he needed directions to the duchess' home, I figured I should escort him."

Caris couldn't quite swallow back a sob, the sound muffled against her fingers. She ducked around Blaine, darting across the room to throw herself into Nathaniel's arms. He caught her like she knew he would, rocking back on his heels. Then his arms wrapped around her and held her close in the way she'd ached to feel since fleeing Amari.

"How?" Caris rasped out, pressing her forehead to his shoulder, shaking fingers clutching at the edges of his open shirt. "How did you get free?"

"I was forgotten in a paddy wagon during the riot. When I was found again, I managed to escape. I hid and was smuggled out of the city by a cog and passed through the chain," Nathaniel said, his lips moving against her hair.

Her lips trembled, breath hitching on a sob, but she still found her voice. "I'm so glad you're here."

Caris lifted her head and unclenched one hand so she could press her fingers to Nathaniel's cheek, feeling the heat coming off his skin from who knew how many days on the road. He smiled at her in a cracked sort of way, taking her hand in his to press a kiss to the back of her knuckles.

"I'm here now," Nathaniel promised. Caris tucked herself in close to him, taking a selfish moment just for them. She closed her eyes and held on, listening to the murmur of voices rise around her. A faint, almost crystalline hum reached her ears as she stood in the circle of Nathaniel's arms, the sound easily ignored in favor of the way he said her name. "I won't leave you again, Caris."

Eleven

HONOVI

The *Katabatic* settled in its anchor berth with a judder, secured in place by the lines thrown over the railing by the airship crew to those on the ground. Honovi blew out a breath and stepped away from the controls, reaching up to loosen the straps of his flight helmet.

"Let's get through the paperwork as fast as we can. I have orders to head straight for the *Comhairle nan Cinnidhean*," Honovi said to his deck master, who was standing in the doorway to the flight deck.

"You want me to handle everything in your stead?" Ingvar asked.

Honovi smiled tightly and tossed his flight helmet on the navigator's table. "No, I'll sign off on everything."

He was captain, after all, and he refused to shirk his duty no matter how tired he was or how much he ached still from the wounds taken while in Amari, despite the additional healing done by the duchess' magician. Magic wasn't a cure, merely a bandage.

Honovi stepped outside the flight deck, already sweating beneath the fur-lined flight jacket. It had been needed in the sky, but here on the ground, with summer heat an oppressive blanket, it left sweat sliding down his back.

Everyone was glad to be home and worked twice as hard to finish what was required of them in order to lock down the airship and head off to their families for a much-needed break. Honovi was met by a clerk who greeted him at the dock after he disembarked. The woman's gown was made of summer-light fabric, though the plaid wrapped around her waist and hips was of a heavier weave.

"*Jarl* Honovi," she said, dipping her head out of respect. Her brown hair was braided back in four plaits, the ends tied with beaded ribbons. "Your father requests your presence."

"Of course," Honovi said.

It took time to leave the airfield behind for the safety of the city wall surrounding Glencoe. She had a motor carriage waiting past the gates, the driver turning the engine on once they were in sight. Honovi slid into the back seat with the clerk, who didn't seem inclined toward small talk.

He'd intended to meet with his father, but he'd hoped for a private moment to discuss all that had transpired—from the attack, to the riot, to the threat of *rionetkas* found in Siv's body that Karla had ferried on ahead.

That was not to be.

The motor carriage drove down the main boulevard from the airfield to the capitol building at the center of Glencoe. The city bustled with people and street traffic in the late afternoon, their speed slower than it would be during off-hours due to the number of vehicles on the ground. The emblem of the *Comhairle nan Cinnidhean* painted on the motor carriage's door didn't allow for their driver to disobey traffic laws.

Eventually, the motor carriage reached the large plaza with its grand fountain bubbling away in the center. The clockwork airship rotated on a pillar above the water, the spray pouring from its prow misting the air and causing rainbows to form.

The driver pulled up to the curb, and Honovi got out, turning to offer his hand to the clerk. She took it with a brief nod of thanks before leading the way up the steps to the massive circular building that was the heart of E'ridia's government.

The pillars surrounding the promenade glinted gold at the top, the constellations carved there meant to catch the eye. One of the heavy wooden doors was propped open, guarded by a peacekeeper who waved them inside. The clerk bypassed the check-in area and proceeded deeper into the building. The mechanical fans hanging from the ceiling between the gaslights had been turned on in deference to the weather. It was cooler inside, and Honovi was grateful for it. He rolled his shoulders, looking forward to removing his flight jacket.

He would know the way blind to the *Comhairle nan Cinnidhean* chambers at the center of the building. After so long away in a foreign country, it was comforting to walk into the two-story chamber with its mechanical astrolabe hanging from the vaulted ceiling. The balcony ringing the two-story chamber was empty of an audience, but every seat at the circular table in the center was filled. The hollowed-out center was empty, as was the speaker's seat, but the adjacent table for ambassadors was full, watched over by the sergeant at arms.

Honovi didn't recognize the men and women sitting there, though he was familiar with their clothing, the tailored style favored heavily by Ashionens. Their colors were muted, lacking the vibrancy of clothes worn by the *cinn-chinnidh* that made up the *Comhairle nan Cinnidhean*. On the opposite side of the room, near the speaker's seat, he spied Karla, who gave him a slow nod in greeting.

The clerk closed the door behind him, remaining out in the hall. Honovi walked alone to greet the ruling body of his country. "The winds were welcoming on our flight home. Well met, *Comhairle nan Cinnidhean*. I understand you have need of me."

"Welcome home, ambassador and *jarl* Honovi of Clan Storm," Alrickson said in return.

His father seemed to have aged in the time Honovi had been gone, or perhaps it was merely distance and time and an absence of the everyday moments he'd left behind when he took up the ambassadorship. His father's expression held no joy, though, and Honovi wondered, briefly, what sort of welcoming he could expect here where politics ruled everything.

"We trust you are well?" Leena, *ceann-cinnidh* of Clan Lightning, asked.

Honovi couldn't stop himself from brushing his hand against his right side, carrying only the ghost of a bruise from the bullet wound now. "Well enough after everything that has transpired."

"Much *has* transpired." Her gaze cut away from him to the ambassadors seated at their table, expression bland. "The *Comhairle nan Cinnidhean* thanks you for your presence. We know how long you have been away."

"I would have returned with Karla, but I was delayed by a brief hospital stay after being shot."

"Yes, that will be discussed. At the moment, we have a different issue on the table."

The foreigner seated in the center of the ambassador table stood, slapping his hands onto the table before speaking in perfect E'ridian. "Your country's airship *fired* on Ashion citizens to aid criminals when they fled our capital. Such an act is untenable."

The sergeant at arms rapped her ceremonial staff hard on the floor, the sound cutting off the man. "If you cannot adhere to the rules of this august body, I will remove you."

The ambassador clenched his jaw before drawing himself up to his full height and inclining his head toward the *Comhairle nan Cinnidhean*. "My sincere apologies."

"Ambassador Fahle requested a meeting upon your arrival home to address the incident that occurred in Amari the other week. The Ashion government is also requesting an extradition of those responsible," Alrickson said.

Honovi cocked his head to the side. "What proof does Ashion have that any of our people were involved?"

"The press captured members of the Clockwork Brigade being airlifted from the riot by an airship of obvious E'ridian make," Ambassador Fahle said tightly.

"An assumption doesn't make anything E'ridian. What I heard before leaving the capital was your own peacekeepers brought revenants into the city to target your countrymen."

The *cinn-chinnidh* seated around the circular table frowned at that statement, murmuring amongst themselves. They would have been told of the *rionetka* by Karla, but this news was a truth Honovi hoped to make them believe.

Ambassador Fahle's lips curled disdainfully. "Slander and lies. The Clockwork Brigade is the only group responsible for the terror that happened, and some of your countrymen aided them."

"I would think your country has more than enough problems with Daijal's occupation of western provinces than chasing down rumors here in E'ridia. If it were mine being invaded, rest assured I wouldn't be chasing *rumors*."

"Your country's airship aided criminals, and Ashion *demands* retribution."

Honovi focused his attention on the *Comhairle nan Cinnidhean,* familiar with the neutral expressions on the faces staring back at him. "Was an airship name identified?"

Alrickson arched an eyebrow. "Ashion has provided no such information."

Of course they hadn't. Honovi had made sure his people had hidden their tracks. "I stand before the *Comhairle nan Cinnidhean* with the opinion the ambassador asks for the impossible. We have never extradited one of ours to another country. We should not begin now when all the proof they have is heresay."

"Ashion will not stand for that," Ambassador Fahle snapped.

"You do not stand in Ashion," Alrickson reminded him. "And it was in your land that *my* son nearly lost his life."

"By one of your own people."

"By a *rionetka,*" Karla spoke up out of turn. "An abomination that no E'ridian would ever condone. Which leaves many who could be accused, but we have not leveled any at Ashion."

Because they didn't have any proof. If they had—if they knew who had carved into Siv and undone her mind—E'ridia would certainly demand retribution through diplomatic channels. Ambassador Fahle was trying to do the same, but his accusations carried no weight here before the *Comhairle nan Cinnidhean* when Honovi had seen the truth with his own eyes—it just wasn't one he'd speak in front of a foreigner.

"If there is, perhaps, hard proof you have of E'ridian participation, we will of course review it. But we have no extradition agreement with Ashion, and we will not be handing over citizens based on the flimsiest of accusations that you have brought us when you cannot even prove the airship was one of ours," Leena said.

Ambassador Fahle's face went red, but he was savvy enough not to yell his ire. "Ashion will not hold your decision favorably."

"Ashion does not rule here. Your concern has been noted, but as *jarl* Honovi has stated, there are more important issues that we must address. You may take your leave, Ambassador Fahle."

The group of Ashionens stood from the ambassadors' table, with Ambassador Fahle leading the way angrily to the chamber door. Honovi watched them leave, not speaking until the door had shut behind them.

"Ashion will not let their demands fall by the wayside," Alrickson said, looking at Honovi.

"I did not lie when I said it was their own peacekeepers who unleashed revenants inside their own city, against their own citizens. It wasn't the Clockwork Brigade who allowed such horror," Honovi said evenly.

"Paired with the *rionetka* that Siv became and the muddled political relationship Ashion has with Daijal while that country creeps past the central border, I would not trust any accusation Ashion levied against our people," Karla said as she stood. She made her way over to where Honovi stood at the speaker's seat.

"If Ashion accuses us of interference and they come back with proof, that will be a diplomatic mess," Aslaung, *ceann-cinnidh* of Clan Mountain, said. "Perhaps we erred in giving you the ambassadorship."

Honovi stiffened, lifting his chin. "If you hadn't, we would not know about the threat of *rionetkas*."

"Perhaps, but neither would we be contemplating the possibility of war."

"Eimarille Rourke is queen of Daijal now and seeks expansion into Ashion," Kele, *ceann-cinnidh* of Clan Sky, said with a frown. "Our ambassador to Daijal confirmed the Twilight Star blessed her coronation and gave her the crown."

Honovi had seen the photographs in the broadsheet once they'd landed in Veran, blurred as they were from starfire. He'd questioned their authenticity, but apparently, they'd been legitimate. "The North Star has not."

Kele shook his head, hazel-eyed gaze sweeping around the circular table before settling on Honovi. "I voted against allowing interference in another nation's sovereign right to rule. I fear that decision and what came after has opened us up to retribution."

"The border between Daijal and Ashion means nothing to Eimarille. I believe she would feel the same way about all the rest on any map of Maricol."

Kele opened his mouth to retort but held his tongue as the door to the chambers opened. Honovi looked over his shoulder, thinking it was the Ashionens again, but the man walking inside was far more welcome.

Seneschal Gregor of Clan Wind was dressed formally in a kilt and tailored jacket, the plaid he wore draped over his left shoulder and pinned in place with a heavy silver brooch. It fell to his knees, a length in deference to his rank.

"Seneschal," Alrickson said.

"*Comhairle nan Cinnidhean*," Gregor replied. His reddish-brown hair was braided back in a thick plait that fell over his shoulder, metal adornments twisted through it as a marker of his rank. He was perhaps only a decade older than Honovi's own thirty-five years, but Gregor had been voted into the position of Seneschal by a majority of each clan. He excelled in the role, shepherding law through with the *Comhairle nan Cinnidhean*'s guidance. Gregor was dedicated to E'ridia and always had been.

So the pistol he unholstered from the small of his back was so atypical that for a moment, Honovi didn't believe in what he was seeing—not until the pistol was aimed at the *cinn-chinnidh* seated around the table.

"Everyone get *down*!" Honovi yelled, already diving for cover, cursing the fact that he didn't have a weapon on him.

But Karla did, pulling her wand from *somewhere* on her person, despite the fact weapons and magic were forbidden in the chamber. Honovi was never so glad for someone to break the rules than in that moment.

Gregor fired the pistol, and someone screamed as everyone tried to make themselves less of a target. The biting crackle of magic erupted from the tip of Karla's wand, a jagged bolt of aether-backed power that wouldn't block bullets but did knock Gregor back onto a bench hard enough to crack *something*—wood or bone, Honovi couldn't tell from his spot on the floor.

Swearing, he caught Karla's eye, her face washed of all color but lips pressed together in sheer determination. "Cover me."

She nodded, tossing her braid over her shoulder and getting to one knee. She kept her arm extended, wand at the ready. Honovi heard someone moaning in pain, but he couldn't think about who had been wounded—if it was his father—not when the threat hadn't been negated.

Honovi hurried toward the Seneschal, finding the man struggling to sit up with a broken arm, eyes glazed over unseeingly. Gregor had lost the pistol from the hit or the landing. Honovi couldn't see it anywhere, but his desire to locate it fell by the wayside once he caught sight of the burns from Karla's wand on Gregor's chest that scorched the same sort of scars he'd seen in Siv.

"*Fuck*," Honovi bit out, pinning the *rionetka* that had once been E'ridia's Seneschal to the bench. He knew, in that moment, the Eastern Spine would not be enough to keep war out of E'ridia. "Karla, I need you! He's a *rionetka*."

"Leena's been shot," Alrickson called out.

Honovi let out a relieved breath even as he tightened his grip on the *rionetka*. Then Karla was there, thrusting her arm over his shoulder to smack the tip of her wand against Gregor's forehead.

"*Sleep*," she snarled.

An aether mist enveloped Gregor's face, and he breathed it in, fighting against the order. Whatever Karla had learned from walking through Siv's mind, she must have employed some of that knowledge there in the chamber. It took nearly half a minute by Honovi's count, but Gregor eventually went lax in his grip, head lolling to the side, eyes half-lidded.

Honovi didn't let him go, watching the way his scarred and burned chest rose and fell, as if a heart still beat beneath his ribs, when it was all a lie.

Twelve

HONOVI

The high priestess of the Star Order in E'ridia curled her hand beneath Gregor's chin. She tilted his head up and to the side as far as the restraint collar would allow, studying the Seneschal with a sharp focus that Honovi was familiar with. His mother had always been one he'd never liked to cross while growing up, more out of fear of disappointing her than fear *of* her. Isla of Clan Storm was kind and loving, but she had guided him down his road with a firm hand that allowed for no diversion.

She raised her left hand, holding on to her brass-plated wand, the metal body of it etched with knotwork. The clarion crystal at the tip glowed from the aether, his mother's magic a warm cloak around her that was comforting in a way, despite the political upheaval they were all unexpectedly stumbling through.

Honovi's mother was a tall woman, taller even than his father. Her graying black hair was braided back in a dozen small braids that blended together into a single plait that fell past her waist. The headdress she wore—six gold rings haloing her head with the star god constellations twisted through the filigree—made her even taller, but Alrickson had never minded looking up at her through the scant few inches that separated them. Honovi always thought they made a striking pair.

She'd been called away from a temple ceremony, and the dusky blue ceremonial robe she wore over her gown was embroidered with gold thread. The gold paint on her face done in intricate lines was meant for prayer in the star temple, not an interrogation in a crowded hospital room.

But Honovi's mother was a powerful magician whose magic she had dedicated to serving the Dawn Star. She was skilled in a level of mind magic meant to be used for healing and guidance. That skill was just as useful in prying out the truth from the *rionetka* Gregor had become and which he didn't recognize himself as.

"I demand to be let go," Gregor said, his words a little slurred from the pain medicine the doctor had given him after the burns on his chest were tended to. "I have done nothing wrong."

"You haven't, perhaps, but someone else has through you," Isla said before pursing her lips. "Be still."

She tapped his forehead gently with her wand, leaving a ghostly stain of magic on the Seneschal's skin. His eyes fluttered shut, body going lax against the restraints he'd been struggling against.

"Is he not a traitor?" Alrickson asked.

Honovi spared a glance at his father, who hadn't yet changed out of his ruined kilt and plaid. The white of his button-down shirt was stained in places with rust-colored dots. Leena had been one of the unlucky ones wounded in the attack against the *Comhairle nan Cinnidhean*. She and two more of the *cinn-chinnidh* had left the chamber on stretchers, bleeding from gunshot wounds Honovi wasn't sure they'd recover from.

"He was made one," Isla murmured, tracing the tip of her wand down the side of Gregor's face to rest against his left temple. "Much like Siv was, I presume."

She touched a hand to Gregor's shoulder, fingers skating over the raised scar of the vivisection mark that crossed his chest. Honovi hadn't gotten a good look at the one on Siv's chest, wounded and hurting as he had been at the time. He'd studied the one on Gregor's chest before the doctors wheeled him into the operating theater, joined by a magician to keep the *rionetka* in check.

He wondered how long Gregor had been a *rionetka*. Honovi would never know how long Siv was not herself, how long she was locked inside her mind, a puppet to some unknown master pulling her strings.

Inside Gregor's chest would be the same sort of clockwork metal heart that had been extracted from Siv's body. Karla had overseen the removal back in Amari, but the device had broken apart during the flight home, some bit of magic causing it to self-destruct, all its magic fading away no matter what Karla did to keep it intact.

What remained were broken pieces of metal, cracked gears, and shattered clarion crystals, whatever magic having powered the mechanical heart gone back to the aether.

It meant none of them knew who was pulling the strings, but Honovi could guess. It wasn't proof, though, and accusing Queen Eimarille Rourke of such atrocities without it would hasten the war coming to their borders.

Honovi watched his mother close her eyes, the tip of her wand glowing softly with magic. Glittering lines of aether wrapped around Gregor's head, casting a colored shine on his skin. The Seneschal breathed slowly through whatever exam Isla was putting him through —right up until he panicked.

Gregor's eyes snapped open, head jerking away from her wand as far as the collar restraint would let him. His lips peeled back over his teeth, eyes going so wide Honovi could see the whites all around the irises.

Despite the strain in Gregor's body—the muscles standing out in his arms and legs, the tendons stark in his neck beneath the padded collar—despite the great gasping breaths he took, he didn't say a single word. Isla removed her wand from his temple, and Gregor sagged against the bed, breathing harshly. His fingers clawed at the white sheet covering the thin mattress, but he stopped yanking at the restraints.

"His mind is his own except where it isn't," Isla said, staring down at Gregor. "He is a prisoner in his own mind and knows it but can't break free."

Honovi dragged a hand down his face. "Was there any hint of who is controlling him?"

Isla shook her head, mouth twisting as she lowered her arm. "No. Only empty places, gaps in his memory."

"How long has he been a *rionetka*?"

She looked at him with a kind of horrified grief that Honovi never wanted to see on her face. "Over a year."

Alrickson swore viciously, banging his fist against the wall hard enough to rattle the medical supplies in the storage cabinet. "This is an unfathomable breach of our sovereignty."

"We shouldn't be discussing anything in this room," Kele said. The older man's blond hair was tacky from blood, the graze across his right temple neatly bandaged. He'd been lucky, oh so lucky, that the bullet from Gregor's pistol had mostly missed its target.

Alrickson gestured for them to follow him out of the private hospital room. Honovi went where directed, eyeing the peacekeepers who stood guard outside the room. One slipped inside once they left to take up a post at the door, attention on the man in the bed.

"We'll need to institute body checks for scars. It's what they've done in Ashion," Honovi said.

Kele nodded grimly. "Can magicians be taught to search for clockwork hearts? The magic powering the devices must be noticeable."

"Gregor has been holding office for over a year, and no one noticed the change," Alrickson pointed out.

"We didn't know of the threat."

"Whatever powers his body, it is a type of invention and magic that is well-made," Isla conceded. "I would not have felt its presence if I didn't already know to look for it. The device works like a heart, and the aether is contained by the clarion crystals inside the body. It's subtle in a way and tied to the mind control. It is, in essence, an elaborate infernal engine."

Honovi closed his eyes, thinking of Siv and wondering when she had been turned—if it was before he'd arrived in Amari or after. How long had he spent in her presence, looking into her eyes, and she was screaming for help in her mind, but none of them heard?

He opened his eyes and met his father's gaze. "We need to call an emergency meeting. We need to set standards on how to ensure someone isn't a *rionetka*. When word gets out about why the Seneschal opened fire in the chambers, it's going to incite panic."

"Let's gather the others who can leave and return to the capitol," Alrickson said before reaching for his wife's hand, giving it a squeeze. "Stay safe."

"You, too. All of you," Isla said, gaze flicking over them.

They couldn't speak openly in the hospital, and the press was clamoring at the doors to the building, wanting answers. If they left, they'd be expected to give a statement, something Honovi knew they were all against providing at the moment. They still braved the shouted questions and cameras that followed their every move as those of the *Comhairle nan Cinnidhean* who could leave the hospital were escorted back to the motor carriages.

Honovi joined Kele in one of the vehicles, but the ride back was made in silence. They both understood the need for discretion, and nothing of substance was discussed until they found themselves pulling into the well-guarded plaza. The fountain in the center was surrounded by candles inside glass cases and so many bouquets of flowers he couldn't see the wall.

The sun was in the west, dipping toward the horizon and the mountains that reached up to the sky there. It was a familiar sight, one Honovi had missed while in Amari, that city sprawled across the Northern Plains and beneath the wide-open sky.

Drifting through the air came the sound of temple bells, offbeat to the pipes and drums that echoed from too many pubs and neighborhood plazas to count. E'ridians prayed differently than those in Amari had, and Honovi was comforted by the sounds he'd grown up with.

Peacekeepers were on guard duty around the capitol building, but Honovi also saw people in military uniform. E'ridia's army was minuscule compared to other countries, but its air force was second to none. Still, it wasn't typical to see soldiers guarding the civic area.

Honovi feared the extenuating circumstance would soon become a new normal none of them would like.

Alrickson must have used his televox to call the *jarls* of the *cinn-chinnidh* who remained at the hospital. They had arrived and waited near the guarded entrance, and it was a whole contingent of E'ridia's governing body that entered the capitol building once more.

The chamber was still being handled like a crime scene, so Honovi wasn't surprised when his father led the group to a conference room used by the *Comhairle nan Cinnidhean* for private purposes. The peace-keepers who had escorted them inside took up guard positions in the hallway.

Kele shut the door, and Honovi didn't blame him for locking it. Honovi gazed at the group of people who took their seats at the table, his attention lingering on Frey, *jarl* of Clan Sun and there because her mother had been injured during the shooting and the mantle of leadership had fallen to her. They'd grown up together amidst the trappings of government and clan needs, though they'd been apart more than together in the last decade or so.

Frey carried herself as if she belonged, much the same way Honovi did. She inclined her head at him in a silent greeting, the metal ranking hair adornments threaded through her braid glinting as she did so. She said nothing, seemingly content to observe first before giving voice to her own clan's needs in this trying time.

Honovi kept his own peace unless directly addressed as the *Comhairle nan Cinnidhean* struggled in the aftermath of the unthinkable. This was a new road they were all walking down, and Honovi didn't care for the steps.

"What of you, Honovi?" Kele asked, turning to look at him. "You brought Siv's body back from Ashion, and she had the same device inside her when she attacked you. Who do you think could have created these monstrosities?"

Honovi leaned back in his chair, frowning. "Accusing anyone without proof would be detrimental."

"Ah, but you think someone ordered this despicableness."

"I do. Most of you know I went to Ashion to be with my husband.

What he uncovered there while working with the Clockwork Brigade is treason against everyone who calls Maricol home. The death-defying machine that turns people into revenants is real. I've seen the blueprints. As for the *rionetkas*? I find it interesting that their attacks have only been directed against those countries who hold no allegiance with Daijal and its queen. Ours, Ashion, even Solaria, if the broadsheets are to be believed."

"All of those countries are ones that border Daijal," Alrickson added grimly.

"What of the Tovan Isles?" Frey asked. "I would think they would be less easily infiltrated on their ship-cities."

"One would think so, but they send ambassadors to other countries the same way we do. Who is to say one didn't return home a *rionetka*?" Honovi asked.

"Accusing Queen Eimarille of such crimes will bring war, and it will affect Ashion first. She'd need to go through that country before attempting to make it over the Eastern Spine."

"She's already started. Daijal forces have occupied Haighmoor under false reasoning. The day the wardens can't handle revenants is the day we all succumb to the poison fields. We all know this." Honovi shook his head before spreading his hands. "She allies with Urova in the north. She wouldn't need to go through Ashion if Urova and its submersibles reach our shores first."

"Urova wouldn't dare."

"And if their government is controlled by *rionetkas*? Wouldn't they? It seems whoever is behind the creation of the *rionetkas* has already tried with us. Who is to say they haven't succeeded elsewhere?"

The room fell into an uncomfortable silence as that sickening possibility settled between them. They didn't have proof, though—either of Eimarille's interference or the status of another country's government—but the doubt sown merely by the *rionetkas* existence was insidious.

"Ashion is under attack. The likelihood of that country falling to Queen Eimarille is high," Kele said.

"She can be queen of both countries, despite the North Star's decree," Alrickson agreed.

"She is a threat, one we need to prepare against," Honovi said firmly. "To that end, I believe I should return to Ashion. Blaine is still embedded with the Clockwork Brigade, and the information they have uncovered so far is critical."

"They can't be our allies. The Ashion government considers them a rebellion, and to acknowledge them will put us at odds with Ashion and Daijal," Kele said.

"Caris Dhemlan can cast starfire. She is the girl Blaine must stand witness for at the behest of the Dusk Star. She can be queen, and she can call for an alliance."

"She isn't queen now."

"There is a bounty on Caris' head that is twice what Blaine's is. I think that speaks enough about the threat Queen Eimarille sees her as. At some point, E'ridia will need to make a choice on where we stand in the face of Daijal encroachment. Staying neutral will not aid us, even with the Eastern Spine between us and the rest of the continent."

Kele eyed him from across the table, a deep frown on his face. "You believe Queen Eimarille will not stop at the borders of Ashion?"

"She's invading one country as we speak, guided by the Twilight Star. If she was never going to be a threat, why did the Dusk Star bring Blaine here? If we are to be pawns, I would rather we be pawns on the right side of this war."

"I find I must agree," Frey said, drawing everyone's attention. "I was there the night the Dusk Star gave Blaine to the clans. I was not aware he'd gone to Ashion, only that he'd been absent from Honovi's side on clan business. Considering what transpired today and the threat levied against us by unknown parties, we cannot remain neutral. The clans will not appreciate us doing nothing."

Honovi nodded agreement. "Sitting idly by is not an option."

He knew what was at stake perhaps better than all of those seated around the table. Eimarille did not strike him as the type of woman to be satisfied until she'd gained control of the entirety of Maricol.

In the end, nothing concrete was agreed to beyond the precautions set down to uncover *rionetkas*. Vivisection scars were easy enough to identify, even if the physical exam would make people uncomfortable. But better a breach of manners than ever wondering if the person standing in front of you was even truly themselves.

It wasn't how Honovi wanted to leave his country behind—a jagged sense of unease and betrayal carved into the heart of their governing body—but he couldn't protect his home if he didn't go where the stars led him. His road had always pointed to Blaine, and if Blaine was meant to fight for Maricol, then Honovi would be right by his side.

In the morning, Honovi took a military crew filled with people from all clans on the fastest airship E'ridia's air force could muster on short notice. The *Celestial Sprite* launched from Glencoe's airfields at dawn, its weapon turrets pulled into its hull to hide its true purpose of being built for war, and headed west toward the burgeoning unrest in Ashion.

Resistance

936 A.O.P.

One

VANYA

"Mother was better at this than I," Vanya said, staring over the balcony railing at the guests below in the vast palace gardens. "She should be here."

"There is nothing to be gained from maudlin thoughts," Taisiya said from beside him. "You've ensured Joelle will be under scrutiny by the wardens. That's a warning that hit home."

"To all the Houses, which earns us no favors."

"Then we must give them something more than what Joelle has offered them."

Vanya offered Taisiya his elbow, and she took it with a flash of a smile before schooling her features into a polite mask. It was their House's turn to put on a gathering for the Conclave in response to Joelle's traditional first foray into the political dance.

In deference to Taisiya's knees, Vanya escorted her to the private lift that ran through the levels of the family wing. The attendant on duty inside handled the gate and controls for them, bringing them to the ground floor. He inclined his head out of respect as Vanya and Taisiya exited the lift.

They made their way through the halls at a sedate pace, eventually stepping outside into the rear gardens. Unlike at the House of

Kimathi, his majordomo knew the proper etiquette when it came to introducing one's emperor.

"His Imperial Majesty Vanya Sa'Liandel, of the House of Sa'Liandel, and *valide* Taisiya Sa'Liandel," Alida said into the voice amplifier device she held. The speakers set about the garden in discreet places transmitted her words for everyone to hear.

Vanya watched those nearest the palace turn to look as he and Taisiya stepped into the sunlight. Unlike at the House of Kimathi, he had no need to cast starfire to gain everyone's attention. The Imperial palace was a grand backdrop of his status. Like the crown he wore, it reminded everyone present of his rank.

The gardens had been decked out with colorful tents to gather under, the coverings providing shade over grassy areas. Mechanical fans had been set up to blow misted air around where people were most likely to gather through the pathways, blooming bushes, and bubbling streams and ponds in the landscaped areas.

The Imperial gardens were walled off from the streets and blocked by old trees that stretched toward the sky, obscuring the view from beyond. Vanya had taken many walks down the paths both as a prince and an emperor when a particularly vexing problem arose and he needed to think of a solution. He'd cherished the walks with his mother, appreciating the guidance she gave, and he missed it now just as much as he did in the immediate aftermath of that loss.

Taisiya gave his elbow a squeeze before stepping away from him to mingle with the Houses present for the Conclave. Vanya wandered in a different direction, intent on gaining other Houses' loyalty by the end of the gathering. Amir, as always, aided in that endeavor.

"Ah, Your Imperial Majesty," Amir said from his spot beneath a tent. "Do come and join us. I've been asked a question I do believe you are better positioned to answer."

"House of Vikandir," Vanya said in greeting as he stepped off the pathway and into the shade provided by the tent above. A servant immediately offered up a tray of wineglasses near dripping with condensation. He accepted one and took a sip of the cold red wine, fruit thick between the jagged ice.

"Might I present *vezir* Cybele of the House of Balaskas."

The *vezir* in question was of a minor House who had never held the Imperial throne, despite their efforts over the past generations. Cybele was perhaps a decade older than Vanya, her curly black hair twisted up in an intricate knot atop her head. Pearl and jeweled combs kept the updo in place.

Cybele curtsied to him, keeping her head held high. The gauzy fabric of her gown fluttered about her as she dipped and rose, the style popular during the summer months. "House of Sa'Liandel."

Only during a Conclave could one get away without a proper greeting to their emperor, but the fact that she offered a curtsey was telling of her stance amidst the talks. "Well met, House of Balaskas."

"I only wish it were under better circumstances."

Amir took a sip of his wine. "She had some questions about the *rionetkas*. I told her you would have a better answer than I."

"I will do my best to answer what I can. My best magicians are still trying to determine the components of the controlling spell," Vanya said.

"So they are controlled by magic?" Cybele asked.

"The clockwork heart works like a real one, but blood would not flow through it without magic. The aether keeps them alive through whatever control their master claims."

"And you truly didn't know of their existence?"

Vanya shook his head. "The *praetoria* legionnaires were themselves right up until they weren't. Every single body that was examined had the same clockwork heart in their chests. The spellwork is complicated and delicate. Any tampering breaks the device, and there are no memories of their master in their minds."

"Convenient," a lilting soprano voice said from behind them.

Vanya didn't bother to turn around as Lady Vesper of the House of Aetos entered the tent, the scent of her perfume subtle on the air. She held on to Artyom's arm, Joelle's son and heir dressed in robes that were nearly as elaborate as the set Vanya wore.

Neither offered any sort of formal greeting to Vanya—Artyom's loyalty to his House obvious, and Vesper still clearly tying her loyalty to Joelle. Vanya met Vesper's gaze over the rim of his wineglass as he took a sip, wondering what verbal pitfalls awaited him.

"That I survived?" Vanya asked drolly.

"That you say you can't find the supposed master of these abominations that have only appeared in your presence," Vesper said.

"Ah, is that an accusation I hear?"

"Merely a musing."

Vanya smiled thinly. "Of course. But these are not the first *rionetkas* we've encountered."

Vesper arched an eyebrow, expression impossible to read. "Do tell."

"The assassin who interrupted my coronation was a *rionetka*, though we had no name for them at that time. I sent the device to the wardens to undergo a study."

"Delivered by your warden, no doubt?" Artyom said with a bite to his voice

"I claim no ownership over any warden."

"Rumors speak otherwise. Much like they say you have no heir."

Vanya couldn't help the way his lip curled at that, a tell that Vesper took as a strike if he judged by the smirk she hid behind her glass. "Raiah is safe."

Artyom waved aside his assurances. "We only have your word, and I would not trust you to keep it."

"Much like we only have Joelle's word that nothing untoward is happening in her *vasilyet*."

Artyom's lips twitched as he fought back a scowl. "The Conclave is gathered to judge our grievance against *your* House."

"And my counterargument has a right to be heard."

"Do you wish to proclaim your ownership over *vasilyets* your House has never governed?" Vesper asked archly.

"My House has held the Imperial throne for the last few centuries. My governance touches every *vasilyet*."

Vesper shrugged, making sure to catch the eye of Cybele, as if she was looking to commiserate. "Your House's governance destroyed a *vasilyet* once before. I would not trust your care, and I would counsel others to be just as wary."

"I'll make my decision on where my House's loyalty shall lie on my own," Cybele said mildly.

"I would think carefully of who is best suited to aid your House."

"You would have them give loyalty to a House who does not have Solaria's best interests at heart? One must wonder what you do in your House's own *vasilyet*. Have you allowed a death-defying machine to be built in Seaville? Would you plead ignorance the same way Joelle has? I would think that a terrible trait for someone who wishes to rule," Vanya said.

Vesper's expression became flat, her fingers tightening imperceptibly on her wineglass. "Your stories and lies will not sway the Houses."

"Ah, but I do not lie. The wardens would not heed such warnings that come out of Bellingham if I lied." Vanya smiled, careful not to show too much of his teeth. "I have only cared for the future of Solaria. I can't say Joelle feels the same when she denies legitimate requests to review her governorship, and the borders she tends are porous."

Artyom's expression darkened, but he kept his teeth clenched together on whatever words he would have said, most likely warned by his mother to not dig any verbal holes they could not climb out of.

Vanya turned to face Cybele. "The *rionetkas* are real, and they are a threat, one I had no intention of keeping to myself. The Houses may play our games, but we play them with our own minds. The threat of *rionetkas* takes that from us."

Cybele inclined her head ever so slightly. "I'll take your words under advisement."

It wasn't a solid commitment, and hers was a minor House, but any he could bring to his side was one less Joelle could claim. Vanya left the tent with his wineglass in hand, hearing Amir hastily make his goodbyes as well. The older man caught up easily enough since Vanya was in no hurry to beg another House for their support.

"Are the major Houses aligned with Joelle? Is that why you spend time flitting between the minor ones?" Vanya asked against the rim of his wineglass to hide his words.

"Not all Houses have taken sides," Amir demurred.

"But enough that it worries you."

Amir gestured vaguely at nothing, careful to keep his expression devoid of worry. "It is only you and Lady Taisiya, and your heir is not here."

Vanya was well aware of the weak position his House appeared to be in. It was why he hadn't summoned any of his extended family to Calhames—he couldn't trust they'd follow the road he needed them to. Vanya swallowed his wine, the sweetness turning sour in the back of his throat at the idea of Joelle winning this game of words. "We've more work to do."

Amir looked at him askance. "Of course."

They parted ways, with Vanya taking a path to a different tent full of different Houses, seeking to sway their opinions about *rionetkas* and a death-defying machine in the face of Joelle's accusations of his betrayal to Solaria. Some, he knew, had already made up their minds, their cool politeness evidence enough of their alliance with the House of Kimathi. Vanya still attempted to sway them, even if there was no swaying Joelle from her goal—he could only try to outmaneuver her.

Vanya remained at a disadvantage, for Joelle had spent weeks already cultivating whispers and rumors to turn the Houses against him. If the Conclave ended with Vanya out of favor, then he would not hold the Imperial throne for long.

That would leave Raiah in Joelle's hands, a scenario Vanya never wanted to happen. Taisiya would not be strong enough to keep Raiah safe, alone as she had been on the coast for years, despite her rank and the starfire she could call from the aether. If Vanya were to keep Raiah from Joelle, then he needed to follow in his mother's footsteps and refuse to bend.

Vanya eventually circled around to her, crossing Joelle's path in one of the center gardens, where the flowering hedges were low and the pond teemed with brightly scaled fish beneath the shade of small trees. The midmorning heat was growing when he turned from one group of guests and came face-to-face with Joelle, the *vezir* of the House of Kimathi having found her way to her son's side.

Vesper, Vanya noted, did not shadow them this time. She was still doing their bidding, he knew. The House of Aetos was lost to him, having already chosen their side in this Conclave. It would be difficult to undo the whisper campaign Joelle and her allies had started against him if she held many of the major Houses.

"I understand you are accusing my House of untruths," Joelle said, her voice carrying to the ears of the nearby guests.

"My accusation has not changed," Vanya said evenly.

"And yet, they remain lies on your tongue."

"You protest much for one who has allowed such horrors into your *vasilyet*."

Joelle shook her head, the jeweled drop earrings she wore swaying with the motion. "I would never condone such cruelty, but your House has a history of doing so."

Vanya would have responded, except the quiet that had surrounded them was broken by the rising voices of his guests, their murmurs taking on an excited tone. Beneath it came the frantic footsteps of someone running. Joelle's eyes widened, mouth parting slightly in surprise, and Vanya found himself turning, hope a tight knot in his chest.

"Your Imperial Majesty," Alida called out, sounding breathless as she hurried down the path to him.

Striding behind her, some distance back, were the only two people Vanya wanted to see.

He'd known Amir's wife had put Soren and Raiah on an airship. He'd known, but he hadn't let himself believe they would arrive, not after everything Soren had said they'd gone through while traveling. But they were here now, and Raiah's voice made him take a step forward, forgetting about the threat at his back.

"Papa!" Raiah shrieked.

She wasn't dressed like a princess—her outfit was typical for a young boy not of any House, and her hair was in need of re-braiding —but he'd know her anywhere. Soren swung Raiah off his hip with practiced ease, setting her on her own two feet between one step and the next. He let her go, and she was off like a bullet, racing toward

Vanya as fast as her little legs would carry her, crying for him all the while.

Vanya met her halfway, swinging her up into his arms to hold her close. Her little arms wrapped tight around his neck as she clutched at him with a sob, too overwhelmed to lift her head where she'd buried it against his shoulder. "*Papa*."

He curved his hand over the shape of her skull, drawing in a ragged breath as he held her tight. "I'm here. I'm right here."

"Papa, I *missed* you."

"And I you. I'm so very glad you're home."

Vanya watched Soren approach, noticing the dark circles under the warden's eyes that spoke of little sleep since leaving Oeiras. He wore his field leathers, the poison short sword for close-quarters combat protruding over one shoulder. The reserved expression on his face never wavered, but the relief in his gray eyes was all Vanya wanted to see—some bit of recognition that Soren was glad to be back.

"Your Imperial Majesty," Soren said as he came to a stop before Vanya. He didn't bow—wardens never bowed to heads of state—but he did incline his head a little in acknowledgment for their audience.

They were arm's length apart, and it felt like a chasm to Vanya in that moment. He had Raiah in his arms, and all he wanted was to pull Soren close, but he couldn't. Rumors already ran rampant about them amongst the Houses. Vanya would typically brush it all aside and do as he liked, but the Conclave complicated everything. Houses already thought he gave too much leeway, too much support, to the wardens. Dragging Soren close for a kiss would only make things worse. He had his House, and his heir, to think of, and that meant sticking to the roles they were born to in the face of prying eyes.

Vanya cleared his throat, staring at Soren. "How was the flight?"

"Uneventful. The crew was examined for vivisection scars before being allowed onto the airship, and Raiah never left my side." Soren nodded at Raiah. "She missed you."

"And I her."

Soren's mouth quirked slightly at the corners, as if he knew what words remained unspoken on Vanya's tongue. "I kept her safe, as promised."

"I had no doubt."

Soren hooked a thumb over his gun belt, gaze moving past Vanya to those behind him. "I have a border report you'll want to hear."

"I'll take it in the palace. You can also fill me in on your time away."

"You gave your daughter to the wardens?" Joelle asked sharply.

Vanya didn't bother turning to face her, not with Raiah in his arms. "I gave her to the one person I knew would keep her safe. Soren isn't a *rionetka*, and he knew what to look for."

"He is beholden to you."

Unsaid went the accusation that she believed the *rionetkas* were Vanya's doing. Vanya watched the way Soren's eyes narrowed, head tilting a little as he took Joelle's measure.

"I take it you're *vezir* Joelle?" Soren asked, tone mild in a way that reminded Vanya of his mother before she went in for a political kill. "The same *vezir* who allowed the death-defying machine to be built and used within the borders of your *vasilyet*?"

Vanya angled himself so that he could see Joelle's face at that accusation, unsurprised to see a flash of anger cross her eyes.

"I see you are a mouthpiece for the House of Sa'Liandel," Joelle said disdainfully.

"I saw the death-defying machine with my own eyes. I saw the revenants Solarians *and* Daijalans were turning the dead into. The quarry was filled with them until I blew it up. That was allowed in *your vasilyet*, and if that is the sort of politics you're conducting, then it's no wonder you barred the wardens from your land. It's no wonder those who made it inside your borders were murdered."

Joelle's sharply indrawn breath could be heard by those standing closest to their little group. Artyom's cheeks had flushed red, but he didn't speak, leaving the defense of their House to his mother.

"Such lies are unbecoming of a warden," Joelle gritted out.

Soren shrugged. "No lies, only a truth that has been reported back to my governor."

The attention of the people around them was shifting, gazes

becoming curious and judging. Vanya could hear the whispers start up as people reacted to Soren's accusation. It didn't matter what they thought of Soren's personal ties to Vanya; the wardens' governor was never informed of a threat that wasn't true.

Movement caught Vanya's eye, and he watched as Taisiya slipped through the crowd on Amir's arm. She didn't hesitate to make herself known, seizing the moment to put Joelle in a corner she could not escape. "Perhaps an investigation headed by the Legion into the House of Kimathi's *vasilyet* would be advisable, Your Imperial Majesty."

"I think that's a fine idea," Vanya said, smiling with all his teeth. "Imperial General Chu Hua will most certainly be agreeable to such an endeavor."

"It is not needed," Joelle snapped.

"We'll see."

Soren nodded decisively, finally refocusing on Vanya. "That border report, Your Imperial Majesty?"

He so very much wanted to hear his name fall from Soren's lips—even *princeling* would be acceptable—but he'd settle for Soren's voice, for him standing real and alive in front of him.

Raiah wriggled in his arms but didn't let go. Vanya hefted her up a little higher, adjusting his grip on her small body. She clung to him tightly, still refusing to lift her head, and he had no intention of putting her down until she demanded it of him.

Soren turned on his heel, leading the way back to the palace. Alida sketched a bow in Vanya's direction before hurrying after the warden to see to whatever needs he'd have after his jaunt through the back roads. Vanya strode after the two, catching Taisiya's eye as he went.

"I'll make myself available here," she said, voice carrying so those of the Houses knew theirs remained in the Conclave.

Vanya's duty at the moment was to see to Raiah and Soren, and he would not be swayed from that path.

Two

VANYA

"Where is Raiah?" Taisiya asked when Vanya entered the private dining room in the family wing for the evening meal.

"Sleeping," Vanya said, fingers twitching with the remembered feel of his daughter's hair beneath them. "Under guard."

He'd not gotten much done since her return, having spent the remainder of the day with her by his side as the servants fussed over her comfort. Raiah had been bathed and fed, her hair combed out by himself and neatly tied back in thick plaits that snugged close to her skull. She'd chattered at him all the while after her tears dried, telling him about her time away, though he knew there were gaps in her telling that she refused to talk about.

She was four, and she'd been hunted by *rionetkas,* made a target by more than just the Houses, he was coming to suspect. Danger came with her position as his heir, but Vanya knew the game the Houses played. He knew the pitfalls of their politics. He didn't know the ones that Joelle had dug herself on a porous border.

He'd wanted to spare his daughter, as any parent did, the horrors of the life that came with being part of a House, much less one that held the Imperial throne. He'd wanted to keep her innocent for just a little longer, for he knew how quickly pain could creep into one's life.

He'd lost his own brother at the tender age of eight and survived numerous assassination attempts before burying his own parents.

Vanya had done his best to use his knowledge of past survival to keep Raiah alive. He'd banked on Joelle's desire to use her great-granddaughter to further her own plans, but that left every other House seeking to murder his daughter in pursuit of the Imperial throne. With the threat of *rionetkas* and the death-defying machine, to say nothing of what was occurring in the northern countries, the world wasn't safe.

He felt like a failure because of it, but Raiah was too young to understand why his heart ached.

"She held up well enough while we were on the road. I tried to shield her as much as I could from what was happening, though it was difficult at times," Soren said.

"You kept her alive. I could ask for nothing less."

Taisiya eyed Soren from where she sat across the gold-gilt table from him, a tiny, delicate glass in her hand half-full with a thick dessert wine the color of pink berries. Both had been seated on either side of Vanya's spot at the head of the table. "Your words today certainly upended how things were going. I spent the rest of the gathering pressing our advantage. For all that the Houses think you little more than a courtesan, the wardens' governor is an entirely different problem I don't believe Joelle was prepared for."

Soren blinked at her but otherwise let no reaction settle in his body. "I spoke the truth."

Taisiya smiled, all teeth, before she sipped at her drink. She favored the sweet wine through every dinner course, something Vanya had learned since her arrival. "Yes. And it was my job to make sure it was heard. We've many more gatherings to attend this week, Vanya. Several major Houses have requested our presence at their estates. Some have even indicated the House of Kimathi will not be present for those gatherings."

That was surprisingly hopeful. Vanya settled onto the cushioned chair at the head of the table. He was still dressed in his robe from earlier, as was Taisiya. Soren, he noted, had at least discarded all his weapons save his two pistols. "Did they now?"

Taisiya nodded before pinning Soren with a steely look. "You will join me at the next gathering, warden."

Soren, hand half-outstretched for his wineglass, froze. "That's not my place."

"Neither is this, yet here you are." She held a hand up at Vanya as he opened his mouth, gaze sliding his way. "You know as well as I that the Houses are right to question the warden's status, even if they will not question the wardens' governor. It is bad politics not to use him."

"I won't be your pawn," Soren said in a low voice, finally grabbing his wineglass.

Taisiya's gaze became pitying, the wrinkles at the corners of her eyes deepening. "My dear, we are all pawns in House games. If you did not wish to play, you should have stayed out of Vanya's bed."

"*Valide*," Vanya said sharply. "Enough."

"He will join me," she said, ignoring his order to not press the issue. "If you had a wife or a husband, they would do the duty he will now take up."

"Soren is not of our House."

"But he is of your household, and he holds your favor. What information he brings is a truth the other Houses are interested in. I will not have the Conclave end with Joelle the victor, and he will aid us in that endeavor." She set her wineglass down and lifted the pearlescent bell beside her plate, ringing it to summon the servants. "Let us eat."

Vanya snapped his teeth together and shook his head. Arguing with her would only give him a headache, and he had no desire to ruin the happy mood he'd been in since Soren and Raiah had arrived home. To that end, he set about enjoying the intimate five-course celebratory meal that had been prepared. Rather than be served from platters on the table, the meal arrived on individual plates wheeled in on a cart and paired with a different drink for each course.

Taisiya kept the conversation flowing, her raspy voice well soothed by the alcohol she drank. She kept the topics lighthearted in deference to the servants around them, asking after Soren's life as a warden rather than his time spent away with Raiah.

Vanya had already received the border report from Soren, the details of their time on the back roads while crisscrossing borders leaving him near sick to his stomach. But that had been earlier, and he had no issue enjoying the meal. Neither did Soren, who knew by now to pace himself for the elaborate meals the royal chef was known to prepare. Not finishing everything on a plate wasn't a sign of dissatisfaction in Solarian culture, and it made it easier to get through all five courses.

By the time the dessert plates of spun pastry soaked in honey and sugar and layered with sweet cheese and nuts were finished and taken away, Vanya was comfortably full. Taisiya leaned back in her chair with a soft sigh. "I would bring your chef to the coast when I leave."

"I pay her handsomely to stay," Vanya said.

Taisiya flashed him a quick smile before pushing her chair back and getting to her feet. "I'll take my leave."

Vanya inclined his head to her. "Sleep well, *valide*."

She'd only had a few hours in the afternoon to spend with Raiah after returning from the Conclave. It had been the first time she'd met his daughter, having not been in Calhames for years. Taisiya had missed the celebrations of Raiah's birth and his own coronation, seeking solace on the coast. He'd not held it against her, and her being here now was invaluable support.

Taisiya left, and the servants slipped inside after her to clear the table. Vanya caught Soren's eye. "Walk with me?"

Soren nodded, pushing his chair back from the table. "Thank you for the meal. Better than the field rations, that's for sure."

"One would hope."

"The rock crystal didn't last long enough for Raiah, but the House of Vikandir rectified that once we were inside their home. Speaking of, I still have your writ."

Vanya waved off that statement as they exited the dining room. "Keep it for now. You may need it again."

He hoped he wouldn't need to send Raiah away out of the line of fire again, but if he did, he wanted Soren to have the means to keep her safe on hand.

Soren fell into step beside Vanya as he led the way through the grand hallways to a side entrance that opened out into a small side garden. It wasn't as large as the one in the rear of the palace, but it bordered them, and a pathway branched off it toward the star temple.

Vanya didn't lead Soren to the star temple but down the pathway that would take them through the heart of the garden. The tents and tables from earlier were gone now, and the moon overhead was nearly full, pale moonlight mingling with the soft amber glow of the gas lamps. The *praetoria* legionnaires on guard duty kept their distance, allowing Vanya some bit of privacy with his warden.

Walking these pathways at night had become a tradition since he'd been crowned. The quiet of the garden was deceptive, as beyond the palace walls lay the vibrancy of Calhames. But this oasis brought him some bit of peace, a false sense of having all the time in the world to work out the problems laying siege to his empire.

He'd missed the nights when Soren joined him, and having the warden by his side again loosened Vanya's shoulders in a way little else did. He reached out and wrapped his fingers around Soren's wrist, squeezing gently.

"I'm not going anywhere," Soren said in an amused voice.

Vanya shrugged. "For now."

Soren deftly twisted his hand free, tangling their fingers together in a discreet hold that no one else saw beneath the stars. Vanya had kept his distance all day, even through the telling of the border report, because Raiah had needed him. Here, now, with his daughter asleep and guarded inside the palace and Soren by his side, all he could think about was the feel of warm skin beneath his fingertips and how he wanted more.

It was enough of a want to shift his feet. He led the way back to the palace after time spent in the gardens, enjoying the evening breeze that had lost some of its heat. They returned through a different entrance, one that brought them into the grand hallways of the public wing of the palace. The quickest way back to the family wing led through the throne room in the center wing, and Vanya didn't hesitate to guide Soren through the grand space.

It looked different at night, most of the gas lamps off and moonlight coming through the stained-glass cupola above the center space. The high windows had been winched open to let in the cool night air, *praetoria* legionnaires standing in pairs on either side of each of the doors leading into the huge space. The dais with the Imperial throne always had a gas lamp burning over it through opaque glass, a mimicry of the eternal flame that burned for the Dawn Star in star temples across the country.

Their footsteps echoed against the marble floor, the portraits of past emperors and empresses hanging on the walls cast in shadow. Vanya was tugged to a halt beneath the moonlit, faintly colored light spilling through the stained glass and catching the gold flecks in the marble floor. He looked over at Soren, who wasn't looking at him but at the Imperial throne.

"You know I shouldn't attend your Conclave," Soren said, breaking the comfortable silence between them.

"I wish you all the best in saying no to my *valide*," Vanya said mildly.

Soren looked askance at him, exasperation clear on his face in the moonlight. "Vanya."

"It would aid us."

"I'm a warden."

"Yes, but you are also mine." He felt the shudder that ran through Soren's body against his own fingertips. Vanya lifted Soren's hand to his mouth without thinking, brushing his dry lips over scarred knuckles. "Do you doubt my words?"

"I've never doubted you," Soren said with a sureness that made Vanya lick his lips. "But your politics aren't mine."

"Aren't they? Do you truly think the wardens can continue to be neutral in the face of what is happening to the borders and the dead?"

"The Poison Accords don't allow us to be anything but neutral."

Vanya lifted his free hand to curl his fingers over Soren's chin, tilting his head up. He ran his thumb over the seam of Soren's lips, staring into eyes made darker by the dim light in the throne room.

"And what if your neutrality would damn Maricol as a whole?" Soren said nothing in the face of this question. Vanya pressed his thumb down until he could feel the outline of Soren's teeth through tender flesh. Then he slipped his thumb between them, stroking over Soren's tongue. "I won't argue with you tonight. That is not how I wish your homecoming to end."

Soren stepped back, letting Vanya's thumb slip free of his mouth. "How kind of you."

Then he planted a hand in the center of Vanya's chest and shoved him gently in the direction of the throne. Vanya raised an eyebrow but didn't fight the silent guidance. He turned and tugged Soren after him across the throne room. He climbed the steps of the dais before taking his rightful spot on the Imperial throne, never letting go of Soren's hand.

He pulled Soren between his splayed legs, hooking fingers over the gun belt and giving it a good yank. Soren didn't lose his balance so much as allow himself to be tumbled onto Vanya's lap and the throne he sat on.

"Hello, princeling," Soren murmured before ducking his head to brush his lips over Vanya's in a teasing sort of kiss.

Vanya ran his fingertips up the middle of Soren's back, over the leather of his waistcoat, until he could tangle his fingers in Soren's hair. He used his grip to tilt Soren's head more, adjusting the angle of the kiss until he could take control and deepen it, holding the younger man in place.

The way Soren moaned into his mouth and shifted against him on the throne sent sparks of heat skittering through his skin. Vanya licked his tongue past Soren's teeth, attempting to breathe for the both of them and failing after a few minutes. He broke the kiss, tugging Soren's head back to better get his mouth on that taut throat, field gear not an issue at the moment.

He sucked an open-mouthed kiss against the pulse of life in Soren's vein, feeling it beat against the pressure of his tongue. He felt

Soren's moan as much as he heard it, the vibrations of it humming against his lips.

"I've missed you," Vanya said against warm skin, the soft light hanging above the throne casting strange shadows across the planes of Soren's body.

Soren's hands swooped over his shoulders, up his neck, thumbing over his temples to cradle his skull in a callused grip he'd hungered for since Oeiras. "Did you now?"

The teasing lilt of his voice caused Vanya to let go of Soren's hair in order to grab him by the ass and jerk him closer. His field leathers and Vanya's own robe weren't enough to hide his desire or Soren's. The growing ache of want had coalesced in Vanya's cock, half-hard in his trousers after only trading kisses.

Soren shifted against him, grinding down in a way that had Vanya trying to dig fingertip-shaped bruises into his hips. The idea of leaving the throne room to make their way back to the family wing and their bed seemed like too much effort in that moment.

He nipped at the edge of Soren's jaw, kissing his way back to warm lips and the taste of the other man in the here and now rather than in his dreams. "Take off your clothes."

The shiver that ran through Soren jerked their hips together, and he heard the other man swallow thickly. "Someone will see."

"Let them."

All three entrances to the Imperial throne room were open to the hallways beyond, allowing anyone to pass by and peer in and see Vanya on the throne with Soren. The acoustics in the space were meant to amplify voices, and the *praetoria* legionnaires on duty out in the hallway would hear everything.

"Vanya," Soren very nearly whined as Vanya shifted on the throne, pushing him off his lap.

He was already undoing the buttons and clasps lining the center of his robe beneath a fold of fabric, peeling it open. His undershirt was light enough, and the belt looped through his trousers was easy to undo.

"Soren," Vanya said, pitching his voice low in a way that brooked no arguments. "I want to see what you look like on your knees before my throne."

He heard the other man swallow, loud in the hushed quiet of the throne room. Soren's gray eyes were more pupil than anything else as he licked his lips before unbuckling his gun belt. It fell off his hips, and he leaned forward to sling it over the top frame of the Imperial throne with a casualness that would make any high-ranked courtier faint at his lack of manners. But the pistols remained in reach that way, and Vanya couldn't fault him for that.

He watched Soren strip out of his field uniform, one piece at a time, until his clothes and boots were scattered over the dais, and he stood naked between Vanya's legs. His scarred skin was cast in odd shadows from the light above, and Vanya traced the history of survival written out there with greedy eyes.

Soren sank to his knees with an easy grace that spoke of control he gave up readily enough to Vanya in moments like this. The gold medallion glinted against his sternum, a promise made and a vow not yet kept. Vanya reached for it, curling his fingers around the metal chain, and tugged Soren forward. He moved without resisting, resting his hands against Vanya's inner thighs as Vanya drew him close.

"Check my pocket," Vanya said. "I want you to get yourself ready for me."

"You'll need to let me go," Soren replied, nodding slightly at the taut chain holding him in place even as he followed Vanya's order.

"No, I don't think I will."

Soren flushed a little at the way Vanya deliberately misinterpreted his statement. He still gamely slipped one hand into Vanya's trouser pocket, coming away with the small metal tin Vanya had retrieved from his bedroom before dinner. Soren popped it open, the lid clattering to the dais with a tinny ringing sound they both ignored. He coated the fingers of one hand in the cream there, reaching behind to prepare himself.

Vanya leaned back against his throne and spread his legs wider, giving Soren room. He let go of the medallion's chain and lazily gestured at the bulge of his half-hard cock pressing against the seam of his trousers. "I'm waiting."

"And if I kept you waiting, princeling?"

Vanya smiled at that, gaze half-lidded as he dragged his fingers through Soren's hair. "I think we both know we've waited long enough."

Soren inhaled sharply before bowing his shoulders and dipping his head, setting the tin aside momentarily to get his hands on Vanya's clothes and undo them, freeing his cock. The slick, wet heat of his mouth on Vanya's cock was enough to make him dig his fingernails into the armrests of the Imperial throne. He watched in quiet awe at the way Soren took him all the way to the root, gray eyes looking right at him with a clarity, a *knowing*, that no one else would ever have.

Vanya groaned, canting his hips upward, driving his cock deeper into Soren's throat. The constriction as Soren swallowed made him harder, and he dug his heels against the dais, rolling his hips again. Soren took the motion with ease, bobbing his head and breathing around the length in his mouth with small, gasping breaths. He wrapped a hand around the base of Vanya's cock to stroke him, his other one working behind him out of Vanya's sight.

On his knees, body on display for anyone who would cast a glance into the throne room, Soren was a sight to behold, and Vanya couldn't resist touching him. He stroked his fingers over the hollowed-out spaces of Soren's cheek, curling them past his jaw to touch his throat. Soren moaned, lips sliding farther down the length of his cock. Vanya sucked in a heavy breath when he pressed his fingers against Soren's throat, feeling out the space his cock took up.

Soren worked him over until he was fully hard, aching with wanting more, and Vanya wasn't shy about taking what Soren so readily gave him in moments like this. He fisted his hand in Soren's hair, drawing the other man off his cock. A line of saliva stretched between Soren's lips and the flushed head of his cock before breaking.

"Come here," Vanya said, his voice loud with want in his ears.

Soren licked his lips and rose to his knees, following Vanya's pull. Soren climbed into his lap, knees squeezed between Vanya's thighs and the sides of the Imperial throne. Vanya let his hair go only to grab him by the hips, steadying him. Soren settled a hand on Vanya's shoulder to brace himself, kneeling over Vanya, his own cock hard and curved and glistening at the tip.

Vanya lifted a hand to snag the medallion, tugging Soren down into a messy kiss, licking the taste of himself out of the other man's mouth. "I want to hear you."

He knew Soren could be quiet, a skill taught to all wardens to keep them safe in the poison fields. Sometimes Vanya indulged in a game of seeing how long it took to fuck sound out of Soren in their bed, but they didn't have time for that here.

"You want everyone to hear," Soren retorted, voice a rasp from Vanya's cock.

Vanya smiled indulgently up at him as he moved his other hand over Soren's ass to slide his fingers through the slickness smeared in the crease, pressing fingertips against his hole. "I don't see anything wrong with that."

Soren flushed, the heat of it spreading down his chest. But he didn't hold back a moan when Vanya slid two fingers into him, the angle not the best for depth but good enough to tease. Soren's head tipped down, eyelashes fluttering. His fingers dug into Vanya's shoulder as he pushed back against the touch, cock bobbing in the air.

Vanya pulled his fingers out and pressed them in again, tugging at his rim. Soren's whine at that touch had Vanya leaning forward to lick at the sweat beading on Soren's chest. "You deserve to let me make you feel good."

Soren's inhale was loud enough it echoed in the air between them. Vanya pressed his fingers in deeper, causing Soren to jerk his hips forward, his cock brushing against Vanya's clothed chest. "And what do you want?"

"Right now? Just you."

It was an easy want, this need he had for Soren like this. A dangerous desire Vanya had spent years clinging to, despite knowing there was no road they could walk that would see them together. Soren was a warden, and Vanya wore a crown, but right now, in this moment, they were merely two people indulging in a heated passion Vanya would not see banked.

Soren shifted on his knees, rising up higher, and Vanya let his fingers slip free. It was the work of a moment for Soren to sink down onto his cock, the heat of him drawing a groan out of Vanya's mouth. Soren had both his hands wrapped around the back of Vanya's neck, thumbs braced against the hinge of his jaw, holding on as he bore down with a slowness that was as much a tease as it was exquisite torture.

Vanya allowed himself to slide forward just enough to give Soren room to fully sink down, one hand splayed against the small of his back to hold him steady. Soren tipped his head back, mouth dropping open on a thick whine as he settled on Vanya's lap, breathing heavily.

"I think about you like this," Soren gasped out as he rose back up before sinking down again. "Every time I'm not with you. I know I shouldn't, but I do."

Vanya scraped his fingernails over sweaty skin, looking up into Soren's flushed face, mouth dry at that confession. He tangled his fingers around the medallion's chain, yanking Soren into a kiss that was all teeth and tongue and gasping breath, forcing him to grind down hard rather than move. The clench of his body around Vanya's cock was delicious, and Vanya couldn't help the stutter of his own hips and the way he jerked upward off the throne.

Soren gasped into his mouth before he batted Vanya's hand away, straightening enough to rise up once more and drive himself down on Vanya's cock with a sureness that came from knowing how to take it. Vanya braced his feet against the dais, holding himself steady on the throne as Soren found a rhythm that worked in the narrow space they were in.

Vanya pushed against the small of his back, changing the angle of his hips until Soren sank down at an angle that drew a cry from him. The sound of it echoed in the throne room, and the flush on his face deepened, eyes wide as he stared at Vanya.

"I didn't say stop," Vanya said mildly, deigning to smack Soren's ass. The stinging hit drew a wordless noise out of him, and Soren started to move again. "There we go."

Soren settled his hands on Vanya's shoulders, gripping at his robe with sweaty fingers as he rolled his hips, driving himself onto Vanya's cock again and again. Every time his hips stuttered away from the angle that drew such delicious sounds from him, Vanya forced him back again. The sound of his cock sinking over and over into Soren's body was drowned out by the cries the warden didn't muffle because Vanya had asked him not to.

"Vanya," Soren gasped out, dropping one hand to his own cock to stroke himself.

"The way you look, it's almost a shame we don't have an audience." Soren's hips jerked at that, and Vanya groaned around a smirk, bracing himself enough so he could snap his hips up as far as he could when Soren sank back down. "Would you like one? I could call in the legionnaires, perhaps some of the servants. Have them watch you fuck yourself on my cock—"

Soren came with a shout that could be heard in the hallways, sinking all the way down and grinding onto Vanya's cock even as his release stained Vanya's clothes. He breathed heavily, slumping forward, body twitching with the aftermath of his orgasm.

"You don't share," Soren murmured, voice coming out on a rasp.

"They'd never touch you, but I'd let them see what they could only dream to have." Vanya's cock throbbed inside the clenching heat of Soren's body, so on edge he was half tempted to tumble the warden to the dais and fuck him into the floor. "Finish what you started."

Soren sucked in a sharp breath before nodding jerkily, biting his lip as he shifted upward again. He couldn't quite choke off the moan as he rolled his hips, oversensitive in the way Vanya liked him to be. He always got louder like this, having just come, still willing to take Vanya's cock.

Vanya drew it out by setting the pace, guiding Soren's hips how he liked. He enjoyed the ache in his gut and the way his skin burned, cock throbbing every time Soren sank down onto him again. Every time he got close to the edge, he stilled Soren's hips, holding him close enough to kiss as he caught his breath, wanting to enjoy it.

Eventually, his need became too much for him to ignore. It was a matter of moments for Vanya to come like that after holding back for so long, driving up into Soren's body with a shout. He held Soren close, grinding into him with jerky motions, letting the release wash through him with a heady groan.

Soren leaned forward and licked his way into Vanya's mouth for a desperate sort of kiss. Vanya kissed him back with a ferocity that made it hard to breathe. Soren turned his head and sagged against Vanya with a gasp, not moving, Vanya's softening cock still buried in his ass.

Vanya turned his head, brushing his lips over Soren's temple, holding him close. "Welcome home."

Three

SOREN

"What they are asking of you is fundamentally not allowed by way of the Poison Accords," Delani said. Her voice came through strong over the receiver in the warden's resupply station Soren had gone to just past dawn the morning after his arrival in Calhames.

"I know," Soren said, fiddling with the wire that connected the handset to the cradle of the telephone. "But the Houses have called for a Conclave, and every *vezir* of a House or their designated representative is present in the city, including Joelle. Her House and *vasilyet* are still a problem we need to address."

Delani's sigh came through as a rough burst of noise. "I'm aware of that and the issues at hand."

Soren allowed himself a wince, knowing she couldn't see it. His report about the *rionetkas* had been ill received—both because of the threat they represented and the lateness of his report. He'd weighed the risk of telling the wardens' governor the truth of that problem without knowing if she herself was a *rionetka,* but if he didn't, he quite possibly risked the lives of his fellow wardens.

By the engineer overseeing the death-defying machine in the quarry's own admission, they'd killed wardens who had passed through and turned them into *revenants*. Soren could not, in good faith, keep the warning about the *rionetkas* to himself. He just had to hope that Delani had full control of her body and mind, considering she hadn't left the Warden's Island in at least three years.

"*Vezir* Joelle has stonewalled our efforts to perform our duties within her *vasilyet*. It's on me for not bringing it up with the emperor before now, but I've had my attention on Daijal more than Solaria recently," Delani said.

"I've heard Eimarille is queen now and that she's sent the Daijalan army across the Ashion border."

"Under the guise of aid and the mistaken belief we wardens can't do our job."

"That's a lie if ever I've heard one."

"Enough people will believe it to consider it truth. People don't understand the job we do and the risks we take to keep them safe. They tithe because they must and hate us for it. This civil war Eimarille seeks will double the revenant count, just like the last one. We'll lose wardens, and we'll need more to replace who the poison fields take."

Soren knew his history well enough when it came to wardens. He knew the civil war that had cleaved Daijal out of Ashion over the right to enact debt bondage as they saw fit had spread revenants through four countries. Only the Tovan Isles and E'ridia had been spared by dint of an ocean and a mountain range barring an influx of the dead from their lands.

Soren shifted on his feet, feeling a twinge of discomfort in his lower back. His time spent riding Vanya on the Imperial throne had done his muscles no favors in the light of day. He couldn't say he regretted it, though. "If the emperor loses support of the Houses during the Conclave, there is a strong chance the House of Kimathi will claim the Imperial throne."

"I will not abide negligence when it comes to our duty. Solaria as a whole has made enough wrong decisions regarding the dead. I need answers, and we need a way into that *vasilyet* that won't see any more of us dead. I'll authorize you to bring up the issue with the emperor and the Houses."

"And if they doubt my word?"

"Solaria is already under threat of sanctions. I'll happily add to it if they like."

Soren winced, thinking of the numbers already promised in tithes that Vanya had said would need to be given up in the future once this entire mess was over. If it ever was. "I'll make them aware. I'll report back with my findings."

"Call when you do. You still have borders to guard, and I may need you to handle a few more. We've lost more wardens than I anticipated over spring."

"Enough to be a problem?"

"With two countries on the brink of war, no matter how the Daijalan press is spinning this tale of neighborly aid? Yes. Tithes take time to train, and we can't replace our ranks as easily as an army can through a draft or conscription."

"I'll keep watch over my assigned borders."

"See that you do. I'll expect an update on access to the *vasilyet* before the week is over."

Delani hung up, the hum of an empty line singing in Soren's ear. He placed the receiver on the metal hooks of the cradle with a sigh before leaving the office. The resupply station's ground floor was empty this early in the morning, save for Soren and the warden whose job it was to run the place. He didn't know if the rooms above the storefront were in use or not, but Soren wasn't planning on sticking around to find out.

"Report what you need to?" the other warden said through a yawn before taking a sip of what smelled like strong black tea.

"Yes," Soren grunted.

The warden nodded and raised his mug at Soren in a vague salute goodbye. "Safe travels."

"You as well."

Soren left the resupply station for his velocycle parked on the street. The rumble of its engine seemed overloud in the early morning light. He licked sweat off his upper lip before kicking up the stand and steering it into the street. The sun wasn't fully up, but the heat of the summer day was a promise in the air.

He drove back to the Imperial palace, winding his way through the streets and inner-city walls of Calhames. His uniform got him through every single checkpoint, and the legionnaires on duty around the palace knew him on sight these days. No one stopped him when he drove back onto the palace grounds, leaving his velocycle with the servants to be brought to the garage. He'd know the way to the family wing blind these days and would have searched out Vanya and Raiah if he wasn't waylaid by Taisiya.

"A moment, warden, if you will," she called out from a parlor he passed, her raspy voice straining as it rose.

Soren slowed his walk before spinning on his feet to enter the parlor, mentally bracing himself for the conversation ahead. *Valide* Taisiya, he had learned over dinner, was a stubborn, politically astute woman.

She was already dressed for the day in a light summer gown the color of sunset orange, heavily embroidered and beaded over her narrow shoulders. Her hair was braided back and twisted high off her neck, held in place by jeweled metal combs. She wore her wealth as befitted a major House and *valide* to the emperor. Despite her absence from Vanya's life, though, she seemed well-informed of the games the Houses played. It spoke to a network of spies she must have who brought information back to the coast.

Soren didn't trust her, but then, he trusted no one of the Houses, save Vanya.

"*Valide*," Soren said politely.

"You're not dressed for the day," Taisiya said, setting down her glass cup, the red tea half-finished.

Soren glanced down at the uniform he wore, the weight of his weapons on his hips and back familiar after so many years carrying them. "I don't know what you mean."

"That is not proper attire for a Conclave gathering. Where are your robes?"

"I'm not Solarian."

"I've been told you have worn them on occasion."

"Once," Soren conceded, thinking of the funeral procession he had marched in at Vanya's request years ago. "I'm a warden and can be nothing else."

"I find that difficult to believe when you've been in Vanya's bed for the past six years." She raised a knowing eyebrow, mouth quirking at the corners. "Or joining him on the throne."

Soren wasn't prone to embarrassment, but the heat that came to his face wasn't something he could stop. He knew the servants would gossip about their tryst last night, but he hadn't known it would reach Taisiya. "I don't expect anything from Vanya."

"You would be the only one who doesn't. The fact that he has taken no one else to his bed, not even a royal courtesan, since you two met has made people talk."

Soren resisted the urge to reach for the vow hanging around his throat and tucked safely out of sight beneath his shirt and leather waistcoat. "I saved his life once. He's always been thankful for that."

"Yes, I am aware of what you did. Our House is ever thankful for your intercession. What he owes you is something of gossip."

"As I said, *valide*, I am a warden. The only thing any Solarian owes us is adherence to the Poison Accords."

Taisiya's smile was indulgent in the way of one who knew a lie when they heard one. "A fact I'm sure Joelle is loath to acknowledge these days. Be that as it may, you still did not answer my question."

"Vanya owes me nothing."

"You would like to think he doesn't." Taisiya rose from her seat, moving slowly in deference to her age. She crossed the room to him, her gaze shrewd and sharp as she took him in. "But I know how this House holds its debts. The legality of your position aside, you saved his life, and our House would owe you a debt. Do you stay because he asks you to or because you told him you would?"

Soren kept silent in the face of that question. He doubted she would appreciate knowing the wardens' governor's order setting his position in Solaria. Soren had been sent to observe the country's politics to ensure its compliance with the Poison Accords and uncover more information about the influx of revenants. That it had coincided with Vanya's demand to see him had made it easier to fit the lie into a mold of truth.

But the reality of the dangerous game Vanya played hung around Soren's neck, and he couldn't quite stop himself from taking Taisiya's wrist in hand when she reached for his throat. The glint in her eyes was almost too knowing. "Ah. I see I was right."

Soren smiled tightly. "About what?"

She raised her other hand to tap at his chest over where the medallion rested against his sternum beneath his clothes. He'd kept the chain of it hidden while in public, or thought he had—habit to hide an indiscretion that would damn him and Vanya both.

"Vanya owes you a debt."

Soren opened his mouth to deny that fact, but someone else beat him to it.

"He has never asked for anything in all the years I've known him, *valide*. Let it be," Vanya said from behind him in a low voice.

Taisiya stared at Soren, arching a neatly painted eyebrow. "Is that true?"

"I'm a warden," Soren said evenly, refusing to think about the broken road he might have once walked if the world was different.

If the star gods were kinder.

She pulled away from him, and he let her go. The sound of the door closing reached his ears before Vanya's hand settled briefly against his lower back. The warm touch slid away as the other man stepped around him to stand between them.

"My mother was aware of my decision at the time," Vanya said.

Taisiya slanted him a look that spoke volumes. "She was a fool."

"She is dead. Your opinion on what my Lady Mother allowed means nothing in her absence. It was my choice, my life he saved. I owe Soren twice over now, for what he has done for myself and Raiah."

"No you don't," Soren all but spit out.

The look Vanya sent him was exasperated and fond. "I do, and you know it."

"If the Houses find out, they would use him to ruin ours," Taisiya warned.

"He almost died in Joelle's *vasilyet*. If she suspected anything, she would have kept him alive to use him against us. If Joelle does not know, it is doubtful any other House does."

Taisiya studied the pair of them for a moment before shaking her head, letting out a rough-sounding sigh. "He is a weakness, Vanya. But I will rectify that today."

Vanya couldn't hide the wariness that came to his eyes, which made Soren tense. "How so?"

"By ensuring he is too difficult a piece to remove. I did say he will accompany me to the next gathering, and there is one this evening."

"I shouldn't—" Soren tried to argue.

"You will, if only to impress upon the Houses your position as a warden. The major Houses know the wardens are aware of the crypt and what that means for the future. The minor Houses have never sat upon the Imperial throne and are not buried beneath the palace. Where the major Houses go, the minor will follow."

"You're so sure about that?"

"What Joelle has allowed in her *vasilyet* will be her undoing. It must be acknowledged. You are uniquely positioned to inform the Houses of what she is doing and what is at stake."

"And in doing so, make it clear that to align their loyalty with the House of Kimathi will be detrimental to them all, but if they align with yours, the consequences won't be as bad?" Soren asked sharply.

Taisiya's lips twitched into a pleased sort of smile. "Good. You understand."

"I understand you think the wardens favor your House. We don't." Soren glanced at Vanya, who stared calmly back at him. "We can't."

"Better our House to see through the sanctions and open borders than a hostile House who would bar you from the poison fields to keep power and put our citizens at risk. Our House countered Joelle's call for a Conclave based on her treatment of the dead. Who better to confirm her betrayal of her oaths than the warden who experienced it firsthand?"

Soren clenched his teeth. With what he knew was happening in the northern countries, it only made sense to keep a House on the Imperial throne that would abide by the Poison Accords. Vanya would see the sanctions through; Joelle, he knew, would not.

"The House throwing today's gathering has declined to invite the House of Kimathi. Enough of the major Houses have accepted the invitation that it would be prudent for you to join me, and you shall," Taisiya said.

Soren knew he could leave—that he *should* leave. That he had no right to insert himself so prominently in a country's politics, but he already had by staying with Vanya. Soren should have walked away long ago, in Bellingham, after taking Vanya from that wrecked train. But it was too late now to amend decisions made. He'd indulged his own wants beneath the wardens' governor's orders, thinking his heart safe while he did his duty.

Oh, what a fool he had been.

"The dead are the purview of the wardens," Soren said.

"Then prove that to the Houses."

She pressed where Vanya wouldn't, and Soren couldn't begrudge Taisiya her desire to see her House safe. He didn't want to ever return from the poison fields one day to discover Vanya dead and buried in the crypt, Raiah with him or forever out of reach in Joelle's grasp, some other House seated on the Imperial throne. That was unbecoming of a warden, but then, he had never been just a warden.

"My loyalty is not to you. I'll not wear your House's attire."

"If he is to be a warden, let him appear as such," Vanya said before Taisiya could argue.

"Very well," she huffed. "With that decided, let us enjoy our morning meal out in the courtyard."

She left the parlor for the hallway, leaving Soren alone with Vanya. He looked over at the other man, noting the regal robes he wore and the crown that sat once more upon his head. He looked dressed not for the Conclave but the Senate. "Did you tell her about the vow?"

Vanya shook his head. "No."

Soren thought he'd hidden the necklace well enough even if he hadn't, in hindsight, hidden the way he felt about Vanya. What were the Houses to think when he returned time and time again to Vanya's side, like a comet orbiting the sun?

Vanya closed the distance between them, his hand catching Soren by the elbow. Those dark eyes searched his own, mouth thinning to a hard line before he let out a heavy sigh. "You could ask me for anything, and I would give it to you. It would free you from this."

From me was clear, even if he didn't speak the words.

But asking would go against everything that made Soren a warden. It would leave his arms empty of the only home he'd ever known when he wasn't supposed to claim any.

He rose up on the balls of his feet just enough to steal a kiss, desperate and hungry, and give up the only answer he'd always ever offered since Vanya had placed the vow around his throat.

"No."

Because what Soren wanted he could not ask for, and there was nothing free found in a heart given under duress.

Four

JOELLE

Joelle smiled her goodbyes at yet another House representative who waxed lovingly about her gathering but still didn't hint at loyalty given. As they were a minor House, she mentally filed them in the column of one who would wait until the last minute to see how the Houses shook out before siding with the majority, whoever that would be.

Then she turned her attention to *vezir* Amir Vikandir, of the House of Vikandir, and knew a lost cause when faced with one.

Well—almost a lost cause.

"A moment, *vezir*," Joelle said.

Amir was one of the last to wend his way to the door of her estate, but he stepped aside for Joelle to say her goodbyes to the last group of House representatives, seeing them on their way. Multiple gatherings were happening today, some of which her House had not been invited to but which the House of Sa'Liandel had. She'd made careful note of those lack of invites, knowing those Houses would need more persuasion to align them with hers.

It was a delicate dance she'd thought would be easier. Vanya's counteraccusation and the appearance of the warden had disrupted her carefully laid plans to strip him of the Imperial throne and bury him in the crypt. It meant she was clawing for support when she anticipated a clear advantage.

"My driver is waiting, but I can spare a few minutes," Amir said.

"Long enough for a cup of tea, I suppose?"

He smiled politely, inclining his head a little. "I had my fill during the gathering today."

"It's bad business to meet without a proper drink. Come now. Our Houses were once close."

"If I remember my history correctly, yours attempted to murder mine some generations back."

It was Joelle's turn to smile as she beckoned him to follow her away from the front door and down the hallway. "As one does in Solaria. Your House still stands, and so does mine. Tea will not make either fall. I'll send a servant to let your driver know he can wait until you summon him."

She had no great desire to kill him, as that would not gain her what she wanted. Despite how tempting it would be to indulge in such actions, his death was not what she was after.

Control was.

"If you wish to ascertain my position, I believe I made it clear over the last several gatherings of the Conclave," Amir said once they'd made it to her personal library, the room windowless to protect the books.

"Clear enough, but this is the Conclave. You can't fault me for laying out my side of the argument."

Joelle took a seat on an armchair whose cushion held firm beneath her weight. Amir reluctantly took the seat opposite hers as a servant bustled into the room, carrying a tea service on a tray. It was set down between them on the low table, with the handle of the ceramic teapot angled toward Joelle as befitted the host.

She knew this tea set quite well and picked up the teapot despite the ache in her finger joints. She poured tea at an angle into Amir's cup, making sure that gravity pulled from the hidden chamber inside the teapot first. She deftly poured herself at a slightly different angle, the tea the same color but coming from the chamber one would see if they lifted the lid.

The key difference between their brew was the three drops of distilled venom drawn from the red-backed snake that called the Wastelands home that would be in Amir's tea. The paralytic toxin it became was quick acting to a degree, its bitterness hidden in the blackness of the tea she'd opted for to cleanse the palate after all the sweets offered at the gathering. Amir seemed appreciative enough of the taste when he lifted the cup to his lips, breathing in the steam.

Joelle did the same, opting to take it plain and without sugar. She watched Amir sip his tea, his gaze never leaving her face. "You must know why I asked you to stay."

"You must know nothing you say will sway me or my House from the road we are on," Amir said almost gently.

"I am aware of that." Joelle lifted her own teacup to sip at it before setting it down. Her knuckles ached, but she refused to flex her hands in front of him. "You've done your best to convince those today that the House of Sa'Liandel is the better option."

"It is."

The plainness of his opinion made her nod. "And if I told you there was no way the House of Sa'Liandel would keep the Imperial throne?"

"The emperor will gain enough support. His counterargument is already finding willing ears."

"Yes, the lies are certainly believable to gullible Houses."

Amir drank deeply of his tea, as if he thought finishing the cup quickly would provide him an avenue of escape. It would, just not the one he hoped for. "Your own actions shore his words up. The other Houses see this."

"Do they?"

He tried to nod, head jerking in a manner that caused his eyes to widen. Amir's gaze dropped to the teacup in his hand, the liquid sloshing against the edges from his loosened grip. A strangled sound slipped past his lips as he tried to set the teacup down. The handle slipped from his grip, the cup clattering to the table on its side, spilling tea everywhere.

His eyes, when they found hers, were filled with a fearful sort of anger. Joelle smiled in the face of the accusation she could read clear in his expression.

"I know your House gave aid to the warden and the princess. I know your House is aligned with the emperor's. Your loyalty to the House of Sa'Liandel will be useful for now."

"I won't—" Amir managed to get out as he slumped in his seat, still staring at her, sweat beginning to bead at his temples and across his forehead.

Joelle shrugged delicately, looking past him as the door to the library opened. The man who stood there wore the gear of a warden, an outfit she'd been unable to convince him to remove. A bitemark scar on his face was a reminder of the dangers he'd survived in the poison fields. These days, the *Klovod* gained wealth and secrets through his skills of alchemy, which Eimarille was not shy of using on anyone.

The *Klovod* had arrived in Calhames the morning after the Conclave began with two Blades, and Joelle had not questioned his appearance in her estate. Neither had she questioned his orders, for they dovetailed well with her own needs.

"His House will be expecting him for their evening meal," Joelle said.

The *Klovod* came farther into the room, his Blades trailing after him. From what she'd gathered, they were either his assistants or his jailer on this trip, but she wasn't keen on asking which.

The *Klovod* stood beside the armchair Amir had taken, staring down at the *vezir* who had caused Joelle so many problems as of late. "The procedure will go quickly enough. The veil we brought may not be large enough to cover the scars."

Veils were intricately cast spells literally woven into fabric. Their construction sometimes took years to make, depending on the size of the fabric needed and the skill of the magician. Joelle knew there weren't enough veils to cover the scars of every *rionetka* in existence, only the ones most critical to Eimarille's plans.

"I trust you to work around that issue. The driver will be dealt with by a magician. He won't know he lost time."

The *Klovod* stepped back, allowing the Blades to approach Amir and haul the heavyset man up between them. They easily carried his weight, dragging the *vezir* from the library to make their way to the makeshift laboratory Joelle had allowed the *Klovod* to set up in one of the storage rooms located in the basement of the estate.

She rather hoped her magician had finished soundproofing the space with magic.

Five

CARIS

"The crystals don't like this cut," Caris muttered.

Wyatt sighed from the other worktable he was hunched over. "You keep saying that, but they can't feel anything."

She frowned at the crystal in her hand and the discordant hum in her ear. It was what made her a good engineer, being able to know the exact shape a crystal needed to be to power a machine. That skill had aided her family's company—barred from her at the moment, funds frozen due to her parents' imprisonment—and now it aided the Clockwork Brigade.

She'd invented things to help people, not to harm them. Recreating the death-defying machine in miniature still felt wrong, but they needed to know how it worked in order to counter it. Still, it made her uneasy, this particular progression of technology.

Caris dragged her forearm across her forehead, wiping away sweat as she squinted through her magnifying goggles at the crystal in her hand. The shape of the rod's edges was almost complete, and she reached for the part it was supposed to slide into and be anchored by. Her fingers closed over the metal at the same time the door to the garage opened.

She looked up and couldn't help but smile as Nathaniel came

inside, dressed in a set of working trousers and a clean linen shirt buttoned up to his throat. She'd missed him so, and having him back after thinking him lost into debt bondage was still a heady sort of relief.

"Nathaniel," she breathed out, setting the clarion crystal down on the worktable.

"I thought I'd find you out here," he said.

"We've quite a bit of work to do."

"What exactly are you working on?"

Caris ran her tongue against the back of her teeth, nerves tingling from a crystalline hum that only got louder the closer Nathaniel got to her worktable. She wrenched her attention away from the sound, focusing on him. "A particular problem that needs to be solved."

"I'm sure you're the one who will solve it."

She grimaced, glancing over at the blueprints taking up half her worktable. "We'll see. I'd rather this hadn't been invented at all."

Nathaniel came around to stand beside Caris, attention on her rather than the tools and machine parts and clarion crystals scattered around her workspace. "I just got out of a meeting with the duchess."

Caris nodded stiffly. She'd known that meeting had been scheduled, and she'd opted instead to bring Wyatt out to the laboratory. He wasn't allowed to work unsupervised, and Caris was still too angry over the situation with her parents and herself to sit across a table from Meleri and pretend politeness.

"Anything of note being discussed?" she asked.

Nathaniel leaned his hip against the worktable, crossing his arms over his chest as he looked down at her. His expression was troubled, and Caris knew she wouldn't like what he had to say. "Could we go somewhere private?"

Caris glanced down at the half-finished clarion crystal and shook her head. "I'm not allowed off the estate. Not without a veil, at least, and Lore has been keeping those locked up. Perhaps the garden?"

"I don't mind taking a meal break," Wyatt said from his worktable, agreeable as always to anything the Clockwork Brigade needed. Caris didn't know if it was out of guilt or not, but she supposed it didn't matter.

Nathaniel nodded at that suggestion, and Caris waved off the guard who would have stayed behind. She didn't need attending to, and besides, her mother had left her alone with Nathaniel once upon a time. If Portia allowed it, then Meleri would have to accept it as well. Besides, who would their privacy be reported to? It wasn't as if they were at a ball during the season. Her reputation was already in tatters if one was to go by certain broadsheets. Others exalted her in a way she was uncomfortable with.

Nathaniel only ever saw her as herself.

The door closed behind the last guard, leaving them in the heat of the garage, with the mechanical fans spinning at their highest settings. Caris clasped her hands together over her bent knee, booted foot resting on the rung of the stool. The faint hum in her ears was persistent, and she did her best to ignore it.

"You look better," Caris said, smiling softly.

Nathaniel reached up to run a hand through his blond hair, fingers catching at the leather tie that held his queue in place. He'd seemed exhausted from the ordeal of escaping Amari, funneled out through cogs that passed him forward along the chains of the Clockwork Brigade. Escape was never sure, but it was made easier by the fact he hadn't yet been tattooed with bank numbers.

But he was the only one of his family to escape. Caris knew that heartache well, for she still wished desperately she could save her parents from the accusations that would see them dead if Eimarille had anything to say about it.

Sighing, Nathaniel let both arms drop to his sides, hands braced against the worktable. "Lore received a coded message earlier this morning. Paradis was raided by the Collector's Guild. Scarlette didn't make it out alive."

Caris flinched at that news. Despite her anger with the secrets kept from her, Caris wasn't willing to walk away from her duty as a cog. The cogs in Paradis hadn't been in her chain, but since her arrival to Veran, Caris had been neck-deep with the others in determining what to do with cogs left behind in Amari. She'd been privy to cogs and chains previously kept separate from her own out of necessity. Losing the burlesque club that doubled as a place where debt slaves were funneled out of Ashion was a critical hit. They'd taken too many of those since the riot.

"Did you know anyone there?"

"They were part of my chain. Scarlette, the woman who owned it, was one of my cogs."

"I'm sorry."

"She knew the risks. We all did." He managed a wan smile for her as he straightened up. "Have you eaten yet? I doubt the duchess would allow me to escort you out, but perhaps a meal in the garden will suffice."

"I'd like that." Her hand drifted up to the necklace hanging from her throat. "I have something for you."

She pulled the chain from beneath her work blouse, the ring the only thing hanging from it. Caris undid the clasp of the chain and pulled it free, letting the ring slide off into her palm. It was warm from resting against her skin, the gold glinting in the light.

Caris offered it back to Nathaniel, biting the inside of her lip. "I never wanted any of what's happened to occur. To you or your family. If this is all you may have of them, I want you to have it back."

Nathaniel touched her fingers and gently curled them over the ring. "Keep it. Please. As a token of my affections, if you must."

Caris' breath hitched in her throat, a flush coming to her cheeks when Nathaniel lifted her hand and turned it so he could brush a light kiss over her knuckles. "I'll keep it safe."

"I know you will. Here, let me put it back on you."

Nathaniel took the ring and the chain from her, threading them together. Caris slipped off the stool and turned around, putting her back to him. She gathered up her shoulder-length hair as best she could, lifting it off her nape. Nathaniel stepped in close behind her, his warmth bleeding through her clothes, making her pulse quicken. Caris had never felt this way about anyone else through the years, unable to understand the ease with which other ladies her age could fall in and out of love.

She'd come to only want Nathaniel, an incremental realization that took four years for her to comprehend, and only then, at the moment he was torn from her. But Nathaniel was back, and his arms went around her how she thought a lover's might, brushing against her body ever so gently.

He looped the necklace around her throat, the ring falling down between her breasts for just a moment. Caris closed her eyes, listening to the sound of him breathing and the distant, discordant hum of clarion crystal cut wrong. The chain dragged upward, pulling against her throat. Caris opened her eyes when Nathaniel's fingers ghosted over her skin, tracing the fluttering line of her pulse.

When they wrapped around her throat, she didn't register the threat—not until they cut off her airway, fingertips digging into the tender flesh over her pulse so hard she couldn't even gag. Caris grabbed frantically at Nathaniel's hand, eyes shocked wide as the hum in her ears drowned out the rabbit-quick beat of her heart.

She panicked, black spots already dancing at the edge of her vision from the limited air left in her lungs, chest aching. Nathaniel's breathing remained calm in her ears, and he said nothing as he sought to choke the life out of her. It made no sense, and all the desperate protests trapped behind her teeth would stay there if she didn't act. One didn't grow up in the Eastern Basin without knowing how to fight when necessary. Being the heir to a barony didn't change that.

Caris kicked out with her leg, high enough her boot caught against the edge of the worktable. She shoved with all her might, succeeding in making Nathaniel stagger back a step, though his grip on her throat never lessened. Her panicked, broken threads of thought crystalized into a single one.

Not like this.

Caris' lips parted, no air coming in or out as Nathaniel did his best to kill her. And perhaps he would have if she wasn't everything everyone else believed her to be.

Caris flexed her fingers, calling forth the aether in its hottest, purest form. Starfire exploded around them like a whirlwind, catching everything on fire, not unlike how she'd experienced it so long ago in the Eastern Basin to hold off a revenant attack. Only her parents weren't here, and the one seeking to do her harm was supposed to love her.

She squeezed her eyes shut, bringing her arm down and back, starfire curling around her palm with a ferocity that never touched her skin. It latched onto Nathaniel's clothes instead, eating away at them, and the shout he let out was full of pain. She could feel the heat of the starfire burning between them, and it was that threat that finally got Nathaniel to release his grip on her throat.

Caris wrenched herself away with a ragged gasp, chest heaving as she struggled to get air into her lungs. She stumbled forward, needing to use the worktable to hold herself up. Black spots still ate away at her vision, but the darkness was receding. Or perhaps it was the dearth of starfire that burned so bright and hot around them that aided her vision.

Nathaniel writhed on the ground, trying to put out the starfire eating away at his clothes, but it wouldn't be put out. It couldn't be—not unless Caris ordered it otherwise. Breathing rapidly, with a throbbing in her temples she wasn't sure was her heartbeat or the start of a headache, she knew she had to act. If she let the starfire burn uncontrolled, it would bring the garage down upon them both, destroying all the vehicles housed inside it and the miniature death-defying machine they were trying to build.

They'd lose whatever edge they hoped to gain against Eimarille, because the Daijalan queen saw her as a threat, Caris realized with a bleak sort of horror. How else to explain Nathaniel's treachery?

The garage door had starfire burning over it, but that didn't stop someone from banging against the hot metal with something heavy. "*Caris!*"

Blaine's voice broke through her fear, making her jerk into motion. She straightened up, still dizzy from the lack of air she'd suffered through, to say nothing of the smoke beginning to build up. She thrust an arm out toward the starfire raging around her and clenched her hand into a fist, thinking about the way a spigot would be turned off, the flow of water choked to nothing, just like the star priest had taught her in secret when she was younger.

She hadn't thought she'd ever need the lessons, warned as she had been to keep the starfire a secret. Only it didn't matter anymore, not after the riot in Amari. Not after this assassination attempt from someone who was supposed to be on her side.

The starfire went out almost instantly, the energy that powered it reverting back to the aether. Caris' head felt heavy, and her knees were weak, but she was on her feet when Blaine wrenched the garage door open and came barreling inside. She watched him race to her in a daze, not quite processing everything clearly yet. She tried to speak, but her tongue felt swollen in her mouth, and her throat protested any attempt at making sound.

"Caris!" Blaine called again, reaching her side in seconds. His hands went to her shoulders, then her face, tilting up her jaw to get a look at whatever bruises were blossoming on her throat. "What *happened*?"

She swallowed, the motion like eating glass, and forced herself to speak when she'd rather be mute. "Nathaniel."

His name came out as a croak, her voice raw and ruined. Blaine's gaze wrenched away from her to where Nathaniel lay on the floor, groaning as the guards who had followed Blaine inside circled him, their pistols drawn.

Nathaniel's clothes had burned on one side, the charred edges of his shirt falling open around his torso. Caris sucked in air and nearly choked on the pain of it, her eyes caught on the damaged curl of blackened cloth peeling away from his skin, revealing the raw, puckered scar of a *rionetka*.

She made a sound, she knew she did, but she didn't know she was crying until Blaine folded her into his arms, turning her head away from the horrible sight before them.

"Shh," Blaine said, trying to soothe her, but there was no making this nightmare better. "I have you. We'll figure this out."

If he thought his words were a comfort, they weren't. But when he tried to guide her away, to spare her, she dug in her heels.

"How did we miss this?" she got out through the rawness of her throat.

"I don't know." Blaine sighed quietly, glancing over at where the guards had secured Nathaniel. "Stay here."

He walked away from her, and Caris followed after him, morbid curiosity pricking at her thoughts, refusing to let go. Blaine knelt in front of Nathaniel, studying him for a moment before reaching to snag the edge of the blackened fabric that wasn't part of his shirt. He tugged at it, and a hint of jagged light shimmered over the unburned portion of it, dying out against the burned edges. His fingers traced their way over the shape of it, snagging on something embedded in Nathaniel's skin that Caris' eyes wanted to move past.

"Someone sewed a veil into his body to conceal the scars," Blaine said after a moment.

"Sir? What do you want done with him?" one of the guards asked.

Blaine straightened from his crouch, stepping back to Caris' side so he could wrap an arm around her waist. She couldn't help but lean into his support.

"Don't kill him," she begged.

Blaine's fingers tightened on her hip. "Put him in one of the storage rooms in the basement under round-the-clock guard."

"Sir," the man said with a sharp nod.

Blaine gently turned Caris, guiding her away from Nathaniel, her feet stumbling over themselves. "Let's get you somewhere safe."

She let out a painful little laugh, for it was obvious there was no safety to be found no matter how far she ran.

Six

NATHANIEL

They threw the body into the basement, locked up inside a makeshift cell that was once a storage room. It was windowless and dark, and the air tasted like dust on the body's tongue. The cold air was like sandpaper on the burns that streaked the body's skin, and Nathaniel knew he *deserved* the wounds.

If he'd only been strong enough, maybe the body would have listened to him and not the insidious control that permeated every part of his mind and body ever since he'd left the *Klovod*'s operating table.

The body lay there in the dark after regaining consciousness, Nathaniel's fury and worry and self-hatred relegated to a corner of his mind. The only thing the body's face allowed an expression for was pain, which didn't seem to surprise Blaine when the other man finally opened the door to the storage room. The sconces in the wall turned on, gas lamps lighting up the emptied storage room, revealing the body still sprawled on the floor.

"Who are you?" Blaine asked as he stepped inside, followed by two men who held themselves with the bearing of military. One carried a pistol and the other a wand, and Nathaniel could *feel* the body calculating the odds of overpowering them to get out and deciding not to.

"I'm *Nathaniel*," the body's mouth protested, words edged with pain as it pushed itself up to a sitting position. The burns on its arms pulled sharply, and it didn't stop the gasp of pain that came to its lips. "What is the meaning of this? What happened to me?"

Blaine stared down at the body, hazel eyes shadowed and unreadable. He stepped closer, and the guards at his back tensed, shifting about so he wasn't in their line of sight. The body bent its knees, raising its arms to look at the burn marks that had yet to be treated. Every motion made his nerves *throb*.

Caris hadn't tried to kill the body, merely warn it off, and Nathaniel ached with the knowledge that it was his hands that had nearly killed her, for all that he'd had no control over them. The body hadn't listened when he'd screamed for it to *stop*, to *let her go*, to *don't touch her*.

It hadn't listened to him, but it had listened to the *Klovod*.

"What do you remember?" Blaine asked after a long moment.

The body shivered, head tilting back so it could look up. Nathaniel peered through its eyes, seeing Blaine looking down, in no hurry to help. "Caris had worked through a meal. I had gone to invite her to dine in the garden. Then I woke up in here. Was there an attack? Did debt collectors find us?"

The stress and fear in the body's voice was pitch-perfect, the way its breath came quick and ragged. Nathaniel tried to get its tongue to shape different words, but that muffled wall between his own consciousness and what lived in place of himself refused to break.

"No debt collectors. Only you."

"What do you *mean*?" The body extended its arms, hands curled up in a beseeching manner. "How did I get these burns? What is going *on*? Where is Caris?"

"Safe from you."

The body jerked back at those words, reacting in the way Nathaniel knew he would if confronted in such a way. "I would *never* harm her."

Blaine flicked his fingers at Nathaniel's chest. "Those scars say otherwise."

The body looked down at its chest, Nathaniel saw the cuts the *Klovod* had sewed up and healed just enough with magic to scar before covering with a veil were now on clear display. The veil Nathaniel remembered being sewn into his body had been removed, scabbed-over marks where the thread had been ripped out in places all the evidence that remained of its placement.

"Blaine," the body said in a weak, horrified voice, swaying where it sat. "What happened to me?"

"That's what we'd like to know." Blaine crouched down, out of reach of the body's hands, and the guards behind him shifted position yet again. "You say you were forgotten in the paddy wagon during the riot and that's all that saved you from revenants. You say Scarlette helped you leave Amari, and then we lost Paradis and that chain. You were taken by debt collectors, but I can't be sure you weren't like this before that."

"You can't possibly think I'd aid Daijal."

"Not of your own free will." Blaine tilted his head to the side, gaze searching the body's face. "But *rionetkas* don't have any."

The body flinched at that word, responding in the exact emotional way Nathaniel would if it had truly been himself facing off with Blaine. "Blaine, *please*. I don't know what is going on."

"Neither do we. And because of that, you will remain down here, under guard, until we determine how best to deal with you."

He stood and walked away, the guards slipping out of the room behind him. The door was closed, lock clicking into place, before the lights were turned off, plunging the room back into darkness.

The body sat there, breathing slow and even now that no one was watching, with Nathaniel screaming in protest where he was trapped in a distant corner of a mind that wasn't his own.

BLAINE

"He's a *rionetka*. We can't afford to leave him alive," Lore argued.

"Nathaniel seemed himself right up until he tried to kill Caris. That speaks to some portion of his mind perhaps still being his own, and I want to know how it was done," Blaine said.

"He's a *threat*. He needs to be put down."

"No," Caris said, the dull rasp of her voice cutting through their argument.

Blaine turned immediately to where she sat in an armchair in Meleri's library, wrapped in a quilt with a cup of tea held forgotten in her hands. The bruises ringing her throat were painful-looking, but the swelling had been reduced with the help of a potion bought from an apothecary and the application of magic from an army magician who wasn't a healer but knew enough field medicine to stabilize a person.

"He can't be trusted," Blaine said gently. "Especially not around you."

She looked up from her teacup, dull gray eyes meeting his gaze. Her lashes were still spiky-looking from the tears she'd cried earlier, but the redness in her eyes had faded somewhat. "I don't want Nathaniel harmed."

Lore huffed out a sigh. "You can't be serious. You must know that the only proper way to address this problem is to eliminate it in its entirety."

"No one is laying a hand on Nathaniel."

"He already laid one on *you*."

Caris straightened up, the quilt slipping off her shoulders a little. "You keep saying you want me to be your queen. Yet here you are, acting like I'm not. You can't have it both ways, Lore. You can't sit there and tell me you want me to rule, then ignore what I want simply because it doesn't align with *your* wants. I won't be a puppet. I won't be *your tool*. I won't be what they turned Nathaniel into."

Lore jerked back as if she'd been struck, mouth falling open a little. Blaine watched as Meleri raised her hand in a quieting sort of manner to her daughter. "Enough."

Lore stiffly settled back in her seat, hands clasped together over her lap. She held her tongue, and for that, Blaine was grateful.

Caris breathed in carefully, nostrils flaring as she winced in pain. "If you kill Nathaniel, then you'll lose any hope you have of figuring out how he became a *rionetka*."

"You want him alive because you care for him," Lore said evenly.

"I'd want anyone alive in this situation for the information they could give us." Caris managed a thin, macabre smile, gaze flat and empty as she stared at Lore. "That's something *you* taught me when I learned how to be a cog."

Lore was too good to show how she felt in the face of that jab, but Blaine rather thought it cut deep. The two women stared at each other for a long, fraught moment, and it was Lore who looked away first. At that, Caris nodded once, more to herself than anything else, and focused on her tea. Blaine settled his hand on her shoulder gently, hating the way she flinched away from him. He pulled away immediately, wishing there was some sort of comfort he could give her that she'd accept.

Next to Lore, Meleri smoothed a piece of the charred veil taken off Nathaniel's body over the table. The magic of its weaving was beyond repair, the veil nothing more than damaged, delicate cloth now.

Veils were expensive and intricate to make, thread magic needing to be woven with intent for the entirety of the spell. Magicians skilled at making such spellwork were few to begin with, the cost of a veil something few could afford. Meleri's store of veils to hide a person's face was a total of five now, after the one damaged in Blaine's fight with Terilyn. Five veils on the smaller size came out to a fortune that could allow a family of poor means to live comfortably middle-class for at least two generations.

The one that had been sewn into Nathaniel's body to cover the vivisection scars had been easily twice the size of the ones used to hide a person's face. Blaine was no magician, but he knew a weaving like that would've taken years to produce and cost a fortune. He wondered if Eimarille had commissioned the piece, and if so, when? How long had she been working toward retaking Ashion?

More importantly, how were they supposed to counter her reach when she was dozens of steps ahead of them?

"The Clockwork Brigade's magicians are looking into Nathaniel's situation. We don't have anyone presently assigned to Veran skilled in mind magic," Meleri said.

"Then perhaps you should find a cog with that skill and summon them here," Caris said.

"As important as understanding how a *rionetka* is controlled, there are other pressing matters we must focus on. Parliament is refusing to bring to the floor eastern provinces' concerns about the occupation of Haighmoor under false pretenses and the breach of our western border. Without the prime minister agreeing to hear such argument, the military cannot be brought into play."

"Something tells me that is not the problem you believe it to be," Blaine said dryly. "The army is preparing itself for a fight, and the officers who believe in Ashion's sovereign right are prepared to go to war. It is the nobility who are digging in their heels at the present time."

Meleri's gaze lingered on Caris. "They need someone to rally around."

"I said before I won't be your puppet," Caris said quietly.

"I understand your concerns—"

"Do you?" Caris cut in, pinning Meleri with a fierce glare. "If that were truly the case, you would have some idea on how to rescue my parents. As it is, they remain imprisoned in Amari, and I've yet to hear of a plan to rescue them."

"That is not an easy endeavor you are asking for."

"You haven't tried." She broke off with a harsh-sounding cough, curling over herself. She put her teacup on the table, the cup and saucer clattering together where she dropped it as she tried to clear her throat. When she straightened up, there were tears in her eyes, but Blaine couldn't tell if they were from pain or anger.

"Caris," Blaine said gently. "Please don't overexert yourself."

"Then help me help Nathaniel, and if you won't, then don't bother to stand as witness," she rasped, getting to her feet. She let the quilt slide off her shoulders, pooling on the couch as she turned to look at him.

"And if he can't be saved?"

"You don't know that he can't be."

"None of us do," Meleri interjected.

Caris made a cutting gesture with her hand. "If we can't bring a magician here to assess him, then we'll go to someone who can. Mind magic isn't the only thing controlling him. His heart—" She broke off with a gasp, and Blaine reached for her, hand hovering over her arm. She batted his hand away, refusing his comfort. "You said Siv's autopsy showed it was a clockwork metal heart in her chest. What are the odds one is inside Nathaniel?"

Blaine dragged a hand down his face. "High."

Caris closed her eyes, expression twisting, but she didn't break down. Blaine rather thought anyone else in her position would, knowing the man she quite possibly loved had been so brutally harmed. "Something like this, what's been done to him. That's not—it's not just magic. It's not just mechanics. It's something else. We need an expert."

"And who, pray tell, would you suggest?" Lore asked sharply. "No one has ever seen *rionetkas* before."

Caris opened her eyes, meeting Blaine's gaze, and the determination he saw in her face was righteous in a way. He fought back a grimace, knowing there would be no persuading Caris from whatever road she was about to set herself down.

Which meant Blaine would have no choice but to follow her down it.

"We can't trust anyone in Ashion who might have the skills to determine what was done to Nathaniel, not even anyone in the Clockwork Brigade. We need a neutral party." Caris glanced over at Meleri before returning her attention to Blaine. "We need the wardens."

"The wardens guard the borders. They deal with the dead. They have no obligation to aid us," Blaine said carefully.

"Nathaniel is practically the walking dead as it is," Lore muttered from her seat.

Caris flinched so hard her entire body jerked. Blaine shot Lore a furious glare before stepping closer to Caris. He reached for her again, and this time, she allowed his touch. "I spoke with him after we put him under guard in the basement. He has no recollection of trying to harm you."

It had been eerie to speak with Nathaniel, to see the confusion in his face through the pain from his burns. He'd asked after Caris, worried she'd been harmed like he had been but refusing to believe he'd been the cause of the attack Blaine spoke about.

However *rionetkas* were made to think, they were themselves until they weren't. Blaine didn't know what triggers were laid into Nathaniel's mind that would cause him to try to murder Caris or any of them. They'd missed the scars because of the veil, revealing that even a lack of scars wasn't enough to prove someone wasn't a *rionetka*.

"He wouldn't," Caris said softly. "That wasn't him."

"We don't know that."

"The wardens might."

"It's dangerous for you to travel right now," Meleri said.

"Staying here, doing nothing, doesn't aid us. If you're so concerned, I'll wear a veil," Caris snapped back.

"Honovi should land here tomorrow. He'd take you to the Warden's Island," Blaine said.

Lore got to her feet in protest. "Blaine!"

"She isn't your prisoner, Lore."

"She's safer here than anywhere else with a warrant hanging over her head."

"And in wanting that you would have her stay here to attend to your family's needs?"

"We fight for our *country*."

"And I'm fighting for the man I love," Caris bit out. Her eyes watered a bit, several tears trickling down her cheeks. She scrubbed a hand over her face, wiping them away.

Blaine knew, deep down, it was a fight she couldn't win. But letting her face this horror alone would break her in ways none of them could afford. "I'll call Raziel. She said she was in town for at least another week before she needed to head back into the poison fields. Perhaps she can provide us some insight into the chances of the wardens aiding us. When Honovi lands, I'll tell him to take us to the Warden's Island."

"*Blaine*," Lore protested. "That is insanity."

"Pray tell how, when you and Meleri lead the Clockwork Brigade and that is your duty, not Caris'?" he asked sharply.

"Nathaniel has proven to be a risk to her life. They shouldn't be around each other," Meleri said.

Caris crossed her arms over her chest, mouth twisting as she turned to glare at the duchess. "It could be argued staying here is a risk. We don't know what secrets Nathaniel gave up, and he knows your bloodline heads the Clockwork Brigade. How many chains are breaking because of that intelligence breach as we speak?"

Meleri flinched, folding her hands together tightly over her knees. "Bringing people in as cogs has always been a risk, but the goal has been worth it."

"Yes, your goal of putting me on the starfire throne." Caris' smile was a rictus, ugly thing that didn't suit her.

Blaine cleared his throat, catching everyone's attention. "Caris is right. Nathaniel knew quite a lot of secrets because of his family's business that the Clockwork Brigade used. He knew the positions of your family, and it would be ludicrous to think that Eimarille will not act on that information."

"I am aware of the risks that Nathaniel's position as a *rionetka* holds at this time," Meleri said.

"Then what do you plan to do about it?"

"My plans have not changed. We will continue to coordinate with the military and rally the bloodlines in the west."

"You need a figurehead for that."

Meleri pursed her lips, glancing at Caris. "I have spent the last few years introducing Caris to many bloodlines that are loyal to the Ashion throne and not Daijal. It has been my hope they will accept her once the truth is known."

"You'd need to be alive in order to do that. If Eimarille knows you are Fulcrum, you will be a target."

"That is a risk I've always been willing to take."

"One you've been prepared for Caris to face? In which case, there is no difference if she goes to the Warden's Island or if she stays." Meleri opened her mouth to argue, but Blaine shook his head. "The North Star warned you about fettering her. Caris has a road. She must walk it."

"As you've walked yours?" Lore bit out.

"I've given up time by my husband's side at the behest of the star gods. I've left my home to come here, to a country that birthed me but is no longer mine, because I understand the threat Eimarille presents to Maricol as a whole. Caris could help end that, yes, but you can't force someone to be queen, no matter their bloodline."

"I never wanted it. I never even knew the starfire throne could be mine," Caris said into the silence that followed his words.

"You can cast starfire. Surely that gift made you wonder?" Meleri said.

Caris shrugged stiffly. "Starfire doesn't make me a queen. I wanted to be an engineer. Now my family's business has been taken over by the government, and my parents are imprisoned."

"Being a queen could change that."

"Would it even be a worthwhile rank if you're the one pulling my strings?"

Meleri's expression became saddened, her shoulders slumping. "I never meant for you to think I wanted to control you."

"Then let me go."

The two stared at each other, and Blaine shook his head at Lore when she seemed ready to jump into the argument. Thankfully, she subsided, and they waited out the silence until Meleri was the one to break it.

The duchess pushed herself slowly to her feet, coming around the low table to stand on Caris' other side. She took Caris' hand in both of hers, patting it gently. "You remind me so much of Queen Ophelia in moments like these. You never knew her, but her passion lives in you, and I am thankful for that."

Caris said nothing, but she didn't pull her hand away. "What was she like?"

Meleri's gaze became distant, her lips curving into a bittersweet smile whose grief had lost all its sharp edges over the years. "Stubborn, but in the best ways. She only ever wanted the best for Ashion and its people. It's why she tried to banish debt bondage. Her idealism made her a target, and we paid dearly for what she believed in. I am merely trying to ensure we don't lose you as well."

"You should have told me who I was. I could have kept that secret."

"Perhaps. But I did what I thought was right, what I thought the North Star wanted." Meleri sighed softly and squeezed Caris' hand before letting her go. "Take Nathaniel to the Warden's Island. The wardens know alchemy better than anyone, so perhaps they can understand how he was unmade. But Caris, you must know, they may not be able to save him."

"I have to *try*."

"And that, my dear, makes you the child of all your parents." Meleri stepped back, looking over Caris' shoulder at Blaine. "I will coordinate with the military and the western bloodlines to begin pushing back against the rhetoric and propaganda about the invasion. I once promised the North Star a revolution, and I will give her one."

Blaine nodded. "Will you remain here?"

"Until you return. The town is defensible enough, and we're scheduled to receive a battalion in the next day or so."

"I'll leave you the code to my televox so you can contact us. I need to call the wardens and prepare for tomorrow."

"I'll come with you," Caris said, sounding a little hoarse. He watched her lean down and grab her teaspoon, dipping it in the honey jar before popping it into her mouth. She licked it clean before dropping it into the teacup and followed him out of the library. She was silent until they reached the stairs, her arm brushing his as they descended.

"All right?" he asked.

"Thank you."

"I carried you out of Amari and promised the star gods I would see you on the throne. My duty is to you, not to the Clockwork Brigade."

"Meleri doesn't see the difference. Nathaniel did." Caris hesitated, her gait hitching the same way her breath did in her throat. "Or I thought he did."

Blaine thought about all the comfort he could try to give her, but it would only be a false sort of care, and he refused to offer that. And Blaine couldn't deny her that desperate desire to help, for if it were Honovi in Nathaniel's place, he'd do anything to save his husband.

A heart was a dangerous weapon, after all.

Eight

HONOVI

The *Celestial Sprite*'s gangplank lowered with a screech of gears, and Honovi was walking down it before the end hit the arrival pier. He raked his gaze over the group of people waiting to board before letting his attention settle on his husband's tense form. He didn't recognize the face, hidden as it was behind a veil, but the clan colors on the plaid wrapped around his waist were Clan Storm, and Honovi would recognize that pattern anywhere.

"Are you all right?" Honovi asked.

Blaine's lips tipped up at the corners in a thin smile that didn't reach his eyes. "Better than you. I'm a little concerned at how often you seem to be getting shot at."

The young woman standing beside him—slim and redheaded, with a dearth of freckles across her cheeks—spoke up in Caris' voice. "You were shot *again*?"

"I'm fine," Honovi said. He couldn't say the same for everyone on the *Comhairle nan Cinnidhean* he'd left behind. "I hear we're not staying long."

"Long enough to board," Blaine said, pointedly putting one foot on the gangplank.

Honovi waved him forward. "Come on, then. Let's get everyone on board."

It didn't take long to load the airship, and the dock master had orders to look the other way when it came to their arrival and departure. Duchess Meleri had used her clout to ensure there would be no record of their presence in Veran that morning. The passengers they took on would never show up in any manifest, especially the one who came on board under guard and only after Caris had been ensconced in the flight deck, out of sight.

The *rionetka* once known as Nathaniel Clementine was quiet when he was escorted up the gangplank, the shackles wrapped around his wrists jangling with every step he took. The shirt he wore had a wide enough collar that Honovi could glimpse the vivisection scars beneath, the puckered flesh red and painful-looking.

"He isn't a magician," Blaine said quietly from his spot beside Honovi. "We're in no danger of a magical attack from him. He'll remain under guard for the entire flight to the Celestine Lake."

"And Caris?"

"She knows not to go near him. Nathaniel has no memory of attacking her."

"Neither did Gregor."

"We think her being alone with him is what triggered the response. We nearly lost her. If she hadn't…" His voice trailed off, and he cleared his throat after a moment. "We checked for scars. We thought he didn't have any, but they'd sewn a veil into his chest to hide what they'd done. I don't know if a visual check will be enough going forward."

"They might be if we add magic into the mix. Veils take a long time to weave. I don't think Eimarille would sew one onto every *rionetka*. Only the most useful ones."

"Did Gregor have one?"

"No."

"I wonder what her criteria are when it comes to being useful."

"E'ridia isn't a threat to her rule at this time, not the way Caris is."

Blaine tipped his head in silent acknowledgment. "The wardens' governor knows to expect us. The wardens here who facilitated the contact yesterday have already left for the Celestine Lake. They very well may beat us to the island."

"We'll see about that."

Blaine laughed softly, his face still not his own. It wouldn't be until after they launched. "I'm going to check on the engines."

"I brought an engineer."

"Well, now you'll have two."

Honovi snorted, refusing to fight the pleased smile that crossed his face. He'd missed having his husband navigate the skies with him. Despite the situation, he felt better having Blaine by his side again.

Honovi followed Blaine into the flight deck, nodding politely at where Caris had posted herself in the corner by the navigation table. She'd removed her veil, holding the fabric bunched up in one hand as she peered through the forward windows. The dark circles under her eyes looked like bruises, and she appeared tired in the way one got where sleep was a missing companion.

The engineer Honovi had brought with him out of Glencoe wisely ceded control of the engine gauges to Blaine, slipping out of the flight deck. Honovi radioed the control tower for clearance and, once approved, began the launch process.

The *Celestial Sprite* lurched out of its berth, the engines a deep rumble in the morning air as the airship took flight. It gained altitude in seconds, rising above the city and surrounding plains, the cloudless sky soon becoming the only thing Honovi could see. His navigator plotted the course, and Honovi steered the airship in a southeasterly direction, aiming the prow at a horizon that always moved.

When they were high in the sky, the chill of altitude making Honovi glad for his fur-lined jacket despite the summer sun, and on a steady course, only then did he step away from the controls. Blaine was busy, and Honovi left him to it, focusing instead on Caris.

"I'll show you to your cabin. We share space on an airship like this, but I've moved crew around to give you your own room to sleep," Honovi said.

Caris nodded. "Thank you. I don't mean to put anyone out."

"You're not. Rest assured on that."

She followed him belowdecks, into the narrow hall that led not toward the cargo hold but the small cabins meant for crew. This wasn't a commercial airship meant for comfort and easy travel. This was one meant for speed and warfare, which meant space was sacrificed as needed.

The cabin he led her to was little more than a closet, with two bunks bolted to the wall for crew to sleep on. Someone had placed her rucksack on the lower bench, along with the small luggage she'd been carrying on the dock. He moved both to the netting underneath the bunk, showing her where to store her things during the flight in case of turbulence.

"How did you do it?" she asked quietly after he stood.

Honovi turned to face her, blinking in the low light of the cabin. "Do what?"

"Let Blaine leave you? How did you…let him go?"

He knew this conversation wasn't about him and Blaine but about Caris and the man locked away in the cargo hold, under constant guard. "Blaine was given to the clans, and mine took him in. We knew—*I* knew—the star gods had a road set out for him. I didn't let him go, as you say. He went, and I followed as best I could."

It had taken some time to convince his father to let him take a diplomatic post, but he'd taken it and found himself in Ashion. He'd kept his duties to his clan and country, different as they'd appeared with his additional title. What hadn't changed was his devotion; the marriage torc he wore had always been a reminder of what he had, even when Blaine wasn't there.

Caris' expression fell a little, and she crossed her arms over her chest, one hand cupping her elbow. "Meleri didn't want me to go. Lore thinks Nathaniel can't be saved, and Meleri thinks my place is as queen in the fight against Daijal."

"And what do you believe?"

"That there must be some way to save him. I can't—" She broke off, gaze sliding away. "He's the first person I've ever loved. For the longest time, I didn't think I could love someone. But he…Nathaniel always said he'd be there for me, no matter how I felt."

"You wonder if it was all a lie."

She flinched, shoulders hunching up toward her ears before she looked at him again. "Yes."

"I can't tell you that. I'm sorry."

"I don't want to lose him."

"I know. But I can't tell you how to let him go." He didn't have the answers she sought, and he wasn't going to gloss over the truth for a lie that would hurt more in the end. "I can't tell you how to walk your road."

"You can only walk yours." She nodded jerkily, eyes looking a little wet. "I know."

He wondered if she truly did. "There are many people who see you as their hope. I can't imagine that is an easy burden to bear."

She curled in on herself, letting out a watery laugh. "How do you do it? How do you rule? Because I don't know how, or if I even want to, but everyone expects me to. Meleri and her family crowned me before I even knew it was mine to take."

Honovi sighed, tucking his hands into the pockets of his flight jacket. "I'm *jarl* to Clan Storm, but whenever I take my father's place, I won't rule alone. My country isn't governed by a monarchy."

"Maybe Ashion shouldn't be one either."

"The North Star says otherwise."

"I don't want the starfire throne," Caris whispered, harsh and low, almost like a prayer begging to be answered. "I don't want to be anyone's queen."

"There were times when I was younger where I resented my family and the responsibilities put upon us. But clan is family and country to us E'ridians. I learned, eventually, that duty is an act of submission. It is no less sacred than love."

She looked up at him at that, bottom lip trembling. "I love Nathaniel."

"Yes, but can you love your country more?"

Caris didn't answer, gaze skating away. Honovi didn't press; it wasn't his place to beg her to rule. Meleri and the rest of that lot could crown her, but a crown didn't make a queen, and Caris seemed to know that.

"I wanted to be an engineer," she whispered.

"So be one. But that doesn't mean you can't be a queen as well."

"I don't know anything about ruling."

"But you know how to build things, yes?" She blinked at him, a frown tugging at her lips, before nodding. "So start there."

Honovi gave her a faint, encouraging smile before slipping out of the cabin, leaving Caris to get settled. He went abovedeck, nearly running into Blaine on his way below. "We have a good tailwind for now and your navigator has the controls. I wanted to check you over."

"Fine by me. I have something for you anyway," Honovi said, smiling.

"Oh?"

"Come with me."

Honovi stepped back down the narrow set of stairs, making his way back to the cabins and the one that was twice as large as Caris', which wasn't saying much. But the captain's quarters were always far more comfortable than the rest. He and Blaine had spent years learning how to navigate around each other in such cramped space. It was easy and comforting, knowing that Honovi only had to reach out and Blaine would be there.

"How is everyone back home?" Blaine asked once he'd shut the door behind them.

"Mostly alive. The *Comhairle nan Cinnidhean* is keeping the Seneschal sequestered, claiming an illness, but I'm not sure how long that excuse will hold. We're in the midst of the summer session, and the Deputy Seneschal can only do so much before people start questioning the situation," Honovi said.

"Do you think they'll reveal the *rionetkas*?"

"It'd do no one any good to disclose them, not when we don't know who officially made them or why. Accusing Eimarille of interfering with our right as a sovereign nation without proof won't go over well."

"And with her already clawing at Ashion's borders, it'd be an excuse to push east faster." Blaine grimaced as he took a seat on the bunk, resting his elbows on his knees. "I hope the wardens have some sort of answer for us. If they do, we could possibly save Gregor as well."

"I don't know if they will. I don't know if they can undo what's been done to a *rionetka*."

"Not their body," Blaine agreed after a fraught few seconds. "Perhaps their mind, if we're lucky."

Honovi thought about the pieces of metal taken out of Siv's body and the power that must have been present to make a clockwork metal heart beat in someone's chest. He thought about the way Siv had been herself right up until she wasn't. "If we're lucky."

Blaine blinked at him, straightening up on the bunk. "You said you had something for me?"

Honovi nodded and went to the narrow, bolted-down desk in the corner. He undid the latch that kept the top drawer secured and opened it, withdrawing a lacquered wooden box. He carried it over to Blaine and lifted the lid, showing what was nestled in soft cloth inside.

Blaine's sharply indrawn breath was all Honovi needed to hear to know he'd made the right decision. His husband reached up to touch the marriage torc he hadn't worn in so long, fingers resting against the woven gold. "I've missed this."

"I missed you wearing it," Honovi said roughly.

He'd missed his husband even when Blaine was in the same city as him because their roads couldn't cross. Honovi had been present in Amari as a diplomat, and Blaine had been hiding behind a false identity as a professor. Their class standing was so far removed as to be laughable according to Ashionen culture. Their clandestine meetings at the embassy had been as much about politics as it was about their own relationship.

But Blaine had known that politics would always come into play when he'd married Honovi, and Honovi had known his husband was guided by the star gods personally. They both had duties they could not walk away from, but their marriage vows still stood, and Blaine's throat had been bare long enough.

Blaine leaned back, tilting his chin up. "You should put it on me."

Honovi didn't hesitate to lift the torc, tossing the box aside. The gap between the ends was the same width from the first and only time Honovi had removed it from Blaine's throat since their wedding day. He hadn't adjusted it back to the original size after removing it, not wanting to risk metal fatigue. It made it easier to press one engraved, rounded end into the softness of Blaine's throat and pull the other around his neck, slipping it back into the only place it should ever truly rest.

He could see the way Blaine's pulse fluttered in his throat as the ends of the marriage torc settled against his collarbones. Honovi pressed hard on the metal with careful fingers to close the gap at the front until barely a finger's width of space remained.

Blaine tipped his head back and let out a thick sigh, lifting one hand to curl his fingers around the gold torc, eyes falling shut. "I love you."

Honovi cupped the back of his head, sliding his fingers through Blaine's hair to get a good grip. "And I you. That will never change."

He leaned down to kiss Blaine, holding him in place, as if this would be enough to keep him there by Honovi's side. He licked in deep, Blaine letting him, and Honovi didn't mind when Blaine's hands found their way to his hips and began undoing his belt.

"I need to get back to the flight deck," Honovi murmured against his lips.

Blaine nipped at his bottom lip, tugging the leather belt free. "You need to do your duty as my husband and fuck me."

"If you insist."

"Oh, I do."

Honovi groaned, all thought of getting abovedeck flying out of his mind. He pulled away long enough to strip out of his heavy flight jacket, tossing it aside. Blaine did the same with his own, both of them scrabbling at their clothes in between kisses. Honovi's fingers brushed across the torc when he shoved Blaine onto the bunk, still mostly dressed. He followed his husband down, settling into the cradle of his hips, kissing the breath from his lungs.

Blaine turned his head away after a moment, and Honovi's lips dragged across the edge of his jaw. Honovi kissed his way down his husband's throat while Blaine shoved his hand between the mattress and the bolted-down frame, coming up with a familiar tin.

"You're still wearing too many clothes," Blaine gasped out as Honovi scraped his teeth over his collarbone.

"So are you," Honovi muttered.

Blaine made an inarticulate sound when Honovi rolled his hips, seeking out friction. "Don't stop."

"I thought you wanted me to get undressed?"

Blaine grabbed Honovi by the shoulder, hooked a leg over his hip, and rolled them over farther onto the bunk. Blaine kissed him fiercely, teeth scraping together as Honovi did his best to undo both their pants and free their half-hard cocks. Blaine opened the tin one-handed, the lid clattering off the side of the bunk to roll somewhere on the floor.

"Yes," Honovi panted against warm skin, licking at sweat beading up on Blaine's throat as his husband took them both in hand, touch eased by the cream. "Like this."

It was too much of an effort to let go, to strip, and fall back into bed. They had duties abovedeck still and an immediate need that was best taken care of quickly. Honovi groaned when Blaine tightened his grip and dragged his hand upward on a heavy stroke. His hips rolled into the motion, and Honovi chased after Blaine's mouth like a starving man.

Lying together like this reminded him of all the times before when they'd flown together, curled up until there was nothing between them but pleasure. It was messy and quick, their hands sliding together as they found a rhythm, holding each other close. The pent-up need he'd carried with him out of Glencoe came undone minutes later when Honovi spilled across his husband's fingers, knuckles pressed against taut muscle as Blaine curled in close, gasping out his name. Honovi pulled him close, making a mess of their skin and the sheets beneath them, their clothes—it didn't matter.

Honovi rolled onto his back, pulling Blaine half on top of him, getting the fingers of his clean hand around the short braid he wore now. He pressed a careful kiss to the corner of Blaine's mouth, breathing in deep and holding on.

"Don't cut your hair again," Honovi murmured.

Blaine pressed their foreheads together, squirming from the mess they'd made. "I have no plans to."

Something settled in Honovi at that soft confession. Blaine's duty to Caris might not be finished, but he could walk that road now as E'ridian and not Ashionen. Honovi curled his hand over the back of Blaine's neck, the gold torc pressing into his palm, the curve of it familiar, right where it was supposed to be.

Nine

SOREN

Soren found Vanya in the Imperial family's private star temple, the entrance guarded by *praetoria* legionnaires, but the soldiers on duty let him pass without a word. His footsteps echoed in the nearly empty worship space as he walked down the aisle toward the altar. Moonlight shining through the stained-glass windows gave the color a different shade than during the day. Marble statues of the star gods stood in recesses between the windows, but only the one of the Dawn Star behind the altar had a candle burning at its feet.

Vanya knelt in the center of the lion head mosaic, hands loose on his thighs, head bowed. The candlelight threw odd shadows on his face, the eternal flame a beacon in the dark. Soren came to a stop beside Vanya, reaching out to trail his fingertips across Vanya's right temple beneath the band of the crown he wore. "I put Raiah to bed. She was asking for you."

"The Senate ran long today. Some bills I expected to sign had to be sent back to a committee for further review," Vanya said, raising his head.

"Why?"

"The Conclave complicates my standing. I'm still emperor, but the unspoken question is for how much longer. My political preference on upcoming potential laws is not the same as another House's."

"What if you dismantled the Senate?" Vanya opened his eyes to glare at him, and Soren shrugged. "What if some other House on the Imperial throne dismantled the Senate?"

"Do you wish to see me dethroned? The Senate is needed to do the work of law."

Soren snorted. "I wouldn't care if you were an emperor or a noble. I just care that you aren't dead."

"You would be the only one."

Soren grimaced, staring down at Vanya. He hadn't moved from his position, attention on the altar in front of them. "Did I interrupt your prayers?"

"It doesn't matter." Vanya rolled to his feet and stood, smoothing down his robe. "Whatever comes of the Conclave, I know I have done what I can for Solaria."

"You're a good ruler."

"That is always up for debate with someone."

"You're staring down future sanctions from the wardens, going against your culture when it comes to burying your royal dead over burning them, and you're doing that despite what it might cost you personally." Soren shifted on his feet, turning so he stood in front of Vanya rather than beside him, forcing Vanya to look at him and not the altar. "You want to keep Solaria whole. There's no shame in that."

He tried not to think about how he was part of the reason the sanctions were being handed down. Vanya had brought him into the crypt, after all, and Delani had told him to report back about anything of interest in the Imperial court. If he was anyone other than a warden, perhaps he could have kept that secret.

But he knew if he'd walked any other road, he might not be standing where he was, by Vanya's side. That absence wasn't something he wanted.

It was why the vow still hung around his throat.

Vanya's smile was bittersweet in a way that made Soren want to smooth it away. "We are nothing if we are not Solaria. We have known that since the Great Separation. But knowing that still changes nothing about where the Houses stand. Letting the wardens know about the crypt has cooled some of the support I'd hoped to find. The rest aren't supporting me because they believe in me, more that none of them trust Joelle."

"I would think that those Houses who support *you* at least see you as a viable option. Who else could they possibly rally behind?"

"If I'm dead, I'm sure they'd find someone."

Soren placed his fingers over Vanya's lips. "Don't talk like that."

"These are the games the Houses play," Vanya murmured, breath ghosting over his fingers. "This life is all I know."

He wouldn't choose something else—he *couldn't*. Seeking power was what the Houses *did*. That's why they existed as they were—families orbiting the Imperial throne the way Maricol orbited the sun. Soren had known that before he ever met Vanya, but the risks of such a culture had never been so personal as they were now.

Soren dragged his fingers over Vanya's lips to rest against the side of his face, thumb pressed to the corner of his mouth. "You have a lot to live for, so try not to die during this Conclave of yours, princeling."

He rose up, brushing his lips over Vanya's in a gentle kiss that didn't stay gentle for long. Vanya's arm came around his waist, hauling him close, and Soren didn't hesitate to deepen the kiss, drawing Vanya in. It was easy to stand like this in Vanya's arms, trading drugging kisses because he'd learned to be greedy whenever he had Vanya within reach. Soren twisted his fingers around the soft fabric of his robes and held on because he was learning he didn't like letting go.

Which was a problem.

When they finally broke apart, breathing raggedly, Soren was uncomfortably hard in his trousers, and Vanya had a look in his eyes that made his gut kick over like an engine sputtering to life. Vanya herded him backward to the altar, guiding him up the handful of stairs to the heavy table draped in velvet cloth.

Soren's hips banged against the edge of the table, the motion rattling the priestly tools used for prayer resting neatly on the altar. Vanya stepped between his legs like he had the right to be there, body solid and familiar, bracketing him in. Soren hauled him down into another kiss, mapping the shape of Vanya's mouth while hands undid his belt and trousers in quick succession, shoving them down. He'd left his weapons in the palace, having not worn them to put Raiah to bed and not detouring to retrieve them before searching out Vanya.

Vanya grabbed him by the hips and yanked him around, kicking his feet out as wide as they would go with his trousers tangled around his thighs. Soren's hands slapped against the table for balance, the altar cloth sliding out from beneath his hands. He went to his elbows, groaning at the way Vanya just manhandled him about. He tried to straighten up, and a hand settled between his shoulder blades, pressing him flat against the table.

Vanya leaned over him, his clothed cock grinding against Soren's bare ass, mouth pressed to the back of Soren's neck. "Such faith you have in me."

Soren clenched his hands around the velvet cloth, the fabric slipping a bit as Vanya rocked against him. "You think so?"

Vanya bit down on the knob of his spine, and Soren arched against the sting of teeth. "Yes, because it's the same faith I have in you."

He shivered at that, a truth he couldn't acknowledge in words, but that didn't matter in moments like this. Not when Vanya's touch was like a brand, his words stronger than any chain that could keep Soren by his side.

He watched as Vanya reached for the vial of holy oil he knew was used in the anointment of prayers. He shivered when Vanya pressed a finger into him, the oil cool until it warmed. Soren tried to get his elbows back underneath him, but Vanya pinned him to the altar with one hand, leaning his weight on him.

"Stay," Vanya ordered, making his point felt by adding a second finger.

The stretch burned, but Soren didn't care, wanting it even knowing he shouldn't. He closed his eyes, rubbing his cheek against the cloth as Vanya worked him open with skilled fingers that made him wish he could get his hand on his own cock. When he withdrew his fingers, Soren whined, unable to swallow the sound.

Vanya flexed his fingers against Soren's back before leaning over him, cock sliding against the crease of his ass. "I'd worship you like this if you'd let me."

"Vanya," Soren got out in a strangled voice as Vanya pulled back far enough that his cock slid down, the head catching on his rim. When he pushed inside, slow and methodical, never stopping, Soren could only try to breathe through the crushing weight of Vanya's attention. When he finally bottomed out, it took a moment for Soren to remember how his lungs worked.

"I'd pray with you like this every day," Vanya said, and Soren could feel the way his cock throbbed before he pulled out. "You have to know that."

When he thrust back in, it was with enough force that the edge of the table slammed sharply against Soren's hips. He scrabbled at the cloth, panting open-mouthed into velvet as Vanya fucked him at a pace that reminded him of the way a choir might chant a hymn rather than sing it—steady and enduring, right up until the pitch changed. Vanya lifted himself off Soren but never removed his hand. It steadied him as Vanya increased the speed of his thrusts, and all Soren could do was press his forehead to the velvet cloth and *take* it.

Vanya came with a groan minutes later, shoving Soren harder against the table, grinding in for the last few thrusts until he was spent. Soren swallowed around a dry throat, his own neglected cock rubbing against the velvet cloth hanging over the side. Then Vanya hooked his fingers over the back collar of his vest, pulling Soren up off the altar, still buried deep inside him.

Soren rocked backward, head falling against Vanya's shoulder as a warm hand wrapped around his cock and stroked him until he came, spilling over the altar and ruining the velvet cloth. He blinked up at the star temple's ceiling, breathing raggedly. Vanya turned his head to brush his lips over Soren's cheek, holding him up, holding on.

"I want you to be my road," Vanya said low and ragged, the words a prayer there at the altar of the star gods.

It wasn't one Soren had the right to answer.

Ten

SORENN

“I think you should join me in the Senate today,” Vanya said over breakfast in the courtyard.

Soren very nearly choked on the bite of spiced egg in his mouth. He chewed furiously and swallowed it. “What?”

“Many, if not all, of the Houses will be there to oversee a vote on the expansion of certain governorship powers. If the Senate passes it, I’ll see about signing off on it. The vote is why no Conclave gatherings are happening today.”

“Is that wise, considering Joelle’s position?”

Vanya smiled thinly and leaned back in his chair. “The bill doesn’t concern borders, merely the regulation over when a *vezir* may call upon the Imperial throne to expand a city or town’s outer walls.”

“They don’t control it?”

“All cities and towns belong to Solaria and, therefore, the Imperial throne. If a population trend allows for city growth and the water table can support it, then we allow it. But building a new outer wall and the housing to fill that new space takes years, even with automatons to aid in the construction. This bill will streamline the bureaucracy of it all.”

“You’re inclined to grant it?”

Vanya nodded. "I would have even if the Conclave hadn't been formed. I've targeted my own fair share of Houses in the past but not this way. I have tried to be less of a destabilizing force after my mother's rule, especially considering I lost House support after her passing."

"She didn't rule fairly?"

"She lost a city under her watch, and we have been paying for that ever since."

Rixham would never hold life inside its walls again. Guarded by wardens and Solarian military automatons, the revenants inside its sealed city walls had yet to fully be eradicated in the years since. It was a waiting game, one that would continue for years to come.

Revenants were the walking dead. They didn't stop unless they were put down.

Eradicating a city the size of Rixham risked sending spores into the air and poisoning the surrounding habitable land. Rixham was a risk at the southern border—to the country but also to Vanya's House.

"I'll go," Soren said after a moment. "It deals with a border, in a way. We can play off my presence through that angle."

Two hours later, Soren was regretting having agreed to be present, mostly because politics, when it got this detailed, was *boring*.

The Senate floor was full, as were the House sections in the mezzanine, though not every House had sent their *vezir*. The House of Kimathi had sent Artyom, who refused to look their way and had only grudgingly given the barest of bows to Vanya when he'd arrived to open the session.

Soren had thought he'd be relegated to the public viewing section, but Vanya and Taisiya had insisted he observe from the House of Sa'Liandel's seats in the mezzanine. Taisiya, for all that she'd spent years on the seaside, was an astute teacher on the intricacies of the decision being voted on today.

"It is a death sentence to be uninformed," Taisiya had explained after she'd near correctly predicted the final tally and Vanya's granting of the bill.

"Even about something as innocuous as this?" Soren asked.

"You never know when a favor may be drawn because of a vote." Taisiya stood, smoothing down her gown. "Come."

They weren't the only ones making their way to the Senate floor to mingle after the vote. Other Houses joined them to discuss the aftermath with the senators, a few even going so far as to thank Vanya for the way he'd ruled on it. Those tended to be minor Houses, and Soren figured perhaps their smaller towns had needed this to pass more than the larger cities.

Soren stayed by Taisiya's side, who never drifted far from Vanya, listening with half an ear as she talked up the results with the Houses who would listen. He ignored the lingering glances cast his way. The bill was essentially about borders, and the few senators who drummed up the courage to approach him for a brief chat got the same answer.

"I'm here to report back to the wardens' governor on the likelihood of changing the maps," Soren said. It wasn't necessarily a lie, and he'd carried the border reports to and from Calhames for years already. Artyom still found a way to twist it.

"I assumed you were here to service our esteemed emperor," Artyom drawled.

Soren stiffened, turning his head to find Artyom standing nearby in the middle of a group of senators. "You are mistaken."

"Am I? You've certainly been presented in a way that says otherwise. It makes one wonder about the vaunted neutrality of the wardens."

"Wardens serve Maricol," Soren shot back, unable to keep quiet.

"I'm sure the emperor enjoys your services *immensely*."

"And I'm sure the House of Kimathi will enjoy the presence of wardens when it comes to establishing new city borders," Taisiya cut in. "I understand some have already been dispatched to your House's *vasilyet*. Tell me, Artyom. Have you done your House duty and allowed them entry, or are you still hiding your deception from those that keep us safe?"

Artyom drew himself up and stepped forward, face going ruddy from temper. "You insult my House, Taisiya."

"*Valide*." Taisiya smiled, thin and knifelike. "Know my place so you know yours."

She was Imperial royalty, and he was not, and the frankness with which he'd addressed her had not gone unnoticed. Soren edged closer to Taisiya, eyes on Artyom's hands as opposed to his face. It was always the hands that gave away the next hit.

"*Valide*," Artyom ground out after a long minute of disdainful silence on his part.

"Is there a problem?" Vanya asked mildly as he approached, the crowd parting to allow him passage across the Senate floor.

Taisiya turned to face him. "No."

Her dismissal of Artyom's House was so thorough that several senators shifted away from Artyom. The rage in his eyes deepened, fingers flexing, and Soren absently rested his hand on his pistol. *Praetoria* legionnaires were nearby, but it wouldn't be the first time he'd drawn a weapon in defense of Vanya and his House.

"The Conclave will see your House diminished. Our prayers will be answered," Artyom snapped.

"Ah, but I haven't heard yours," a clear, ringing voice said from the center of the Senate floor.

The entire crowd shifted as if an earthquake had jolted the Senate building, pulling back to give ground to the star god in their midst. Soren moved on instinct, putting himself between Vanya and the newly arrived threat. He'd unholstered his pistol without conscious thought, staring over the barrel at the Dawn Star shining in all her glory there on the Senate floor.

Callisto wasn't as he'd seen her last—surrounded by starfire, in a quarry that was nothing but charred dirt and ashes once he'd finally gotten his bearings. The gown she wore had a low collar to better show off the golden Lion constellation tattoo wrapped around her throat. The white of the fabric stood out starkly against her dark skin, trimmed in matching gold. But it was her eyes that caught Soren's attention like nothing else could—dark and deep and fathomless like a clear, endless night sky full of stars.

She looked at him as if she could scrape out everything that made him who he was until there was nothing left, not even the lies he lived by.

As if a gear had shifted, everyone surrounding them kneeled in a wave, showing their respect to a star god. The fierce murmur of the crowd was like the buzz of insects in Soren's ears. Vanya moved to stand beside Soren and settled his hand on Soren's outstretched forearm, pushing down until the pistol pointed at the floor. He leaned in close, breath ghosting over Soren's ear. "Let's not shoot my country's guiding star, hm?"

Soren clicked the safety back on after a moment, feeling the gears shift in the pistol, and holstered it. He never took his eyes off Callisto. She paced forward, a smile playing at her lips and starfire flickering around her fingertips. Vanya bowed because even the star gods outranked an emperor. Soren didn't bother with manners, remembering all too well his last meeting with the Dawn Star.

"My lady, you honor us with your presence," Vanya said before straightening up. The calmness with which he greeted the star god made Soren wonder if he, too, had ever been visited by one before now.

"I am not here for honor," Callisto drawled.

"Then why are you here?"

"To give a blessing." She came to a stop an arm's length from them, the edge of her being shimmering like a heat mirage. "The Houses are at a crossroads, and I find my children are in need of a guiding hand."

Around them all, those belonging to the Houses stiffened at being singled out. Some faces went pale, Artyom among them. The slack-jawed expression on his face would have been amusing at any other time.

Vanya inclined his head regally. "I am at your command."

Soren said nothing, silent because he had no choice but to be. Callisto knew all his secrets, after all, though she seemed disinclined to share them.

"I hear the prayers sent to me, but not all Houses pray as they should. A pity." Callisto tilted her head, eyes going half-lidded. "But you pray, House of Sa'Liandel."

She raised her hand, starfire dripping from her fingers, and touched her thumb to Vanya's forehead, just beneath the band of the crown he wore. Starfire burned incandescent white as it twisted around the gold, overtaking the shape of it until it looked as if Vanya wore a crown of fire, not one of metal.

"And I have heard your prayers," Callisto murmured, her voice carrying like a thunderous echo in the Senate building.

The starfire became blinding so suddenly that Soren had to squeeze his eyes shut. When he opened them again, blinking spots out of his vision, the Dawn Star had disappeared, but the starfire on Vanya's crown remained.

The crowd still knelt, every face turned toward Vanya, and Soren's skin crawled at the focused attention. He stayed still, stayed his hand, and watched as Vanya closed his eyes, catching the spill of starfire in his palms, the heat of the aether harming him not at all.

As blessings went, the favor of a star god could not be more obvious. Soren could only guess how this would shake the Houses apart.

Eleven

EIMARILLE

"He has the backing of a star god."

Eimarille frowned into the telephone receiver pressed to her ear. "Are you certain?"

Joelle's harsh laughter was grating. "*Yes*. The Dawn Star herself blessed his rule. The Conclave will not end with the support I require now."

"A pity."

"You promised me the throne in exchange for aid at the border. If you can't provide—"

"I have given you every tool to create the outcome you so desire. Your failure isn't laid at my feet," Eimarille cut in coldly. "My plans will not change."

"You need control of my *vasilyet*'s border. Tell me how this doesn't change them?"

"I *have* control of your *vasilyet*'s border."

Two battalions of the Daijal army were currently running war games on the southern Daijal border there, preparing to cross the eastern border. Eimarille had confirmation that Meleri had retreated to her bloodline's ancestral estate in Veran but that Caris was no longer there. The army was well positioned to advance once her hold on Haighmoor was assured. She was due an update from High General Kote within a day or two on that.

"The emperor will use that backing to send legionnaires north. The border will be compromised for our needs. As it is, the wardens are demanding access to my *vasilyet*."

"They do so because of the damage done to the quarry. Despite you losing a death-defying machine, perhaps it is for the best at this time. The Legion has already examined the quarry, and they have no proof of what was produced there. The wardens will find the same."

"I can't hold them off forever. If I had control of the Imperial throne, I could thwart them. But the Dawn Star gave support to the House of Sa'Liandel and not *mine*."

An arm reached out to set a teacup and saucer on her desk. She looked up and nodded her thanks at the guest who had provided her tea. "You don't worship her."

"No, but the Dawn Star's favor would have aided our plans."

"She could never favor your House. You know why."

Joelle's silence was a furious sort that lasted half a minute. "The Conclave is scheduled to last another two weeks. That time is meaningless now. What Houses I have convinced to my side will flee to the emperor's."

"Then you must provide a different road to them. That is why you reached out, is it not? The House of Sa'Liandel has held the Imperial throne for too long, I remember you saying. Don't tell me you'll give up on it now."

"I haven't," Joelle ground out.

"My contingency will see us through this. You will remain in Calhames until the package is delivered to you. For all the Dawn Star's supposed favor, it can't compete with the dead."

"And when can I expect this package?"

"I'm sending it by way of airship tomorrow."

"If I do not get the Imperial throne—"

"I know what you *want*, *vezir* Joelle. But it is not what I need at this moment, and my needs *must* come first if we are to do right by your House." Eimarille gentled her voice, coaxing the conversation to a more pleasant tone. "I told you when we agreed to work together that I would help you gain the Imperial throne. We need the Houses to look away from you and the border we share. I will ensure that happens."

"I insist you do so *before* the Conclave officially ends."

The line hummed from an ended call, and Eimarille set the receiver into the telephone cradle. She leaned back in her office chair and turned her head to catch Innes' eye. "Such atrocious manners. I do regret to inform you that your sister has given her favor to a House, my lord."

Innes crossed his arms over his chest and leaned a hip against her wide wooden desk. He wore a rather fashionable day jacket in lilac, with trousers to match. Dark blue embroidery at the cuffs and collars pricked with gold were offset by the cravat tied around his throat. The gloves he wore were cream-colored to match the waistcoat he wore, his button-down shirt a bright white. He could have passed for any courtier—and did—but no one would ever see the truth of him unless he allowed it.

"How interesting," Innes mused.

The Twilight Star appeared unconcerned with the news, though Eimarille knew from considerable experience that he would never truly reveal how he felt at any given moment. He was inscrutable when it came to the truth of his emotions—if he even had any.

"Interesting is one way to look at it. Why would the Dawn Star show favor to the House of Sa'Liandel after decades of silence?"

"She'd favor any House sitting on the Imperial throne at a time like this."

"Not Joelle's."

Innes' lips curved in a smile that never reached his eyes. "Her prayers belong to me."

"I do hope you'll answer them appropriately when it's time."

Innes laughed, leaning over to press a kiss to the top of Eimarille's head. The gesture was almost paternal, though she knew he'd never see her in the way of a child, only a pawn. "Have no fear. Her road is set."

"I was going to wait to send the strike force, but now I think it's best I dispatch them tomorrow for the east after I send Terilyn south." She pursed her lips, dropping her gaze to the folios on her desk that held updates from the military brass on their ongoing annexation of Ashion provinces. "I'll need to speak with Kote first."

"You have a meeting," Innes reminded her just as a knock sounded on the door to her private office. "Ah, right on time."

The door was pushed open by Terilyn, the Blade garbed in brown tailored trousers, a russet-colored corset belt, and a snow-white blouse embroidered at the sleeves and collar with delicate lace. Her hair was pinned up, the jeweled stiletto securing the updo a gift from Eimarille two years ago. Terilyn inclined her head, sweeping an arm out behind her as she turned. "Your next appointment, Your Royal Majesty."

The Urovan ambassador entered, clicking his booted heels together before bowing deeply to Eimarille. The heavy brocade overcoat he wore was perhaps too warm for the summer weather, but the embroidery and gold embellishments on it provided a visual of his rank that Ambassador Maksim had always been loath to part with.

"Your Royal Majesty," Maksim said in greeting.

Eimarille smiled sweetly at the man. He was two decades older than her own thirty years, but the years had been kind to him, or perhaps it was his wealth. He'd been born the third son into a high-ranking noble bloodline in Matriskav and hadn't been satisfied with his lot in life until he'd fallen into politics. From there, he'd earned the trust of Urova's Isar, enough so that he'd made a name for himself in foreign courts.

Maksim had come to the Daijal court long before her marriage. Eimarille had spent many an afternoon over the years discussing politics with the man, Terilyn ever by her side. Eimarille had a soft spot for Maricol's most northern country. Her Blade had come from there, and she would spare its people if she could. She'd promised Terilyn that, and Maksim had come around to her way of thinking after an encounter with the Midnight Star.

Xaxis could be persuasive—or he could simply take your mind.

Despite his reluctance to build a war against his siblings, the Midnight Star had taught the *Klovod* how to make *rionetkas*.

Maksim had been the first one Eimarille had ever seen made.

It was always interesting to see the personality still shining through after all these years.

"What news from Urova, my dear ambassador?" Eimarille asked.

"I've heard from my institution back in Matriskav. The Urovan court has received outreach asking for aid from Ashion that does not come from its parliament," Maksim dutifully reported.

"How interesting," Eimarille murmured. "The duchess' doing, I presume?"

"They claim to represent the western provinces on behalf of the true queen of Ashion."

Eimarille curled her hand into a fist before realizing she'd made the gesture. Such a tell was not something she wanted to reveal and was glad it was only the four of them in her office and this wasn't court. "And what do these liars want?"

"Aid to stop Daijal's push past the border."

Eimarille laughed and pushed her chair back. "They'll not have it. Isar Dávgon has agreed to treaties with Daijal. Urovan support belongs to us, not to traitors."

She'd pulled those strings for over a decade behind Bernard's back once Maksim became what he was now. It had taken subtle, intense effort on her part to lay the groundwork for a political relationship that had drawn tighter after the Inferno. Urova's clarion crystal mines were too important to the war effort to give up to another country's needs.

Maksim's hands on the treaties drawn between Urova and Daijal in recent memory were as much the diplomat's own as they were hers. Bernard had never seen that, too pleased with getting what he thought he'd wanted when in fact, it was what *she* had wanted.

"You'll advise Isar Dávgon of what your country owes mine in the wake of these overtures," Eimarille said, pinning Maksim with a hard look. "I'll not have him playing two sides."

"I'll endeavor to bring my cousin to heel."

"See it done."

Maksim bowed deeply and left. Terilyn closed the door behind him and locked it, gliding across the office to come to Eimarille's side. She pressed a soft kiss to Eimarille's cheek, wrapping an arm around her waist. "Lisandro is with his governess for the rest of the afternoon."

Eimarille wrapped both her arms around Terilyn's waist, absently counting the hidden weapons on her lover's body with touch. "He may join us for dinner tonight. I'll need a respite from today's many problems."

Her son was a joy and always would be. She adored him, as much as she adored her Blade. Terilyn hummed agreement, fingers stroking over Eimarille's hip, rucking up the fabric of her gown there. "What did Joelle have to say?"

Eimarille huffed out a sigh. "Apparently, the Dawn Star has shown favor to the House of Sa'Liandel."

Terilyn pulled back to look Eimarille in the eye, frowning prettily. "That's unusual."

"And a problem. The Conclave was supposed to rally the Houses to Joelle. Now it won't, and I need a distraction so the Legion will not be focused on Solaria's northern border."

"Am I to be that distraction, then?"

Eimarille ghosted a kiss over Terilyn's subtly painted lips. "Yes, for I trust no one else. I'm sending you to Calhames tomorrow. See that the dead are properly handled."

"Your will be done."

Eimarille glanced over Terilyn's shoulder, eyeing Innes where he still leaned against her desk, watching them. Maksim hadn't acknowledged him once, the star god most likely influencing the man's awareness so as to go unnoticed. "Will you join us for my call with the high general?"

"I trust you to see these initial battles through to the next stage. I find my attention is needed elsewhere," Innes said.

He gave them both a little nod before sweeping out of the office, off to handle whatever pressing need required him. Eimarille never claimed to know how the star gods lived their lives.

"Perhaps he's off to speak with his sister," Terilyn mused, pulling away.

Eimarille smoothed her hands down the skirt of her gown. "I'm sure whatever he is doing will aid us. His goal is our goal."

"Of course."

"I'll ask Kote to deploy the strike group and have them make their way to the Warden's Island. Kote picked the soldiers personally, but they'll need to move discreetly."

"It will be a good chance to test the new long-distance war machines."

"If they do well there, then they will certainly do well against the Legion."

The factories in the north of Daijal had been working day and night on the production line to provide the war machines the Daijal army would need to take the continent. The nobles who owned the mines that supplied iron and other metals to the companies handling the production had been more than happy to acquiesce to the crown's needs for the right to keep control of the mines.

The war machine designs—both short and long-range—had been something Kote had overseen before Eimarille was crowned. The military budget had been ramped up toward the end of Bernard's reign, ostensibly at his orders, but Eimarille had been the one to coax the expansion out of him by manipulating others. These days, she no longer needed to work behind the scenes to obtain her goals.

Ashion could beg for help from outside their borders all they liked. Urova would not lend them aid, and Solaria was occupied by internal issues. The Tovan Isles kept to their ship-cities, and E'ridia would be dealt with once Ashion was under her control, and not even the Eastern Spine would keep her forces out.

The North Star might have kindled the flames of the starfire throne, but Eimarille would wear the crown that mattered. Maricol would fall in line, or it would burn.

Betrayal

936 A.O.P.

CARIS

The Celestine Lake pooled at the southern end of the Eastern Spine, the range there smaller than the highest peaks that separated E'ridia from the rest of the continent. Under guidance of the Poison Accords, Maricol's countries had built railroads and paved roads to pass through the mountains to reach that body of water and the people who claimed it as neutral territory, held by no country.

The waters were a brilliant blue at the height of summer, but they were deceiving. The Celestine Lake was always poisonous to some degree, carrying runoff from the mountains and drifting spore-filled fog. At the center of the lake was the Warden's Island, an outcropping of land dotted here and there with trees and mountain scrub. Rising from the earth was a massive fort where wardens were made and trained out of tithes.

Caris peered over the *Celestial Sprite*'s railing, squinting through the lenses of her gas mask. Despite the clear skies, Honovi had ordered everyone to wear one as they began their descent. The Eastern Mountains were one of the last areas on the continent the wardens had not yet cleansed. Their vastness made the job exceedingly difficult, much like the Wastelands. Sometimes it was easier to simply contain an area and guard its borders rather than lose wardens by the dozens in an endeavor that may prove fruitless.

"They know to expect us?" Caris asked over her shoulder.

"Yes. Honovi received clearance to land," Blaine said as he came to stand with her by the railing, his own gas mask firmly in place. His voice came out distorted through the filters, but she could understand him well enough. "They have a small airfield on the north side for us to anchor in. Come, you should strap in for the descent."

She didn't linger at the railing, following after Blaine to the crew cabin. She felt the descent in her gut and ears, pressure building in her head until it popped. No colored smoke marked their berth, but Honovi guided them down into a hangar with impressive skill.

Caris watched through the cabin's windows as the sky and mountains gave way to the edge of an open roof and metal walls, drifting down into a space lit by fully enclosed gas lamps. The ground crew who guided the airship into its anchor berth wore the uniforms of wardens, all of them armed in some fashion. It left her wondering about the reception they were about to receive.

The *Celestial Sprite* settled into its anchor berth with a judder, the shouting quieting down once the airship was secured. Caris undid the safety belt and darted out of the crew cabin, finding Blaine and Honovi on the flight deck near the gangplank. A crew member winched it out while a warden on the pier secured it on their end.

A tall man dressed in a field uniform strode up the gangplank, flinty brown eyes taking them all in. A pistol was holstered to his hip, framed by the blade of a long-poled double-headed battle axe he carried across his back. The clarion crystal embedded in the pommel glittered over one shoulder. "Air is clear today. The gas masks most likely won't be needed for now, but keep them on you. The weather can change quickly, and we'll warn you when it's not safe."

Blaine pulled his gas mask off, hooking the strap around his belt to secure it to his hip. "We know how that is. I'm Blaine of Clan Storm. This is my husband, *jarl* Honovi, also of Clan Storm and our captain."

The warden nodded curtly at them. "I'm Yufei. I'm to take you to the governor. I understand you have cargo that needs to be secured?"

"We do, but it can't be offloaded until our charge is out of sight." Blaine nodded at Caris, who slipped her gas mask off to meet the warden's gaze. "The *rionetka* was somehow triggered to harm Caris. I'd like her in the fort before you transport the cargo."

"He has a name," Caris said tartly.

"Cargo is cargo. We'll deal with it." Yufei looked over at Honovi. "Your crew will be escorted to the guest barracks. You three will follow me."

Honovi gestured for Caris to precede them down the gangplank, and she hurried after Yufei, clenching her hands and refusing to duck her head at the sharp-eyed curious gazes that watched them disembark the airship. She was used to attention, but the wardens were intense in a way she wasn't comfortable with.

A few wardens on the ground nodded at them. She recognized Raziel from Veran, the older woman giving her a friendly smile. The hangar was stuffy from heat, and it was warm outside as well, making her sweat beneath the fur-lined flight jacket she'd been wearing. Caris stripped it off and tied it around her waist, all the while taking in the open area between the hangar and the fort. The graveled path they were on was patrolled by a pair of spiderlike automatons with Zip guns bolted to the top of their casings.

"Is it dangerous here?" Caris asked, eyeing one of the machines.

"Anywhere is dangerous if you're not careful. Revenants swim, so we always have a guard on duty. Don't worry, none have been sighted for several weeks, and our live training exercises are held off the island," Yufei said.

"Live training exercises?"

Yufei glanced back at her, an amused smile twitching on his lips. "How else do you think we learn to handle revenants?"

She knew Maricol needed wardens, that their livelihoods rested on the wardens always monitoring the borders and poison fields and eradicating revenants. She just hadn't ever thought about what that training might entail, about the tithes who were sent here to become what Yufei was. Ignorance was a comfort she could no longer wrap herself in, she was coming to realize.

The trek up the winding path passed a training oval where tithes ran loops in two column formations beneath the watchful eyes of older wardens standing on watchtowers. Inside the oval, on the grassy field, wardens ran through various forms of physical training with pairs of tithes. Not all the tithes were the same age, but every single one of them was focused on the task at hand and never looked over once.

The fort loomed ahead, its walls built high, with more automatons in a more humanoid form pacing the ramparts, their Zip guns larger than the ones on the spiderlike automatons. The metal doors of the gates were thrown open, with a warden on duty in the guardhouse. The grizzled man waved them on through before turning his attention back to the book he was reading. The automaton crouched beside the guardhouse would surely notify him if something was amiss, as would everyone else still out on the field.

They passed through a short tunnel, coming into an open space dotted with buildings built close together. It reminded Caris of Amari's Aether School of Engineering, a campus built for learning, save for how this one was built to house and train wardens.

It was like a mini-city, held within the confines of the protective outer walls and surrounded by the Celestine Lake. Trees lined the pathways leading to buildings, providing much-needed shade from the sun. Caris wiped sweat from her brow as they trudged along, passing wardens on errands. She didn't see any tithes outside, but a glimpse through some windows showed many sitting in classrooms.

"How long do classes last?" she asked, curious despite the reason for their visit. She didn't know of anyone who had ever visited the Warden's Island. Tithes and supplies were delivered at the designated time of the year, but she had never been involved in that process. The Clockwork Brigade had never found fault with it, not the way they'd found fault with debt bondage.

"Once a tithe has been processed formally into our ranks, they begin their education and training immediately. When wardens return from the borders and poison fields, we are expected to collaborate on the data and chemical analysis we bring in," Yufei said.

"What happens if a warden can't go back out into the poison fields again?"

"We find a place for them, either here or at a resupply station somewhere across the continent. Wardens are always needed." He said that proudly, with not a trace of bitterness for a life given up from whatever country had tithed him.

The rest of the walk was done in silence, following twisting paths and streets to a squat, unremarkable building. It was warm inside, and Caris licked sweat off her upper lip as they traversed stairways. They were finally waved into an office overflowing with folios, a sofa with sagging cushions and threadbare seams that looked comfortable for a nap, and maps of all kinds pinned to one wall.

"Governor," Yufei said with a head tilt in greeting. "I've brought *jarl* Honovi, Blaine, and Caris for you, as requested."

"Thank you," the governor said. "Dismissed."

He slipped out of the office, closing the door behind him. Caris laced her fingers together behind her back as she stared at the woman before them. The wardens' governor sat behind the wide wooden desk and studied them with a gaze that startled Caris—not because of the woman's attention but because of her eyes. One eye was her own, while the other was made of black glass with hints of gold flecks in it. She wore a monocle over her good eye, the leather straps securing it in place wrapped snugly around her skull.

"I'm Delani, governor of the Warden's Island," she said in a raspy voice. "It's rare we get a request for citizens to want entry here, especially on such short notice."

"I don't believe the Poison Accords ban citizens from the island," Honovi said carefully.

"It doesn't." Delani stared at him for a long moment before her gaze slipped away to focus on Caris. "But you're not here as tithes, nor are you here as oversight, are you, princess?"

Blaine bristled beside her, and Caris tried not to flinch at that title. "I'm no princess."

Delani raised an eyebrow, expression clearly disbelieving. "That's not what the broadsheets out of Ashion are saying."

"Do you get many here?" Blaine asked sharply.

"Wardens send reports in every day through telegraph machines and telephones. I'm well aware of what has occurred in Amari over the last few weeks. I am not the one who named you princess, who espouses you can be queen. That is your public."

"They aren't mine," Caris said. "My name was never written down in the royal genealogies."

"You wield starfire" was Delani's blunt reply. "That's mark enough of royal blood, especially in Ashion."

Blaine stepped forward, edging partway in front of Caris, as if he could hide her how he had with his silence all these years. "She isn't why we are here."

"Somehow, I doubt that."

"Governor—"

"Peace. I'm a warden. We have no say in your politics and don't want any. Our duty is to the borders and always has been."

"And to the dead," Honovi said. "Which is why we are here."

"Nathaniel isn't dead," Caris protested.

"No, he's merely been turned into a *rionetka*."

Delani's good eye narrowed slightly behind the glass monocle she wore. "I understand he still breathes."

"He's *not* a revenant. I won't let you harm him," Caris said sharply.

"We've only received dead *rionetkas* and broken hearts. It will be interesting to see a breathing one."

"He's *alive*."

"For a given definition of such."

Caris opened her mouth to argue, but Blaine shot her a pleading look. "Caris, please."

Unspoken went the warning that they couldn't afford to anger the wardens if they wanted help. Nathaniel's life depended on the people here, so Caris held her tongue, for all that she wanted to protest Delani's opinion of Nathaniel's current state.

"You know of *rionetkas*?" Honovi asked after a moment.

Delani nodded. "We wardens first became aware of them a couple of years ago, though we did not know what they were called back then or their true purpose."

"That long ago? And you didn't warn anyone?"

"The one in question was used as an assassin against a head of state. We still don't know who sent that particular *rionetka*. We learned the name of them and uncovered the mind magic that controls them only recently."

"Do you know how they are made? Can you unmake them?" Caris asked.

Delani drummed her fingers against her desk and sighed. "You *would* be here for answers we can't give you."

"But you've known of the existence of *rionetkas* for years. Surely you've uncovered something that could be helpful?"

"We know *of* them. Our understanding of their creation is limited. We've seen from autopsies that what magic binds the clockwork metal heart to the body and mind is set with a self-destruct spell. If any magical interference is detected, the hearts shatter, along with the spells holding them together. The hearts we've tried to work on have all been collected after the *rionetka* ceased to function, but the results were the same. We've only pieces left."

"You're not talking about them as if they were alive, but like they're machines."

"Aren't they?" Delani asked in a terribly bland voice. "They are organic constructs powered by the aether that runs through the replacement mechanism, controlled by someone else. They are an infernal engine."

Caris flinched, digging her fingers into her palms behind her back. "Nathaniel is *alive*."

"No, he isn't. Not with a clockwork metal heart beating where a real one should. That's machine work, no matter how you look at it."

Caris opened her mouth, but no words came out, stomach sinking somewhere down near her feet.

"Their minds aren't their own. Magicians have said as much after one attacked me in Amari and another in Glencoe. But these *rionetkas act* like they always have, like they are the person we believe them to be. Some part of them must still remain for that to happen," Honovi said.

Delani's gaze sharpened, and she leaned forward intently. "Interesting. That would take a very precise application of mind magic to ensure the personality shines through and still adheres to the controls laid over it."

"They aren't *things*," Caris growled, frayed temper finally snapping. "They are *people*. And right now, one of them needs your help."

Delani pushed her chair back and stood, coming around her desk to face them. She looked them each in the eye, her attention lingering on Caris. The scrutiny made Caris' shoulders rise to her ears, mouth twisting in a stubborn scowl.

"You remind me of someone," Delani said, never blinking.

Caris grimaced. "Do I?"

Delani shrugged off the question. "Wardens give aid every day of our lives. We do what you can't—what you *won't*—because your countries tithe for the grace you live with. We see things you never will, and we live by those truths. This, right here, is something you will need to live with, too."

A curl of shame twisted through Caris' chest, warming her cheeks. She couldn't blame it on the summer heat, but neither did she try to hide from it. Instead, she raised her chin, squaring her shoulders as she brought her hands back around in front of her, splaying them in a pleading gesture. "If we can fix the problem for the better, if we can save a life, isn't that worth trying? Isn't that your duty?"

Delani's smile was small and humorless, her single-eyed gaze empty of all emotion. "Isn't it yours, princess?"

Caris drew in a breath, curling her hands into fists and letting her arms fall back to her sides. She thought about what Honovi had told her on the airship at the beginning of the flight. How duty was a form of love and there was no shame in that.

"Please," she whispered. "There has to be a way to save him."

Because it wasn't just Nathaniel; it was everyone else whose heart and mind and soul had been ripped from them and enslaved in a way far worse than debt bondage to banks.

"I can't promise anything but that we'll try." Delani waved at them to follow as she walked to the door. "My wardens would have taken the *rionetka* to our laboratories. I'll escort you there, and we can see what a living *rionetka* has to tell us."

Two

BLAINE

The laboratories where tithes were turned into wardens over the course of years were built below ground, in the rocky earth, the walls of the rooms and halls smooth, seamless metal that Blaine couldn't help but take a second look at. It reminded him of the catacombs in Amari and the oldest civic buildings in Glencoe. Architecture from a long-ago Age that had somehow survived by way of engineering lost to them.

The spaces were lit not with gas lamps but with clarion crystal chips at the tips of wire encased in thin blown glass. The flameless lights ran on aether power from a generator deep below the labs, the earth blocking the sound of it. The invention was one Blaine wished he had time to study.

"The generator runs much of the power for the island. We built it underground to protect it from winter storms," Delani explained as she led them down a windowless hall.

Some doors to laboratories were propped open, giving them the chance to peer in at the wardens working on alchemy experiments with poison. Some doors were closed, with colored lights over a warning sign indicating an experiment was in progress.

"Tithes taking on a round of poisoning," Delani said when a high-pitched shout startled them as they passed a room.

"Poisoning?" Honovi asked.

"Yes, how else do you think we become tolerant? It takes years to build up resistance."

Blaine hadn't given much thought on how wardens were trained, but the idea of being poisoned for years in order to survive in the poison fields and take on revenants left him feeling ill at ease. "Isn't most of Maricol cleansed?"

Delani shook her head. "Spores ride the winds and seep into ground water. A land can be cleansed for a generation, and the next will find it tainted again. We are always striving to record the poison levels in every quadrant we are assigned along borders to ensure Maricol's children do not succumb to the land. There are frontier towns that are here in summer and gone in winter because of poisoned mist and fog. Cleansed doesn't mean safe."

No wonder the Poison Accords was the oldest set of treaties on record. Wardens might not have a country, but they were a people still, one everyone else looked to for survival. That skill with poison and alchemy and dealing with the unknown was why they'd brought Nathaniel to them.

Still, it was a shock to see Nathaniel strapped down on a lab table, bared to the waist, putting the vivisection scars on full display. A warden was tending to the burn wounds on his arm and side when they entered the laboratory. Blaine had to grab Caris by the shoulder to hold her back from approaching the lab table, keeping her there by the wall with him and Honovi.

"What are you doing?" she cried out.

"Figuring out a puzzle," a warden wearing a leather apron said as she approached the lab table. She wasn't tall, her build wiry, and her features favored a Urovan ancestry even though Blaine knew wardens called no country home. "We aren't removing the clockwork heart."

"Yet," the other warden muttered.

"You won't be removing it at all," Caris snapped furiously, pulling against Blaine's grip.

"Ksenia," Delani warned.

The leather-apron-wearing warden looked over her shoulder at them, a white curl falling into her eye. She was perhaps close to Honovi's age, hair dark save for a thick white streak that cut at an angle over her head. Blaine wondered if she'd been born with that absence of color or if it had been acquired in the poison fields.

"Governor," Ksenia drawled. "If you want answers, we will need to cut."

"No," Caris snarled.

The bright burst of light that sparked at her fingertips had every warden in the laboratory shouting out a warning. "No magic!"

Ksenia glared at them, pointing a finger at Caris. "Control yourself, magician. We're running a lot of delicate experiments down here, none of which I want disrupted because you lack control."

Caris glared at her, still trying to shrug off Blaine's grip. "I'm no magician."

Ksenia shot her a withering look. "That was magic."

"It was *starfire*. Don't think I won't use it to protect him."

Blaine winced at that threat and how every warden in the laboratory came to attention, gazes snapping their way. Ksenia put down the needle and glass syringe she'd been holding onto a rolling tray table. She shoved her goggles up onto her head, white and black hair sticking out every which way.

"The governor may be in charge above, but down here is my realm, girl. I am the master alchemist, and my word is law. When I say you will control yourself, you will do so, or I will remove you," Ksenia bit out.

Caris opened her mouth to argue, but Blaine tightened his grip on her shoulder, giving her a gentle shake. "Calm down. Arguing is not going to get us anywhere."

"But they're going to hurt him!" Caris protested, trying to knock his hand aside.

Ksenia snorted. "He's sedated, and we're running tests. How else are we supposed to figure out what's going on?"

"You wanted our help," Delani reminded them. "We are experts when it comes to alchemy and mixing it with magic. Your friend is the first living *rionetka* we've had to observe. If you want us to find a way to possibly undo what was done, we will need to run experiments."

"I don't want him hurt," Caris said.

Delani gave her a pitying look. "He's already hurt. Now, stay back."

Ksenia watched them for a few seconds longer before turning her back on them. She rolled the tray table with its line of tools and vials over to the lab table, where she set about drawing some of Nathaniel's blood.

"We'll take his vitals and find a baseline for what he is now. A pity we don't have a control record from before he was changed," Ksenia said.

Caris stopped fighting against Blaine's grip, and he let her go after a moment. The three of them watched in silence, Delani guarding them, as the pair of wardens worked on Nathaniel's unconscious form. Machines were rolled out of large storage cabinets and winched down from the ceiling.

Ksenia was in charge as the master alchemist, but Blaine didn't miss the wand hooked to her belt. She was a magician as well, blending science and magic together, which was the cornerstone of alchemy on Maricol, one the wardens understood better than any academic in any university.

"You said all the clockwork metal hearts you've had before have broken. How will you keep his intact?" Blaine asked.

"We've mapped bits of the spells and have researched several foundations that could possibly build them, but we've never had an active version within our laboratories to study," Ksenia said, not looking up from the second blood draw she was performing on Nathaniel. "We know about the self-destruct aspect of the control mechanism and are prepared to work around it."

"You'll need someone well versed in mind magic. Whoever does this to people, their control goes deep," Honovi warned.

"We know." Ksenia withdrew the needle from Nathaniel's arm and inserted it into a vial that contained a substance at the bottom. She emptied the syringe before capping the vial and setting it aside. "Our initial examination will take a while. You can find something else to do."

"I'm not leaving him alone with you," Caris said.

Blaine sighed, sharing a glance with Honovi. If Caris was allowed to stay, then he would remain as well. Whether or not Nathaniel was unconscious and strapped to a lab table, he wouldn't risk Caris being in the same room as the other man, not when he was a *rionetka*.

"Will they be in the way?" Delani asked.

"Not if they stay quiet and stay where they are."

"Very well. I'm needed above. Radio me when you've some information."

Delani left, marching off to handle her duties as governor, whatever those might entail. Blaine, Caris, and Honovi remained in the laboratory, pressed up against the wall, watching as Ksenia and her assistant worked diligently for several hours. They moved between Nathaniel's unconscious body to machines and microscopes set up on counters around them.

The sound of the machines was a hum that came and went, pressed into purpose for exams that Blaine couldn't follow. He knew better than to ask their purpose, keeping quiet as Ksenia worked.

Blaine noticed when she must have found something. The way her shoulders went tight and how she waved her assistant over to confirm some result was impossible to miss. Caris picked herself up off the floor, brushing off her trousers. "What have you found?"

"What did I say about being quiet?" Ksenia said. She stood over Nathaniel, stethoscope still in one hand, wand in the other.

"But you've found something, haven't you?"

Blaine held out his arm when Caris would've stepped closer. She flashed him an annoyed look but settled back against the wall. Ksenia didn't answer, merely put down her tools and went to pick up the radio. "Governor, I need you back down here. Can you tell me if Petra is on the island still?"

The radio crackled after a moment, Delani's voice coming through a little broken due to depth. "She's not fully recovered and hasn't been assigned a border for the season."

"Good. Tell Petra to bring her cat with her."

"I'll locate her and bring them down."

Ksenia set aside the radio and returned to Nathaniel's side. She picked up her wand, the clarion crystal at the tip pulsing with a soft green-blue hue of magic. She kept it resting against Nathaniel's chest, right over where the scars crossed, rising and falling with every breath he took in unconsciousness.

Eventually, Delani returned, though she didn't arrive alone. On her heels was another warden, who walked with an obvious limp, a metal brace screwed in place around her right knee for extra support. But it was what came in behind both of them that had Blaine tensing.

When Ksenia had mentioned a cat, he thought it would be a living creature, like the sort noble-born women had as pets, long-haired and demanding. This, though, was no living creature that padded into the laboratory.

The clockwork cat was made of gears and metal plates, no wind-up mechanism in sight. Its bottle-green crystal eyes shone with an eerie light, strange head swinging their way, metal eyelids half closing as it seemed to stare at them. Blaine thought perhaps it was steam-driven, but it moved with a fluidity that not even automatons had. Flickering at its center was the illuminating presence of magic that gave life to its form in a disconcerting way.

"Since when do we perform autopsies on revenants?" the new warden, who must be Petra, asked.

"He's not a revenant," Ksenia said, eyeing the newcomers from across Nathaniel's bare, scarred chest. "He's a *rionetka*."

"A what?"

"Something enslaved," Delani said, proving to Blaine that the existence of *rionetkas* must not be well-known through the general ranks of wardens. "Have you found a control mechanism?"

Ksenia pursed her lips. "I've found a framework, and it's familiar."

"How so?"

"Petra, I need to borrow Tock."

Petra settled her hand on the dull brass metal between the clockwork cat's ears. "Why?"

"I won't harm its making."

"Let her have access," Delani said.

Petra appeared annoyed at that, but she still urged the clockwork cat forward. It went to sit by Ksenia, obedient in a way an automaton might be, but Blaine didn't trust it. It wasn't like Fred, left behind back in Amari, or any of the small clockwork devices he'd handled while teaching at the university.

Tock acted alive in a way that was highly unusual.

Caris ducked around Blaine and moved closer to the lab table. He missed grabbing her by mere inches, swearing softly under his breath. When the wardens didn't order her back to the wall, he and Honovi joined her. Beneath the lights, Nathaniel looked washed-out pale, the vivisection scars standing out starkly against his chest. The burns were wrapped, hopefully healing, but there was no magic or medicine that could heal what had been done to his heart.

Blaine watched out of the corner of his eyes as Caris reached for Nathaniel's limp hand, curling her fingers around his, unable to lift his arm, seeing as how it was strapped down by thick leather straps reinforced with metal. Her attention wasn't on the wardens but on Nathaniel's slack face.

"You know we couldn't figure out the spell structure of the broken hearts we've received before. The one in his chest beats just fine, and it resonates in a way I have only seen in one other device," Ksenia said.

She tapped her wand against Nathaniel's chest, and magic flowed from the tip, spreading down the length of his scars. It flickered in time to a heartbeat that Blaine couldn't hear, peeling up out of skin and scar tissue to latch together in a fine knot, forming in the air over where Nathaniel's heart used to be. He watched as Ksenia's magic shaped itself into a glittering image of a clockwork metal heart that pulsed like a real one. He wasn't a magician and didn't know what kind of spell she was casting.

Ksenia looked down at the clockwork cat that waited beside her. "Up on the table."

It vaulted onto the lab table, metal paws clattering loudly when it landed. It picked its way to seat itself between Nathaniel's strapped-down legs, strange, gear-made face tilted in Ksenia's direction. Its bottle-green eyes looked right at her, spring-tipped tail moving from side to side.

When Ksenia pointed her wand at it, Tock's plated ears flicked backward like a real cat's would, but it didn't move. The glow in its center—what magic animated it—filtered out over screws and plates and gears, rising out of its body like a fog edged in light.

Petra made a sound, reaching toward Tock. "Ksenia."

"Stand down. We need to know if the spells are similar. Let Ksenia cast the comparison one," Delani ordered.

Petra dropped her arm back to her side, face a wooden mask as they all watched the shape of a heart form over the clockwork cat in magical lines, eerily similar in design to the one that shimmered above Nathaniel's chest.

Ksenia looked across the table at Delani, expression grim. "This is warden's work."

Tock hissed, the sound like metal shearing, and the clockwork cat suddenly launched itself at Ksenia. Half the people around the lab table were wardens, used to reacting quickly and decisively to a sudden threat, but Ksenia was fastest. Magic snapped from her wand and slammed into the cat. It writhed in midair, gears grinding, before going limp, like a puppet with its strings cut. Then it fell to the lab table, half hanging off the edge between Nathaniel's feet, the weight of its design pulling it all the way over seconds later.

It clattered to the ground, nothing but gears, the glow of the aether that powered it fading in guttering flickers that eventually burned out.

The one in Nathaniel's chest kept beating, the image of its making that Ksenia had summoned for them to see keeping time in a steady rhythm.

CARIS

"Should you be down here?"

The warden who asked didn't move from their position guarding the heavy steel door to the laboratory Nathaniel was held in. Caris squared her shoulders and lifted her chin, looking the warden in the eye. "I was summoned by the master alchemist."

It'd been a surprise to receive the missive from a tithe, the young girl panting from her run across the island. Caris had just finished breakfast when the note had been delivered, Blaine and Honovi gone off on their own for the day as they had since their arrival.

The warden blinked at her before turning to rap his knuckles against the door, the sound ringing in the air around them. "The Ashionen is here for you."

Caris resisted the urge to shift on her feet as she waited. Less than a minute later, the door to the laboratory was pushed open, Ksenia peering at her through the crack. "Good. You came."

Caris stepped forward. "You said I could see Nathaniel."

"I need to run a test." The shrewd look in Ksenia's bloodshot eyes didn't comfort Caris at all. "You'll be helping me with it."

"A test?"

Ksenia pushed open the door to the laboratory, gesturing for Caris to enter. "It's taken round-the-clock work, but we've mapped the spell that keeps the clockwork metal heart beating. Back when Petra was first given Tock, she allowed several wardens to study it when she came in from the poison fields. We were able to work off those reports in the archives, and it helped cut down our research time immensely. We still have work to do, but I'm having difficulties with the mind magic portion of it. I need to see how he reacts with his trigger."

Caris' heart sank at that statement, but she entered the laboratory anyway. It was different from the one where the initial exam had taken place. It still had a wealth of machinery tucked out of the way, alchemist tools scattered across worktables. It was not unlike the laboratories Caris had worked in while at university, but none of them had what amounted to a cell built into the corner.

She took a step toward that walled-off space and the man who sat on the cot there. Two days since they landed and discovered the shocking origins of the spell that bound Nathaniel's will and Caris hadn't had a moment to herself or with him.

"Nathaniel," Caris said, his name unsteady on her tongue.

He stared at her through the bars, fingers plucking at the blanket wrapped around his shoulders. It was cool down in the underground laboratories, a chill never quite leaving the air. Someone had given him a shirt, the linen wrinkled and threadbare at the cuffs, but it covered his chest. Caris could admit that seeing the vivisection scars on his body left her wanting to cry.

"Caris," Nathaniel said, letting the blanket pool on the cot he'd been given as he stood. It revealed a metal collar around his throat, studded with clarion crystals. While it wasn't a bank number tattoo, it was still a reminder of his status.

She made to go to him, but Ksenia stuck her arm out, blocking the way. "Not yet."

"I just want a moment with him," she begged.

Ksenia shook her head, unmoved by Caris' pleas. "We need to discuss what must happen first. Follow me."

Ksenia led her to a door that opened up into an adjacent laboratory, one whose cabinets were filled with vials and jars of various liquids, neatly labeled with names that made Caris recoil. The amount of poison stored in the room could wipe out a small town. Growing up in the Eastern Basin, she was intimately aware of the dangers poison could inflict on a population.

She looked away from the cabinets, attention snagging on the exam table in the center of the laboratory. Gears were neatly lined up on it in the shape they'd been taken apart in, showcasing the remnants of the clockwork cat that had faithfully followed Petra around before it attempted to murder Ksenia. With the revelation that the clockwork cat and Nathaniel's clockwork metal heart shared a foundation —one apparently of warden origin—the alchemists had been working nonstop on the problem.

The knowledge had been like disturbing a beehive. Caris wasn't privy to the inner workings of wardens, but even she knew that their magic and science wasn't meant for the atrocity that had been done to Nathaniel and all other *rionetkas*.

Caris shivered when she looked at what remained of Tock, teeth set on edge from the discordant hum that rang at the very edge of her hearing. The clarion crystals used in the clockwork cat's creation certainly weren't pleased with being broken down to their components. It reminded her of the sound she'd heard when around Nathaniel after he'd arrived in Veran and before the orders that turned him into a puppet tried to kill her.

Ksenia shut the door but didn't lock it, crossing her arms over her chest as she stared at Caris. "You want to speak with him?"

"Yes," Caris said.

"Good. I need you to have a conversation with him when I'm not in the room. I need to see what the orders do." Ksenia peered at her with a keen gaze. Caris felt as if the master alchemist was taking her measure and finding her lacking. "You may discuss whatever you like. I will leave the laboratory, and you will remain in it."

"Are you certain he'll think we're alone?"

"I've set tracers into his mind to map the damage, matched to a clarion crystal in the lab. The chemicals we put into his veins will neutralize the self-destruct spell and allow for the spell to work for a limited time."

Caris' heart lurched in her chest. "You found a way to stop his heart from breaking?"

"I am a warden and master alchemist, princess. A warden's job is to undo a wrong. If I couldn't do that, I'm not worth the title the last governor gave me." She shrugged, never looking away from Caris' face. "It's not a cure, mind you, more of a temporary reroute that needs sustained application."

"I see." Caris eyed the dark circles underneath Ksenia's eyes that looked like bruises. "Have you even slept?"

"That's what stimulants are for. Now, what I need to know is how he acts when the orders are activated. Tock provided an illuminating map of the heart. I need you for the mind."

Caris bit her lip. "Will it hurt him?"

"I can't promise it won't."

There was no hesitation in Ksenia's answer, no attempts to prevaricate. Caris appreciated the warden's forthrightness, no matter how much it made her want to flinch. "What should I ask him?"

Ksenia shrugged before moving away from the door. "Whatever you like."

Ksenia tapped her free hand against the wand on her belt, the sturdy brass hilt of it extending from the casing. From what Caris had discerned, few on the island were magicians. She assumed the demographics here were the same as across Maricol—magicians simply weren't as numerous as the general population. The genealogies had recorded fewer and fewer over the generations. It made Caris wonder if there'd ever come a day when magicians ceased to exist.

If it ever came to pass, the wardens would still do their duty. Of that, she was certain.

Caris steeled herself before reaching for the knob, opening the door wide enough for her to slip back inside the main laboratory. Ksenia followed on her heels, making a show of rifling through a stack of folios before grabbing one and leaving for the hallway.

Nathaniel hadn't moved from his spot inside his cell. It was more a cage than anything else, the metal bars of equal length and height, bolted to the floor and laboratory walls in the corner. Caris could see a tray with empty dishes on the floor near a locked pass-through space.

She swallowed, crossing the laboratory on slow feet. "Hello, Nathaniel."

"I'm so glad you're safe," he said, sounding so much like himself that she ached. "The wardens won't let me out of this cage. I don't know why I'm being kept down here."

"It's to keep *you* safe."

Nathaniel curled his fingers around the iron bars that separated them, staring at her with an intensity that made her skin crawl. It wasn't *him* in that moment, there and gone in a flash. Nathaniel's expression softened, as if he'd seen her hesitation. "I'd never hurt you."

She had the ghost of bruises on her throat still from when he had. Caris swallowed against the memory of that horror and managed a tremulous smile. "I know. But the wardens are adamant you must stay down here. They're trying to help you."

"Why? What do they think I've done?"

Caris stepped closer to the cage, fiddling with the signet ring hanging from around her throat. "It's not what you've done. It's what was done to you."

"Nothing has been done to me. I don't know why the wardens have imprisoned me here, why you've let them." His voice became cajoling, all wounded eyes and a painful grimace on his lips. "You know what I've worked for, what my family has worked for. We're cogs. We believe in the Clockwork Brigade and what it stands for. Caris, I believe in *you*."

And *oh*, his words sounded so much like Nathaniel. So much like the man who'd encouraged her curiosity and called on her and never once tried to cage her. Caris found herself drifting closer, swaying toward him, wanting to believe the words he spoke were his own.

He moved so quickly, this *rionetka* he'd become. He thrust his arm through two of the bars, reaching for her, fingers skimming the air where her throat had been before Caris jerked back. She called starfire instinctively, the hot sparks of the aether flaring at her fingertips. Nathaniel never flinched from the heat, arm outstretched, grasping for her on orders of someone else. He stared at her and didn't know her, and Caris had to turn away, hand over her mouth to stifle the sound of a sob that wanted to leave her throat.

The laboratory door was flung open, and Blaine hurried through, racing to her side. "Caris! Are you all right?"

She threw herself at him, wrapping her arms around Blaine and burying her face against his chest. She squeezed her eyes shut against the tears that wanted to fall, gritting her teeth. "I hate Eimarille for doing this to him. What if she's done the same thing to my parents?"

She'd had nightmares of that last night, getting little sleep, still worried about her parents left behind in Amari. Thinking about what Eimarille had done to the people she cared about hurt in a way not even a broken bone could, because at least a bone could mend.

Blaine hugged her close, stroking a hand over her hair. "I'm sorry. You shouldn't be down here."

Caris stopped herself from wiping her nose on his shirt and sniffed hard before pulling back. "No, I needed to be. Ksenia needed my help."

Blaine frowned at her as he put her at arm's length and gripped her shoulders, looking her in the eye. "They're the experts here, not you. It's okay to walk away."

She wiped at her eyes, clearing her vision. "Walking away wouldn't solve anything. I'm needed here."

Ksenia had entered the laboratory again, along with another warden, both of them looking at the thin clarion crystal sliced a half centimeter thick, held between two padded clasps on the work counter. The delicate circles embedded in the crystal reminded Caris of tree rings. Cutting through all of those lines were fractal-like designs that rang, distantly, like a broken song to her ears.

It sounded like Nathaniel had—still did—ever since he'd come to Veran, she realized. Caris glanced behind her, seeing only worry in Nathaniel's eyes, no recognition of what he'd tried to do just now.

Blaine made a wordless sound before guiding her away from the cage and over to where the wardens stood.

"Are you done with her?" Blaine asked.

"For now," Ksenia said, not looking away from the clarion crystal.

"What is that for?" Caris asked, digging in her heels when Blaine would've guided her out of the laboratory.

"The crystals on the collar he wears were cut from this one to be spell seekers. They are connected. They mapped the mind magic in his head and relayed the pattern to this one. This"—Ksenia tapped a fingernail against the flat clarion crystal—"is what the compulsion spell looks like in his mind."

"It's a mess," the other warden said with an irritated sigh. "It will take weeks to try to unravel, and there's no guarantee we can replicate the undoing in his mind. One wrong notation and he'll be made catatonic or dead."

Caris could admit that none of what they spoke about made sense to her, but the only way through ignorance was by asking questions. "How will you map the pattern?"

"On the crystal?" Ksenia shrugged. "We have instruments that can measure the pitch of the song the fractal cuts give off. The discordant notes will be where the compulsion anchors sit, but we can't distinguish those until we've the whole of it marked off. Knowing where they are here means we could possibly find and undo them in his mind."

"But see here and here?" The other warden touched where the fractals branched off the crystal slate in patterned flares. "These areas have a different spell tied to it. You can tell by the pattern. Most likely, it's the one that keeps the clockwork metal heart beating. There's a chance undoing the mind magic will undo that spell, and the self-destruct portion of it will activate."

"So the status quo remains," Blaine said.

Ksenia tossed a withering glance his way. "If we were mere magicians, yes. But this is warden work, and there's alchemy involved. I've two wardens mixing a potion that will aid in altering his state of mind so that we may attempt to separate the two spells without triggering the self-destruct one."

Caris reached out and touched the slate, delicately tracing over the fractal patterns, feeling the edges of the magically made cuts beneath her fingertips. "I can hear the song."

Ksenia turned and stared at her in surprise. "You can?"

Caris nodded jerkily. "I always have. I always know where to cut. My father let me work in our company's laboratories since I was a young girl because I always knew how to shape a clarion crystal for any device. The crystals sing."

"Yes. They've sung throughout our entire history, but very few have ever been recorded having the ability to hear them." Ksenia looked back at the slate and narrowed her eyes. "Can you read this? Can you find the discordant notes?"

Caris traced her fingers upward, following the curls of Nathaniel's thoughts, wondering if any of them had been about her. "Yes."

"Good. You're working down here with us today. If you can map his mind, then perhaps we can free him within a few weeks rather than months."

"Are you sure?" Blaine asked.

"The song is the difficult part. If she can hear it, then that reduces the time by quite a lot."

Caris pulled her hand away and made a fist to hide the way it shook. "Set me up somewhere quiet, and I'll get started."

She'd do anything to help save Nathaniel, and if the saving of him helped others, so much the better.

HONOVI

"Here." Honovi set the bowls of Solarian spicy noodle soup down in front of Caris and Blaine, balancing the serving tray on his other hand. "You need to eat."

The prodding was more for Caris than for his husband. Blaine didn't look as if he'd been put through a clothes wringer and spat out, still needing another wash. The circles under her eyes were stark against her skin, dark hair pulled back in a queue, shorter strands curling around her narrow face.

She flinched at his words or perhaps at the noise in the refectory. The communal dining hall they were in was large, and nearly all the tables around them were filled with tithes and wardens. The line of those with meal trays waiting to be served their portions of the evening meal was still steadily streaming past the kitchen and its serving areas.

Honovi had noticed since their arrival that wardens ran everything on the Warden's Island: from patrols to kitchen duty to training to everything in between. They didn't employ any citizens from any country within the fort, maintaining a self-sufficient society dedicated to the protection of everyone else. Every job that needed to be done was done by wardens who were still healing from a stint in the poison fields, were retired, or were assigned permanent duties on the island for a length of time.

Their table was tucked away in a corner, surrounded by wardens as opposed to tithes. Honovi's airship crew were scattered throughout the room at other tables, having somehow made acquaintances with some of the wardens for the few days they'd been present.

He sat on Blaine's other side, placing the tray he'd used to carry the bowls onto the table. Ksenia was seated across from him, looking far more rested than Caris, despite both of them having spent all their time below in the laboratories, working on Nathaniel.

"How is everything coming along?" Honovi asked.

Ksenia took a bite of her salt-and-pepper pork chop and shrugged. "It's going quicker than it would, thanks to Caris."

"Oh?"

"I'm helping to map his mind using clarion crystal. Ksenia put the spellwork on the crystal, but I can hear the song. If we know the areas where the compulsion is tied to, Ksenia thinks she can undo it," Caris said.

"Will it work?"

"Not without alchemy intervention, and even then, there's a risk," Ksenia cautioned.

"If you fix him, it doesn't quite negate the risk of him leaving under someone else's control," Blaine pointed out.

Caris reached for her yogurt drink, the thickened liquid freshly made and one Honovi had chosen for his own meal to combat the spicy heat. "I've thought about that. The wardens have clarion crystals in storage, and they've the kind that Meleri has for the catacomb keys and maps."

Blaine made a surprised sound that had Honovi glancing at him. "How old is that crystal?"

Ksenia snorted. "Old enough to be useful. So will the map I'll have drawn for you to take with you."

"How will that work?" Honovi asked. Magic ran on his mother's side of the family, but he hadn't been graced with that power. He was no magician and made a better aeronaut. He'd lived around magic, though, been privy to how magicians practiced, and it had always fascinated him.

"The crystals will be paired from a whole. Caris will cut them, and I'll imbue them as well as the ink used to draw the maps with a tracking spell. They'll act as a compass when placed on the map. You'll be able to find Nathaniel no matter where he is."

"Until he loses the crystal or the person attempting to control him orders him to discard it."

Ksenia raised an eyebrow. "Mm. He'd have to carve into himself to get rid of it."

Honovi's hands went still in the process of twirling some noodles for a bite. "Come again?"

"Ksenia thought it prudent to implant the clarion crystal shard in Nathaniel's chest," Caris said flatly. She took a mechanical bite of her soup, slurping at the noodles, and wouldn't meet anyone's eyes.

"I take it you don't agree?"

Caris' voice was full of self-loathing when she spoke. "No, but I was overruled. I just wish it wasn't necessary."

"Will you tell him?"

Caris hesitated before shaking her head. "Ksenia thought it was better he didn't know so that he wouldn't end up hurting himself if he was controlled again. I'll carry mine on my necklace."

Honovi could only imagine the sort of bodily autonomy Nathaniel had lost and was still losing. It was a nightmare, no matter how one looked at it.

"The spell will be embedded in the grain of the crystal and will remain dormant unless paired with the map. It's subtle enough it should go unnoticed unless someone knows what to look for," Ksenia added.

"Can you make a set for me?" Blaine asked.

Ksenia tilted her head in Caris' direction. "For you and your charge?"

"Yes. I'll pay as needed."

"You don't have to do that," Caris protested.

"For my own peace of mind, I want to."

"I'll order another map from our cartographers and get Caris to carve you some crystals. I won't take payment," Ksenia said.

"Trying to clear a debt?" Honovi asked.

Ksenia's gaze was steady, face impassive. "The governor has told us to aid you. Consider this me following orders."

So, not out of the goodness of her heart, then, but a debt paid, if they viewed it as such, the way the Houses of Solaria might. Honovi couldn't say which would be better in the situation they'd found themselves in, but they couldn't really decline such an offer.

Dinner passed quietly after that, conversation reduced to nothing as they ate their fill. When they finished, they deposited their trays and dirty dishes in the collection bins, parting ways for the evening. Blaine followed him out of the refectory and into the cool night air, the breeze having a faint mountain chill to it despite it being well into Tenth Month.

Blaine laced their fingers together, and Honovi didn't need to think about keeping pace with him. The sun had gone down past the mountains some time ago, the sky dark enough now for the stars to shine through. Gas lamps lined the pathways, flickering steadily through orange-tinted glass.

"Want to head up to the wall? I've been stuck in the laboratories for most of the day, and it'd be nice to stretch my legs," Blaine said.

Honovi could well understand the desire to see the sky and stretch his legs. Since their arrival, they'd been confined inside the fort walls for their own safety. Honovi had spent hours exploring the area he'd been allowed into aboveground, the fort laid out much like any other military base.

He tugged on Blaine's hand. "I know a way up."

He led Blaine down a pathway that eventually merged into a narrow street. From there, it was easy enough for Honovi to find his way to the wall surrounding the fort and the nearest set of stairs that led up to it.

The way wasn't barred, though the top was guarded by a spider-like automaton. The boxy body with its miniature Zip gun attached spun around on its legs. Gears clicked over before it trundled closer to the outer edge of the ramparts, clearly deciding they weren't a threat.

"Their automatons are well-developed," Blaine said.

Honovi let go of Blaine's hand in favor of wrapping an arm around his husband's shoulders. He leaned in close to kiss Blaine's temple. "I don't think they'd let you pick one apart to look at the underlying engine."

"I could ask. I'm not doing much in the laboratories except watching Caris work."

Honovi laughed, guiding Blaine down the ramparts. The wall surrounding the fort was wider than the length of a motor carriage, providing enough space up top for them to walk side by side. Defensive towers rose up a single level in evenly spaced intervals, armed with weaponry. They passed through the arched entrance of one, bypassing an unmanned Zip gun.

He knew the Eastern Spine was a propagator of revenants the same way the Wastelands were. Spores weren't eradicated in those areas, and the dead—be they human or animal—had a tendency to rise again and look for the living. In the trailing edge of the mountains, the Celestine Lake was a draw, specifically for the island the wardens called home. The Zip guns and automatons on patrol with the night shift of wardens kept an eye on the land around the fort.

The moon was half-full, giving off enough light to reflect on the water of the lake. The Leviathan constellation had pride of place in the sky, and Honovi's gaze tracked the set of stars, mentally giving shape to the beast it represented.

"Do you think the wardens can free Nathaniel?" Honovi asked.

Blaine sighed, gesturing vaguely with his left hand. "Their alchemy is far more advanced than anyone else's, and I think they have a chance to undo it. It's not saving him, though. Not with what was done to his heart."

"They aren't condemning him to death, though."

"I think they see him as an interesting experiment over an actual person, but that may just be Ksenia."

"Do you trust they'll do right by whatever they find, even knowing one of theirs perpetuated it?"

"We can't blame all of them for the actions of one."

"Do they know who it was?"

"I think they have an idea, but they haven't been forthcoming about it."

Wardens kept secrets more than most, and with good reason. For all the good they did guarding borders and working in the poison fields to cleanse the land, they weren't always treated fairly. The stigma of poison and handling revenants was something they couldn't always escape, no matter the country. The clans dealt with spores and revenants more than most other countries save Solaria with its Wastelands. They knew what horrors wardens kept at bay, and wardens were always welcome.

Honovi steered Blaine over to the edge of the ramparts to lean against the wall overlooking the training grounds. He couldn't see much of anything past the glow of lights around the walls. Blaine leaned against him, a line of warmth against the cool air.

"If word gets out a warden created the *rionetkas,* that will put a target on their backs from people in governments across Maricol," Honovi said.

"Countries can't keep wardens out of their borders. The Poison Accords don't allow for that."

"But if people distrust them, governments could keep them out of cities and towns. Perimeter walls protect us. There will be those who argue wardens don't belong inside, not when they handle the dead so often."

"That aids no one."

"Are you sure?" At Blaine's questioning look, Honovi continued with "The last civil war between Daijal and Ashion ended up with over a hundred thousand dead. Who do you think dealt with the bodies and the revenants that rose from the battlefields? It certainly wasn't the armies."

"Wouldn't starfire have made a difference?"

Honovi shook his head. "The queen at the time only had a nominal amount. Some Ashionen historians blame her lack for the armistice that happened. The Iverson bloodline didn't have starfire to aid them. She could have theoretically won that war."

"But she didn't."

"By the time she agreed to go into the trenches, it was too late. Too many more people would have died on both sides. She opted for an armistice instead. After the civil war, the Rourke bloodline married based on genealogy records, not for love. They chose people for their ability to cast starfire or the strength of it in their bloodlines. Queen Ophelia could cast starfire, but not to the extent her children can. She meant them to be a deterrent."

Blaine snorted. "I don't think she'd be proud of the road Eimarille has walked."

"Agreed." Honovi absently rubbed his hand up and down his husband's arm. "But what does Eimarille gain by turning people against wardens? If she's intent on war, she'll need them just like they were needed during Ashion's first civil war. Otherwise, she puts her own troops at risk when revenants rise."

"She doesn't strike me as the type of person who cares about that."

"She'll pretend to and blame the wardens for a high death toll."

"Wardens are supposed to be neutral."

"Do you think that matters if everyone believes it was a warden who created the *rionetkas*? If the wardens are pushed aside, unable to do their duty, then the Ashion army that Meleri hopes will stand against Daijal will have to fight the living and the walking dead."

"Damn it." Blaine dragged his hand down his face before turning to wrap his arms around Honovi's waist, resting his forehead against Honovi's shoulder. "I want to say you're wrong, but I don't think you are."

Honovi turned to better hold his husband. "The diplomatic corps were certainly useful in showing me just how cutthroat politics can be."

That wasn't to say E'ridian politics were easy. Clans disagreed all the time, but Honovi wanted to believe no E'ridian would ever do what Eimarille had done when it came to controlling other people's lives. First the continued use of debt bondage, and now clockwork metal hearts. It was slavery, no matter how one looked at it.

"Caris needs to survive," Blaine said after a long moment where the only sound was the distant waves lapping at the shore and the hum of insects.

Honovi held him tighter, thinking of that long-ago night when Blaine had arrived in E'ridia, a refugee from a country that was still breaking apart.

"So do you," Honovi murmured.

He turned his head enough that he could see the night sky and the stars, sending a silent prayer to the star gods, asking for the only thing that mattered to him.

Honovi hoped they listened.

Five

VANYA

“I hear congratulations are in order,” Amir said as he joined Vanya on his walk out of the Senate building in the early afternoon.

“Nothing came of today’s deliberations,” Vanya said.

Amir smiled, matching Vanya’s pace, his metal-tipped cane clacking against the floor. Senate aides bowed as *praetoria* legionnaires guided them through the hallway. “Ah, but the House of Kimathi’s gathering this morning was not as robust as it could be.”

Vanya knew better than to show his pleasure at that and so bit back the smile he wanted to share. “I hadn’t heard.”

Taisiya had been set to appear at that gathering before the midday heat became truly unbearable. He’d expected to receive an update from his *valide* once he returned to the palace, but it appeared Amir had beat her to it. “My wife attended and rang my televox to let me know few of the major Houses deigned to appear.”

“We’ll see where they stand if they attend my gathering in a week’s time.”

Vanya knew they would. His majordomo had been fielding press inquiries, social invitations, and political requests since the moment Callisto had appeared in the Senate chamber the other week. By now, news of her favor had reached every corner of Solaria and quite possibly beyond. Broadsheets were still writing opinion pieces about the appearance, as it wasn't every day a star god showed favor. Innes had done so for Queen Eimarille mere weeks ago. Callisto's favor would certainly bolster Solaria when it came to international agreements.

"Might you have a moment this afternoon for a meeting about the Conclave?" Amir asked.

Vanya tilted his head toward the *vezir*. "For you, always."

The Conclave was still ongoing. Callisto's appearance had upended the guest list at every gathering since as Houses maneuvered between Vanya's grip on the Imperial throne and Joelle's false promises. Amir had been kept busy and away from the palace but had made himself available when needed. Certainly Vanya wasn't going to turn down his request, not when Amir had done so much to aid the House of Sa'Liandel.

Vanya led the way to his waiting motor carriage and its escort. He took the back seat with Amir, rolling the windows down to allow for a breeze to circulate through the vehicle. The drive back to the palace didn't take long, and someone must have been alerted to their return, for Taisiya was waiting for them, framed by the arched entrance that overlooked the forecourt.

She was still dressed in the elaborate summer gown she'd worn to the morning meal before leaving for the gathering at the House of Kimathi's estate. The shimmer of sheer gold-and-cream fabric was embroidered at the hem with crimson thread, depicting the Lion constellation. The jewelry she wore was all gold and rubies, a match for the ones in the crown Vanya wore.

"Ah, *vezir* Amir. Well met," Taisiya said. "Will you be staying on for the evening meal later?"

"Alas, my lovely wife has bid me return to our estate. His Imperial Majesty has granted me a meeting to discuss issues of the Conclave."

"I'll join you. My time at this morning's gathering was certainly interesting."

"As was Malia's."

"We'll meet in my office," Vanya said.

They waited in the foyer only long enough for the *praetoria* legionnaires to perform the physical inspection for scars on Amir, who never protested the precautions. Vanya kept an easy pace through the palace to allow for Amir's and Taisiya's slower steps. One of the many servants must have alerted the staff, for Alida was waiting for them outside his office, afternoon tea tray in hand.

"I thought perhaps you would like some tea for your meeting," Alida said, the many keys on her belt jangling softly as she straightened up.

"The gesture is appreciated," Vanya said as he entered his office.

Taisiya came in after him, with Amir mere steps behind. The moment Amir crossed the threshold, the spell-detecting device that Chu Hua had discreetly ordered placed in his office went off for the first time since it had been smuggled into the palace.

The device had been attached to the gaslight fixture in the ceiling, replacing the base of it, and painted to look like brass. Clarion crystals thought to be decorative glass pieces inserted into the light were now glowing a vibrant hue of purple in warning. The chime of the alarm built into the device rattled through Vanya's skull.

He froze for all of a second before whirling on his feet, facing his guests. Taisiya looked confused, as did Amir, while Alida had stopped just short of the threshold, still out in the hallway holding the tea tray. Two *praetoria* legionnaires bracketed her, having left their posts at the sound of the alarm, their pistols raised for a threat.

"What is that noise?" Taisiya asked.

Vanya's mouth went dry as he stared at her. "A warning."

"For what?"

He didn't answer. Instead, Vanya strode over to his desk to pick up the telephone. He pressed the button for the palace operator, who picked up almost immediately. "Put me through to Imperial General Chu Hua's televox."

The operator patched him through. The line rang several times before a click indicated it had connected. Chu Hua's calm voice filtered through to his ear. "Yes, Your Imperial Majesty?"

"Send me a magician you trust. It activated," Vanya said, teeth clenched tight as he stared at the two people who had done so much for his House lately.

"Expect us within the hour," Chu Hua replied before ending the call.

"Your Imperial Majesty?" Alida asked in an uncertain voice, her grip white-knuckled on the tray.

He stared at where she stood, out in the hall, and thought about the number of times his majordomo had flitted in and out of his office. The spell-detecting device had never triggered upon her appearance, but he could not take a chance with her.

"Put the tray down and remain here," Vanya said.

Alida nodded slowly before obeying, stepping inside to set the tray on his desk. She posted herself up in the corner, out of the way, watching them with wide eyes.

"What is the meaning of this?" Amir asked.

Vanya stared at him, wondering if there was something else other than *rionetkas* they'd have to worry about now. The satisfaction of knowing he had managed to outmaneuver Joelle was bitter in the wake of this uncertainty.

"Sit down, *valide*. You as well, *vezir*. There are things we must discuss." Vanya looked past them at the *praetoria* legionnaires who had taken it upon themselves to enter the office, their pistols trained on those who were supposed to be loyal to his House. "Send Soren to me."

"What is going on?" Taisiya demanded, hands curled tightly over the armrests of the chair she sat in.

Amir appeared just as tense, and Vanya let his attention linger on the *vezir* of the House of Vikandir. "A precaution."

Vanya curled his fingers loosely, as if to cradle starfire, and had to force himself to relax. He went behind his desk and sat in order to reach several hidden buttons that opened up a secret compartment. The seam of the small door was hidden in the grain of the wood underneath. When it unlocked, it barely popped free, and he had to use his fingernails to open the small door. Inside was a hidden space where he'd stored the spell-detecting device's control mechanism.

The square bit of metal and brass with its singular button and toggle was powered by a clarion crystal chip. The crystal in question was flickering the same purple as the ones in the device above. Vanya pressed the button to deactivate the spell-detecting device, and the alarm that had been sounding abruptly stopped.

The hallway outside his office had become quite crowded with *praetoria* legionnaires. It shouldn't have been a surprise when Captain Javier Molina shoved his way through. "Your Imperial Majesty!"

"I'm fine," Vanya said.

Javier swept his gaze around the office, hand resting on the grip of his pistol holstered to his hip, wand in his other hand. "We should move you."

"I'm waiting for Imperial General Chu Hua's arrival. This was a warning device we set up together. I'm in no danger."

"A warning device?" Taisiya repeated.

Vanya smiled thinly. "Yes."

"For what?"

"For *rionetkas*."

Taisiya recoiled, eyes going wide. Amir reacted the same, while Alida's head jerked up, a horror in her eyes shared by the other two. Vanya wondered, distantly, just how deep the mind magic went to make someone appear as they always had been, even when they weren't.

"Vanya," Soren said from the doorway.

Vanya's gaze snapped to Soren standing framed in the doorway between two *praetoria* legionnaires, one hand gripping the hilt of the poison short sword protruding over his shoulder. Vanya shook his head slightly, and Soren's arm fell down to his side as the warden came into the office. Soren's gaze flicked from those seated to the *praetoria* legionnaires before tracking upward at where he knew the spell-detecting device had been installed, the only other person outside Chu Hua and a single engineer to know where and what it was.

Soren's lips twisted slightly. "It went off."

"Yes. I don't know who triggered it. All present have supposedly passed the security examination," Vanya said.

The visual inspection for vivisection scars had been incorporated into the palace security since the attack at Oeiras. It wasn't foolproof by any means, but it had been a stopgap that had been working.

Or so he thought.

"You think *I* am a *rionetka*?" Taisiya demanded.

"I don't know what to think, *valide*."

She didn't press the issue, staring at him with narrowed eyes. Taisiya eventually folded her hands together over her lap and lifted her chin. "Very well. I won't hold your lack of faith against me."

Vanya's mouth twitched at the corners. "How kind of you."

He wanted to believe she'd been herself this entire time—that they all had—but it was so difficult to trust these days. Before it had merely been House games, and now it was so much more than that when one counted *rionetkas*.

"Your orders?" Javier asked after a moment.

"Stay your hand for the moment. This is no attack, and I don't want rumors to say as much."

Javier nodded and set himself up near Alida, wand still in hand, and barked out an order for the *praetoria* legionnaires to resume their normal positions. If they could keep the appearance of normalcy for now, that would be ideal.

"Raiah?" Vanya asked.

"Safe," Soren said.

Vanya nodded and leaned back in his chair, playing the waiting game with long practice. Eventually, Chu Hua arrived with several officers in tow. She bowed deeply to Vanya in greeting, and he quickly brought her up to speed on the situation.

Chu Hua narrowed her eyes before facing the others. "You will disrobe."

"We have already passed muster. Surely this is not needed?" Amir said.

"Surely your protestations would not be needed if you had nothing to hide, *vezir*. Strip, or we will do it for you."

Taisiya had stood, as her gown's ties were done up in the back and she was incapable of reaching them herself. She put her back to Soren, calm in the face of so many eyes, knowing what it meant when members of a House were pitted against each other. "I find I am in need of your assistance."

Soren went to her and picked apart the buttons that held her gown in place. The fabric of it fell down her shoulders, sliding to her waist, where she caught and held it. She kept her chin high amidst the eyes on her, meeting Vanya's gaze with steely intent. She carried no scars on her body, only the passage of time.

Javier stepped forward at a nod from Chu Hua and traced his wand around the shape of Taisiya's body before tapping her on the forehead. Her eyes went half-lidded, and she swayed on her feet. Soren put a hand beneath her elbow to steady her.

"She is herself," Javier said before stepping back.

"Satisfied?" Taisiya asked.

Vanya met his *valide*'s gaze and smiled grimly. "You know why I must be certain."

Taisiya inclined her head as she sought to redress herself with Soren's help. "For our House."

Amir had yet to stand, had yet to disrobe, while Alida's gown was pooled at her feet. Vanya gestured for Javier to see to Alida, focusing on where Amir sat, the older man calm in the face of so much attention.

"*Vezir*, I gave an order," Vanya said.

Amir huffed out a sigh, pushing to his feet with the help of his cane. He didn't protest, nor did he ask for help to undo his robes. The fabric parted, revealing the wide expanse of his hairy chest, no scars to be seen.

Vanya stared him down. "Disrobe."

There was a moment of hesitation, just enough that could be played off for the older man needing balance with the aid of his cane, but Vanya had not lived so long by trusting in someone else's lies. He tensed, but it wasn't Javier who came to his unspoken disquiet. Soren moved from Taisiya to Amir and gripped the edges of the *vezir*'s robes from behind, pulling them back over his shoulders.

Amir's protesting cry was drowned out by the horrified gasps of those in the office with them. Vanya stood, hands pressed flat against the top of his desk as he stared at the mess of scar tissue carved into Amir's skin that peeked out from beneath a veil sewn into his chest. The play of magic was difficult for his eye to hold, but it didn't matter, not when the truth cut so deep.

The House of Vikandir had been compromised.

Six

TERILYN

Calhames in summer was hotter than New Haven, a temperature change that made Terilyn glad for the Solarian robes she wore rather than the closely tailored design of Daijalan fashion. She did not look out of place amidst the staff that scurried around the House of Kimathi's estate, though she was by no means employed by Joelle. Terilyn took her role as oversight seriously and so remained in Joelle's office despite Artyom's clear desire to have her elsewhere.

"What do you *mean* they've uncovered the *rionetka*?" Joelle hissed into the telephone receiver.

Terilyn cocked her head to the side, straining to hear the voice on the other end of the call. They'd been in the midst of a meeting when one of Joelle's handmaidens had interrupted to send the call through to Joelle's telephone. The *vezir* seemed displeased by whatever news had been relayed.

She mentally ticked through the problems it could be and ultimately decided it wasn't about any of Eimarille's orders. They didn't have *rionetkas* operating in the Imperial court. They'd pulled the handful from other areas of government after the destruction of the laboratory in the quarry and the Imperial general's attempts at uncovering them.

"Are they suspicious of you?" Joelle asked. "Good. See that they continue to be ignorant of your place. I will notify you through the usual measures when my plan is in motion."

She ended the call by dropping the receiver into the cradle, dark eyes snapping with anger. Terilyn studied the old woman. "Bad news, *vezir?*"

Joelle's gaze cut toward her, mouth twisting. "I have been reliably informed that the *rionetka* the *Klovod* recently made for me has been discovered."

"The star priestess?"

"No. Those are still within our control."

"Someone of the Houses, then? The Conclave is still ongoing. Who have you sought to control?"

The sour expression on Joelle's face told Terilyn she'd guessed correctly. Solarian politics weren't her politics, but that didn't mean Terilyn wasn't a student regardless. Words were just as sharp as the bladed weapons she carried on her person, and she'd learned that lesson well when standing by Eimarille's side at the Daijal court.

"I sought to mitigate our social losses after the Dawn Star's appearance. It seems my efforts have been cut short."

"Can it be traced back to you?"

Artyom curled his lip. "If it can, then the blame will be placed on the *Klovod*."

Terilyn smiled, lips cutting against her teeth. "I doubt that. The choice in target falls to you. If you missed in that area, it is no fault of the *Klovod*."

"We—"

"My queen allowed for the *Klovod* to come south to aid your attempts at keeping everyone's attention *here,* in your capital, rather than the border that separates our countries. Do not mistake allowance for ownership. The *Klovod* gives aid on our orders, not yours."

Artyom snapped his teeth together at a glare from his mother. A pity. If the man had continued on his chosen topic, Terilyn would have opted to take offense in Eimarille's name and dealt with such insult by carving a line through his throat.

Joelle still had a daughter, angry as Karima was at being replaced. Artyom was less malleable than Karima, but Terilyn played with the cards dealt her. She turned to face Joelle in a motion meant to dismiss Artyom without fully putting her back to the man.

"We allowed the *Klovod* to come and replace the *rionetkas* you inelegantly lost searching for your great-granddaughter, who recently returned to the capital despite your best efforts to catch her," Terilyn continued. "We never condoned using him to take a member of a House."

It wasn't because Eimarille thought the Houses were impossible to infiltrate, merely that they were difficult to control. Unlike most other foreign ranks of nobility, the Houses could split any which way, with loyalty breaking and reforming along all manner of social and political lines that could change on a whim and end in death. The Houses weren't anchored to one way of thinking, even amongst those who claimed the title of *vezir*. Loyalty was currency, and the Houses spent it every which way they could.

Ultimately, the Houses preferred dealing with power exchanges through murder, and Eimarille was loath to risk the *rionetkas* they used for political gains that could not be guaranteed. Aside from that, the social bathing culture in Solaria meant such scars the *rionetkas* carried would be nearly impossible to hide, even if they could afford to dole out veils for every *rionetka* made.

Eimarille had been forced to infiltrate Solaria in other ways, though Terilyn was beginning to think the outreach to the House of Kimathi wasn't worth the headache. But her queen still found Joelle useful.

For now.

"It was necessary."

Terilyn arched an eyebrow. "Was it?"

Joelle's glare could have flayed iron it was so heated. She did not give in to her wrath, though. "I have handled the Houses how I see fit. *You* are not Solarian. Don't pretend you know our ways."

"And now the House of Sa'Liandel has been made aware of someone's effort to infiltrate a House allied with theirs. I'm certain the emperor will feel obligated to search out the perpetrator, and it may lead him to your door."

Joelle's lip curled at that. "We will not be here for such accusations."

"The Conclave is not finished."

"It finishes in a week with Vanya's gathering."

"My understanding was the Conclave would finish at the end of Eleventh Month. The month has barely begun."

"The Dawn Star's appearance has moved up my agenda."

"Has it now?" Terilyn hummed wordlessly. "What of the star priests?"

"The key has been obtained and copied, no one the wiser. The secondary defense will be accessible to us as well. We have the papers that will get my people past security and gain us access to the star temple."

"Forged?"

Joelle shook her head. "Completely authentic. My spy in the household was able to obtain what was needed. We are *prepared*. I do hope your queen is satisfied."

The words were bitten out, Joelle clearly annoyed at having her authority questioned. Terilyn didn't care. She was here to see her queen's will done. "If anyone you assigned to this endeavor is a *rionetka,* they will be removed from the plan. My fellow Blades will take their place."

"My plan is *set*."

Terilyn's smile was small and tight, displeasure seeping into her voice like poison. "No, it is not. Your plan is mine to change as I see fit. The palace will be putting security measures into place because you tipped your hand early. You should have waited to infiltrate the *praetoria* legionnaires. Then you turned a House member into a *rionetka* and sent them into the one place they should *not* have gone. The House of Sa'Liandel is on guard because of your actions."

"And you think your Blades will do better?"

"Blades have taken out a government before. What makes you think we can't do it again?" She let the reminder of Ashion's past settle between them like a promise, holding Joelle's gaze. Terilyn was not the first to look away, and she nodded slightly at that win. "My fellow Blades will handle this task. They're well suited to it. You, however, will find an excuse to leave Calhames."

"If I leave before the Conclave is over, the Houses will see it as mine giving in."

"If you stay, you'll die."

"Your queen would like that."

"She'd like many things," Terilyn said lightly.

She didn't elaborate on what those wants were, and Joelle didn't ask. Terilyn left the office without another word, finding handmaidens and a Blade waiting in the room beyond. The handmaidens entered the office while the Blade fell into step beside her. Witten was dressed in nondescript robes of someone not worth a second glance. The look was intentional.

"Check our munitions and ordnance supplies that I brought with me. We'll be handling the excavation, not the *vezir*. And find out which star priests will be handling the delivery. If they are *rionetkas*, remove them. If they are not, then set our magicians to them to make sure they are loyal," Terilyn said in a low voice.

"And those who belong to the House of Kimathi?" Witten asked.

Terilyn pursed her lips. "Leave them in place for now. They still have a purpose."

Joelle may have been forced to stop playing fast and loose with *rionetkas*, but Terilyn wouldn't put it past the woman to try to sabotage Eimarille's plans in favor of her own. Terilyn was here to see that didn't happen.

NATHANIEL

Nathaniel woke up disoriented, the world wider than it had been, pain a deep ache he felt in his bones. He sucked in a breath, air catching in the back of his throat, and he held it, lungs locking up at the half-formed thought running through his mind.

His body listened to him.

It *listened.*

He snapped his eyes open, the order one he was sure came from him, blurred vision taking in an unfamiliar ceiling. He tracked his gaze from one corner to the other, giddy in a way that left him light-headed even while prone—*this was him.*

This was his body.

He unstuck his tongue from the roof of his mouth, swallowing convulsively. The taste was horrendous, all chemical traces that would not wash away. Nathaniel gagged and tried to roll over but found that he couldn't. Panic gripped him, made him gasp and pull against the restraints holding him down.

A cool hand touched his forehead, and a face bent over his, blocking out the light. "Shh, shh. It's all right. Calm down. You're still recovering."

Nathaniel forced his vision to focus, eyes watering as he stared up into Caris' beloved face and—couldn't stop the wordless, guilty moan that slipped past his lips. He tried to move away from her touch, but Caris never lifted her hand. The tremulous smile on her face wasn't one of joy but of exhausted worry. It widened once she realized he was tracking, that he was awake.

"Sorry," Nathaniel finally got out in a scraped-raw voice. "I'm sorry."

She stroked her fingers over his forehead, trailing down to his temple. "It wasn't you."

But it had been, and he'd have to live with that for the rest of his life.

However long it was.

"What do you remember?" Caris asked.

He closed his eyes, unable to meet her gaze. Most of the blank spots in his mind were gone, impossibly filled up again with moments he'd rather forget. "What I did to you…"

"It wasn't you," Caris repeated. "I know it wasn't you."

Nathaniel opened his eyes when something cool and wet dropped onto his cheek. Caris' eyes were watery, the skin beneath them bruised dark from little sleep. He wanted so very much to hold her, to wipe her tears away, but all he could do was lie there, weak and in pain and riven with guilt.

"It was my hands," he managed to say.

"It wasn't your intent."

As if that mattered. As if the insidious control that had suffused his entire being had cared about *intent*.

"Ah, he's awake," a new voice said. "Let's sit him up."

Caris smoothed his hair back away from his eyes one last time before stepping back, out of sight. The clanking grind of gears filled the room, and the table he was lying on moved. His head rose up as his feet sank down, the table tilting to an angle that let him better see the room they had him in.

It was a laboratory, he realized, different from the one he'd been caged in. Those memories were flashes in his mind, like bits of shattered glass, glimpses of a fractured whole. But he remembered enough to know that Caris shouldn't be around him. He tried to think back further than that, but much of it was difficult to grasp. The more he prodded at the memories, the more gaps he became aware of.

Movement caught his eyes, and he stared forward. The warden who planted herself in front of him had been there from the beginning of his stay here below. She studied him with the distant, exacting attention of an alchemist running experiments, with himself the puzzle at her fingertips. He certainly felt like one.

"What do you remember?" Ksenia asked.

It seemed to be the question of the hour, and while his recent memory felt like a sieve, there was one that cut through it all like the sharpest blade. He doubted he'd ever forget it; the healing burns on his arm and torso would never let him. "Caris shouldn't be here."

"So you remember that. What else?"

"Ksenia," Caris said tiredly.

The warden held up her hand, and Caris lapsed into silence. "The compulsion set upon your mind was extremely intricate. It was chemical-based and aether-made, powered by the clockwork metal heart in your chest."

"Did you take it out?" Nathaniel rasped.

Ksenia's mouth thinned into a hard line. "The compulsion? It's been unraveled from your mind, but I couldn't remove it completely. It's tied too closely to the other spells that keep you alive. Your mind is your own again, for now, but not without some damage to some of your recent memories, though I was able to recover others. As to your clockwork heart? No. It remains inside you."

Nathaniel closed his eyes and let his head fall back against the slanted table, breathing in through his mouth. He held it in his lungs, stoppered up, listening as the pulse in his ears pounded overloud like drums through every inch of his skin. He'd not been able to focus before, but now he could *hear* the difference, subtle as it was. He could feel it as well, had been able to sense that cold weight in his chest since leaving Amari. "Why aren't I dead?"

Caris' cool fingers wrapped around his clenched hand, and when he opened his eyes, she was looking right at him, bottom lip bitten raw between her teeth. "Because I couldn't live with myself if I left you as you were."

"I'm a danger. To you, to the Clockwork Brigade—"

"I know what to listen for now," Caris cut in. "I know what a *rionetka* sounds like. And if it can be undone, why wouldn't I try to help you?"

"Will it *stay* undone?" He dragged his gaze away from Caris, focusing on Ksenia, who didn't bother lying to him how anyone else would have. For that, he was grateful.

"We don't know. The framework of the compulsion spell is etched into your clockwork heart, along with the self-destruct one. There is always a risk you can again become what they made you," Ksenia said.

He licked his lips, dry skin catching on his tongue. "A puppet."

"Yes." He couldn't hear pity in her voice or see it in her eyes. The warden looked at him from the precipice of a life lived in the poison fields and all the uncertainty and danger that road offered. No, there was no pity in her gaze, only a tired sort of understanding that made bile crawl up his throat.

He swallowed it down.

From one puppet to another—*rionetka* or tithe, the syllables meant the same thing—they both had their roles to play, a road to walk.

A life to live, if one could call it that.

Caris picked at the leather strap of the cuff holding his left wrist in place. "Let's get you out of here. You've been down here for almost two weeks and haven't seen the sun."

"I shouldn't be around you," he protested.

Her gaze snapped up to his, gray eyes wide in her face and filled with a steely sort of determination that he'd never had cause to doubt. "None of this was you."

She ducked her head, working on the restraints that kept him bound to the table. Both Caris and Ksenia were there to help him off once they were undone. His legs didn't want to hold him up, shaky and weak from days of experimentation. The clockwork metal heart in his chest steadily beat as he went down to his knees, cradled in

Caris' arms. She kept him upright, her grip tight, and Nathaniel found himself curling into her touch.

"You need to be careful." She ran her fingers through his dirty, sweaty hair and pressed a chaste kiss to his forehead. "The wardens don't know how long their magic and chemicals can keep your heart going. The self-destruct spell was rerouted and contained within the clarion crystals but not eradicated. It was too dangerous to try. Nathaniel..."

Her words came out in a whisper, the fear in them louder than if she'd screamed. Nathaniel curled one arm around her waist, fingers scraping over the cool leather of her corset belt. Yes, the wardens had given back his mind and control of his body, but the specter of death lingered in what passed as his heart.

If he wanted to save himself—to save *her*—he'd walk away from Caris, from the Clockwork Brigade, to find some distant corner of Maricol where perhaps the tangled strings of a puppet master's control could never find him. He didn't think anyone would blame him if he did, but that wasn't how his parents had raised him.

Nathaniel lifted his head and touched his fingers to Caris' jaw, urging her to look at him. He brushed aside some of her dark hair to better see her eyes, managing to dredge up a smile somehow. It cracked the edges of his mouth, dry lips bleeding a little.

"I will love you until my heart breaks," Nathaniel promised.

Caris' expression crumpled, and when she kissed him, there on the laboratory floor deep below ground, he could taste the salt of an ocean on her lips, and it drowned him.

Eight

CARIS

Caris wiped her clammy hands on her trousers beneath the table where no one in the room could see. Blaine sat on her right and Honovi beside him. Nathaniel was elsewhere, Delani

having been adamant he wasn't allowed to be present during their meeting because of what had happened to him. She didn't trust him, even if Caris wanted to. It wasn't his fault, after all, but she could understand why the wardens wanted to keep him ignorant of their plans.

Delani had a spot at the head of the table, and every seat left was filled by wardens, with yet more standing against the wall. She recognized a few. The intensity of everyone's attention was not unlike when she'd presented her graduation project for final approval.

Laid out in the center of the table were the broken pieces of what had once been the clockwork cat belonging to Petra. The warden in question was seated at the table, her face an eerie emotionless mask. Whatever her feelings on the destruction of the clockwork device that had been by her side for years, apparently, it wasn't enough to make her leave.

"The *rionetkas* are based on our alchemy, our science twisted for someone else's gain. The same spell that powered Tock and gave it life is the framework for the one keeping Nathaniel breathing," Delani said.

"Olet died in the poison fields," Petra said.

"How do you know if a warden is truly dead rather than run off?" Blaine asked. Caris winced at the rude looks thrown his way. It was a tactless question to ask, but it had to be voiced.

"Wardens have a duty, and we are trained never to abandon it," Delani said.

"Surely some must have in the past? Your dead who never return?"

The archivist—a warden in her eighth decade whose sole job was to record the names given to tithes, their time as a warden, and their deaths—had her finger on a line in a massive tome with yellowed pages. "Olet was recorded as dead fifteen years ago. He'd been assigned the northern border of Daijal at the time. The way station in his section never received his border reports."

Delani sighed, folding her hands together over the table. "We allot three years to be certain a warden is deceased. Sometimes we are able to find bodies, lost vehicles, and tools. Mostly, we find nothing."

Because even supposedly cleansed land had its risks and dangers. Caris had seen enough of that in the Eastern Basin.

Honovi eyed the archivist's book. "You said Daijal. Was that always where he was sent?"

The archivist ran her finger across the row to a different column. "According to the records, most of the time. He occasionally handled the northern span of the center border between Daijal and Ashion."

"We don't switch up borders between wardens often unless there are problems that need further addressing. If the land is growing more toxic, we'll send a team of wardens to handle the alchemy needed for a cleansing. If there's a settlement turned into revenants, we'll send support. But wardens know the borders they guard year after year. They know what's out of place beyond the chemical records they bring back," Delani said.

"But there's nothing stopping a warden from walking away and becoming a civilian of any country," Honovi pressed.

"The countries of Maricol would not be what they are today if wardens consistently left as you are suggesting."

"You said it was warden work that created the *rionetkas*. Nathaniel said the one who performed the operation looked like a warden. This *Klovod* could be one," Caris said. She had no skill with mind magic, but Ksenia had been able to uncover some of his memories the *Klovod* had tried to hide. They were flashes, glimpses, really, of a scarred face, Nathaniel had said, and a name.

He didn't remember the operation itself. Trauma, the warden had told her. Sometimes the brain refused to remember some things, burying those moments so deep no amount of mind magic could draw them to the surface. But he'd given them a name—the *Klovod*—and that was more than what they'd had before leaving Veran. It was information they needed to send back to Meleri and the others, but Caris didn't trust sending it over wire.

This was a message that needed to be relayed in person.

Delani shook her head. "Whether or not he is one, it's our teachings that have been used to harm. We cannot turn our backs on that."

"So what will you do? Will you ally yourself with those fighting against Daijal?"

"We are neutral."

"Neutral won't mean anything if Eimarille conquers the continent."

It was strange to think Eimarille could be—*was*—her sister. Caris couldn't understand how someone who claimed to be a Rourke would do such harm to their people.

"The Poison Accords have stood through Ages and war before, as have wardens. This will be no different."

The wardens around the table nodded agreement. Caris couldn't fault them their loyalty to a way of life that let others live, but this time was different. Of that, she was certain. The Age of Progress had been a long one, and the star gods typically didn't show their favor until it was time for a new Age. She didn't want to be the catalyst for something new, but Caris doubted she'd get a choice in the matter.

"While we are incredibly grateful for your aid in helping

Nathaniel, this is information we need to get back to Fulcrum," Blaine said after an uncomfortable silence. "When we find more *rionetkas,* we would like to bring them to you."

"Your politics aren't ours," Delani said.

"*Your* politics infringed on our sovereign rights," Honovi said sharply. "My country's Seneschal was made a *rionetka*. That was only possible by your own admission. It was warden work that did harm. It should be warden work that undoes it as much as possible."

"Wardens are neutral. We guard the borders. We cannot pick sides under the Poison Accords."

"Your neutrality doesn't absolve you of aid." Honovi stood, leaning his weight against the table, dark eyes snapping with anger. He commanded the room with an ease Caris couldn't help but be envious of. "Word will get out that one of yours perpetuated this horror. Whether it was on Eimarille's orders or someone else out of Daijal, you cannot escape the ties the *Klovod* wove with her. Daijal is a threat to all of us. If you ignore that, if you ignore what your alchemy wrought, then you damn the world you're so hell-bent on saving."

The silence in the conference room was tense, most of the wardens appearing displeased by the accusation, though Delani had grace enough to look resigned.

"How will breaking the Poison Accords further aid any of us?" Delani asked. She held up her hand when Honovi sought to argue, silencing him momentarily. "We know Daijal is a threat. I've had wardens watching the Daijal court for years since the Inferno. It is not the only court we keep an eye on. Your politics leave bodies behind, and *we* are tasked with cleaning up those messes. We are *trying* to contain what damage we can find."

"Not well enough," Honovi bit out. He pushed away from the table, jerking his head at the door. "This is information I can't deny my people from knowing. Our Seneschal deserves the same chance you gave Nathaniel. If your duty is to Maricol and her children, then you won't decline the *Comhairle nan Cinnidhean*'s request when it comes."

Delani stared at him with an unblinking gaze and promised nothing in her silence. Caris wasn't politically savvy enough to know how the fallout would be dealt with those affected. Meleri would, perhaps, but she wasn't here.

"We thank you for your aid, but we must get back to Ashion," Caris said, drawing the room's attention. "I would ask for a supply of pain pills for Nathaniel and the authority to request such from resupply stations."

She knew an apothecary would not be able to mix the cocktail of chemicals Ksenia had come up with to medicate Nathaniel over the course of attempting to undo what the *Klovod* had done. Chemists weren't the same as alchemists, and wardens were in their own class compared to any who would call themselves such in any country.

Nathaniel hadn't complained much, but she'd seen the pain lines etched into his face when he thought no one was looking. Caris wanted to have the medication on-hand even though Nathaniel was adamant about not taking it, fearful of becoming dependent. The medication was of a strength she was certain only hospitals would be able to dispense, and even then, only under strict observation.

Ksenia shoved her chair back with a huff. "I made enough pain pills to last you to Twelfth Month. They lose potency after that, and you'll need a new batch. It'll be winter at that point, and a resupply station will be easier to reach rather than trekking back here. I'll issue an alchemist's script for you."

She didn't ask for permission, and no one protested her decision, not even the wardens' governor. Caris stood from the table as Honovi turned to address them. "I'll get the *Celestial Sprite* ready for launch. We can leave within the hour. Meet us at the hangar once you have everything."

"I have a few more questions, if the wardens' governor doesn't mind," Blaine said, remaining seated.

Delani waved a hand at him. "We'll continue."

Caris figured Delani would be happy to see them gone as much as they would be to leave. She followed Ksenia out of the room and down the hall to where Nathaniel waited at the far end on a bench. He stood when they stepped out of the room, waiting for them to approach.

"We're leaving the island," Caris told him.

"So soon?"

"We accomplished what we needed to by coming here, and there is news people must hear."

Nathaniel offered his arm, and she curled her hand over the bend of his elbow. They followed Ksenia down hallways and stairs toward the exit. The mechanical fans didn't do much to cool the heavy air inside, and it was almost a relief to leave the building. The sun was past its zenith, sliding into the early afternoon. Their flight west would chase the sun for hours.

"Will every resupply station have the chemicals to make the pain pills?" Caris asked as they walked.

"Caris," Nathaniel sighed.

"You don't always have to take them, but I want them to be available when you feel you need to."

"The smaller resupply stations most likely won't. You'll be better off sourcing the medicine from one in a city. Supplies there are more likely to be in stock. The pills only help with the pain, though. As I've said before, they aren't a cure," Ksenia said.

Nathaniel grimaced. "I know they won't stop me from being controlled again. Is there anything that could?"

"We need to research the spell construction more. If the *Klovod* gets his hands on you again, he'd be able to take control. The clarion crystal Caris wears will let her know if the control has returned, so at least your people will have a warning."

Caris couldn't stop herself from lifting a hand to touch the slight lump beneath her blouse that was Nathaniel's ring and several shards of clarion crystal. One was a small oval-cut piece marked with the fractal base pattern of his mind. The pale rose color would bleed red if the *Klovod*'s control returned. The pendant acted like the tip of a clarion crystal–tipped wand, the focus for the aether-backed magic that Ksenia had performed. It was a different cut from the shard that had been spelled to act like a compass. Nathaniel still didn't know about that one, hidden in his chest.

"I'll keep watch," Caris promised.

She meant it to be comforting, but she knew all the ways that the precautions could be subverted—that Nathaniel could be subverted, as he already had once before.

The entrance to the laboratories was inside a squat building whose thick walls and slanted roof were made of concrete and metal. The lines etched into every available space weren't images of constellations but precisely laid containment spells meant to hold in all manner of disasters that might befall the laboratories below.

The building was always guarded, both by wardens and by automatons. The bipedal machines with their Zip gun arms recognized Ksenia and didn't so much as twitch in their direction. The heavy metal door with its wheeled lock wouldn't be out of place in a bank vault. Few wardens had keys to the entrance, as it was a restricted location, but Ksenia was the warden in charge of the laboratories below. Her key gained them entry into the building, the baked-in heat of the space like an oven.

Caris started to sweat almost immediately, waiting as patiently as she could for Ksenia to open the solid metal door built into the ground. This, like the ones set into the building, was reminiscent of a vault door or, perhaps, the entrance to a bomb shelter. The door, when it broke apart in the middle and rose open on quiet gears, was even thicker than the one leading to the building.

As safety measures went, Caris wasn't sure if it was to keep people in or out. Considering what was done in the laboratories—tithes made into wardens, dangerous experiments on poison, to say nothing of the revenants that were dissected—she supposed it didn't matter, so long as the doors could be locked and hold against a threat.

They descended into the laboratories, the air cooling as they went. Ksenia led them to a laboratory whose setup wouldn't be out of place in an apothecary. The wardens working on mixing chemicals barely looked up at their arrival, each wearing goggles and gloves, though no gas masks. Caris absently touched the gas mask hooked to her corset belt, assuring herself it was still there.

"The chemicals used in the pills have an aether base due to magic, but it won't interfere with the spells keeping your clockwork heart beating and the self-destruct spell at bay," Ksenia said.

Ksenia passed over a tin rather than a jar, a multitude of tiny, pale green pills piled inside. Nathaniel took it with fingers that didn't shake, staring at the warden. Caris so very badly wanted things to be different than they were, but that was an impossible prayer to be answered.

Nathaniel swallowed audibly. "Thank you. For everything."

"Don't thank me. What was done to you is an abomination that should not have been created. Consider this an attempt to right a wrong."

Nathaniel nodded and tucked the tin into his trouser pocket. He opened his mouth, but whatever he was going to say was cut off by a terrible, echoing boom that thrummed through the walls of the underground laboratory. The floor didn't shake, but Caris instinctively braced herself even as she hunched her shoulders.

"What was that?" Caris asked, looking at the ceiling. "A training class?"

Ksenia stared upward, eyes narrowing, one hand reaching over her shoulder for the poison short sword strapped to her back and the other for the wand at her hip out of what must have been pure reflex. "No. We don't train with ordnance on the main island."

Caris sucked in a breath. "Ordnance?"

Before Ksenia could respond, the only aether light in the laboratory not switched on suddenly flared to life, shining through crimson glass as small mirrors spun around it at the base, eliciting a flashing effect. Then a sound rolled through the underground laboratories like a wave, pulsating in her ears, the tones of a warning siren something Caris knew in her bones.

"It's an attack," she breathed.

She didn't have to think very hard about who must have ordered it.

Nine

BLAINE

Blaine was in the middle of arguing a point—salient, in his mind, about how E'ridia would perceive the wardens' actions, or lack thereof, when it came to his country's situation with the Seneschal—when the entire building *shuddered*. He jolted in his seat as the roar of an explosion too close for comfort echoed through the walls.

The piercing warning sirens that ripped through the air seconds after sounded closer, one right outside the conference room, but that felt a little too late in his opinion.

"What was *that*?" Blaine got out as he stood.

No one answered him, most of the wardens already racing out of the room, shouting at each other about things he didn't understand. Others raced down the hallway outside the room. A warden who hadn't been in the meeting skidded to a stop in the doorway, looking at him. Raziel waved her hand at him, scowling. "Come *on*! You can't stay in here."

"Is it revenants?"

"Revenants don't have bombs" was her acid retort.

He sucked in a breath, hand brushing against the grip of his pistol before he unholstered it. If it was bombs, that could only mean one thing. "Do you have defenses?"

Raziel's look was scornful. "We're *wardens*."

Who were, to a person, the last line of defense against Maricol and all the poison and spores the planet had to throw at them. He didn't doubt they'd know how to guard their home. He only hoped it would be enough against whatever force Eimarille had sent east, for it could be no other who would break the Poison Accords so savagely.

An attack on the Warden's Island would be seen as an attack on all of Maricol. He couldn't comprehend what had driven Eimarille to approve such a horrific act.

Blaine followed Raziel into the hallway, pistol in hand, and got halfway to the stairs before his televox started chiming on his hip. He unclipped it, thumbing the casing open to take the call. "Honovi?"

"Where are you?" his husband snarled, the sound of explosions background noise for both of them.

Blaine stayed on Raziel's heels. "Leaving the administrative building. Caris and Nathaniel haven't returned from the laboratories."

"I need to launch. There are submersibles in the lake and soldiers on the shores, and I can see two airships flying our way. They haven't hit the hangar yet, but it's only a matter of time."

Blaine knew his position in relation to the hangar and the distance between them. He would not reach the airship in time. "I need to find Caris."

Honovi grunted, didn't argue, and said, "Keep your emergency flare on you. I'll get you when I can."

"What will you do?"

He could hear the bite in his husband's words, could imagine the teeth-baring smile on his face. "Shoot those Daijalan airships out of the sky and start dropping bombs of our own."

The *Celestial Sprite* was of military design, even if she didn't look it. Honovi had left E'ridia with a full compartment of ordnance when he'd flown to Veran, and they hadn't needed to use it yet. Honovi might not be a military officer, but the air force captain he'd brought along with him as part of the military crew *was*, and Blaine had faith in the aeronauts on that lone airship to hold the line as long as they could.

"May the wind steer you true," Blaine said before he jabbed at a button to end the call. The crystals in the device dimmed before brightening as he put in Caris' code. It chimed and chimed but didn't connect, and he swore. She must be out of reach, which hopefully meant she was still below ground. The only problem was the entrance to the laboratories was halfway across the fort from their current location, and the fort was currently under siege.

Raziel burst out of the building, Blaine only a second behind her, both of them racing into summer heat. The sky above was hazed by smoke drifting from several buildings that had caught fire in the immediate aftermath of the first volley from the assault. Blaine didn't know what the protocol was here, but his best bet was to stick close to a warden until he could make it to the laboratory entrance.

The whistling sound of something cutting through the air made his head snap around. His eyes tried to track the streak of a bomb launched from the shore, but he couldn't get it to focus. He only saw the aftermath—an administrative building three blocks over exploding into so much rubble, debris and smoke rising into the air.

His stomach lurched, thinking about the wardens who might have been inside, who would've been crushed by the collapse if they weren't dead from the initial hit. But there were wardens running down the street, weapons out, some with wands, all of them shouting—to each other and into televoxes—with automatons scurrying past. Blaine didn't know where Delani had gone, but he couldn't worry about the wardens' governor. His duty was to Caris, and he had to get her off the island.

Somehow.

"I need to get to the laboratories!" Blaine shouted, instinctively ducking as another whistling sound—*too close,* he thought—pierced the air.

Raziel didn't respond, merely grabbed him by the arm and sprinted across the street. They made it into the space between two buildings when the one they'd just left exploded from the hit. The force of the blast nearly drove Blaine to his knees, but Raziel kept him on his feet, kept dragging him forward.

"Keep moving," she said, not looking back, never letting go.

Blaine matched his stride to hers, breathless by the time they made it to the end of the alleyway, onto another street. He pulled his arm free of Raziel's grasp, trying to orient himself. "I'm getting Caris."

Raziel cut him a vicious look. "The entire fort is a blast zone. You really want to risk it?"

He didn't look at her, attention on the sky and the hideous sound of the fort under siege. The warning sirens were still going, a ceaseless, skin-crawling noise that hadn't yet been cut off. "I have no choice."

The star gods meant for Caris to be queen. They'd tasked him to stand as witness. Blaine was the tie between the past and the present and a future Eimarille was doing her damnedest to burn.

He couldn't let it all be for nothing.

"You risk dying."

"I'm *going*," Blaine ground out. To the laboratories. To save Caris. To find a way to get her off this island the same way he'd gotten her out of Amari, no matter the impossibility of the task.

This was his road. He would not leave it.

Couldn't leave her.

The Westergards had *always* protected the Rourkes.

He started down the street, heading in the direction he knew the laboratories to be, when Raziel swore behind him, footsteps loud on the cobblestones. She grabbed him by the elbow and spun him about, jerking her head in the other direction. "You go straight there and you're liable to get blown to pieces. We'll go around and aim for one of the other entrances."

"I thought there was only one entrance into the laboratories." Delani had said as much when she'd taken them below upon their arrival days ago.

Raziel shook her head and headed the other way. Blaine didn't hesitate to follow. "There are others for safety purposes. Tithes don't know about those. Not until they're wardens. And do you think we'd give up all our secrets?"

He didn't want to think about why tithes would want to find an escape from below. "All right."

Raziel led him away from the center, heading toward the fort walls. Blaine could see the spiderlike automatons patrolling the ramparts, Zip guns aimed outward and going off with a heavy *rat-tat-tat* that was a nonstop counterpoint to the sirens.

There wasn't any cover to be found, and the wardens they passed were heading for the walls to fight, though what good they'd do, Blaine didn't know. It wasn't until they turned a corner and he staggered midstride at the sight of what was walking toward them did he realize the wardens were better equipped than he thought.

The two-story-tall, human-shaped automaton made out of metal and gears walking on two mechanical legs toward the fort wall at a steady pace had Blaine rearing back. "That's a Solarian sentinel-class automaton. How do you even have one of those here?"

"We need them to guard Rixham."

"Rixham isn't *here*."

Raziel dragged him out of the street so the automaton could pass. Blaine looked up, seeing a warden seated in the torso of the clockwork machine, working various levers as it maneuvered forward what was essentially a war machine to protect the fort. Blaine had only seen a sentinel-classed automaton once before, on a trade run to Calhames, where the machine had stood guard in front of the Legion's military headquarters.

"Solaria tithes gear just like all the other countries." Raziel picked up the pace, not even close to being out of breath. "Let's keep moving."

More wardens were choosing the fort wall over looking for cover, if the stream of people heading for the fight was anything to go by. Blaine swallowed against a dry throat as he followed Raziel, hunching his shoulders every time a bomb fell within the fort, praying to the star gods none would fall where they ran.

An explosion outside the walls had Blaine's head snapping up as an airship flew high overhead, the hull of the *Celestial Sprite* cutting across the sky. The doors of the bomb bays on either side of the hull were open, which meant it had already dropped a payload.

Relief coursed through Blaine with a sudden punch, but it was a momentary high because the *Celestial Sprite* was the only airship in the sky on their side.

Another bomb launched from beyond the wall found its target, hitting close enough the ground shook. Blaine kept looking at the sky for falling debris as the building a block and a half away lost half its structure from the hit. "Where exactly is the nearest laboratory entrance?"

"Close by, just keep running," Raziel called out.

She knew the fort better than he did. Blaine only hoped they got to where they needed to be *soon*. They turned a corner and reached another street, this one wider than the others, and the fort's outer wall loomed high to Blaine's right. He didn't know where they were in relation to the main laboratory entrance, but he didn't see any building that had a vault for a door. All he saw was a smaller fort gate, guarded by half a dozen wardens on the ground and a cluster of automatons up on the rampart. Two of the wardens were crouched next to a third, who appeared to be wounded.

This gate wasn't the main entrance to the fort that led to the docks or the airfield. Blaine didn't know what it led to, but it certainly wouldn't take him where he needed to go. He realized seconds later, when Raziel unholstered her pistol and shot her fellow wardens in the back, that he was nowhere close to where he needed to be.

Blaine raised his pistol, finger curling over the trigger. He pulled it without aiming first, which made Raziel jerk to the side and turn toward him, still standing, still alive. A knot formed in Blaine's gut, cold sweat breaking out across his forehead despite the heat of the day. "There isn't any other laboratory entrance, is there?"

Raziel didn't seem concerned he had a pistol pointed at her. "You've quite a bounty on your head, but I'd have brought you in even without it."

His mouth went dry at her words. "You're with the Daijalans."

He couldn't think about how many other wardens might be as traitorous as her—couldn't think about what kind of danger Caris was in with bombs raining down and the enemy within.

Something small and round was flicked away from Raziel's other hand. When it hit the ground and shattered, a cloud of chemical smoke erupted right in front of Blaine. He breathed it in before he could stop himself, coughing harshly, whatever it was stinging his eyes and throat. He fumbled for his gas mask with his free hand, still keeping his pistol up.

He saw Raziel's shadow through the smoke and fired off another shot, but he didn't hit his target. The world had gone blurry, and he stumbled back, intent on running, when a high-pitched whistle sounded through the air for a few seconds until it cut off.

Too close, he thought frantically, trying to stay out of Raziel's reach.

The bomb was too close.

The building directly across the street from them exploded, the blast wave throwing Blaine off his feet. He landed on his back hard enough to drive the breath from his lungs, but it couldn't fix the way his vision spun. The chemical smoke wasn't thick enough to hide the debris flying through the air and crashing to the ground from the damaged building.

He lost his pistol when he landed, the gun sliding away across the ground, out of reach. Blaine tried to scramble to his feet, to move, but he wasn't quick enough. The crumbled piece of concrete that slammed down onto his outstretched left arm drew an agonized scream from him, pain whiting everything out.

He collapsed, tried to pull his arm free, but the agony that stabbed through the rest of his arm and into his chest made him stop. Blaine lay there, gasping for air, heart rabbiting against his ribs. The white-hot pain from his lower arm overrode everything. The smoke he'd inhaled only moments ago stole his ability to think, black spots pricking the edge of his vision.

A shadow fell over his face, and Blaine turned his head, breathing rapidly like a trapped animal. Raziel knelt beside him, and he flinched back, tried to get away. Nausea made him want to retch, but he swallowed it back.

He blinked up into Raziel's grimly determined face and tried to speak, but his throat felt as dry as the Wastelands must be, and his vision swam. "*Rionetka*."

"No," Raziel said as something cold and sharp pricked his neck, a coolness spreading through his body from whatever she'd injected him with, numbing the shock and pain. "Just a warden who was offered a better road."

He lay there, trying to stay awake, as she somehow levered the debris off his arm, pulling him free. Blaine got a glimpse of the damage done below his elbow before he had to turn his head away, gasping, thinking, *I can't fly like this*.

He couldn't feel his fingers.

He didn't know if that was from the drug now coursing through his veins or the injury itself. His ability to think became difficult, everything fuzzy and distantly sharp-edged. Raziel hooked her hand beneath his good arm and dragged him forward, past bodies, to the gate. She left him lying on warm stone, cheek pressed to the ground, breath stuttering in his chest as he watched her access the levers and winch that would undo the barricades locked into place over the gate.

Raziel opened the way for whoever was beyond, but they were only shadows to Blaine's worsening vision, pain bleeding through it all. Darkness smeared across everything, the sound of Zip guns like thunder in his ears, but Raziel's words were clear enough.

"The debt collected, as promised. They'll be expecting him in Foxborough," Raziel said.

"We were told you'd have the girl for us as well."

"Change of plans."

Blaine parted his lips, trying to find words to protest or maybe scream, but nothing in any language came to him. A tall figure came to stand by his side, face indistinct to his drugged mind. Unconsciousness was grasping at his focus, threatening to pull him under, anything to save him from the heated agony of his left arm, but he still tried to turn away from the hand that reached for him.

The last thing he heard was someone shouting amidst the crack of gunshots before everything slipped away.

Ten

HONOVI

"Get the guns ready," Honovi snarled as he yanked at two different levers on the control panel. "We're launching hot."

Air force Captain Caoimhe of Clan Sky stood right beside him, radio in hand as she barked out orders to the crew, her altitude mask dangling from one strap of her flight helmet. "I want all turrets out, best shooter on the Zip gun, and bombs ready to drop. We've got ordnance incoming. Brace for fast flying, stay hooked to your anchor wire, and everyone better have their jump vests on."

Caoimhe was around his age and had been an officer in E'ridia's air force for over a decade. He hadn't protested her posting to the *Celestial Sprite* and he trusted her ability to command the military aeronauts that made up the crew. His job was to keep them airborne.

"Anchor is clear!" someone bellowed from the open deck. "Hangar roof is open!"

Caoimhe clicked the radio on, her voice echoing through every active speaker on the airship. "Brace for launch."

Honovi was already working the levers and toggles that would send the *Celestial Sprite* into the sky at a rate of speed he hoped would ensure any enemy fire would miss them. E'ridian airship engines were far more advanced than other countries' when it came to speed and maneuverability. He only hoped that still held true in the face of Eimarille's foray into war.

The *Celestial Sprite* launched fast, Honovi's stomach swooping in a familiar way, ears popping at the rapid ascent. The walls of the hangar and roof disappeared, replaced by smoky blue sky and the Warden's Island coming into full view through the windows surrounding the flight deck.

A crew member ducked inside, nearly banging her shoulder against the door frame, spyglass in hand. "Got two airships flying our way, and looks like there are at least two dozen Urovan submersibles lining the shore. They already sank the steamboat and destroyed the pier across the lake. There's smoke rising from that location. Lots of soldiers on the ground."

"Urovan submersibles?" Honovi repeated, half his attention on the horizon and the rest on the gauges lining the control panel.

"Yes, manned by soldiers who aren't in uniform. I couldn't see anything that would identify them as Daijalan when I looked through the spyglass."

"We can't say they're Daijalan without proof," Caoimhe said, scowling.

"We all know there's only one country who would order this atrocity. Blaine is still in the fort, and half the wardens in there are *children*," Honovi said.

The ping of bullets hitting the steel-lined hull and air balloon could barely be heard over the thrum of the engines, but it proved they'd been spotted. Honovi scowled, steering the airship higher on a vertical launch that had him bracing his feet against the decking out of habit.

An explosion echoed through the air, sounding close below, and his mouth twisted as shouts from the deck filtered in. "That was the hangar."

"Hold ascent trajectory." Caoimhe clicked the radio back on. "Drop a payload if you have a target in sight."

Honovi was used to flying airships meant for trade, not for war, but the logistics of flight were the same. He kept his hands steady on the controls even as two more explosions sounded below—their airship's bombs creating havoc on the ground.

But the ground wasn't the only thing they had to worry about.

"Let's knock those airships out of the sky," Honovi said.

His navigator, standing on the other side of Caoimhe, offered a tight nod of agreement. "They're flying in from the west, and we're currently higher in altitude than they are."

"Aim for the engines," Caoimhe said.

Altitude and speed were the kingmakers in an aerial fight, and Honovi had claimed both by dint of superior flight mechanics. He banked the airship west, guided by his navigator into a dive that made the body of the airship pull against the cabling attached to the balloon. The ballasts groaned with the sudden change demanded of them, but the gauges were far from the red of warning, and he kept his vector steady.

Caoimhe clicked the radio on again. "Take the shot when you have it."

The horizon tilted, mountains coming into view once more, blue sky disappearing. The dive brought them swooping down over the Celestine Lake, the pair of airships well within sight and Zip gun range. Honovi's job as captain was to fly, and his grip was steady as he guided the airship down.

The edge of the control panel dug into his thighs as he braced his feet against the decking, half listening to his navigator rattle off numbers as the needle on the gauges moved. He could see the way the other two airships started to rise, hoping to get above the *Celestial Sprite,* but no matter their make, they weren't running E'ridian engines.

Honovi didn't particularly enjoy the idea of a two-against-one aerial dogfight. They didn't have time for that, not with the Warden's Island still under attack. Honovi had to stay above them, get his airship's heavy artillery in range, and take them out, engine first.

One at a time.

The military crew he flew with was used to the speeds of a military airship. They'd be hooked into the safety lines and manning their positions, so Honovi didn't worry too much about the steep angle of the dive. Mere seconds later and the sound of the heavy-caliber Zip gun spitting out a rapid volley could be heard over the engine.

The Zip gun was in the fore section of the airship, belowdecks, and so Honovi couldn't see it from his position in the flight deck. But he saw the aftermath of its attack, the way the balloon on the other airship *ripped* across the entire length of the unprotected top as the gunner shot a line of bullets down into the enemy's flight deck and hull and finally its engine.

The balloon didn't deflate—it'd take at least a day, really, for the gas to disperse—but the damage done to the other airship's engine meant it would never fly again. Black smoke poured from the stern of that airship, tongues of red-orange fire erupting from the damage. The explosion, when it came, tore through the decking and hull and burned through the balloon. The cabling snapped over the stern, the weight of the airship breaking the rest. Fiery debris fell toward the water, the balloon a fluttering, burning tail.

Honovi pulled out of the dive, airship groaning as the engines changed pitch. He caught a glimpse of a handful of that other airship's crew pitching themselves into open air. If they had jump vests, with chutes to slow their fall to earth, they might survive the downing of their airship. Except they were over the Celestine Lake, and even if they survived the fall, they might not survive the poison that lurked in the waters below.

Honovi hoped they didn't.

"Keep your eyes on the target," Caoimhe barked into the radio. "We're going to make another pass. Priority is taking out the sky support."

Honovi tuned out the shouting coming from all around him, eyes flicking across the control panel before focusing on the horizon again, a continuous pattern that fed him information. He yanked at a lever, wanting more altitude, listening as the engines changed pitch and wanting desperately to have Blaine with him.

Caoimhe kept her attention focused forward as Honovi fought to climb faster than the last remaining airship. "You're a good aeronaut captain."

"Just making sure we all get out of this alive," Honovi grunted.

He had no intention of losing this battle—at least, not the one in the air. He only hoped the wardens had enough weapons to hold off the attack on the ground.

He only hoped Blaine wasn't caught in any of the bombs.

Honovi shunted that thought aside, knowing better than to dwell on things that weren't immediately before him in a situation like this. Right now, he was pushing to get and stay above the last airship, trying to orient their position in the sky. It meant working in partnership with his navigator, and he was thankful it went smoothly enough for them to finally gain altitude.

Honovi scanned the horizon as crew members shouted back and forth on the open deck. The radio crackled, coordinates spitting out of the speaker from one of the aeronauts. The navigator checked against their position in the sky before saying, "Plotting vector."

He listened intently, guiding the airship back into another dive, less steep this time. The cabling stayed taut, the frame of the airship pulling against the balloon as Honovi piloted them toward the enemy. Flashes of light spat through the air, but the other side's Zip gun couldn't angle high enough to reach them. Honovi adjusted the angle of their descent slightly, letting the navigator guide a path through the sky.

The *Celestial Sprite*'s portside turret guns started firing, the gunners more maneuverable than the one at the fore. Honovi dropped the airship with a quick change of the ballasts, bringing them alongside the other airship's balloon, the length of three airships between them in the sky. It was still close enough for their gunners to focus fire on the other airship's engine as Honovi banked to keep them circling so the enemy's engines remained in view.

He held position, braced against the pull of gravity as the gunners kept firing until the engine exploded. Then Honovi yanked on the controls, guiding the airship higher in a bank that would bring them back around.

"Let's hope they don't have any anti-airship guns," Caoimhe said in a grim sort of voice. "I'd feel more comfortable dealing with those weapons with a squadron of aeroplanes to assist than just one airship."

"It's difficult to transport heavy artillery up the trailing edge of the Eastern Spine. Whatever they hauled up here, I think they focused more on the lake rather than the sky," Honovi said, thinking about the submersibles encircling the Warden's Island.

"I think we should do something about that." She clicked the radio on again, steady on her feet. "All right, let's focus on dropping some bombs and give the wardens aerial cover."

Honovi piloted them back toward the island, hands steady on the controls, eyes on the horizon, the sound of war in his ears. They were closing in on the shoreline at an angle, their bombers confirming readiness over the radio, when some of the submersibles began to dive rather than remain, leaving soldiers on the shore.

The bombs didn't reach them first.

Starfire did.

It erupted along the ramparts and spilled over the side, racing like a prairie wildfire toward the soldiers still on the shore and the submersibles in the shallows. It moved like a living thing, stealing ground and taking lives in seconds. The glare of it was nearly as bright as the sun above, dangerously beautiful and elegant in its destruction. The only thing left behind when it recoiled back like a wave leaving the shore was blackened earth that glinted like glass.

Caris, Honovi realized in that moment, was a weapon unto herself.

Eleven

CARIS

A line of tithes rushing down kept Caris pushed to the right as she reached the last landing. Looking up the stairs, she saw a tall, burly warden standing guard at the open vault doors above, bellowing at the tithes under his watch. Ksenia and Nathaniel were in front of her, but only Nathaniel looked behind him to make sure she was still with them.

"What's going on?" Ksenia demanded.

"Soldiers on the shoreline and in the sky. We're under attack," the other warden said.

Ksenia swore and sprinted up the last set of stairs. Nathaniel reached behind for Caris' hand, and she took it. Together, they made it to the top, Caris' calves burning from all the stairs they'd taken at double time. With the ground no longer muffling the sound of attack, she could clearly hear explosions happening around them in the fort.

"Keep the vault open and funnel the tithes and any wounded below. Have you heard from the governor?" Ksenia said.

"No, but any capable wardens are to man the wall."

Ksenia nodded, wand already in hand. "I'll make my way to a defensive station."

"What about us?" Caris asked.

"Stay below."

Caris stepped around Nathaniel, trying to keep her voice steady. "We can help."

"Caris, no," Nathaniel protested.

"You're no soldier," Ksenia said.

Caris raised her hand, palm up, spreading her fingers. She reached for the aether and called forth a spark of starfire, the brilliant heat of it forming above her palm. "I know I'm not, but I wield starfire."

Ksenia's jaw ticked. "Can you control it?"

She curled her fingers over the flame, unburned by the heat of it. The spark snuffed out, and Caris drew in a deep breath. "Better than I used to."

Ksenia narrowed her eyes. "I won't see wardens harmed because of your lack of training."

"Would you rather see them harmed by the enemy, then? I can *help*, Ksenia. So let me."

"You aren't trained for war."

"Are you?"

Ksenia's expression appeared as if carved from stone. "In more ways than you."

The ground shook again, and Caris braced her knees to stay standing. Ksenia strode out of the building, and Caris swore, following after her, ignoring Nathaniel's protesting shout. They stepped into sunlight made hazy by dust and smoke. Ksenia had her televox in hand, the device open and crystals humming with power.

"Governor, are you there?" she barked into the speaker. "What are your orders?"

The line must have been active because Ksenia's shoulders slumped after a moment, relief flickering across her eyes before being replaced with a grim sort of determination. "No, I don't know where Blaine is, but I have Caris with me."

Caris' heart lurched and missed a beat at that news. "Wasn't he with the wardens' governor?"

Ksenia ignored her. The call lasted less than a minute, for Caris had come to understand that wardens were a very direct, matter-of-fact kind of people. Ksenia closed the televox and slipped it into the case on her belt.

"The governor wants you on the wall if you're still willing to fight, but you have to know there's a risk of you being hurt or dying," Ksenia said, blunt in a way Caris could appreciate.

Nathaniel grabbed Caris by the elbow, worry in his voice, in his eyes. "Blaine would tell you not to."

Caris curled her hand over his before gently pulling free. "The soldiers are here because of me."

"You don't know that."

"Why else would Eimarille send troops to attack the Warden's Island?"

"You can't be certain she's in command of them."

"Who else would do such a thing?"

No country in their right mind would levy such an attack on the people who kept Maricol safe. Governments may not care for the costs of abiding by the Poison Accords, but those costs were still paid.

Another explosion on the other side of the fort had Ksenia turning her back on them and heading down the street at a dead run. "Quit arguing and make your decision. If you're coming with me, then put your gas masks on."

Caris yanked her gas mask off her belt and raced after the warden, putting it on with practiced hands as she ran. Nathaniel made it to her side seconds later, his own gas mask in place. They caught up with Ksenia, shadowing her through the fort as they ran for the nearest section of the wall to help with the defense.

The warning sirens were still going, and they passed small groups of tithes from time to time. Each group they passed, Ksenia paused long enough to direct them to the laboratories, which were deep enough to act like bunkers amidst the hell raining down on the island.

They turned a corner, a high-pitched whistling sound abruptly cutting off, when Ksenia spun on her feet and shoved both Caris and Nathaniel into the alcove of a doorway. A roiling concussive blast ripped down the street, making her ears pop. Caris squeezed her eyes shut against the dirt and dust it kicked up, Nathaniel shielding her from most of it.

"What are they targeting?" Nathaniel asked.

"Everything," Ksenia retorted.

"What about the gates?" Caris asked.

"They would have been shut and barred per protocol."

"Was anyone in the training fields?"

"A live exercise was scheduled for today with older tithes, but that's held off the island."

Caris winced at that, not relishing the thought of tithes learning to fight against revenants, but she supposed that sort of training was better than being cut down on the shore by the enemy.

Ksenia leaned back out of the alcove to see if it was safe to move. "Let's go."

They moved back onto the dirt-choked street, a building at the corner nothing more than rubble now. Caris hoped no one had been inside it when the bomb hit, aching with the thought of how many senseless deaths were most likely happening right now.

They were perhaps a quarter mile from the section of the wall, having missed two more bomb drops flung from the enemy's position on the shoreline, when the passing of an airship overhead had Caris looking up. She hunched her shoulders out of instinct before recognizing the *Celestial Sprite,* its hull bristling with weapons.

"Honovi's in the air," she gasped out, throat dry from their frantic run across the fort.

"Do you wardens have any airships?" Nathaniel asked, sounding just as out of breath.

"Nothing meant for a fight like this. We use them to haul our alchemy machines for deep cleansings of the land," Ksenia said.

They turned another corner, the narrow street they found themselves on leading directly to the fort's walls. At the end of the street, Caris could see a sentinel-class automaton walking up the stone steps to the ramparts, Zip guns raised and ready to fire. Other wardens were in position on the ramparts as well, crouched down and returning fire when they could.

"Has anyone breached the walls yet?" Nathaniel asked.

"Sirens would've changed pitch if that happened. Let's get up there."

They sprinted toward the stone stairs as another bomb whistled overhead, arcing through the sky to land well beyond their position. The explosion still made Caris' shoulders rise to her ears in the wake of the noise. Nathaniel grabbed her hand, giving it a squeeze as they both nearly rebounded off the fort's wall in their haste to make it to the ramparts.

They reached the top, after the sentinel-class automaton did, skirting past its massive bulk while its Zip guns that doubled as arms clicked into place and started firing. The warden in the cage at its center aimed at where the enemy was massed at the shore below.

Nathaniel pulled Caris into the sentry tower, Ksenia already inside and conversing with a pair of wardens manning a large grenade launcher. The bulk of the tripod-mounted contraption sat below the top of the tower wall, but the barrel pointed at the sky. Caris eyed the weapon and the crate of grenades that sat near its base.

One of the wardens ducked away from Ksenia to position himself behind the grenade launcher to load it. He yanked at a couple of levers to load the grenade, waiting on his partner to sight the target through a spyglass.

"The shore is lined with submersibles still offloading soldiers," Ksenia said, raising her voice to be heard over the sound of Zip gun fire down the wall. "We need to target their escape vehicles. Cover your ears!"

Caris slapped her hands over her ears, but it wasn't enough to block out the sound of the grenade launcher releasing with a deafening *crack*. The sound made her whimper, her gas mask trapping the noise inside metal and leather so no one else could hear it. The wardens handling the weapon both had earmuffs to help shield them from the noise.

"Since when do you need war machines?" Nathaniel shouted. Caris could barely hear him over the ringing in her ears.

"Ranged weapons work better when there's a horde to eradicate," Ksenia said.

Caris wasn't sure blowing revenants into pieces was safe, considering the spores that would aerate, but she supposed wardens weren't worried about that threat as much as everyone else.

"That took out a few submersibles, but there might be more in the water we can't see," the warden handling the grenade launcher said. "They have us surrounded."

Ksenia grimaced. "The wall is holding."

"For now."

Caris stayed low as she moved closer to Ksenia. "Do you need the shore cleared?"

Ksenia stared at her through dusty goggles. "Do you understand what you're offering to do? Are you still willing to do it?"

To fight in defense of a people who had only ever spent their lives guarding Maricol's children against poison and revenants. To strike back against an unprovoked attack.

To *kill,* when she was no soldier.

"Caris," Nathaniel said, his hand settling on her shoulder as more explosions filled the air. When she looked at him, her eyes were drawn to the way the collar of his linen shirt gaped open, giving her a glimpse of the scars he carried. "You don't have to do this."

She covered his hand with hers, taking in a steadying breath. "I have to."

If Eimarille was willing to go to war to conquer, Caris had to be willing to go to war to fight back. She didn't think she could live with herself if she stood by and did nothing.

"Let's have you take out this section of the shore first," Ksenia said.

Caris nodded jerkily, cupping her hands together in front of her. She squeezed her eyes shut and reached for the aether, channeling it into their plane until it seeped out of her in the form of starfire, all flickering, white-gold heat in her hands. She fed it more power until it coiled around her forearms, almost like a living thing. Caris gripped the starfire in both hands and half rose from her crouch, raising her arms over her head and casting it outward over the security tower's wall.

She spread her fingers wide as the starfire fell to the ground, expanding in size and rolling like a wave once it hit. It felt like a thread unraveling from the center of her chest, her awareness spreading outward without her say-so. She coaxed the starfire to burn hotter, to move quicker, guiding it toward the water as if it were a prairie wildfire with nothing to limit its spread.

The screams of those trapped on the ground were filled with agony, but they didn't last all that long. Their eventual silence wasn't a comfort, for Caris knew it was her power, her magic, her hand that had killed them. She straightened up, her head clearing the edge of the stone railing, watching as the sea of starfire swallowed the ground between the fort and the water and burned it black.

She clenched her hands into fists and yanked her arms back, pulling the starfire with her. It faded as it rolled back, leaving behind nothing, not even bodies, because bone could burn to ash at a high enough temperature.

Nothing on Maricol burned hotter than starfire.

Caris staggered once she released her connection to the aether, head throbbing, but less so than it had in the past. Then Nathaniel was there to hold her up, arm wrapped around her waist to steady her. "Are you all right?"

Caris swallowed against a throat gone dry. "Yes."

He asked her that same question over and over throughout the many hours it took to withstand an attempted siege of the fort, and she always, always lied.

Twelve

HONOVI

The Warden's Island was burned black around the fort, the shrubs and summer grass nothing more than ash when the *Celestial Sprite* anchored by the main gate inside the wall. The few hangar bays in the airfield were nothing but rubble now, so the crew anchored as if they were in the mountain peaks.

Temporary anchor berths were dropped, the clawlike contraptions digging into the fort wall for support, the only stone around. Lines were winched tight as the airship dropped nearly to the ground, its hull hovering a few meters over scorched dirt. Honovi stayed at the controls until Caoimhe gave the all clear.

"I'm keeping the crew on watch," Caoimhe said grimly as they left the flight deck.

Honovi nodded, glancing up at the darkening sky. The battle to keep the Daijalan forces out of the fort had lasted hours. They'd run out of bombs well before that, forced to ration their limited supplies on targeted drops. They only had one war airship, while the soldiers had plenty of Urovan submersibles.

What no one had accounted for was Caris and her starfire.

That sort of power had ravaged the land and the submersibles surrounding the fort, melting metal along the shoreline and leaving no one alive. The Daijalans had resorted to firing from the water, intent on bombing the wardens into submission. There'd been more forces on the land past the lake, ready with more submersibles to bring to the fight. Honovi had passed along that information to the wardens halfway through the battle.

The wardens' governor's response had been curt at the time. "The tithes will prove their worth."

Honovi hadn't known what that meant until perhaps an hour after that brief communication. They'd done a wide circle back to the mainland to get eyes on the enemy forces there and had arrived in time to see a horde of revenants—both humanoid and animal—attacking the soldiers in the launch area. The revenants had been followed by wardens and tithes, the soldiers unprepared to be flanked by such a threat.

Honovi had done another flyby over that area before the sun fully set. Submersibles had been set aflame in shallow waters, body parts scattered across the pebbled beach. The *Celestial Sprite* had picked up the wardens and tithes once the fighting had died down on the island, bringing them on board. The outside deck was crowded, but the wardens and tithes were good about staying out of the way as the crew worked.

Rope ladders were thrown over the railing, and Honovi saw the wardens and tithes off the airship first. A few had minor wounds they'd seen to themselves, but none which made it difficult to disembark. Once they had boots on the ground, Honovi hauled himself over the railing with practiced ease and descended the rope ladder to the rubble-strewn street.

The main gate had taken a beating, its doors damaged and hanging off broken hinges. Sentinel-class automatons stood guard around it, their Zip gun arms pointed at the shoreline and lake. The dark would hide the damage to the fort, but Honovi had seen enough while in the air to know recovery would take time.

He turned to face the small group waiting for him amidst the damage of a building that had been bombed. Caris stood there, covered in dust and dirt, her gas mask hanging off her belt. Nathaniel stood beside her, carrying a pistol in his hand.

Blaine wasn't with them.

Honovi stilled, gaze settling on Caris' tense figure. She looked a little too pale, exhaustion giving her skin an almost gray cast in the gas lamp light. "Where is Blaine?"

She stared at him, eyes wide in her narrow face. "Alive, but not here."

"*Where?*"

"We had a traitor in our midst who sold us out for a profit. Sold your husband, too," Delani said from behind Caris.

Honovi lurched forward a step, ears ringing as if he'd taken a blow to the head. "*What?*"

Delani was covered in dust, blood staining a bandage that had been wrapped around her upper left arm. A long scratch was scabbed over her cheek but not stitched. The wardens' governor walked with a faint limp as she approached the group, pistol in hand, gloved finger resting against the trigger guard. She came to a stop beside Caris, eyeing him. "My thanks for your air support."

"I don't want your thanks. I want my *husband*. What happened?"

Delani sighed and holstered her pistol. "A warden opened a side gate. She handed Blaine over to the Daijalans. They got him in a submersible and off the island."

Bile crawled up his throat, hot and terrible. "We bombed the shore. We bombed the *lake*."

"He's alive," Caris said, stepping forward and reaching for Honovi as if to comfort him, only Honovi didn't want her pity. "Once the fighting was over and the laboratories were opened up, I checked the map. My tracking crystal shows he's traveling west."

"That doesn't guarantee he's *alive*."

"The crystals won't move if the one it's tied to is dead," Delani said.

Honovi wanted to demand the map, wanted to tear free the crystal hanging from Caris' throat and use it to find Blaine. He wanted to follow wherever it led and rescue his husband from whatever horror he'd been betrayed into. "Your wardens handed Blaine over to the enemy."

Delani pursed her lips, her single eye dark and betraying nothing. "Only the one."

Honovi stepped close to her, hands clenched into fists. "One was *enough*."

Delani said nothing to that, merely inclined her head in acknowledgment of his anguish but offered no words of comfort. He wondered if wardens even knew how. "Raziel is alive if you'd like to question her."

He jerked back, gaze snapping to Caris. "Raziel? The same warden from Veran?"

Caris nodded tightly, crossing her arms over her chest. "Yes."

"Is she a *rionetka*?"

"She doesn't carry any vivisection scars. She did it of her own free will."

"Apparently, she was promised a large sum of aurons, enough to retire handsomely in any town she chose if she handed over Caris and Blaine during the attack." The disdain in Delani's voice did nothing to ease Honovi's fury. "She wouldn't dare try to fight Ksenia, and prying Caris out of the laboratories would have been too difficult. Blaine made the easier target."

"E'ridia won't stand for your betrayal," Honovi promised harshly.

Delani's expression never changed. "Raziel will be punished."

"I want her given over to me."

"Your country—"

"Don't preach to me of politics and neutrality when it was one of yours who *took* him. I am *jarl* to Clan Storm, and Blaine is my husband. She committed a crime against my clan, and she will pay for it."

Delani was silent for a moment before letting out a harsh sigh. "You may have her if your people don't blame the wardens as a whole for her betrayal."

"Do not worry, governor. I have no intention of suggesting E'ridia break the Poison Accords." Honovi looked at Caris. "Where is the map?"

"Still in the laboratory," she said.

"Retrieve it. I need to make a call to Glencoe. The *Comhairle nan Cinnidhean* needs to be apprised of the situation so they can send someone to take custody of Raziel."

"Unless your airship's radio reaches over the mountains, then your call won't go through. The Daijalans targeted our communications tower. It's damaged and unable to send or receive calls or telegrams," Delani said.

"I can fix it," Caris said, looking between them. "The underground generator is undamaged, and the laboratories would probably have the clarion crystals I'd need. We can dismantle any other machines or automatons to use their parts to rebuild it."

Nathaniel wrapped his arm around her shoulders. "I'll help. Between the two of us and with wardens to help, we should be able to get it up and running while you focus on relief efforts."

"We have the dead and wounded to see to," Delani agreed.

Honovi grimaced at that reminder of the threat that came in the aftermath of any battle. "Take me to Raziel."

Caris and Nathaniel peeled away from their small group, following another warden to the communications tower and the task ahead of them. Honovi wanted more than anything to board the *Celestial Sprite* with map in hand and go after the bastards that had his husband, but he had his duty as *jarl*, and that meant informing the *Comhairle nan Cinnidhean* of what had befallen the Warden's Island and Blaine's kidnapping.

As Delani led him through the rubble-strewn streets of the fort, Honovi got his first up-close look at the damage he'd only seen from the sky. Gas lamps still burned outside buildings that had escaped the bombs, but many more were damaged and left areas in the dark. Wardens resorted to setting up field gaslights to shine on the collapsed buildings as automatons scuttled about. Delani's handheld gaslight provided much-needed illumination in the areas where light couldn't reach.

The damage was extensive, Honovi realized with a sinking heart. The Daijalans had come with the intent to eradicate the wardens and their home, striking at the heart of Maricol's stability. For without wardens to walk the poison fields and guard the borders, no country would be truly safe.

"How many dead?" Honovi asked in a quiet voice.

"We don't know yet," Delani said, sounding tired. "The lecture halls, barracks, and refectory were destroyed completely in the initial volley of bombs. The administrative buildings were next. The Daijalans knew where to do the most damage, though I don't think they were expecting Caris. Her starfire kept them on the defensive, but it didn't stop them from fighting. They just couldn't breach the wall."

He thought of the children and teenagers he'd seen throughout his stay on the island and couldn't quite hold back a wince. "Your tithes?"

Delani's expression never changed, hard in the way of one who understood the risk of living a dangerous life. "Many of them never made it to the laboratory entrance. It was the tail end of the midday meal for one rank, and classes were in session."

"I'm sorry. They'll dance among the stars."

"Wardens are nameless and starless. There is no guiding star for us."

Honovi could hear no bitterness in her voice, and he wondered at the sort of faith she carried to do her duty on a road many wished never to walk. He wondered if she would let herself grieve.

They walked in silence through the rubble, past buildings still standing and others not. The smell of smoke hung heavy on the air, the mountain breeze yet to blow it away. Magicians must have kept any fire from spreading, but the damage was bad enough that Honovi wondered what they would do during winter.

Eventually, Delani led him to what might have been a courtyard once, lit by a gas lamp and filled with debris. Half a dozen wardens stood guard around a single one of their own whose bruised face was familiar from Veran.

Raziel had been stripped of her weapons and her uniform, left to kneel naked in the cool night air and bound by metal cuffs. She was bruised and bloody, one eye half-swollen shut, and one arm appeared as if she still had a bullet lodged in it. Pain etched lines in her face, but her cheeks were free of tears, eyes vacant in a way Honovi knew meant mind magic was at play.

"How did you know it was her?" Honovi asked.

"Wardens saw Raziel fire on her brethren and open the gate to let the Daijalans in. They saw her hand over Blaine but were too far away to stop the soldiers from leaving with him. Wardens shot her and managed to capture her," Delani said.

"And then you broke her mind?"

Delani shrugged. "I wanted answers."

"Did you find them?"

Delani tipped her head in his direction, single eye looking at him askance. "A Blade out of Daijal recruited her late last year on behalf of Eimarille."

Honovi went still, thinking of the Blade who had nearly killed Blaine in Amari. "Terilyn?"

"That was her name in Raziel's memories."

Honovi frowned. "That means Eimarille had this attack planned before we fled Amari."

"Capturing Caris or Blaine was an opportunistic moment. Whether or not they'd been here, Raziel still would have aided the Daijalan forces. She still would have opened that gate." Delani's mouth pressed into a thin line, twisting briefly and tinged with grief. "She still would have told them where to target for the most damage and lives lost."

If Eimarille had planned this attack to happen while she invaded the eastern provinces of Ashion, then he had little doubt she would target the rest of the continent. No country had ever attacked the wardens in such a way in their entire history. Wardens were needed; they always had been. Attempting to eradicate them like this spoke of trying to weaken Maricol as a whole.

"Can Raziel speak on any of this?"

"You'd be better off letting a magician handle her."

He stared at Raziel, the warden's gaze looking right through him, as if she didn't even see him. "Once the communication tower is back up and running, I'll request reinforcements from Glencoe."

"All that effort for just one warden?"

"No." Honovi looked past where Raziel knelt, at the pockets of light glowing in the dark amidst the rubble, thinking of the bodies that must be buried beneath some of it. "You'll need help to evacuate your wounded to somewhere safe and gain access to the dead. E'ridian airships will provide that."

As furious as Honovi was, he knew Blaine would never forgive him if he let the wardens suffer. And he couldn't, in all honesty, turn his back on the people who guarded the borders against revenants. The Warden's Island wasn't safe, and if it couldn't be defended, then its people would have to be transported somewhere else until recovery efforts could begin in earnest.

"We won't abandon the island," Delani said.

"You need to coordinate your wardens from somewhere else, at least temporarily. Somewhere Eimarille won't expect you to be."

"I'm needed here."

"Then appoint another to either handle the coordination effort or the recovery efforts, but you need to split your forces."

Delani stared past where Raziel knelt, into the dark that hid the damage and death of all she knew. "When the communications tower is back up and running, I'll send out a notice to all the resupply stations."

"About the attack?"

"No. About pulling out of Daijal."

Honovi's eyes widened slightly, though the wardens guarding Raziel didn't seem surprised. "You'd leave a country to fend for itself against revenants and spores?"

"The Poison Accords allow for sanctions. Until new rulership heads Daijal, I won't risk my wardens' lives. Queen Eimarille is already spreading false rumors about wardens in the western provinces of Ashion. That was her justification for crossing the border."

"She'll take your decision as a further excuse to advance."

Delani smiled, wide and vicious. "She won't have much of a country in even half a generation if we leave Daijal and stay gone. We wardens know the poison history of every country. We keep border reports for a reason. We know what to look for in the poison fields and how to fix it. Spores travel, bogs fill, and without alchemist intervention, the land dies."

"You'd damn even those who had no say in the attack against the island?"

"Eimarille damned them with her actions today." Delani finally turned to look at him, real and glass eye glittering in the gas lamp light. "I have tithes to burn."

She walked away, shoulders straight, head held high, to go deal with the living and the dead. Honovi turned his attention back to Raziel, the warden's gaze still empty of anything but pain. He dragged a hand down his face, wanting desperately to take the map, get on the *Celestial Sprite*, and fly after Blaine.

But he couldn't leave the wardens unguarded. He didn't know if Eimarille would send anyone else to attack again. The wardens needed support while they recovered, and E'ridia could provide that with their air force. He needed to facilitate that first because if they lost the wardens and all their knowledge, no one on Maricol would be safe.

Then he could go after Blaine with more than a single airship.

"Find her some clothes and keep her alive. I'll be sending her back to E'ridia under guard," Honovi said. Raziel wasn't going anywhere at the moment, and there was plenty that Honovi could do to help. He needed to do *something* to take his mind off Blaine.

He made his way back to the *Celestial Sprite*, the airship's rope ladders still hanging over the side. Honovi hauled himself up to the decking and found Caoimhe waiting for him, something sorrowful in her gaze as she looked at him.

"We heard what happened to Blaine," she said. "Your orders, *jarl*?"

Not captain, not for this. "Delani has agreed that the warden who betrayed us and her brethren will be extradited to E'ridia to face charges there. Caris and Nathaniel are working to get the communications tower back up and running, but that's going to take time. The *Comhairle nan Cinnidhean* needs to be warned."

"We can't get a clear connection to Glencoe from here."

"If there are passing airships, we might be able to reach them. The likelihood of them being war airships is slim, but whoever hears would be able to at least help transport the wounded and relay a message back home."

Caoimhe nodded. "We'll start the outreach. What will your message be?"

"Tell them..." He paused, thinking about Delani's words and all that they implied. "Tell them Daijal has broken the Poison Accords and acted against the wardens in a direct attack. Tell them E'ridia stands with the wardens and all airships who can provide aid are asked to make their way here."

"I'll assign shifts for the calls." She hesitated a moment before continuing with "What will you do?"

Honovi turned his head to stare at the scattered points of light throughout the fort, knowing there were so many wardens in the dark trying to save their livelihood. "Put myself to work."

Those who survived the attack worked through the night, and Honovi joined them during those long hours. Wardens tended to the wounded, gathered their dead, and took stock of the damage left behind. Caris, Nathaniel, and other wardens worked nonstop to get the communications tower up and running again.

It had been an easy target, being one of the tallest buildings within the fort, meant to act as a relay to the ones scattered over the Eastern Spine to reach E'ridia and all across the rest of the continent. It was integral to the functionality of the wardens in the poison fields. Now, it tilted dangerously, wires severed and clarion crystals shattered. A bomb had taken out a nearby building, the subsequent collapse damaging the top of the communications tower and one of the support beams. A sentinel-class automaton was being used to help shore it up.

Caris was in the midst of that organized chaos, in charge of cutting clarion crystals while Nathaniel helped wardens assess the engine that powered the communications tower. Thankfully, the large underground generator had escaped damage by virtue of its location. It was everything else that needed work. Caris and Nathaniel were Ashion-trained engineers, but machines didn't run based on cultural mores. It was math and science and a little bit of magic drawn from the aether when steam engines weren't in the mix.

It was everything Blaine would've known how to help with, and Honovi didn't. He flew airships; he didn't fix and maintain the engines that gave them flight.

The moon tracked across the sky for hours, and the recovery efforts never waned. When the deep black of a starry night sky began to fade to gray in the east, then to the pink hues of dawn, the gas lamps began to slowly turn off as daylight approached. Mist had crept over the Celestine Lake sometime during the night. The wardens had tested the air for poison and found it within acceptable parameters for non-wardens to breathe. Tithes who hadn't yet built up their resistance to all of Maricol's poison, as well as Honovi's crew, didn't need to wear their gas masks.

Honovi had spent the two hours before sunrise helping wardens sift through the rubble of destroyed buildings, looking for survivors. He hadn't slept, eyes gritty behind the goggles he wore to protect them from dust, and his focus was dialed into the task at hand so deeply so as to not think about Blaine. It took two shouts of his name before the voice finally penetrated. Honovi looked up from the section of building he was working on with several other wardens, frowning at the crew member racing toward him.

"*Jarl* Honovi!" the man called out. "Airships are to the south of us!"

Honovi drew in a sharp breath, stepping away from the damaged building. The wardens around him had all turned to face the runner, hands drifting to their pistols. "Ours?"

"All hailing E'ridian names and codes. Caoimhe told them to anchor on the shore. She's informed the wardens' governor of their impending arrival so no one shoots them down."

"I'll go out and meet them."

He'd called them to port, after all. It was his duty to give them their orders upon arrival. Honovi left his current task behind and made his way to the main gate of the fort, the damage there extensive from the initial attack. Ksenia met him there, giving him a tight-lipped smile in greeting, wand in one hand and pistol in the other. The hilt of a poison short sword protruded over one shoulder, the clarion crystal there a deep blue.

"Caris said they'll have the communications tower jury-rigged to work within the hour. The governor is with her in order to send out the recall messages as soon as communications are restored. I'm here to judge who has answered your call," Ksenia said.

"My people won't harm yours," Honovi said.

"We've already been attacked by one country. You'll allow us our paranoia."

Honovi and Ksenia walked out of the fort together. Honovi's boots crunched over damaged earth, the mist thinning out now that the sun was creeping over the eastern horizon. Six airships bearing clan crests and E'ridian company designs skimmed low over the Celestine Lake, flashing their lights in a code Honovi could easily read.

Friendly-aid-anchor.

Whoever was manning the radio on the *Celestial Sprite* must have given the all clear because the airships started to descend, coming in side by side to anchor on the shore. Honovi could hear the crews calling out in E'ridian, the language a balm after so long speaking the trade tongue while on the island.

Rope ladders were tossed overboard, the knotted ends landing in ashy dirt. Beyond where the airships anchored, the twisted, melted remnants of submersibles stood out in the shallow waters of the shore like broken field markers.

The first ones off the airships were aeronauts who claimed the rank of captain, the collars of their fur-lined flight jackets with the plaid panels over the shoulders glinting with the ranking pins. Honovi was distinctly aware of the lack of metalwork woven into his braid, but the men and women who jogged to greet him called him by the appropriate rank regardless.

"*Jarl* Honovi, I'm captain of the *Catskills*. We received your message," the lead captain said in greeting, expression grave. "How can we help?"

The other captains echoed his offer of assistance. Honovi nodded a silent welcome to all of them before looking at Ksenia. "It's your call."

Ksenia's gaze wasn't on the captains but the half dozen airships anchored on the shore, ready to take on passengers. "You're certain your hospitals in Glencoe can handle the influx of patients?"

"Yes."

"Then let's get the wounded and the youngest tithes on board. They can't be tended to here."

Honovi nodded and set about coordinating the transfer of evacuees to the first wave of E'ridian airships who'd answered the call to help.

Thirteen

BLAINE

Blaine was jolted out of unconsciousness when he hit the ground. The impact sent fiery agony stabbing through his crushed left forearm up to his shoulder, spiderwebbing across his ribs. For a moment, Blaine could only pant into the dirt, the scent of loam thick in his nose, as he tried to get more air into his lungs in order to scream. He swallowed, tasting bile, the familiar churn of nausea creeping up his throat.

This wasn't the first time he'd swam into awareness, but it was the first time it felt as if it would stick.

He couldn't decide if that was a blessing or not.

A boot knocked against his chest, making him want to curl around the bruise-like pain it invoked, but moving only made the rest of him hurt worse. So Blaine stayed still, trying his best to orient himself through the haziness of his thoughts when all he wanted to do was sink back into unconsciousness. But the agony in his arm was too sharp to ignore anymore. Whatever drugs they'd pumped into him were finally wearing off, and what replaced it was a level of pain that made it difficult to think.

Blaine slitted his eyes open, taking in the slope of the hill they were on, the underbrush surrounding them, and the dappled sunlight streaming through the tree canopy that haloed the soldiers around him.

"He's awake," the soldier who'd kicked him said.

"Where's the doctor? We need to keep him alive long enough to get him to Foxborough," someone else said.

"Last I saw, the doctor was checking on Corporal Aubreo's wounds."

"He still bleeding?"

"No. Doc is checking if he was bitten."

Blaine tried to lift his head but found that made the world spin dangerously. He squeezed his eyes shut, panting softly as he tried to will his stomach not to rebel. A kick to his ribs meant he lost that battle, and Blaine turned his head to the side to vomit up bile, all that was left in his stomach. It wasn't much, but it still burned, and he gasped for air afterward.

A shadow fell over his face, and he looked up, blurry vision settling on a man in the brown and dark green uniform of a Daijalan soldier. Blaine didn't know the man's name or his rank, but the expression on his face—as if Blaine was an animal to be dissected—left him feeling chilled.

Or perhaps that was the beginnings of the fever.

Fingers tangled in his hair, jerking his head off the ground. Blaine couldn't stop the moan that left his lips, the fingers of his right hand curling into the dirt beneath him. He couldn't feel the fingers of his left hand, couldn't make them move. His hand and forearm were a mangled mess that his gaze skittered away from, not wanting to believe the damage was real. Someone had tied a tourniquet around his forearm just below his elbow, but he couldn't feel that either.

Blaine knew—distantly—that wasn't good.

"Are you with us, my lord?" the soldier asked mockingly in the trade tongue.

"Not a lord," Blaine mumbled, voice coming out in a rasp.

Fingers curled over the torc around his neck, giving it a tug. Panic made him try to jerk away from the touch, but all he ended up doing was choking. "Bounty says otherwise. You're wanted for treason against the crown."

Blaine bared his teeth, tongue pressed to the back of them. "Not my queen."

"That's what traitorous cogs always say."

The hold on his torc released, and Blaine slumped back against the ground. The soldier stood, staring down at him with cold eyes. "Someone fetch me the doc."

"She's still with the corporal."

The soldier sighed loudly, the sound very put-upon, before unholstering his pistol and checking for a bullet in the chamber. "I'll remedy that."

He walked away, but his absence didn't make Blaine feel any less afraid. The soldiers standing or sitting around him were simply further proof of his status as a prisoner of war. He rolled carefully onto his side, dragging his damaged arm with the motion and nearly puking from the pain it caused.

A gunshot sounded, loud and echoing in the air. Blaine flinched with his entire body, gasping at the wave of pain that rolled through his left arm. Sweat made his shirt stick to his skin, and he couldn't tell if he was hot from the summer heat or the creeping claws of a fever.

"The corporal could've lived," an irritated female voice said.

"I'm not wasting time on the wounded other than the one we're being paid to bring back. Put him under. I won't have him fighting us while we head for the rendezvous point. The airship is scheduled to leave in an hour, and we better be on it."

If Blaine had the wherewithal to fight, he would've tried. As it was, two soldiers pinned him to the ground by his shoulders and feet while the doctor handled his good arm with steady hands. The prick of a needle entering a vein made him moan in protest, but his ability to think lasted only so long. He blinked, the sunlight smearing across his vision until everything faded away.

He sank into a blackness so complete that he didn't know he was dreaming, not at first. The stars above looked so real from the roof of the clan home in Glencoe, the constellations bright to his eyes. The expanse of E'ridia's capital was how Blaine knew it must be a fever dream, for he hadn't been to Glencoe in years.

"Ah, but you consider that city your home and not Amari," a vaguely amused voice said from behind him. "It is the place I left you, after all."

Blaine stiffened, slowly turning around, coming face-to-face with someone he hadn't seen since he was ten years old. "My lady."

The Dusk Star smiled at that honorific, her dark hair braided back, a crown of ranking hair adornments glowing from starshine around her head. She wore the fur-lined leather flight jacket of an E'ridian aeronaut, hands resting on her hips, her trousers with their split seams on the side open enough to show the golden Eagle constellation tattooed there on her right thigh.

"Aaralyn can believe what she likes, but you're still mine, for all that you have Westergard blood flowing through your veins," Nilsine said.

"I've kept to my road."

"I know. You've walked it well, my child. But you must keep walking."

Blaine wrapped his right hand around his left wrist, squeezing tight around bone that was whole when he knew it should be in pieces, flesh soft and mushy in a way muscle was never meant to be. "It will kill me."

Nilsine stepped closer, reaching up to cup his face in both her hands, the intensity of her gaze rooting Blaine where he stood in this dreamlike space that felt so real. "Perhaps. Perhaps not. You must have faith to stand witness. You are the only one who can."

Caris' name could not be written down in the royal genealogies without a witness to her past. He might not have been there for her birth, but he'd carried her out of the old palace and Amari at the behest of Queen Ophelia. He knew Caris' truth better than she did.

He knew, too, that he could not deviate from his road.

"Eimarille wants me dead."

Nilsine kissed his forehead, her lips warm enough to burn, the heat of her touch consuming the city all around him. "Then don't die."

Blaine opened his mouth on a scream that felt as if it was ripped from the depths of his bones—raw and unending in the way it shredded his throat as reality set in. He arched against the restraints keeping him strapped to a table, the swaying of nearby gas lamps spinning shadows across a nightmare's face.

The cloth mask over her mouth moved, but the whine of a steam-powered oscillating bone saw was all Blaine heard, all he *felt*, as metal teeth cut into his left arm. The agony was like nothing he'd ever felt before as she carved away at his body, severing the mangled mess of his crushed forearm just below the elbow.

His teeth clacked together, sound forced between them, high and shrill like a cornered, dying animal, tasting blood in his mouth. The pain spiraled deeper, sharper, an incandescent agony he couldn't escape until a blackness swallowed him whole.

There were no stars to greet him this time as he slipped under.

Crossroads

936 A.O.P.

One

TERILYN

Terilyn went through the motions of her training exercises in the empty estate courtyard denoted for guest use. The air was hot and heavy still, despite the late hour. Most of the estate's servants were abed, the numbers more than halved since Joelle had left for Bellingham yesterday with most of her House. Only Artyom had stayed behind, overseeing their guests—Terilyn and other Blades who'd come to Daijal with her.

The only sound this late was her heavy breathing beneath the light of gas lamps. Sweat slicked her skin as she kicked and punched the air in a pattern that became almost meditative. She didn't complete the final set of exercises, concentration broken by Artyom entering the courtyard with loud footsteps.

"I would think you'd be reviewing the itinerary for tomorrow," Artyom said.

Terilyn eased back out of her lunge, flexing her fingers as she turned to face him. He was dressed in thin sleep trousers and a robe that was open down the center, revealing a bare chest that had lost its definition by way of rich foods and expensive drink. He stared at her sweaty form with disdain rather than lust, a change from some of the others she'd dealt with while in Solaria. Artyom, at least, knew what she was and treated her accordingly.

"We know the plan. It isn't something we need to review again," Terilyn said.

"I have suggestions on the timing. The *vezir* said I should speak with you about them."

Terilyn reached up to wipe sweat off her brow, flicking it off her fingers. "No."

Artyom scowled, a thunderous expression crossing his face, clearly not used to being denied. He stepped forward, attempting to loom over her. Terilyn merely stared him down, not bothered by being weaponless in that moment. She didn't need a blade or pistol to kill someone. Artyom seemed to recognize that, stumbling to a halt midstride.

"No?" Artyom growled.

"The plan remains as it is. If you're worried about surviving it, you know when you need to leave the gathering."

"You risk my niece's life with how things will go. I do not want to leave her behind."

Terilyn smiled in the face of Artyom's seemingly affronted attitude. "You mean we risk your path to power."

"Raiah is of our House."

"The princess will be handled as we informed you. That will not change." Terilyn made her way to the stone bench where her gear sat. She picked up a small towel to wipe her face and neck clean of sweat. "It is late. You should rest for tomorrow."

It was a polite dismissal, one Artyom obeyed with an annoyed huff, but he left. Terilyn watched him go, making a mental note to tell Witten that Artyom may be a problem tomorrow. The House of Kimathi always did seem to want to do things their way.

Her televox chimed, drawing her out of her thoughts. Her braid slid over one shoulder as she bent to rummage through her bag, unearthing the televox from where it'd slipped to the bottom. Terilyn opened the casing to answer the call, Eimarille's voice coming through clearly.

"Darling," Eimarille said, the fondness in her tone bringing a smile to Terilyn's face. "I've news from the east."

Terilyn sat on the bench and reached for the pitcher of water on a tray a servant had kindly left her earlier. The water had turned tepid, but she still poured it into a glass. "It's late. Was the strike force successful?"

"In as much as soldiers can be against starfire."

"Ah." Terilyn set the pitcher down, refraining from drinking just yet. "Caris was on the field, then?"

"Unfortunately, yes. The new grenade launchers proved useful in battle up until she melted them."

"Were the soldiers able to capture her?"

"No, but our spy managed to deliver the professor to us. They're en route to Foxborough."

"If that is the case, then I will leave for Foxborough in the morning to oversee the transport of the prisoner to Daijal."

"Are you certain you can leave Calhames?"

Terilyn tipped her head back to look up at the night sky above, some of the stars hazy from thin clouds limned in moonlight. "Joelle and most of her House have already left Calhames. The emperor's final Conclave gathering is tomorrow. My intention was to oversee the morning preparation for the attack and depart once everything was in order. I can leave that to the Blades that are here. They will follow my orders."

"I never doubt you, my dear, but the Blades—"

"The Blades have their orders and will see the plan through."

Eimarille huffed out a sigh at Terilyn's interruption, but she didn't lash out because of it. Terilyn was the only one who could speak to Eimarille in such a way and be assured there would be no punishment for interrupting her queen. Eimarille might rule a country and be well on her way to laying the groundwork to rule Maricol, but in certain moments, Terilyn ruled her.

It had been a heady realization when she was younger, but not once had Terilyn ever thought to use such power for any sort of gain. She was content with her position beside Eimarille as lover and confidant, knowing there was no other person outside a star god who had the ear of the most powerful woman in the world.

"I would rather you not be in Calhames at all for what we have planned, though I was willing to go along with your initial plan. I want you safe," Eimarille said.

The worry in Eimarille's voice left Terilyn feeling warm. "I'll leave in the morning."

"Good. I miss you. I always sleep terribly when you're gone."

Terilyn had received updates every morning and evening when the sun rose and set over New Haven in Daijal of her lover's status. They still hadn't been enough to quell her worry over the last few weeks while she'd been deployed to Calhames. She always carried a lingering tension from being parted from her queen on these missions she carried out.

"Are you in your office?" Terilyn asked.

"I've too much work to do to be anywhere else at this hour."

It wasn't as late there as it was in Calhames, but Terilyn didn't need to look at her discarded pocket watch to know Eimarille should be finishing up for the day. She would be if Terilyn was there with her. "Go to our room, darling. Get ready for bed and try to get some sleep."

"There is still so much to do."

"It will keep." Her tone brooked no argument, and Terilyn was pleased when Eimarille caved to her request.

"Very well. Come home to me soon, darling."

"I will," Terilyn promised.

She ended the call, snapping the televox case closed and setting it aside. Terilyn gathered her things to leave the courtyard, coolly planning out the next few hours and the tasks still needed to be completed.

By morning, the queen's Blade was gone, heading north as promised.

Two

SOREN

The final gathering of the Conclave of Houses was set to occur at the Imperial palace, in the late afternoon once the heat of midday had faded. The palace servants had gone all out to prepare for it, and the work still wasn't done. Vanya's robes for the occasion had been laid out the night before by a body servant in the dressing room. When Soren woke at sunrise from an uneasy sleep and slipped free of Vanya's arms, he discovered a second set of robes had been laid out with the first.

The clothes had obviously been made for him, the sizing meant for his stature, not Vanya's. Soren fingered the white robe and trouser set neatly laid out on the chaise, the cuffs and trim embroidered with gold and crimson thread. He could see the constellations twisting through the design, the Lion more prominent than others. The fabric was soft, the tailoring and detail expensive, but it wasn't his field uniform.

He left the robes alone, pulling on the clean field uniform the palace servants had returned yesterday. He holstered his pistol and strapped on his poison short sword before retreating back to the bedroom where Vanya was still abed.

"You're not dressed for today," Vanya said in a low, gravelly voice, clearly awake, if not up.

Soren approached the bed, reaching out to slide his fingers through the tight curls of Vanya's hair shorn close to his skull. "You know I can't wear your House's colors."

One warm hand slid free of the sheets they'd slept beneath to grab Soren's wrist. "I wish you would reconsider."

"I'll stand with you at this last gathering as a representative of the wardens, but I can't be that if I'm out of uniform."

If the Conclave didn't end in Vanya's favor, the wardens would need to know how the loyalties of the Houses lined up. Joelle had proven that the Houses could push back against the right of unhindered travel granted to the wardens. It was a dangerous precedent the wardens couldn't allow to continue. It was why Soren had stayed for the Conclave when he should have already left for his border duties beyond the city well before now.

Vanya said nothing, merely leaned up on an elbow to draw Soren into a kiss that left Soren's toes curling in his boots.

"Come back to bed," Vanya murmured when they broke apart.

Soren kissed an apology to the corner of his mouth. "I need to retrieve the border reports from the resupply station. I'll be back after my errand."

Vanya reluctantly let him go and Soren extricated himself from the bed. He knew full well if he didn't put some distance between them, he'd find himself tumbled back onto the sheets, weapons and clothes discarded, with Vanya's hands keeping him there.

He left before Vanya could convince him to stay.

The palace bustled with servants still preparing for the gathering ahead. Soren had requested his velocycle be ready for him in the morning, and he found it resting on the stand in the forecourt, the metal polished to a shine. He slung a leg over the seat and started the engine, kicking the stand up and driving out of the palace.

Heat was baked into the city as he drove through the twisting roads and past inner-city walls. The trees lining the streets and dotting the public parks and squares he passed could only provide so much shade. The air was already warm by the time he braked to a halt in front of the resupply station, gaze lingering on the door. It was closed, and the shutters were drawn over the windows.

Soren turned off the engine, settling back in his seat as he took in the building. The rooms above the resupply station on the first floor all had their windows closed as well, when usually they'd be open if occupied to let in a breeze.

He got off the velocycle and approached the door, ringing the bell there. Wardens arrived at resupply stations at all hours. While the doors were sometimes locked to keep the supplies secured, the warden on duty would always answer if the bell rang.

No one came.

Soren gripped the doorknob with tight fingers, frowning at the wood. He glanced at the street on either side of him before retreating to his velocycle and digging through the storage box behind the seat. He pulled out his tool kit, flipping open the flap and rummaging through it for the set of lockpicks he always traveled with.

He hadn't needed to pick a lock in quite some time, but he hadn't forgotten his training in that area. It took a couple of tries, but Soren eventually got the tumblers and gears to move, and the mechanism unlocked itself with a soft click. He pocketed the tools and kept one hand on the grip of his pistol. The door opened on silent, well-oiled hinges, the chime from the bell echoing in the empty room.

Everything looked in place, no signs of a burglary or fight. Soren did a circle in the shop, unease crawling through him. It didn't go away when he climbed the stairs to the rooms above meant for traveling wardens.

They were all empty.

He stood in the hallway at the top of the stairs, frowning at all the open doors that led to empty rooms. It was as if everyone had left and locked up behind them when resupply stations were never to sit empty.

Soren returned to the ground floor and went to the small telegraph room all resupply stations had. It doubled as a records room, folios lining bookshelves of supply inventories over the years, along with copies of maps.

Soren approached the telegraph machine, the notepad used to write down messages sitting beside it, the cover open. Nothing was written on the top page, but there were faint indentations on it, as if someone with a heavy hand had copied down a message and ripped that page free to take with them. He picked up the notepad and a nearby pencil, holding it at a slant to gently rub graphite over the indentations until the shadow of words appeared.

"Recalled wardens meet in Veran," he read out loud. "Governor's orders."

That wasn't a city in Solaria. It had an Ashionen name, and when Soren found a folio of maps on the shelf that included one of Ashion, he located the town after reviewing the legend. He set the map down and stared at the notepad in his hand. Wardens weren't recalled all that often, not without another replacing them.

He bypassed the telegraph machine in favor of the telephone on the other desk. He lifted the receiver off the metal cradle and used the rotary dial to call a number every warden memorized when they were tithes. The line to the archives on the Warden's Island always had someone manning it, day or night. A call always went through.

His didn't.

Soren pulled the receiver away from his ears and stared at it, a knot forming in his gut. He tried calling again and got the same response, nothing but a dead line. The next time he stuck his finger on the dial, Soren called a different number, the governor's direct line, which few wardens were privy to.

It connected, but the warden on the other side wasn't Delani. "Station warden, you were given your orders already. Why aren't you on the road?"

"You aren't Delani," Soren said.

"No, but I'm authorized for her jury-rigged line. Who is this?"

"Not the station warden. I'm Soren. I'm the warden assigned to the border around Calhames in Solaria. The resupply station was unmanned when I arrived for my updated reports to manage my assigned border."

There was a brief pause before the warden on the other side of the line cleared their throat. "Your border isn't on the recall list."

"*What* recall list?"

Another pause. "Daijal attacked the Warden's Island. Significant damage was sustained."

Soren's knees went weak, and he caught himself against the side of the table. "*What?*"

"No warden is to guard a border in Daijal until the governor says otherwise. Available wardens who can leave their borders or stations are being recalled. Replacement wardens will come from the poison fields to take over the resupply stations within the next week. The secondary list will find out in the next forty-eight to seventy-two hours. Now, you're holding up the line, and I have other stations to call."

He swallowed dryly. "Am I recalled?"

"I don't have your name on my current list."

"Where is the governor?"

There was a pause before the other warden answered. "Glencoe. She's alive."

The line clicked off, call ending, and Soren stood there, frozen in place, staring blankly at nothing. The news didn't seem real—that the Warden's Island had fallen to Daijal. That a country would go against everything dictated by the Poison Accords and bring harm to the very people that kept the world safe.

Soren drew in a ragged breath, wondering about the tithes, about the wardens too old or wounded to survive the poison fields. The Warden's Island was supposed to be a respite from the roads and borders. It wasn't a home, but it was all any warden had.

And now they didn't even have that.

Soren shook his head, crumpling up the piece of paper and dropping it in the bin by the desk. He took himself out of the resupply station, locking the door behind him. His skin had goose bumps, and not even the heat of a summer day could warm him.

Soren didn't know how Vanya would react to news of the Warden's Island being attacked. Sanctions were primed to be levied against Solaria. Even with that punishment in play, Soren liked to think Vanya wouldn't take pleasure in the deaths of Soren's fellow wardens and too-young tithes.

He reached for his belt, belatedly realizing he'd left his televox in the bedroom back at the palace, not expecting to need to fully gear up for a simple roundtrip to the resupply station. He could use the telephone inside the resupply station, but Vanya would not expect the call from that number and would not answer on his personal televox. Calling the household line was out of the question. Neither could he reach the Chief Minister's office and hope the news wouldn't spread.

Ever since the discovery of Amir's status as a *rionetka*, Vanya had become deeply distrustful. That lack of trust was something Soren understood, leaving them both on edge, despite all the precautions Vanya attempted to take to safeguard his House and country.

If a call wasn't possible, the only other option was to return with the devastating news in person. Soren didn't recall much of the drive back to the Imperial palace. The streets passed in a blur as he guided his velocycle through the traffic. The *praetoria* legionnaires on guard duty at the palace gates sent him through with a crisp wave, and he drove into the forecourt.

Rather than leave his velocycle for a servant to deal with, he drove it at a low speed to the garage detached from the main wings of the palace. He needed the tools there to do a check on the engine. He'd been planning to perform that maintenance after the gathering today and before he got on the road, but it needed to be done now. It couldn't wait.

Neither could Vanya.

Soren drove into the garage and got off his velocycle, walking it toward the mechanics bay. He parked it in an out-of-the-way spot before leaving the garage and returning to the palace proper. Soren stopped the first servant he found who wore the colors of one assigned to the royal household as opposed to the general palace staff.

"Where's the emperor?" Soren asked.

The maid bowed her head respectfully, carefully keeping the vase of flowers she was carrying upright. "I haven't seen him this morning. Perhaps try the star temple? He spoke yesterday of wanting to pray this morning."

It wouldn't be out of character for Vanya to pray before a gathering, despite already having Callisto's blessing. He was dutiful that way. Soren nodded his thanks before striding down the hallway, making his way across the palace wings again for an entrance that would take him to the private star temple.

It was a place he was familiar with, ever since entering it the first time for the funeral of Vanya's parents. He'd long moved past the quiet fury of realizing what lay beneath the palace, working to better secure the entrance to the crypt. Vanya had agreed to all his suggestions, including the creation of a secondary door built by warden engineers, with a key given to the House rather than the Star Order.

It was meant as an extra precaution, requiring the presence of a member of the ruling House or someone they designated from the royal household to enter the crypt. There was no recent cause—for Vanya and Raiah still lived—to open the crypt within the star temple. So it was strange to find the way barred by a star priest, door closed behind him, and the *praetoria* legionnaires who normally patrolled the star temple missing.

"The temple is off-limits today," the star priest said, refusing to move. His Solarian was faintly accented, sounding as if he were from one of the *vasilyets* around Bellingham or even Karnak.

"I'm looking for the emperor."

"He isn't here."

"I was told he came to pray."

"There is no sermon set for today. Again, I must ask you to leave."

The star priests assigned to the star temple here knew Soren. They knew this was his border, knew he had explicit permission to enter at any time. He had never been barred from the premises, for the only one who had the authority to do so was Vanya.

And Vanya never would.

A chill coursed down Soren's spine, unease settling in his skin. He stared at the star priest, whose serene expression never wavered. He contemplated sliding free the Imperial writ tucked safe into the inner pocket of his vest to gain access but decided against doing so.

"I'll look for him in the greenhouse, then. He likes to wander there after a prayer session," Soren said, lying through his teeth. Vanya almost always returned to the palace after praying, busy as he was.

The star priest nodded, waving Soren away with one hand. "May the stars guide you."

The greenhouse was within the palace gardens but set beyond the star temple. It was an excuse for Soren to follow the path around the circular building to the rear entrance typically used by star priests and *praetoria* legionnaires. The door was plain-looking and unguarded but locked.

Frowning, he withdrew the lockpicks and slipped them into the keyhole, fumbling a bit with the tumblers and gears. It took a minute or so for him to pick the lock, pushing the door open slowly, looking up in case there was a bell he had to be aware of. But the way forward was unalarmed in any way, no spell set down to seal it off or give warning of someone entering or leaving.

Soren pushed the door open wide enough to allow himself to slip through, letting it close quietly behind him. The service hallway was low-lit by a single sconce, throwing gaslight on the smooth-tiled walls and the pair of bodies sprawled on the floor. Soren stilled, automatically unholstering his pistol. He approached the bodies of the man and woman dressed in the robes of star priests, the white panels of their robes stained dark with blood. The backs of their robes were ripped from stab wounds, blood congealing around the bodies.

Soren crouched beside them, attention focused on the hallway ahead of him. He touched two gloved fingers to the throat of the nearest body, not checking for a pulse but for rigidity. Flesh gave beneath the pressure, speaking of the star priest having been murdered recently, most likely within the last hour.

He straightened, moving farther into the star temple rather than retreating outside. The safer option would've been to leave and come back with reinforcements, but if he didn't know who the enemy was, he wouldn't be able to warn Vanya. So Soren followed the sound of voices that came from the sanctuary at the center of the star temple, keeping to the shadows, pistol raised and ready to fire.

Soren slowly crept into a side chamber, his movement masked by a half-open door leading to the sanctuary. He stayed low, kneeling behind an altar set up in the center of the small space. He peered around it, taking in the people who wore the robes of star priests but who carried themselves more like mercenaries than religious servants. Some were speaking in Daijalan, others in Solarian. What he could understand made Soren's breath catch in his throat.

"We can't blow the charges until we know all the Houses are within the palace for the end of the Conclave. Can you ensure the star temple will be inaccessible until then?" a blond man said in heavily accented Solarian.

Soren had to bite his tongue to keep his shock choked back when he saw who came to stand by the stranger and answer his question. The woman in question stepped over a body on her way, gown clutched in slim hands to keep the hem from dragging through blood.

"I forged the emperor's signature on a change of duty order. The *praetoria* legionnaires typically on guard duty around the star temple have been reassigned for the day. You'll have free movement so long as you keep your robes on beyond these walls," Alida said.

The majordomo of the royal household, one of Vanya's closest confidants when it came to the safety of his House, calmly unclipped a large brass key from her key ring and handed it over to the stranger. The key was one Soren recognized, even from a distance.

It was the key that opened the secondary door meant to keep the crypt locked.

"You hope," the man said, taking the key from her.

"No one questions me. They think I'm loyal. I've proven that fact to the emperor's satisfaction over and over again. He suspects nothing."

Vanya hadn't, Soren knew with a sinking sensation in his stomach. Neither had Soren. Alida had been checked for vivisection scars time and time again, coming away as human. She had been with Vanya's household since he was a teenager, rising from servant to majordomo, never straying from service to his House. Her steady presence had been a balm to Soren amidst the politics of the Imperial court as he came and went over the last few years, always ready with an answer to any question he had when Vanya wasn't there to hear him.

She'd been loyal.

She'd been *trusted*.

The incandescent rage that suddenly suffused him made his lungs constrict, made his skin hot. He tightened his grip on his pistol, finger pressed hard against the trigger guard. He clenched his teeth together, forcing his breathing to stay quiet and steady. Something hot and vicious unfurled in his chest, the aether a mere breath away.

It would be so easy, he knew, to reach for the power long denied him and burn everyone in the star temple to ash. But doing so would only implicate himself in the act when a warden wasn't supposed to command starfire at all. If Vanya knew what Soren had kept from him, then Soren would be no better than Alida, and he didn't want to be that.

A sound came from behind him, and Soren moved on instinct, twisting out of the way of the Blade that sought to slide a knife between his ribs and very nearly succeeded. The motion caused the candles and incense burners on the altar to tumble to the ground, clattering on the tiles.

Soren kicked out with one foot at the stranger's knee, but the other man dodged out of the way with an agile twist. Shouts from the sanctuary made Soren swear, knowing he only had a moment—seconds, really—to *get out*.

He didn't bother to engage in close quarters with the man who'd sneaked up on him. Instead, Soren swung his pistol around and pulled hard on the trigger. The loud sound of the bullet exiting the chamber made the shouting in the sanctuary only get louder. He'd aimed blindly, wanting to create some room to maneuver in, and while the first bullet hadn't hit the enemy, his second punched through the man's shoulder.

A lucky shot, but his luck ran out seconds later.

Soren was on his feet when the man Alida had been speaking with kicked the chamber door all the way open, leading with his pistol as he entered the now crowded space. Soren would've chanced a run for the hallway, already half turned to flee, but the bullet that cut through the air mere inches from the side of his face to embed itself in the stone wall had him freezing where he stood.

"I thought everyone in the star temple was handled?" the man snapped, staring down the barrel of his pistol with cold eyes.

Soren's gaze didn't stray from the pistol, not even when Alida sidled up behind the man, blanching when she saw him. "That's Vanya's warden. You can't kill him, Witten."

The barrel of the pistol was aimed directly at Soren's head, his own uselessly aimed at nothing. "Give me one good reason why I can't?"

"Because Joelle wants him alive."

Soren stiffened at that statement, his gaze snapping to Alida. "Your loyalty is with the House of *Kimathi*? You'd betray your emperor?"

Alida raised her chin, color having returned to her face, though her lips were still pale. "My loyalty lies with the House of Laxsom. It always has."

Soren stared at her, clenching his hand tighter around his pistol. "Rixham is a dead city."

Something fierce and prideful filled her eyes. "Its people *aren't*."

"You—"

"I had a family once," Alida spat, the serene countenance she always seemed to carry twisting into something filled with hate and an old kind of grief. "They died in Rixham. I'll see Vanya bury all of his before he dies."

Soren wanted so badly to shoot her, pistol twitching in his hand, but he never got the chance. What felt like a straight-lined windstorm slammed into him with enough force to lift him off his feet and send him crashing against the wall at his back. He hit hard enough to drive all the air from his lungs, head cracking sharp and painfully hard against smooth stone.

His teeth clacked together, catching the edge of his tongue, and copper flooded his mouth. His vision didn't fade, but it constricted at the edges from the blow to his head. By the time he managed to force his lungs to draw in air, someone was kneeling over him, sliding a needle into his wrist. It took two blinks for him to focus on Alida's face, struggling to sit up, feeling as if he was about to vomit.

"I'd let the Blades kill you if you weren't worth more alive. *Vezir* Joelle has questions about what happened in the quarry, and you will answer them," Alida said.

She stepped back before Soren could grab her, someone else taking her place. Soren lashed out at them, the world tilting from the head wound he'd taken. Whatever Alida had given him wasn't poison, but he could feel *something* creeping through his veins that made his limbs less coordinated.

Drugs were something his body could handle—no one ever medicated correctly for a warden's resistance to toxins and poisons. But a bone-bruising concussion was something else. Pain throbbed down his neck and jaw, a splitting headache already creeping through his skull. It made fighting back difficult when two men—Blades or others, he couldn't tell—sought to secure him.

Someone grabbed him by the arms, another by the feet. Soren twisted in their grip, trying to get free. He slammed a hand against someone's chest, fingers curling over fabric and a thin chain. He lost his grip on the robe when someone punched him in the face. The world blurred, going dark at the edges as spots erupted across his vision, but he managed to keep hold of the necklace, the chain breaking. He spat blood to clear his mouth, not letting go of whatever was tangled around his fingers.

"Why isn't he unconscious yet?" Alida asked from somewhere he couldn't see.

"He's a warden. Your drugs won't work on him," Witten said.

Soren bared his teeth, snarling, but there were enough people to hold him down, keep him still, that he had no chance to escape. Another prick of a needle, this time in his neck, had him trying to kick out. A tiredness washed through him almost immediately, making it difficult to concentrate. He couldn't even focus well enough to call up starfire, feeling as if his skull was ready to split apart when he tried.

"Let's get below. We need to set the charges and clear out before anyone knows we've been here," Witten said.

"We need the warden alive," Alida said.

"We can't walk out with him when he's like this and has seen you. We'll keep him below until it's safe to retrieve him after the revenants are freed."

Soren drew in a breath, icy fear making his breath stutter in his throat. He couldn't find the words to protest as he was hauled up between two Blades and half dragged, half carried out of the side chamber and into the sanctuary of the star temple itself.

He watched, almost as if from a distance, as the intricately mosaiced floor was opened with the high priestess' staff. He could feel the thrumming of gears through where his knees rested against the floor. The new iron door that had been specially created to seal the entranceway beneath the floor was opened with the key Alida had handed over.

Then he was dragged down into the cold darkness of the royal crypt, filled with its iron tombs and the dead that scratched inside of them, always looking for a way out.

Soren's breath came out of his mouth in ragged little gasps as they hauled him far into the crypt, to the alcoves with empty coffins, plaques carrying no names of the dead. He was stripped of his weapons and manhandled into a cold grave, head glancing off the edge of the coffin, the blow enough to send bright streaks of light cutting across his eyes. He went limp, gritting his teeth against the pain, eyes squeezed shut as he struggled to stay conscious.

When he could see again, he found himself weaponless and in near total darkness, the iron coffin lid settled above, with only a sliver of space open near his head to let in air. The space was growing warmer, and he realized why after a long, agonizing moment as he clawed his focus back into place.

They were welding the lid in place.

Soren pressed his hands against the coffin lid, fingers scraping against warming metal, his breathing frantic and ragged in his ears. “Let me out.”

They either didn’t hear him or didn’t listen.

They only left him there in the dark, buried in the crypt, with the dead for company.

VANYA

"This isn't how I thought my marriage would end," Malia, of the House of Vikandir, said with a grief Vanya could see etched into her face.

The older woman was dressed grandly for the gathering set to start later in the day before sunset, but there was no joy in the way she carried herself. Vanya had invited Amir's wife to the midday meal because that House, for all the damage done to it, was still loyal. A magician whose skill in mind magic was unparalleled had confirmed that.

Amir had been relegated to a suite in the House of Vikandir's estate in Calhames, under round-the-clock guard by legionnaires assigned to that House's *vasilyet*. Amir was himself in all the ways that mattered, an eerie puppet mimicking the man who had given Vanya so much advice and support since his parents' passing. But he could no longer be trusted and would remain a prisoner within his household until he could be saved—if that was even possible—or until he died.

Sometime after Chu Hua had set up the spell detector devices in his office and during the Conclave, Amir had been turned into a *rionetka*. No one could pinpoint the exact moment it had occurred, though Vanya had his suspicions. Malia did, too, ones which Taisiya had no qualms about giving voice to.

"What will you say to the House of Kimathi?" Taisiya asked.

Malia folded her hands together over the edge of the table, having barely touched the platters of food on offer. Her plate was mostly empty, and not because she'd eaten. "My spies have informed me Joelle has fled the city, returning to Bellingham. Her actions speak of guilt."

"They speak of failure on her part."

Vanya nodded in Taisiya's direction. "I have to agree with my *valide*. Since the Dawn Star's blessing, the Houses have realigned behind mine, even many of those who bought into Joelle's lies. There are several holdouts, but not enough to be a threat."

He didn't like to think about what would have happened if Callisto hadn't shown up. Joelle had been on track to gain loyalty from a good many Houses, both major and minor, during the Conclave. If she was behind the travesty that had occurred with Amir, then it was merely a last-gasp effort to claw her way into power at the destruction of someone else's life.

It seemed her habit.

Vanya reached for the wine carafe but froze when the sound of rapid footsteps caught his ear. He watched as Chief Minister Caelum hurried through the courtyard entrance, making a beeline for their shaded table.

"Your Imperial Majesty," Caelum said with a sketch of a bow, out of breath and harried-looking.

"What is it?" Vanya asked, frowning.

Caelum thrust out his hand, a folded piece of paper held between his fingers. "My sincere apologies for the interruption, but I have news that cannot wait. This just came in from the Warden's Island, at the behest of the governor's office."

Vanya took the note, unease settling in his chest. He unfolded it and read what was transcribed there, the message diligently recorded from a telephone call to the Chief Minister's office, as Caelum was generally the point of contact for wardens and their border reports.

Daijal attacked the Warden's Island. Severe damage occurred. The wardens' governor is recalling a percentage of wardens. The border Solaria shares with Daijal will be affected. We will reach out once our defenses are secure.

The words didn't make sense at first—the inconceivable actions of Daijal's queen impossible to accept as he read the note over again. Even knowing the sanctions he'd brought upon Solaria that had yet to be levied, not once had Vanya ever thought about attacking the people who guarded Maricol's borders to spare his country the higher number of tithes.

Quickly following that thought was the desperate relief that Soren had been delayed in returning Solaria's border reports to the Warden's Island. If he'd been there, the likelihood of him being injured or killed by such an attack was high.

Taisiya leaned forward. "What has happened?"

Vanya handed the note to her. "Daijal has attacked the Warden's Island. Queen Eimarille has broken the Poison Accords."

Taisiya nearly dropped the note, eyes shocked wide. Malia made a strangled sort of sound, half rising from her seat. "*No.*"

Karnak had strong ties with wardens by virtue of being the closest Solarian city to the Warden's Island for transit purposes. All of Solaria's tithes went through Karnak, and wardens were welcomed inside that city's walls. The House of Vikandir had always been a huge supporter of wardens.

Vanya stood, looking at Caelum. "Summon the Daijalan ambassador and Imperial General Chu Hua to the palace. I will speak with them in the throne room before the Conclave commences this evening."

"Of course, Your Imperial Majesty," Caelum said with a bow of his head.

Caelum left, and Vanya wanted to do the same, but Taisiya's voice stopped him. "If the wardens stop guarding the borders, there will be an uproar."

"I know."

Taisiya looked at him, still holding the note. "Where is your warden? He should know what has happened to his people."

Vanya didn't argue that Soren wasn't his, because in that moment, he wished it were true. "I'll find him. He was supposed to be back by now."

A trip to the resupply station in the city shouldn't have taken so long. Vanya had expected Soren back for the midday meal—the servants had even set a place for him—but it had remained empty. He hoped Soren hadn't heard the news and left without saying goodbye.

"We have the gathering tonight," Taisiya reminded him as she handed back the note. He folded it up and put it in his pocket.

Vanya grimaced. "I am aware. I won't cancel it."

He realistically couldn't. For his House, for his country, he had to let the Conclave play out. While he wouldn't come away with debts, he'd come away with loyalty, and he could ill afford to lose any of it.

Vanya strode from the courtyard, meal forgotten, and headed toward his office. Caelum's aides would know where to find him once the ambassador and general arrived. He entered it right as Alida came bustling down the hallway, a clipboard in hand and pencil in the other. His majordomo was overseeing the preparations for the gathering and had been busy all morning.

She was unscarred, unlike Amir. The spell-detecting device had never activated for her, but Vanya couldn't help feeling a twinge of unease whenever she or anyone else entered his office, waiting for the warning system to go off.

It didn't, of course, and Alida dipped into a respectful bow. "Your Imperial Majesty. The entertainers for this evening's gathering have all been cleared."

He grunted. "Have you seen Soren?"

Alida shook her head. "No. The servants said he returned on his velocycle some time ago, but I have not seen him."

Vanya frowned, moving around his desk to sit. "He was supposed to join us for the midday meal."

"Perhaps he is working in his office? I can send a runner to check."

"Do so. Once he's found, send him to me."

"Of course. Now, your robes are laid out and ready for you to change into later. I've requested the crown—"

"Changing will have to wait, but I want the crown brought to me here. I'll be meeting with the Daijal ambassador shortly."

Alida blinked at him, pencil going still over the page on her clipboard. "The Daijal ambassador?"

"Yes. I require an explanation of their country's actions. I'll meet them in the throne room. Have it prepared to receive them."

Alida took the new instructions in stride, as she always did. "Of course. I'll tend to that now."

She left, closing the door behind her. Vanya took the note out of his pocket and folded it open to read the words again. "Where are you, Soren?"

As much as he wanted to, Vanya didn't have time to dwell on Soren's absence or go searching for him. The crown arrived from the vaults, brought by the Imperial jewelers, one of whom offered it to Vanya with a respectful bow of their head. Vanya took the crown and settled it on his head before striding out of his office.

The palace bustled with servants and other political aides, busier than usual in anticipation of the Conclave ending tonight. Vanya made his way to the throne room, knowing it would take time for the ambassador and general to arrive but wanting to prepare regardless. He found Caelum waiting for him in that grand space, the chief minister holding a folio stamped with a seal meant to mark it as private government communications.

"More news?" Vanya asked.

Caelum nodded gravely. "E'ridia has issued a temporary border closure. The *Comhairle nan Cinnidhean* has recalled their trading airships from Solaria."

"We have done nothing wrong."

"My understanding is it is precautionary."

Vanya dragged his hand over his mouth. "And their ambassador?"

"Still in Calhames. I've received no recall notice from the E'ridian embassy."

"Summon them as well. I'll be damned if E'ridia thinks we had any part in this atrocity. I'll meet with them after I hear what the Daijal ambassador has to say."

"I will put a call in to their embassy." Caelum handed over the folio. "Will you be notifying the Senate today of what has transpired?"

"I need to close out the Conclave first, and I want more information than we have on what's going on before I bring this problem before the Senate. They'll want input on any action I decide to take where our borders are concerned. Considering the Conclave, it's best if I allow it."

He could issue such an order on his own, but it would cause more problems than it was worth right now. He was so close to solidifying enough support to challenge Joelle's actions that he couldn't afford to act alone, even when he had that right as emperor.

Flipping open the folio, Vanya skimmed the typed-out memorandums and telegram messages, turning pages quickly as he absorbed the beginning of an international problem that was becoming Solaria's as well.

Vanya had finished reviewing the last page when footsteps on the marble floor made him look over at the entrance. Imperial General Chu Hua strode across the throne room in full uniform, straight-backed and grimly determined. "Your Imperial Majesty."

Vanya snapped the folio shut before offering it to her once she was within arm's reach. "Review this."

She took it, and Vanya retreated to the throne, the memory of having Soren there lingering in his thoughts as he sat. He couldn't banish his worry over the other man, and Vanya was half tempted to send legionnaires out on a search for the warden.

Chu Hua was quick to absorb the information before closing the folio and tucking it under one arm. She met his gaze easily enough. "I've been reliably informed by the Imperial outpost between Karnak and Seaville that an E'ridian *jarl* requested evacuation support over the radio from any available E'ridian airships during the night."

"E'ridia shouldn't be the only country providing aid."

"The wardens haven't requested any."

Vanya would have replied but fell silent as a *praetoria* legionnaire stepped inside the throne room, acting in the absence of a political aide to announce an expected arrival. "Your Imperial Majesty, the Daijalan ambassador is here to see you."

The ambassador swept in before the *praetoria* legionnaire even finished speaking, dressed in what Vanya supposed passed for Daijalan fashion. There was far too much lace, constricting tailoring, and gaudy brocade in an eye-searing mix of colors for his tastes. He and his entourage clearly expected more of a crowd, their footsteps echoing loudly in the throne room without courtiers to break up the sound.

He dipped into an elaborate northern bow before rising and greeting Vanya in accented Solarian. "Your Imperial Majesty, how may I be of service?"

"Ambassador Ansel," Vanya said coolly. "I've been informed your country has broken the Poison Accords by attacking the Warden's Island."

The ambassador was in his early forties, more than a decade older than Vanya, and well versed in the realms of politics. He didn't immediately react to Vanya's accusation, expression a mask of bland neutrality. "I must confess, I know not what you speak of, Your Imperial Majesty."

"I'm certain you don't. It wasn't your orders that caused the unthinkable. It was your queen's."

"What you accuse my queen of is madness."

"It *is* madness. Who in their right mind would try to annihilate the people who guard our borders and cleanse the land?"

Ansel firmed his jaw, blue eyes narrowing. "I sincerely request you do not speak ill of my country's queen."

"Your country's queen is asking for war. From Ashion, and now, it seems, from the wardens themselves."

"Again, I know not of this hearsay you speak of."

"Of course you don't." He stared at the Daijalan Ambassador, weighing his options, before abruptly deciding on the one that would most certainly create an unfortunate political mess. "You are summarily expelled from Solaria, Ambassador Ansel. I expect your people to be out of my country by tomorrow evening."

Vanya heard Caelum breathe in sharply, but his chief minister didn't speak up to try to change Vanya's mind. Neither did Imperial General Chu Hua. Her piercing, judging gaze remained on the ambassador, and silence was all the confirmation Vanya needed of her agreement.

Ansel, however, appeared momentarily taken aback before his expression smoothed out. His voice, when he spoke, was flatly controlled, giving no hint of his emotional state. "Your accusations have no basis. Whatever has happened to the wardens was not initiated by my country."

"I look forward to hearing what the surviving wardens have to say about that. I assume it will match Ashion's displeasure of the invasion currently happening in their western provinces."

Ansel pressed his lips into a thin white line before squaring his shoulders. "Ashion is under Daijal's rulership. There is no invasion, merely outreach to cities and towns who cannot rely on the wardens."

"Is that what they're calling war these days?" Chu Hua asked in a mild voice.

Ansel refused to respond to her jibe. "Daijal will depart from our embassy by tomorrow evening. I am certain you must be aware this insult will not be accepted lightly in the Daijal court."

Vanya knew it wouldn't. He knew the moment Ansel made it back to his country's embassy, he'd be ringing his people back in New Haven. Vanya expected an official denunciation of the expulsion from Queen Eimarille and had little doubt she'd expel his own diplomats from Daijal. "The rest of Maricol won't stand for the actions of your queen."

Ansel kept to protocol and bowed. "Your Imperial Majesty."

Vanya dismissed him with a wave of his hand, watching as the ambassador and his small entourage left the throne room. The meeting had taken bare minutes, but the fallout would take days, if not weeks, to settle.

"I'll send a small platoon to watch the embassy. We'll search the premises once they are gone," Chu Hua said.

"They'll burn any documents they can't take with them," Caelum warned.

"If we're lucky, they'll miss some."

The destruction of diplomatic cables and other classified documents was to be expected. It was standard procedure anytime an embassy was closed. Vanya sighed, leaning back in the throne. "Would it be better or worse to recall our diplomat and embassy workers in New Haven before Eimarille expels them?"

Caelum rubbed at his chin. "There is a chance Eimarille won't expel our people."

"She'd never trust any diplomat I allow to stay, and that puts our people at a risk beyond a border we can't cross."

"The risk isn't worth it, not with the threat of *rionetkas* at play and the wardens reeling from the attack. Queen Eimarille cannot be trusted," Chu Hua argued.

Vanya grimaced and looked over at Caelum. "Recall our Daijal ambassador and everyone at the embassy. Let Eimarille send an envoy here to argue her actions."

Caelum bowed. "I will send the order on your behalf at once. What will you tell the Senate?"

"Nothing today. I must meet with the E'ridian ambassador and then close out the Conclave."

Tomorrow, he would inform the Senate of what had happened to the Warden's Island and his decision regarding their embassy in Daijal. Tonight was dedicated to cutting Joelle off from the power she craved.

Four

HONOVI

The *Celestial Sprite* settled into its assigned anchor berth outside Veran, the airship crew deftly handling the anchor and ropes in concert with the ground crew. Five other war airships—part of the squadron the *Comhairle nan Cinnidhean* had sent to the Warden's Island—had beaten them west by a day. Those airships remained airborne, lashed to the earth by long anchors, weapons protruding from their hulls.

The rest of the squadron remained east, with orders to evacuate wounded wardens and ferry them back to Glencoe. Half a dozen airships would remain at the lake to guard the wardens who stayed behind to begin the difficult process of rebuilding while retaining control of the Warden's Island.

Honovi secured the controls before handing them over to Caoimhe and heading out onto the crowded deck. They'd packed the airship to the hull with the last of the wardens needing to come west to handle the extraction of their brethren out of Daijal. Ksenia had been deputized by Delani as the wardens' lieutenant governor, a post intermittently filled in their history and typically only in emergencies. She'd been on an earlier flight out to Veran to handle logistics.

Honovi figured a burgeoning war counted as an emergency.

Caris met him on the decking with Nathaniel by her side. She had a leather travel tube slung across one shoulder, the map inside it drawn with spelled ink to assist the movement of the clarion crystal shard she wore. That bit of magicked clarion crystal was all that could lead them to Blaine.

"Meleri and Lore are on the docks with Ksenia," Caris said.

Honovi nodded. "Good. We need updates on what the western border is like and the readiness of the Ashion army."

"Won't be much of an army if parliament has any say over it."

"Then we better hope Meleri's Clockwork Brigade has enticed a rebellion with the provinces that matter."

Their welcoming committee on the pier greeted the wardens gamely enough before Honovi, Caris, and Nathaniel stepped off the gangplank. Meleri wore a gown as befitting her station, though there was little decorum in how she strode forward to sweep Caris into her arms for a fierce sort of hug. Caris tucked her head against Meleri's shoulder, holding on tight for a moment while Meleri whispered something into her ear Honovi couldn't hear.

When the two parted, Meleri's eyes looked a little watery, but her voice was steady when she spoke. "I'm very glad you're safe."

"Did you have trouble while we were gone?" Caris asked.

"Not particularly." Meleri's gaze slid to where Nathaniel stood. "Did you?"

Caris stepped back, reaching for Nathaniel's hand without looking, the same way Honovi would have if Blaine was standing near. "The wardens figured out a way to bypass the compulsion spells that control a *rionetka*. Nathaniel is himself again."

"I want to apologize profusely for putting everyone in danger," Nathaniel said stiffly, as if he'd had a choice in the matter.

Meleri nodded slowly, expression unreadable. "We'll need to adjust your chain."

Nathaniel's expression tightened, but he didn't argue. If Honovi were in Meleri's place, he'd fully remove Nathaniel from any critical information. The wardens had worked a miracle, but there was no guarantee it would last.

Honovi turned his attention to where Ksenia stood, arms crossed over her chest and laden down with weapons. She'd been directing her people down the pier, giving them instructions on where to go once inside the town walls while Meleri finished greeting Caris. Now, she stepped closer, squinting against the sunlight. "I hear you want to head to Foxborough."

"That's where the crystal stops on the map for now," Honovi said with a sharp nod. They'd checked not even an hour ago, and Honovi itched to check again.

"There's always a chance they'll have found the crystal on him and he won't be there."

Honovi bared his teeth. "I'm going."

"You and part of your country's air force, it seems," Meleri said, frowning up at the sky. "Foxborough will see it as an invasion. They'll try to shoot you down."

"We'll chance it, even if Eimarille has equipped every town with anti-airship guns."

"Her bombs were top-tier during the attack on the Warden's Island, but she wasn't expecting airships of your country's caliber over the Celestine Lake," Caris said.

"I wouldn't underestimate Eimarille," Lore warned. "You should prepare for the possibility that she's planned out an attack on E'ridia that takes into account your country's superior air force."

"She won't be ready to face us right now," Honovi said.

"You hope."

"It doesn't matter. She ordered the attack on the Warden's Island. Her people took my husband prisoner. We have no proof she's behind the *rionetkas*, but who else stands to gain from destabilizing other governments? If it's war she wants, it's war she'll have."

Meleri met his gaze with a regretful sort of sadness in her own. "I wish this wasn't anyone's road, but if you are set to walk it, then you should know the Marshal sent cogs to Foxborough after they warned me about the troop buildup along the southern portion of the central border. We'll have allies in that city, but they won't be military-trained and won't have clout to override any government orders. Foxborough is governed by Ashionens loyal to Daijal despite its populace's sympathies for the Clockwork Brigade."

"I have no qualms with Ashionen citizens who have refused to abide by the will of the Daijal court."

"They'll still be within your field of fire. If you drop bombs on that city, they'll be among the death count."

Honovi clenched his teeth together, unable to argue that fact. "It's not my intention to fire on innocent people. I just want my husband back. If you want Caris as queen, you'll need him."

"Do you think the Clockwork Brigade could rally support if it's known I granted E'ridia's war airships the right to travel within our air space?" Caris asked.

"You aren't queen yet," Lore reminded her.

Caris smiled thinly. "And I won't be, not legally, not without Blaine. He's the only one who can confirm I am who I say I am. Without him, my name won't be written down in the royal genealogies, and that must happen. There are those who prefer the tradition of a Rourke on the throne continue on, even if their only perceived choice is Eimarille."

"You could sit on the starfire throne. You could put out the decree the North Star lit after the Inferno. That would prove you are Rourke."

"Maybe so, but since the riot, since Daijal crossed the western border, how likely is it that Amari is accessible?"

Lore's mouth ticked downward before she nodded in pained agreement. "My sister Brielle and her family are stuck in the capital. Parliament enacted an emergency order to close the city walls. No one gets in or out now. They've effectively sealed the city."

"We have wardens inside those walls," Ksenia said, planting her hands on her hips. "If the Ashion parliament follows Daijal orders, then my wardens will be recalled."

Meleri drew in a sharp breath. "From the entire country?"

Ksenia shrugged, clearly not put out by their concern. "We'll carve out exceptions province by province if need be. *We* weren't the ones who broke the Poison Accords."

"Eimarille's word is law as far as she views it, and she clearly doesn't care for wardens. Her recent actions prove as much," Lore said.

"Could we get the wardens out through the catacombs?" Nathaniel asked.

Caris' expression became hopeful. "And my parents? Could we try to rescue them as well?"

"The catacombs do extend past the city walls," Meleri said slowly. "But many of the routes aren't fully accessible. It's a risk, especially if Daijal has gained access. And I'm sorry, Caris. The cogs left behind in that city got word out that your parents have now been sent west."

Caris covered her mouth with one hand, hunching her shoulders. Nathaniel wrapped an arm around her waist, pulling her in close. To her credit, she didn't break down sobbing, but Honovi could see the tears in her eyes.

Lore glanced at her mother before focusing on Ksenia. "The Daijalans wouldn't know where to go if they entered the catacombs. We could try to reach your wardens that way if you're willing to risk it. We have cogs that need to be evacuated as well."

Honovi was aware the catacombs beneath Amari were extensive from what Blaine had once told him. Whether they were a way to gain access to the Ashion capital was an argument for another day. "Blaine isn't in Amari. He's in Foxborough. Unless you tell me there are catacombs in that city, then we'll be flying in."

Caris wiped away a couple of tears with the back of her hand. "You should spread the word to the Clockwork Brigade and the army through coded messages that I'm heading to Foxborough with allies."

"No, you are not," Meleri said firmly.

Caris drew herself up to her full height, a stubborn look coming to her eyes. "I won't leave Blaine to Eimarille's mercy."

"And if you go, we risk losing you. No, Caris, I must insist you stay here."

"Meleri—"

"Mother is right, Caris," Lore interjected. "We can't risk losing you. We've managed to obtain support from bloodlines in the eastern provinces, but all of that is predicated upon your survival. If we lose you, we lose Ashion."

"But—"

Nathaniel touched her shoulder, drawing Caris' attention to him. "I'll go where you go, but if the *Klovod* is in Foxborough, I'd rather not test the warden's alchemy against his when it comes to my clockwork heart."

It was a calculated request, one that had Lore's shoulders easing from their tense line. Caris' expression twisted, but whatever position she had wanted to take to join the fighting forces in Foxborough, it wilted beneath Nathaniel's concern. "I don't want to put you in danger."

"Then stay with me here in Veran."

After a moment, Caris gave a reluctant nod. Lore let out a soft sigh that Honovi barely heard over the sounds coming from the surrounding airfield. "You'll be there in spirit if not in person. If it eases your mind any, I'll go with Honovi to Foxborough while you work with Meleri to solidify support with the bloodlines."

"You'd have me be a figurehead," Caris said.

"You always were." Lore spoke firmly, not unkindly, but Caris still flinched. Then she drew in a breath and slid the travel case off her shoulder, handing it to Honovi. He took it and the clarion crystal that she pulled off her necklace, cradling both in careful hands.

"Thank you," he said.

Meleri clasped her hands together as she stepped back. "Well, I suppose there's nothing for it, then. Ashion citizens will have to choose sides, and I chose mine years ago. The Ashion army is mustering in the eastern provinces, and we have representatives in the Urovan court asking for aid. We will work to defend Ashion from Daijal."

Ksenia shook her head. "Call your people back from Urova. Every submersible used in the attack on the island came from that country. If Eimarille has Urova's Isar as an ally, they won't be yours."

Meleri pursed her lips, appearing tired in the face of that unexpected news. "I'll pass that information along. Right now, we've a battalion bivouacked throughout Veran. Half of them can be mustered as your reinforcements within an hour. The rest must remain here for defense purposes. There's a steam train waiting at the station that can carry people west, but it won't match the speed of your airships."

"It doesn't need to. Our best bet for the least amount of casualties is a nighttime arrival. Wardens are legally allowed entry past the time a city gate is locked. The army can come through that way," Honovi said.

Ksenia nodded agreement. "I'd normally not advocate such deception, but these are not normal times. We wardens will assist as needed."

"What weapons and supplies does the Ashion army have?"

Meleri frowned. "Nothing for a siege."

"That isn't our intention here."

"I was informed by the quartermaster that the battalion came equipped with Zip guns, automatons, and military vehicles. Not all of those can be shipped off with you. We need some to remain here."

"Do they have any racing carriages?" Caris asked, causing Nathaniel to glance at her in alarm.

"Transport and attack vehicles, mostly. Veran has a few racing teams, though."

"Let me speak to the owners and see if they'll let us borrow a few racing carriages and allow for some modifications. You'll want fast vehicles to chase after whoever has Blaine."

Honovi wasn't going to argue with her. He'd heard from Blaine all about Caris' inventions when his husband had still been working under the false identity of a professor. Caris knew her way around an engine. That she knew her way around a racing carriage was a bit of a surprise, but he had to believe she knew how to modify one.

"Let's talk to your military," Honovi said, looking at Meleri. "My air force captain will want to coordinate with the commander of the ground troops who will be going west with us."

Meleri gestured toward the distant gate at the end of the airfield pier. "The officers are waiting past the wall to speak with you."

Honovi could only follow his country's tentative allies down a road none of them had ever wished for.

Five

TERILYN

Terilyn pushed open the door leading to the hidden basement room built inside a well-to-do home in a Foxborough neighborhood populated by rich merchants. It was owned by a transplanted Daijalan family whose loyalty to the Daijal court had never been in question. Their daughter had gone into the Star Order and been summarily inducted as a Blade. Terilyn had used their home many times over the years, safe in the knowledge the family was sworn to secrecy.

The basement wasn't a laboratory. It wasn't a place for the *Klovod* to conduct his gruesome operations. But it was a place where particular people were brought to extract information.

The room Terilyn entered was little more than an underground cell, the concrete floor and walls stained from moisture and other things. A single gaslight hung from the ceiling, casting a harsh orange glow over the prisoner when she flicked the switch.

The man sprawled on the floor didn't flinch away from the light, eyes closed, face flushed from the onset of fever. His right wrist was secured by a metal cuff, the chain leading to an anchor bolted to the middle of the floor. The protocol for transporting prisoners was to cuff both hands, but seeing as how he was missing his left arm from just below the elbow, she could understand why that standard hadn't been adhered to.

"He's alive," Captain Kendrick Gladstone said. The Daijalan army officer sported a bandage on his forehead and a splinted right wrist from the attack on the Warden's Island but was otherwise fine.

"Not in the best of health," Terilyn mused as she stepped inside the room. She crossed the short distance to the unconscious man and knelt, eyeing a face she'd seen once before through a torn veil.

The warrant put out by the Collector's Guild for Tristan Arquette had quite the bounty on it. They'd been after the man since the fight in the pub when Caris had first become a threat, both of them unknown adversaries until that moment.

Eimarille had lucked out that Raziel had crossed paths with Caris and Tristan in Veran, reporting the interesting news that Tristan was married to *jarl* Honovi of Clan Storm. He'd made a very good spy, passing as an Ashionen so well Terilyn hadn't questioned his nationality.

Terilyn stood and looked over at the doorway where a Daijalan government magician waited. "Wake him up."

The magician nodded and entered the room, withdrawing her clarion crystal–tipped wand from the case hanging off her belt. It looked to be made of antiqued metal, the end of it twisted coils molded to her grip. Kendrick closed the door behind them but didn't lock it, giving them privacy. Terilyn stood back, allowing the magician space to work.

The tip of the wand glowed softly, magic drawn from the aether slipping free in a coiled loop of foggy light. It fell onto the prisoner's slack face, sinking into his flushed skin. Terilyn counted three breaths before he jerked to awareness, eyes snapping open, body arching against the compulsion running through him.

"Wha—" he slurred, not quite all there, despite being awake. Fever and infection would do that.

"Do you remember me?" Terilyn asked.

He blinked slowly up at her, brow furrowing after a moment. His answer, when it came, was a long syllable of sound. "Yes."

Terilyn quirked a smile that wasn't friendly at all. "Good. Tell me your name."

He tried to lie. She could see the fight in the way his tendons stood out in his neck. In his current state, magicless as he was, he couldn't win against a magician. She expected the name from the warrant, but it wasn't the one she got. "Blaine Westergard."

Terilyn dropped to her knees, blade in hand out of instinct. The edge of her stiletto pressed against his throat, snug against his jaw. Considering the way he swallowed, she didn't think he knew it was there. "The Westergard bloodline is dead."

She should know. She'd read the reports of the Blades who had gone after it during the Inferno, killing generations of the people who'd claimed that name. No one of that bloodline should have been left alive.

And yet.

Blaine's lips parted, and he panted for air. "I'm not."

She held the stiletto so close to his skin she could slice it open with just the barest hint of pressure. His identity as the professor had been a lie all along. "Who is Caris?"

His expression twisted, eyes squeezing shut as he fought magic that was better than an alchemist's potion to coax the truth out of an unwilling target. "Rourke."

Terilyn was so startled her hand slipped, a motion her trainers would have beaten her for. The blade cut into the edge of his jaw, drawing a red line over the angle of bone. "How?"

She didn't want to believe it, but starfire of the caliber Caris wielded would realistically only be found in royalty. All the cadet bloodlines should have been eradicated. If Meleri had found a survivor of any of them, then that would explain it, but the Blades had been thorough.

Innes had been thorough.

Blaine opened his eyes, staring up at her. He bared his teeth, trying to keep them together, but the words slipped out anyway through the compulsion. "I carried her out of Amari after fleeing the palace."

Terilyn went cold at that revelation, breath stilling in her lungs.

Caris wasn't from a cadet branch, then, but a direct descendent of the royal family that once sat upon the throne. Eimarille had once had a younger brother, thought dead since the Inferno. Queen Ophelia had died with her unborn child—or so everyone assumed. Yet here Blaine was, lying at her feet, claiming to have rescued a princess whose name was never written down in the royal genealogies.

But could be, with a proper witness.

She should kill him now, Terilyn knew, except the act of bearing witness could also be used in Eimarille's favor. She'd never given up her name, never given up her right to the throne, but there were Ashionen bloodlines who refused to support her simply because of her Daijalan upbringing. If the last living representative of the bloodline that once protected the royal Ashion family threw their support behind Eimarille rather than Caris, then alliances might shift.

The choice between two women who would be queen—one born to it, another a mere noble and engineer—would hopefully be obvious to the nobility. Except Queen Ophelia had born three children, and no one had heard even a whisper of Prince Alasandair Rourke's survival.

"What of the prince?" Terilyn demanded. "Did you give him aid as well?"

Blaine tried to turn his head away from her, but she slipped the stiletto underneath his jaw to the other side of his throat, between skin and the gold marriage torc, stilling him. His gaze slid her way, the fever brightness in his eyes stark in the dim gaslight. "I didn't."

Oh so telling was that confession. "Who did?"

"The star gods."

An interference Terilyn was well familiar with. She'd been brought to Eimarille by the Midnight Star himself, Xaxis happy to deliver her to that train in Istal all those years ago. She'd never regretted being bound to Eimarille's service—had learned to care for and love the woman she lived for. She stood by Eimarille's side because Xaxis had chosen *her*.

It seemed other star gods had been generous with their own favor as well.

"Where did they take him?"

Blaine tried to swallow back the words, but the compulsion was too strong. The glow of the aether flickered across his eyes, across his teeth, and the words came out anyway. "The Serpentine River."

"Were you with them?"

"No."

So he wouldn't know where the prince might have been taken or if Alasandair was still alive. Caris came from Cosian, a city as far east as one could get in Ashion. Terilyn doubted the star gods would have hidden the two children in the same geographical area. That left one child going east, and if Eimarille had gone west, north and south were the only other options.

Urova had seen no signs of someone who could wield starfire at the level of Rourkes, and that country was loyal to Xaxis and Innes, which made them loyal to Eimarille. She doubted the North Star would have risked a Rourke child growing up in supposed enemy territory.

Which left the south, but for all that Solaria was trouble, there'd been no sign within the Houses of someone who could rival Vanya's vaunted strength when it came to starfire. Terilyn settled back on her heels, lifting her stiletto away from Blaine's face, thinking about how he'd recently lived as someone else while in Amari and been raised as E'ridian since he was a boy. How Caris was registered in the nobility genealogies as part of the Dhemlan bloodline, raised up as far from the political heart of the country as one could get.

The star gods had stripped them both of their identities, giving them new roads to walk, new names written into genealogies. If they'd wanted to hide the prince—if they'd wanted to fully strip Alasandair of his identity and keep him out of the fray—the Houses would not be the best choice.

But the wardens would.

They'd lost the quarry and laboratory housing a death-defying machine in Solaria, the location burned by starfire. When Joelle had reported the loss, Eimarille had thought Vanya responsible for the destruction, despite Joelle's assurances it couldn't have been anyone belonging to the Houses. Who else could have had that degree of starfire held at their fingertips?

It seemed, perhaps, Eimarille had been mistaken.

If the prince was somehow still alive, Terilyn could only hope he'd been caught up in the attack on the Warden's Island. Regardless, it was a possibility Eimarille needed to be warned about in person, not something voiced over the wire.

Terilyn stood and sheathed her stiletto, staring down at Blaine. "We'll take him with us to New Haven. I want—"

She broke off at the muffled, distant *boom* that filtered down to her ears. Terilyn's gaze snapped to the ceiling, her free hand going for the snub-nosed pistol holstered at the small of her back. Her fingers trailed over the grip before she spun on her heels. "Secure the room."

She stepped into the main area of the basement, nearly running into Kendrick. The captain reared back at her appearance. "My lady, there's smoke coming from the airfield."

Terilyn strode toward the stairs. "Was there a crash?"

"We don't know."

"Then find out."

If an airship crash-landed, the cascade effect of the explosion would be tremendous. If her airship got caught in the destruction, she'd have to look to a steam train to get out of Foxborough.

Unfortunately, her luck didn't hold. Word came within the hour that the airfield was unusable. The thick black smoke rising from the north wasn't from just a single airship berth but all of them—destroyed, the military scout said, by wardens. The shock of who the perpetrators were was reverberating through the city, all anyone could talk about as the fire brigade sought to keep the fire from spreading across the prairie.

"The attack started with the crown's airship," the scout said with a grimly apologetic look on his face.

"Of course it did," Terilyn murmured, lips twisting in displeasure. "We didn't think they'd retaliate so quickly. It would have been better if the entire population of the Warden's Island had been eradicated."

Kendrick bowed his head at that indirect chastisement. "Apologies, my lady."

"They know a representative of our queen is in Foxborough but not our exact location. We'll need to leave immediately."

"The mayor has ordered the city gates closed under an emergency order. The rail stations have all been evacuated, as it's expected the wardens will target those next," the scout said.

Terilyn was too well trained to show how much the news made her want to curse. She turned to face Kendrick, staring him down. "Find us a way out of this city."

The wardens couldn't lay siege to Foxborough, but they could and were making it difficult to flee. Terilyn refused to become a sitting target.

She refused to leave Eimarille to fight this war alone.

Six

VANYA

"You are distracted," Taisiya said.

Vanya sipped his wine, the glass slippery in his fingers from condensation. He tightened his grip. "Soren is beyond late."

"Perhaps he heard word of the attack and is reaching out to his fellow wardens." Taisiya kept her voice low, pitching it to a level only Vanya could hear as they left one tent behind for another farther down the garden path. They passed an acrobat standing on a pillar, performing feats of the body that had drawn enthralled admirers.

The rich hues of sunset colored the sky in the west while gas lamps glowed above everyone's head. Strategically placed mechanical fans helped keep everyone cool. Servants bustled down pathways and through tents, ferrying cool drinks and finger foods on silver trays to the mingling guests. A small orchestra played an upbeat tune, their music drifting through amplifier speakers discreetly positioned throughout the gardens.

Vanya was acutely aware of Amir's absence amidst the gathering, used to having the older man's counsel and now left to forever second-guess it. While Malia swore she'd seen his unscarred chest weeks ago when he was in Karnak, that didn't excuse the scars he now carried, nor the meticulous changes to his mind that magicians were able to confirm.

Amir's status as a *rionetka* now undercut whatever support from other Houses Vanya could hope to claw away from Joelle, even with the Dawn Star's blessing. He'd been waiting for Joelle to arrive, but so far, the House of Kimathi's *vezir* had not deigned to grace them with her presence. He'd been told her heir had, though of course, Artyom was keeping his distance.

"Vanya."

He pushed his thoughts aside, focusing on his *valide*. "Have we swayed a majority of Houses?"

"The Conclave will close with our House claiming enough support to continue to rule despite Joelle's accusation." Taisiya paused, lips twitching with a faintly humorous look in her eyes. "Or until we are all murdered."

"A challenge, to be sure."

"I would hope so." She brushed her hand against his arm, curling her fingers around his elbow. "Now, I do believe the House of Balaskas is awaiting us."

Vanya let Taisiya steer him toward the parterre and the long, rectangular fountain that stretched from the palace steps to the distant statue of the Dawn Star. Desert plants bloomed in intricate designs around the fountain amidst stone benches and elaborate cushions scattered on the flagstone beneath colorful tents.

Cybele greeted them with a smile inside one of those tents, secure in her vaunted position of having rallied enough minor Houses and not a few major ones to Vanya's side. She'd given him loyalty even before Callisto descended on the Senate, and he'd trust her more than the others, just not with his life. He'd trusted Amir with that, when he'd sent Soren and Raiah to the House of Vikandir's *vasilyet*, and look where it got him.

"House of Sa'Liandel," Cybele said as she curtsied rather than bowed. A wise choice, considering the height of her headdress with its delicate jeweled adornments and tiny golden bells that chimed every time she moved.

"House of Balaskas," Vanya returned in kind.

Cybele's gaze flicked to Taisiya before settling on him. "My understanding is the last gathering of the Conclave goes to the victor."

"I've yet to lay eyes on the House of Kimathi. A poor showing before our guiding star's choice."

"One can't expect well-wishes from a House that is better than yours," a cool voice said from one of the many cushions scattered in the shade.

Vanya's gaze cut to the side, finding Vesper of the House of Aetos lounging amidst ladies and young men near her age, if not her status. She lingered amongst Houses who favored him and not Joelle, and he knew she didn't stay out of an abundance of manners. She always seemed to be Joelle's eyes and ears in these situations. Vanya had long since slotted her House into the group of ones he could gain no loyalty from.

Vesper rose gracefully to her feet, the gown she wore carrying the colors of her House with shades that wouldn't be out of place on Joelle's clothing. The support was subtly applied, but it was unmistakable. She offered no bow or curtsey in greeting, holding her chin high instead to look him in the eye.

Vanya still greeted her with a smile. "When the House of Kimathi is blessed by the Dawn Star herself, then perhaps I'll look upon them differently. As that House's illustrious *vezir* is not present, I'll take her absence as the forfeit of the Conclave that it is."

"Your House is not fit to rule. Yours has torn Solaria apart enough over the years. I stand by my vote and allegiance with the House of Kimathi," Vesper said.

"Solaria remains whole because of what my House has accomplished."

Vesper's lips curled into a vicious smile. "Yes. The destruction of a city and eradication of a House. Such a legacy for your daughter to carry. But you stand here alone with your *valide*, and I know I am not the only one who thinks you weak for that."

He tamped down his temper, feeling Taisiya's fingers dig harder into the bend of his elbow in a silent warning. "I stand with the Houses who believe in Solaria's future."

Vesper's gaze raked up and down his body, one brow rising in disdain. "Some future."

"A future most of the Houses have put their support behind."

"Misapplied faith" was Vesper's serene answer. "I'll give mine elsewhere."

"Joelle is not what Solaria needs."

"I find what Solaria needs isn't something you can offer," Artyom said from behind him.

Vanya made a show of glancing over his shoulder. "The Dawn Star thinks otherwise."

Artyom narrowed his eyes as he came around to stand by Vesper. It appeared he'd come alone, dressed as if he were royalty, wearing an elaborate robe heavy with embroidery. All that was missing was a crown.

"I've heard Joelle left Calhames," Taisiya mused. "She seemed so invested in the Conclave. A pity she couldn't see it through to the end."

"I am more than capable of representing my House."

"Yes, a House who called a Conclave and could not win it, much like the throne."

Artyom glared at her, looking for all the world as if he wanted to raise his hand to her for the insult. Taisiya always knew how to get under people's skin.

"You can tally up the Houses all you like, but you don't have the support," Vanya said.

Artyom raised his chin. "You don't know who stands with us."

"Not anyone who matters."

Vesper stiffened, an affronted expression settling on her pretty face. "I won't stand for your insults."

"No one is keeping you here. Joelle has already left Calhames. Perhaps you should follow her."

Artyom's lips twitched, as if he wanted to smile, but he didn't. "You won't be emperor forever."

"No one ever is."

Vesper swept past him on Artyom's arm, spine rigid in the way of a noblewoman who knew her place in society. She'd done her part, spread what doubt she could, but there were few Houses who followed them out of the tent. Vanya doubted the pair would stay for the meal. Vesper had made her choice known, and Artyom would find a frosty reception from the other Houses.

"She'll have left a prayer cake on the table despite her words," Cybele mused.

"Poisoned, no doubt," Taisiya said dryly.

"Many are, I'm certain."

"Yours?" Vanya asked, keeping his voice light.

Cybele tipped her head to the side, smiling. "It is tradition, is it not?"

Tradition to gift, even if Vanya had no plans to eat any. "Your thoughtfulness will be appreciated."

At that, Cybele did laugh. "I'm certain it will."

He'd not offered anything poisoned to anyone at the gathering today, choosing to rely on the knowledge that he was Callisto's best choice to rule. He no longer needed to prove himself, prove how far he'd go to keep control of the Imperial throne. Vanya had no desire to make anyone else prove their loyalty by drinking or eating something laced with poison when he could guilt them onto his side by reminding them the Dawn Star had blessed him and not Joelle.

"You have the Houses that matter. Enough to keep ruling," Cybele said.

Vanya nodded. "I am aware."

"Don't waste this chance."

The blunt request was given with a respectful nod before Cybele moved away, only to be replaced by someone else who wanted to take his measure. Taisiya gently squeezed his arm before leaving his side and the tent to join people in a different one to further their outreach. Vanya moved from one group to the next, greeting the Houses and confirming which ones actively supported him and which had done so merely because of a star god's blessing.

But they supported him and not Joelle, and in the end, that was all that mattered.

The sun was halfway below the horizon when Alida announced the evening meal was ready to be served. The crowd made their way to a large tent set up past the long fountain, brightly illuminated with gaslights on wire strings. Two dozen tables were situated beneath the tent, each one's centerpiece incorporating the Houses assigned to it. People found their seats on the low cushioned benches while servants came around with platters of food. The table with the House of Kimathi and House of Aetos centerpiece was half-empty, missing their namesakes.

Vanya had just been handed the voice amplifier device, ready to make his closing speech to end the Conclave, when the ground shook in a way historical records described the eastern coastline shaking every now and then. Vibrations thrummed underfoot, making Vanya widen his stance to brace himself. Before he could even search out where Taisiya sat, *praetoria* legionnaires swarmed the tent, leaving their posts in favor of extracting the Imperial family.

"This way, Your Imperial Majesty," Javier barked, getting his hands on Vanya.

Vanya was immediately encircled by *praetoria* legionnaires, hustled out of the tent and toward the garden path that would lead back to the palace. Other guests shoved themselves away from the feast-laden tables, demanding to know what was going on.

Vanya swore, trying to shrug off Javier's grip but couldn't. "Taisiya?"

"Another squad has her. We're bringing her back to the palace."

They'd separated for the meal to better press their argument with the Houses. The Conclave was supposed to officially conclude at the end of the meal, with support offered to the House of Sa'Liandel that Vanya desperately needed. All he could think of right then was how Joelle hadn't shown, how her most ardent supporters had left, and now *someone* was attacking the palace.

An eerie sound rose through the air, the siren high-pitched and pulsing in a way that made Vanya freeze and Javier miss a step. They stumbled into each other as the tones of the warning siren only ever used for revenants drowned out everything.

People screamed and ran back down the long stretch of the garden for the palace. Javier yanked on his arm, and Vanya stumbled into a run, surrounded by *praetoria* legionnaires who refused to leave his side.

"Don't leave anyone behind," Vanya snapped.

Javier looked over at him with a grim sort of expression on his face. "You and your House are the only priority."

"I won't lose everything I've sought to gain by refusing to give the Houses aid. Give the order to the legionnaires."

Javier swore viciously before making a gesture with his left hand at the legionnaire closest to him. The woman peeled off, shouting out orders. Vanya craned his head around and caught a glimpse of a huddled knot of *praetoria* legionnaires hurrying toward them. Through the surge of bodies, he saw Taisiya's pale face, his *valide* held safe in a *praetoria* legionnaire's arms.

The sun was sinking beneath the horizon, still enough sunlight casting long shadows across the palace grounds that, at first, Vanya thought the figures rounding the distant wing were groundskeepers. But that long-held instinct every Solarian was born with crept up his spine, turning his skin clammy despite the heat.

People had a way of moving, and so did the dead.

What careened through bushes and past desert trees, heading their way, were revenants—inside Calhames' walls, on the palace grounds, past every conceivable defense. It hadn't been an earthquake, Vanya knew with sudden certainty.

It was something worse.

"Raiah," Vanya said, heart pounding so hard he could barely hear Javier over the rush of blood in his ears. "She needs to be kept safe."

"Get to the palace!" Javier yelled, voice booming in that trained way all officers learned for the battlefield.

Vanya lengthened his stride as several *praetoria* legionnaires went for their clarion crystal–tipped wands and all the rest went for their pistols. The Houses who had been invited—representatives or heads of Houses of nearly all in existence—scrambled to make it to safety. Some had fainted from the sight of the revenants, and while a few loyal members of their Houses carried them onward, others were abandoned to lie on the garden grounds, left for legionnaires to try to protect.

The sirens still rang through the air when *praetoria* legionnaires started shooting, muzzle flashes sparking in the air. Everyone's screams got louder, and Vanya had to force his own panic down as the crowd finally reached the palace steps at the same time a revenant riddled with bullet holes crashed into a straggling guest and dragged them to the ground.

Javier put his hand in between Vanya's shoulder blades and shoved. "*Move.*"

The *praetoria* legionnaires carved a brutal path through the guests between them and safety, but Vanya dug in his heels before Javier could drag him through the doors. He saw Alida over the tops of their heads, already inside and staring back at him with a pale, pale face. The captain whirled to face him, eyes snapping with fury.

"We need to buy everyone time to make it into the palace," Vanya said.

"All due respect, we need to get *you* inside where it's *safe*."

"What kind of emperor would I be if I cowered while every other House was left to the mercy of the walking dead?"

"You'd be *alive*."

Yes, he would—and be blamed for the destruction of the Houses the way his mother had been once upon a time. She'd done what was necessary back then to keep Solaria whole, to keep hold of the imperial throne, to keep their House in power.

Vanya could do nothing less.

He looked at Alida, gaze boring into hers. "See to Raiah."

Then he wrenched himself free of Javier's grip, stepping back and turning to face his scattered people. Javier reached for him before jerking his hand back, away from the starfire crawling up Vanya's arms, licking across his torso. The circle of *praetoria* legionnaires guarding him fell back, giving him space to walk, the heat of starfire creating room in the crowd.

Someone gave a cry of relief, calling out his name, calling for the Dawn Star. Vanya paid no attention to the voices, more focused on creating a wall of white-hot heat between the encroaching revenants and the few they'd lost to the dead already.

"Get everyone inside the palace!" Javier shouted to the soldiers under his command, even as he never left Vanya's side. "We could certainly use your warden for this."

Vanya grimaced. "He was supposed to be here tonight."

But he couldn't think about where Soren was, not when spore-driven revenants lurched through the starfire burning across the garden pathways, becoming nothing but dangerous ash the wind caught and carried, drifting over the crowd.

No one was equipped with gas masks, but many placed the sleeves of their robes over their noses and mouths as they desperately tried to enter the palace. *Praetoria* legionnaires corralled as many guests as they could and directed them inside, trying to keep people from being trampled. Javier and a dedicated group stayed by Vanya's side as he kept the curved wall of starfire burning between the revenants and his people.

But the revenants had been his people once before, long ago.

Embalmed and buried for decades, centuries, even thousands of years—the royal dead of Solaria filled the snaking crypt beneath the palace, and now they'd crawled out of their prisons to walk the world again. Spore-driven, fast in the way of the long dead, the revenants would not be stopped.

"We need to barricade the palace," Vanya said, arms outstretched before him, fingers curled as if he could grasp the starfire he wielded from a distance.

"We'll secure the doors and windows once you're inside, Your Imperial Majesty," Javier snapped.

Vanya let himself be led backward to the palace entrance, unwilling to fully spread the starfire out until he knew the last of the Houses were safely inside. He didn't know if anyone else was trapped in the gardens and couldn't risk setting fire to it all. When he made it to the palace doors, he drew down the starfire until he could see beyond it, and what he could make out in the half circle he'd burned around the area made him go cold.

Dozens of revenants surged their way. Some were little more than dried, cracked skin over bone, while others could have been recognizable in the oil paintings lining the palace hallways.

He wondered if his parents were in that horde.

If his brother was.

Some part of him knew they must be.

Javier yanked on his shoulder, hauling him through the doorway. "Get inside, Your Imperial Majesty!"

Vanya let the starfire die out, but not before some revenants lurched past the burning line of defense, flames licking up their dry, dry bodies. They staggered forward as pillars of fire, unbothered by what consumed them, driven in pursuit of the living by the spores that never let the dead rest.

The doors slammed shut. A *praetoria* legionnaire locked it with only seconds to spare before the sound of bodies hitting it from the other side made the doors rattle on their hinges. Vanya looked to the side at the glass windows, staring at the revenants beyond the flimsy defense.

The Imperial palace didn't have the metal shutters and defensive attributes found in way stations throughout Solaria or any of the other pockets of civilization where walls were foregone. Calhames had walls. It was supposed to be safe behind them.

Only it wasn't.

Perhaps it never had been.

The window on the left shattered when a revenant head-butted it and crawled through, glass shards sticking out from its skull. Vanya wanted to throw starfire at the damned thing, but he risked weakening the palace's walls if he did so.

Javier grabbed his wrist and dragged him away from the door and farther down the hallway to get beyond a rank of *praetoria* legionnaires. The men and women behind them took aim and fired, targeting the dead, for what little good their bullets would do against things that wouldn't ever stay down, not without a warden's intervention.

"We need to get you to the family wing," Javier said.

Vanya nodded jerkily, starfire sparking at his fingertips. Raiah would be there, he knew. He'd sent Alida on ahead, and he knew his majordomo would keep his daughter safe. They just needed to find a route through the maze of a palace the walking dead were hunting in.

He just needed Soren and the warden's skill with eradicating the dead.

Seven

SOREN

The sound of something clawing at the coffin made Soren's jaw twitch, teeth tingling.

He swam toward consciousness by sheer will alone, forcing himself to ignore the hideous throbbing in his skull. He opened his eyes, darkness greeting him in the tomb he was trapped in. He turned his head to the side, the motion sending sharp agony spiking down his neck and jaw, pulsating behind both eyes.

He squeezed his eyes shut, able to feel the world spinning in his gut. Soren swallowed bile, breathing slow and deep to keep the nausea at bay. When he managed to pry his eyes open again, he found the thin sliver of space between the lid and coffin edges that let in cold crypt air was blocked in places where bony fingers had shoved their way through.

Revenants.

His fingers twitched automatically for weapons he no longer had. Soren drew in a shaky breath, pressing his palms against the side of the coffin. He slid them up slowly to the lid covering him, knowing that it wouldn't move. The Blades had welded it shut, intent on hiding him away until whatever horror came to pass aboveground.

Vanya, Soren thought bleakly. *Raiah.*

They didn't know Alida was a traitor. It would gut Vanya, Soren knew, when he discovered Alida had betrayed them all of her own free will. But Vanya wouldn't know unless Soren got out of the predicament he'd found himself in.

He scratched at the iron lid. The revenant's bony fingers gripping the edge of the coffin suddenly tried to shove in deeper, but the last knuckle got in the way. Soren held his breath, held still, trying to quiet the rabbit-fast beat of his heart.

The air was thin and hot in the coffin, the strip of breathing hole the Blades left him barely enough to keep him breathing. Soren couldn't tell if the pounding in his head was from the blow taken in the star temple or oxygen deprivation.

It didn't matter.

He had to get out.

Soren flexed his feet, using his boot heels to drag his body down the coffin a few inches, all the space he could move, to stay out of reach of the revenant's scrambling fingers. He flattened his hands against the coffin lid and closed his eyes. The world seemed to spin, even there in the claustrophobic darkness. He tried to drag his thoughts into some semblance of order, to center himself.

Whatever drugs he'd been given had been burned through by the resistance he'd built up as a tithe. The head wound was what hindered him, making concentration difficult. He'd been trained to push through worse, though, because a warden who didn't get back up on their feet was a dead warden.

The lid was cool to the touch now, which meant hours must have passed. If he were anyone else, Soren would be stuck there, left to wait for Alida and the Blades to return and smuggle him out of the palace or until he died, missing and forgotten.

If he couldn't command starfire, he'd be reduced to a pawn.

Except he could, and he wouldn't be anyone's bargaining chip against Vanya.

Soren drew in a breath, the air warm on his tongue, tasting rotten. He swallowed dryly, ignoring the scraping sound of bone on metal outside the coffin. He focused inward, reaching for that part of him which could touch the aether, could pull it out of where that power existed just out of reach, just a sideways step from the world they inhabited.

It poured through him the way a branding iron might feel pressing into skin. Soren couldn't choke back the scream that escaped his lips, a band tightening around his skull as starfire crawled away from his fingertips, spreading out like a death vine. He forced the white-hot flames into the edges and corners where the lid met the coffin. It ate at the air in the coffin, making Soren pant in quick, harsh breaths, sweat sliding down his face and throat. He licked salt off his dried lips, unable to tell if it came from sweat or tears.

The pain in his head grew and grew, as if someone was slamming a pickaxe into his skull over and over again. His control of the starfire wavered, the flames flickering, nearly guttering out. The revenant let out a sound that was like wind blowing through a distant, broken tunnel—hideously raspy and horrifying.

Soren squeezed his eyes shut, swallowing back bile, refusing to stay where the enemy had put him. He dug his fingernails into the warm metal, skin on the tips burning, and strained the heels of his palms against the coffin lid. Pressure built and built—in his chest, in his head, beneath his skin.

It had to go somewhere.

When starfire exploded out of him, it shattered the coffin lid into molten pieces that cut through the air above him, ripping through revenants. A thin barrier of it kept molten metal from falling onto his body. Soren sucked in air as he scrambled to a sitting position. The world spun, sparks of starfire illuminating half a dozen revenants around the coffin, red molten metal eating through bone.

It wouldn't stop them.

Soren's head spun, and the nausea that assailed him couldn't be ignored any longer. He leaned over the side of the coffin and vomited, gut heaving as he tried to clear his throat. He blinked wetness from his eyes, nose stinging from bile, risking an even worse headache when a still-upright revenant lunged at him. Soren swept his arm around in a clumsy half-arc, starfire streaking outward and lighting up the dead. They didn't scream the way humans did, but they burned to ash all the same.

Soren hauled himself out of the coffin, falling knees-first with a twist of his body. Something rammed into his stomach when he landed, and he grunted, panicking before he realized it was his poison short sword leaning against the side of the coffin. His gun belt had been dropped there as well—all of it too incriminating, he supposed, for people masquerading as star priests to carry around.

Soren wrapped his hand around the sword sheath and hauled it over his shoulder, clumsily buckling the pauldron back into place. The weight of it across his back settled something in him, even if it didn't make the world stop spinning. Soren wrapped the gun belt around his waist, buckling it back in place. Both pistols were missing. While he no longer had a distance weapon in hand, the pouches hadn't been emptied. More fool them, as Soren came up with a tin every warden carried in their belt.

The pills inside weren't a cure-all, but they were a pain reliever mixed with a stim to keep a warden on their feet, enabling them to get to safety in the poison fields. It wouldn't knock him out, but it would keep him clearheaded as much as his body would allow.

Soren swallowed a pill dry before using the coffin to drag himself to his feet. He swayed there, blinking at the smoldering remains of the revenants, like coal embers in a fire. The starfire still burned, and it took effort to draw it back into the aether, all but a flicker of flame to light his way out. He stomped out the glowing bits of fire still burning through the dead before leaving the alcove on unsteady feet, poison short sword in hand and a wealth of anger urging him onward.

Eight

HONOVI

They'd chased the sun as far as they could before holding position, watching from the decking as the night sky formed in the east and spread west, blanketing the world in darkness. Honovi had given the order to kill the running lights on every airship, flying dark as the stars came out.

Foxborough had been a smudge on the horizon during daylight hours, made indistinct by a haze of smoke, as they waited for the hours it took the steam train to catch up. Caoimhe's communications officer reported on the damage done to the city's airfields and rail stations. The frantic warnings from the city's government were being broadcasted on an open line, easy to listen in on.

"We'll need to warn the Ashionens the rail station isn't viable if they haven't heard already," Caoimhe had said after the first few reports trickled over the radio.

"I don't think Ksenia's plan to talk her way through the city gates will work. The airfield's control tower reported it was wardens who set the bombs," Honovi had replied.

Caoimhe's smile had been wolfish. "Then we'll open the gate for her."

Now, the time for waiting was over. The *Celestial Sprite*'s lookout had finally spotted the steam train's lone gaslight shining like a tiny beacon on the ground. When Honovi got on the radio to contact their ground support, he wasn't surprised to hear Lore answer his hail. "Does the map still show the package in Foxborough?"

Honovi glanced over his shoulder at the map spread out on the worktable, pinned down, the flat shard of clarion crystal settled over the ink dot marking out Foxborough. "Yes, but you can't make it to the city. The rail station was destroyed by wardens."

"We heard those warnings. Ksenia is stopping the train a few miles out from the city walls. Will you remain in the sky?"

It was where he operated best, but he wasn't going to leave rescuing Blaine to anyone else. "I'll ride with the ground troops into the city. Once we're notified the train has come to a stop, we'll descend."

"Very well. We'll see you soon."

Lore signed off, and Honovi set the radio back down in its cradle, focusing on the sky. It was perhaps fifteen minutes later when the radio crackled to life again, with Ksenia on the other side of the line giving him the go-ahead to descend.

Night flying was always tricky, but Honovi reversed the ballonets and let the airship sink, the only one to break formation. He listened as Caoimhe called out slight adjustments from her spot near the railing out on the deck. Honovi kept his eyes on the gauges rather than the impossible-to-see horizon.

It wasn't like that night raid, where he'd needed to match speed with a steam train. This time, the train was already stopped, and it was only a matter of maneuvering to get the airship low enough alongside the engine car for a crew member to toss a rope ladder overboard.

Caoimhe took over the controls, giving him a firm nod as she slid into his spot. "We'll see you on the other side. May the stars guide you."

Honovi stayed only long enough to roll up the map and shove it back into the travel case. He hooked the crystal pendant back around his throat and left the flight deck for the ladder. It was a matter of muscle memory to swing himself over the railing and climb down. When he was a few feet up from the dirt, he jumped the rest of the way, landing with a grunt.

Headlamps shining from helmets and handheld lights gripped in fists were all the illumination Ksenia had allowed for the moment. She and Lore waited for him by the engine carriage, the heat coming off the metal warming the air around them. Honovi jogged to their position as behind him, the airship's engines changed pitch to the tones for ascent, the *Celestial Sprite* rising back up into the night sky where it belonged.

Down the length of the steam trains, Ashion soldiers disembarked train carriages and worked to unload supplies. Light was kept to a minimum, which left everyone in dim pockets of illumination that made the hair on the back of Honovi's neck stand on end. Everyone knew that being outside in the open, past the walls, was a risk, even if the land was cleared by wardens. The Northern Plains was still home to wild beasts, and people were known to die out on the roads. Spores traveled on the wind, and the night had never stopped revenants, only made them difficult to see and kill.

"I have wardens patrolling and the ones positioned outside Foxborough have reported no revenant sightings," Ksenia said, correctly reading Honovi's wary glance over his shoulder at the dark behind them. "This land was cleared back in spring."

"Doesn't mean anything with the influx of revenants in the west," Lore muttered.

"That's not our doing."

"I didn't say it was. We can blame the death-defying machine on that mess." Lore jerked her thumb over her shoulder. "Let's get our racing carriages. Caris was kind enough to add a Zip gun to one of them before we left Veran."

"You let her put vehicular weaponry on a racing carriage?" Honovi asked.

Lore gave him a droll look as he fell into step beside her. "There was no letting involved. Caris was adamant we have a way to protect ourselves while driving. We let her work on that rather than work herself up in a strop about not coming along."

Ksenia snorted. "You can't keep a person leashed all their life if you want them to actually walk their own road."

Honovi agreed, but he knew if Caris had come along and they lost her, Blaine would blame himself for not being there. "I know."

The racing carriages in question were stored in one of the forward train carriages. Lanterns hung from hooks on the inside, providing light to see by. The steam train must have been one used by the Ashion army. Unlike civilian freight steam trains, even the train carriages used for storage were connected with covered walkways, allowing people to walk the length of it while it was in motion.

The racing carriages were secured on the left-hand side. The modified one had a low-built body, two narrow seats, and a low-profile windshield frame, the glass removed. The paint had been pristine once —that is, until Caris had welded the Zip gun onto its hood. The quick-firing heavy-caliber gun had been placed in front of the passenger-side seat, its handles protruding through where glass once sat. It was maneuverable, and a belt of bullets was draped down into the footwell.

Lore patted the top of the Zip gun, a grimly pleased smile on her face. "It'll be good protection once we're in Foxborough."

"We don't know where Blaine is in the city," Honovi said.

Ksenia waved aside his worry. "I had a warden retrieve a Foxborough map from the resupply station in Veran. I traced over the ink with the kind we used on your map. Your crystal will work the same on it as the world map."

Honovi didn't think twice about undoing the pouch on his belt and passing over the clarion crystal shard. "Caoimhe is ready to drop bombs on the city gate to get us inside."

"The Clockwork Brigade is prepared to keep Daijalan supporters at bay on the other side. I've been coordinating with them in code on the ride over. We're hoping to keep civilian casualties to a minimum," Lore said.

"Will your cogs be enough?"

Lore crossed her arms over her chest as she watched a soldier undo the heavy-duty straps hooked over each tire of the racing carriages used to secure them for transport. "My understanding is the Marshal sent quite a few Daijalan chains west. They're ready to assist."

"We'll have backup from the wardens standing guard beyond the wall as well. They're prepared to act as escort once we're inside," Ksenia said.

Honovi stepped closer to the modified racing carriages, settling his hand on the cool barrel of the Zip gun. When he looked up from it, he found Lore staring at him, never blinking. She gave him a tight smile. "Ready to get your husband back?"

Doing so would see E'ridia commit itself to a war not even the Eastern Spine could hold at bay. While Honovi knew Eimarille would say the attack was unjustified, the *Comhairle nan Cinnidhean* and E'ridia's air force had been invited by Caris. She was queen enough for that, and Honovi was prepared to acknowledge her as such if it meant he could save his husband.

He'd come this far already. He wasn't leaving Foxborough without Blaine.

"Let's go," Honovi said.

Nine

VANYA

Gunfire made Vanya's ears ring as the squad of *praetoria* legionnaires attempted to hold back a trio of revenants ripping apart a servant in a hallway. The skeletal revenants in faded and ragged robes didn't look like they should have the strength to take someone down, but the evidence lay in scattered bloody bits around them.

"We need to circle back," Javier snapped, holding on tight to Vanya's arm and trying to pull him back the way they'd come.

The only problem with that idea was it would take him farther away from where his daughter hopefully was. Alida hadn't answered her televox when he rang. Vanya could only hope she was busy hiding and not dead. "We're pressing on."

"Your Imperial Majesty—"

Vanya stepped forward, thrusting out his arm. "I'm going to Raiah."

Starfire flickered at his fingertips before erupting in a burning ball of heat. Javier shouted out an order Vanya barely paid attention to. The *praetoria* legionnaires ahead of them dropped to their knees and ceased shooting, giving Vanya all the room he needed to incinerate the dead.

The revenants turned into columns of flame, starfire eating through bone until nothing but ash was left. The heat had everyone traveling with them flinching away, skin flushing, but no one retreated.

Vanya made a fist, snuffing out the starfire. All that remained were scorch marks on the floor, walls, and ceiling of the hallway and the ashes that drifted lazily to the floor. He pressed the sleeve of his robe over his nose and mouth, not wanting to breathe in the ash and lingering smoke as their group continued on.

"I don't suppose you could simply fling starfire at any revenants that appear?" Cybele asked from some ways behind him. The small group of survivors had opted to stay with him rather than chance a run to the palace gates.

"I'd rather not risk the structure of the palace or breathe in whatever spores might be left in their bodies if I don't have to," Vanya said flatly.

Taisiya cleared her throat. "I concur on that. Let's continue how we have been."

Javier released Vanya's arm but never left his side as *praetoria* legionnaires scouted farther ahead, seeking safe passage through the maze of hallways. One legionnaire swiftly reloaded a pistol without looking and lengthened his stride to overtake the other two. Everyone else followed at a fast pace, eventually turning a corner into a hallway that overlooked the palace's grand forecourt.

The hallway was lined with windows on one side, scattered doors leading to empty rooms on the other. The gaslights were all on, and none of the windows had their shutters or curtains drawn. Javier swore under his breath before dragging Vanya to his knees.

"I'm not losing you to a head shot if whoever released revenants into the palace has marksmen in their employ," Javier said. "Stay down and move as fast as you can. Goes for everyone."

Vanya didn't argue the order, merely did as he was told. Javier stayed in front, and Vanya followed close behind, staying below the line of windows. They were halfway down the long hallway when a clanking sound came from the corner up ahead. Before anyone could react, a delta-class automaton stepped into view.

About Vanya's height but bulkier, it walked with a jerky gait on mechanical legs. Rather than a Zip gun arm, the delta-class ones were outfitted with grenade launchers. Their assigned positions were on the roof of the palace as ever-vigilant guardians. Vanya wondered what had caused this one to leave its post when there were plenty of revenants crawling across the grounds for it to target.

The star priest that followed in its wake was a surprise. The man jerked when he caught sight of them, and it wasn't relief that flitted across his face.

"Shoot him," Vanya ordered before he could really process what he was seeing.

Because yes, those were the robes of a star priest on the man, but no star priest assigned to the temple on the palace grounds had a face like his—untidy beard, pockmarked cheeks, and the body of one used to fighting rather than praying. Neither did any star priests carry a rifle favored by the Daijalan military.

The man ducked behind the automaton, bullets missing him and ricocheting off metal. The automaton planted its feet and swiveled its torso with a crank of gears to better aim the grenade launcher at them.

"Someone has control of the override keys," Javier said before grabbing Vanya and diving for the safety of the room across from them. They hit the floor at the same time, the impact sending Vanya's crown flying off his head.

Just in time, as the grenade that flew through the air landed with a *boom* that made the wing of the palace shake. Plaster dust shook free of the ceiling, making Vanya cough as it fell around them. The ringing in his ears had gotten louder, but it wasn't loud enough to drown out the pounding of his heart.

"Taisiya," he croaked. "Make sure she's okay. I'll handle the automaton."

Javier looked back at him, then at the office—two stories up and no way out but the doorway they'd fallen through—and swore. "I shouldn't let you risk yourself."

Vanya smiled, the feel of it wrong on his face. "You don't let me do anything, Captain."

He got to his feet, left his crown wherever it had rolled, and called forth starfire. It erupted from his hand, spilling out into the damaged hallway. He raised the temperature higher, until the flames flickered pure white and the blowback of the heat was so intense Javier had to curl in on himself.

Vanya walked right through it.

He wielded the core of the heat—that dangerous, metal-melting power—with expert ease, the way his mother had taught him. He pushed it outward, slamming it into the delta-class automaton, using the starfire like a cudgel to send it crashing through the window and out of the palace. Vanya didn't hear it land over the sound of the grenades going off, the explosions making the remaining windows rattle and fracture in their frames.

The man masquerading as a star priest rolled on the floor, trying desperately to put out the flames. Vanya helped with that, drawing back the starfire, but it wouldn't save the enemy. Starfire had burned away the stolen robes, searing flesh down to bone on his arm and torso and part of his leg. Nothing but blackened flesh remained, and if the burns wouldn't kill him, perhaps the shock would.

Vanya looked behind him at the damage done to the hallway. The grenade had ripped a hole in the building, and half their group was now on the other side of the gaping space. Some were injured, having not been quick enough to dodge the blast. Vanya could see someone in uniform lying unmoving on the floor past the blast radius.

At least Taisiya was alive, still carried in the arms of the *praetoria* legionnaire. Vanya wished there was a place in the palace he could put her, locked behind a door no revenant could get through. But nowhere was safe, not with the enemy having infiltrated the palace.

Javier stepped into the hallway, took one look at the situation, and scowled. "Someone bridge the gap."

A *praetoria* legionnaire stepped forward, wand in hand and pointed at the empty air between them where the floor used to be. Aether curled at the clarion crystal–tipped wand as trapezoid shapes snapped into place out of thin air. The shield turned bridge covered the distance between them, a temporary way out.

"Move," Javier said, gesturing at everyone on the other side of the hole.

No one balked, hurrying across the glowing trapezoids, many refusing to look down. The wounded were carried across, and those that could still walk were set down. Vanya reached for Taisiya's hand when she made it across, giving it a gentle squeeze. "Are you hurt?"

She shook her head, face washed of all color. She was too old to be at war like this. "Try Alida again."

Vanya pulled his televox from his robe's pocket, having not lost it like he'd lost the crown in their dive for safety. As before, Alida never answered his call. He put the televox away and focused on their situation and not any of the ones concerning his daughter his too-imaginative mind could think up.

Javier waved at him from down the hall. "He's dying. Do you have questions, Your Imperial Majesty?"

"Deathbed confessions can never be trusted, but I want to know who he's allied with," Vanya replied.

Javier knelt beside the burned man, not giving aid, wand in hand and pointed at a ruined face. The man was crying out of his good eye, the other scorched to the point of bursting. For all that Vanya wouldn't trust what the enemy would say, memory was something else entirely. He could spare the minute it took for Javier to claw information out of a dying mind.

"He's a Blade," Javier said, disgust dripping from his words as the aether faded from the dead man's remaining eye. "That's all I could get before he stopped breathing."

The implication of that was something Vanya didn't have time to pick apart. But Blades meant Daijal, and the fact Queen Eimarille had interfered so deeply in his country's sovereignty made Vanya *furious*.

"We'll deal with that later. We need to move," Vanya said. He walked past the dead man, letting the *praetoria* legionnaires surround him once more. Their group hurried down the long hallway, slowing only long enough for the *praetoria* legionnaires to clear the area around the corner.

Right as Vanya turned down the hallway, every gas lamp hanging from the ceiling and attached to sconces in the walls flickered ominously before guttering out, plunging the Imperial palace into darkness.

In that moment of panic, Vanya thought he heard the scrape of bone against the floor and the raspy sound of air moving through a dried throat and mouth in a parody of spore-driven breathing at the far end of the hall.

He raised his hand and snapped his fingers, sparking starfire into life. He pushed the illumination brighter, sending the flicker of flames dancing down the hallway to light the way. It pierced the shadows up ahead, reflecting dully off old jewelry the dead had been buried with, throwing into temporary high relief the small horde of revenants now standing at the end of the hallway like a nightmare no one could escape.

Waiting.

Ten

SOREN

Soren passed many broken-open tombs on his way out of the crypt but saw no revenants. He remembered the sounds they'd made during the funeral some years back—the ever-scratching noise of something trapped forever, looking for a way out.

Well.

Someone had given it to them.

The coffin covers had all been blown open by way of dynamite and magic, breaking the welded seals that kept the dead contained. Almost every single alcove of the royal dead that Soren passed on his trek out of the crypt was empty. Some had body parts scattered on the floor, the explosive charge to open the coffins too strong or the body inside not spore-riddled.

The border had been untended, and that was his fault. His failed duty.

The only way to fix that was to eradicate the revenants. Wardens should have been called for that fight, but he knew those assigned to the resupply station had left the city. He was the only warden left to stand against the dead, and the only weapon Soren had on him was his poison short sword. The Blades had stripped him of his guns, and the rest of his gear was in the palace.

Soren flexed the fingers of one hand against the wall he used to steady himself. He was reluctant—incredibly so—to call upon starfire in the midst of Calhames where so many people could see it. Considering the state of his head, he wasn't certain he could even reach the aether and summon its power.

He paused for a moment at the bottom of the stairs leading up to the star temple, tilting his head back and breathing through his mouth. The pill he'd taken was fast-acting, and he felt more aware than when he'd been trapped in that coffin. But the hit to the head he'd taken wasn't healed in any meaningful way. Soren had worked through worse, though.

He shoved away from the wall and pitched himself up the spiral staircase, out of the dark and into the star temple. Only a few gaslights were burning, and the only sound he could hear other than his breathing was the warning siren piercing the air beyond the star temple's walls. The crypt entrance had been left open to allow the revenants a way to leave. None of the Blades nor Alida had stayed behind. They'd be dead if that were the case.

A pity.

Soren traversed the sanctuary, poison short sword in hand, and headed for the main entrance. The doors had been thrown open and the star temple abandoned. A quick scan of his surroundings showed dark shapes moving around the palace grounds, flitting through the illumination cast by gas lamps. Soren squinted, making out broken windows in the palace up ahead. Gunfire echoed through the night, paired with the shouts of *praetoria* legionnaires and the occasional scream.

He knew he should head for the palace's golden gates, get it locked down so the revenants couldn't escape the grounds and make their way into Calhames proper. He should find someone who could spare a pistol so he'd have a distance weapon again. He should coordinate with a legionnaire officer because he knew there weren't any other wardens inside Calhames to respond to the warning siren.

Soren should do many things—things a warden was bound to do

by the Poison Accords—but his feet took him away from the gate and toward the palace itself.

To where he knew Vanya and Raiah would be.

He'd lost so much time already. He'd gone into the star temple in daylight, and now the sky was dark, the Leviathan constellation glimmering against the blackness. He'd missed the Conclave, missed warning Vanya about Alida.

Soren's breath hitched as he lengthened his stride, easing into a skull-jarring run. He pressed his thumb over the button beneath the cross guards of his poison short sword three times before holding it down, then releasing it. The vibration from gears shifting within the hilt as they opened up one of the internal vials thrummed against his palm. He couldn't see it, but he knew poison was dripping down the channel in the blade, coating the sharpened steel.

He might not have his pistols, might not be able to be in the position to safely summon starfire, but that didn't mean he couldn't fight.

Soren only hoped the *praetoria* legionnaires wouldn't mistake him for a revenant and shoot him on sight. The risk of that happening was high. He'd have to face it, though, because it was the only way for him to get inside the palace and locate Vanya and Raiah.

He cut through the gardens, sticking to shadows, steering clear of the gas lamp–lit pathways for now. Soren didn't pass any revenants for the first few minutes. Only when he came upon the garage and the open land between him and his destination did Soren hear movement in the dark around him.

Soren went still, the warning siren fading out before rising again. In that moment of near quiet, he heard the rasping breath of the dead. He gripped the short sword with both hands, bringing it up in a ready position, gaze searching the dark.

When the shadows moved, Soren moved as well.

It was habit ingrained down to his bones ever since he was a tithe —and he couldn't help but worry if any were even left after the attack on the Warden's Island—to cut through the dead. The poison coating the blade of his short sword meant when the revenants were cut down and fell, they *stayed* down.

Soren carved his way through a dozen revenants before he finished dispatching the ones in his immediate vicinity. Panting for breath, he ignored the throbbing in his head and turned back to the palace, wondering if running would be the better option.

A hiss of voices from inside the garage caught his attention. Soren turned and saw the side door to the garage had been cracked open, a fearful servant peering out at him.

"It's the warden," the woman said over her shoulder, relief palpable in her voice.

Soren headed for the garage, angling his poison short sword away from the figure in the doorway as he reached it. "How many are inside?"

"Not many. Some of the guests made it to safety, though," she said, stepping back so Soren could enter.

Soren closed the door behind him, and a different servant set about barricading the door again. The lights in the garage were bright enough he could make out a group of people huddled around parked vehicles. Some appeared wounded, but Soren didn't have time to give anyone aid, especially if they'd been bitten.

"What do we do?" a woman cried out. She was better dressed than anyone else, clearly a member of a House, but Soren didn't know which one.

"Cover the low windows. Put any storage cabinets in front of them if you can. It's too dangerous for you to try to make it to the palace gates," Soren said as he pushed his way unsteadily through the crowd. His velocycle was somewhere in the garage. It would have the rest of his gear. He hadn't thought to pack an extra pistol, but his explosives and poison kit would have to do.

"The gates are closed. The order came from the emperor himself through our officer's televox," a *praetoria* legionnaire informed him.

Soren swallowed dryly. "Good."

"You'll stay to protect us, won't you?" the woman from before demanded.

"No."

He ignored her cry and kept walking, the crowd of people hastily pulling away from him. He must be a sight—covered in blood and bits of revenant pieces—but Soren had never cared about that, even if other people did.

He found his velocycle parked where he'd left it. Soren leaned his poison short sword against the vehicle and set about hauling open the travel compartments, withdrawing anything that might be of aid for the fight ahead: explosives, antidotes, poison, and other tools to fight the dead.

"Here." Soren looked up, blinking sweat out of his eyes as he stared at the *praetoria* legionnaire standing on the other side of his velocycle. The soldier offered Soren his pistol in one hand, grip first, and an extra belt pouch of ammunition. "I noticed your holsters are empty. You'll need this."

The extra ammunition in his gear wasn't the right gauge for Solarian pistols, but he accepted the weapon and pouch regardless. "Thanks."

"Everyone ran for the palace when the revenants attacked."

"Do you know if Vanya is inside?"

The *praetoria* legionnaire grimaced. "I don't know."

Only one way to find out. Soren picked up his sword again and turned on his heels, walking back across the garage for the side door. He looked through the nearest windows to check the area outside for any revenants before moving the barricade so he could get through.

"Good luck," the *praetoria* legionnaire said behind him before firmly closing the door and barricading it again.

Soren's head *ached*, but he kept moving. He was only a few yards away from the garage

when all the lights in the palace and on the grounds flickered madly before going out. The area plunged into darkness, the only light to see by the distant burn from the city beyond the palace walls. Soren tightened his grip on the poison short sword, listening as voices shouted in fear, some turning into screams.

He'd bet the vow hanging around his neck that Alida and her traitorous allies had sabotaged the steam engines that powered the gas lines. Soren swore and headed for the palace at a run. With no light to see by, he wasn't as worried about getting shot so much as he was about getting ambushed by revenants.

That changed when the automatons on the palace roof began shooting indiscriminately.

He was yards away from the palace when the heavy *rat-tat-tat* of a Zip gun firing overhead ripped through the air. Soren sprinted the rest of the way, instinctively ducking his head against the rain of bullets falling somewhere behind him.

The door was broken open, glass underfoot that crunched beneath his boots as Soren threw himself inside, leading sword first. He skidded to a stop, forcing his breathing to slow as he tried to get his bearings. He put his back up against the nearest wall, fingers flexing around the sword hilt.

Soren licked sweat off his upper lip, dredging up a mental map of the palace, despite the headache that made his teeth throb in his jaw. He was in the public wing opposite the private family wing of the palace, where Raiah would've been during the Conclave. He could fight his way across the central wing to the other side of the palace or risk the forecourt.

Soren knew he could search for Vanya all he liked, but the one place the other man would always go—the same way a compass always pointed north—was to where his daughter was. Soren only hoped Raiah would still be there.

Decision made, Soren straightened up and steeled himself to make his way through a palace filled with the living and the dead.

Eleven

HONOVI

They were already driving when the bombs dropped on the main eastern city gate to Foxborough and some of the towers where the anti-airship guns were located. The precision strikes—calculated to occur at the same time—caused explosions to light up the sky.

The gate and sections of the wall on either side collapsed from the attack. Ksenia had been worried about debris blocking their way into the city, but Caoimhe had promised the bomb's concussive blast would clear them a route. The bombs being used tonight were restricted for military airships. While Honovi didn't have firsthand familiarity with their results, he trusted Caoimhe's promises. Whatever rubble was left behind, the Ashion army had a couple of armored crawlers being hauled along on transport trucks that could take care of the rest.

"Eyes on the road," Ksenia said, sounding far too calm beneath the thrum of the racing carriage's engine.

The master alchemist sat in the passenger seat, holding the Foxborough city map book in her lap and clutching the clarion crystal shard in her other hand. The racing carriage they were in didn't have any additional weaponry attached to it, but it had speed. Honovi's goggles, with their special lenses capable of seeing in the dark, had been borrowed from wardens. They allowed him to make out the road they drove alongside as well as the automatons moving into position on the surviving section of the city's eastern wall.

The Ashionen battalion captain had said the dark would make it difficult for the automatons to target effectively. It wouldn't stop them completely, nor would it stop the remaining anti-airship guns from shooting into the sky. Their side only had six airships, after all, and the city had far more defensive postings than that.

But E'ridia's air force was unmatched when it came to aerial warfare.

The deep, heavy sound of the artillery going off made Honovi wince, and he sent a silent prayer to the Dusk Star to watch over the airships in the sky. He gripped the steering wheel tighter, maneuvering up beside the modified racing carriage that Lore and another warden were in. Lore sat in the passenger seat, handling the Zip gun. Ahead of them both were several troop transport trucks positioned behind a gun truck and a transport truck carrying an armored crawler on its flatbed.

Their group was one of several racing toward the city under cover of darkness. The surprise attack would hopefully buy them time to get control of the gate while Honovi's group went in search of Blaine. If the anti-airship guns were all taken out in time, then they could leave by way of an airship and not have to backtrack through an unfamiliar city again.

A small explosion on the top of an intact section of the wall briefly caught his eye. It wasn't a bomb dropped from above, but *something* had targeted the automatons, landing a direct hit on one if the miniature bonfire burning into existence was anything to go by.

"Must be the cogs on the inside," Honovi said.

They'd received coded confirmation back from the Clockwork Brigade in Foxborough that the cogs would be ready to assist the Ashion army's push to take control of the city. Their aid meant less of a threat targeting those beyond the city wall, and Honovi was grateful for every second that passed without being shot at.

The gun trucks ahead of them began shooting once they were in range, attempting to take out the remaining automatons on the wall and the handful of soldiers that had belatedly taken up position there as well. The group Honovi drove with adjusted position as they ate up ground. Their speed slowed, but the gun trucks were able to provide cover fire as they approached the ruins of the gate.

Their group wasn't the only one laying down cover fire. Honovi watched as the truck transporting the armored crawler slowed down. The soldier sitting in the protected seat threw the machine into reverse as soon as the truck's ramp folded down. Honovi slowed their own speed to stay behind the armored crawler as it got into position.

The solid steel plates of the armored crawler's continuous track ate up ground as it rumbled toward the damaged gate. Caoimhe's bomb had definitely eradicated the gate itself and a large section of the wall, but some rubble remained. The armored crawler's U-shaped blade—partially lifted while it got into position—was maneuvered down once it reached the road and was within range of debris.

Sparks skittered up from the edge of the blade as it ran over the asphalt before coming across the first chunk of debris. The rubble was gathered against the blade as the armored crawler drove forward, clearing a path into the city.

"Steady on," Ksenia said.

The reverberating roar of velocycle engines erupted in the air as nearly two dozen wardens came riding from the north and south out of the dark. The wardens astride their two-wheeled vehicles fell in around their group as they entered Foxborough behind the armored crawler. One pulled up right alongside their racing carriage, the rider's head turned toward Ksenia. "We've kept watch on the city gates. No one has left Foxborough since we blew the rail stations and airfield."

Which meant Blaine was hopefully still somewhere in Foxborough.

"Follow us," Ksenia ordered, raising her voice to be heard over the thunder of engines. "We're pushing deeper into the city."

The wardens weaved into a different formation, allowing the two racing carriages to pull ahead while the troops stayed behind to secure the area. The cobblestone street made Honovi's teeth clack together as they put distance between their group and the city gate. He pressed his foot down harder on the gas pedal. "Where to?"

Ksenia gripped the leather cord the clarion crystal hung from, dangling the shard over neatly drawn lines depicting Foxborough on paper. Honovi kept his eyes on the road, but when Ksenia said, "Turn left," he obeyed without question.

The outer section of any city tended to house poorer citizens. It was the least safe area in the event revenants somehow got past the outer wall. The air raid sirens and the attack on the wall seemed to have been warning enough for everyone to stay inside their homes. Honovi didn't see anyone on the streets they drove down.

According to the map, Foxborough had four inner-city walls, delineating the city's expansions over the centuries. They didn't come across anyone until they reached the tunnel through the inner wall leading to the next area of the city. Honovi expected the gates there to be closed, that they'd have to fight their way through to the other side. As they approached, he saw the gates to the tunnel were open, with bodies lying scattered on the street. If Honovi had to guess, he'd say the Clockwork Brigade had cleared the way.

Lore's racing carriage took the lead, and Honovi moved into position behind them. The wardens smoothly drew in close, riding two abreast through the short tunnel until they reached the other side of the inner wall. The moment they exited the tunnel, Lore started shooting. The warden driving her racing carriage turned suddenly, and the vehicle skidded across the intersection at an angle, providing Lore with a better shot.

The reason for the defensive shooting scuttled down the street. Two spiderlike automatons exploded after taking bullets from the Zip gun. Then Lore's driver spun the wheel to reorient their vehicle. She stopped shooting so several velocycles could drive past, weaving in and out as wardens went to dispatch the threat.

"Keep driving," Ksenia said.

"Which way?" Honovi snapped, turning the wheel quickly with both hands to steer around Lore's vehicle.

Ksenia pointed right, toward a well-lit street whose buildings were all locked up tight, windows shuttered. "We need to get farther into the city. The map is showing Blaine's location within the second city ring."

"Once we have Blaine, I'll send a flare into the sky to mark our position. We're too deep to try to drive back out. Caoimhe will be on the lookout for it."

"She risks being shot down by any remaining anti-airship guns."

Honovi bared his teeth, engine thrumming as he picked up speed again. "Not if the anti-airship guns are taken out first."

Any city's major defense was almost always consolidated on the outer wall in deference to the threat of revenants. Ashion was the only country to have suffered a civil war, and its major cities still had defenses built into their walls from that time period. The airships would target the anti-airship guns first. Until those were taken out, flying low was a risk, but he knew it would be one Caoimhe would take.

He also knew E'ridia's war airships were very, very good at hitting their targets.

Five blocks later, an explosion echoed in the air. From their position on the ground, weaving through streets, Honovi couldn't see where the bomb had been dropped, but he knew his people had taken out yet another anti-airship stand. If Caoimhe's luck held, the airships wouldn't need to target any other part of the city.

Honovi's luck didn't.

A pair of wardens were ahead of them and had crossed an intersection when gunfire sounded, and one of the wardens went down, velocycle skidding out from under them. Honovi swerved so as to not hit them while Lore's racing carriage braked to a halt so she could fire down the street at the peacekeepers who'd finally shown up.

Another warden drove to their fallen brethren and stopped only long enough to haul the downed warden onto the back of their own velocycle and get out of the line of fire. They didn't retreat the way they'd come, though, and the warden who'd had their velocycle shot out from beneath them seemed conscious enough. When Honovi pulled up alongside them on the other side of the intersection, he could see the man bleeding from a gunshot wound in his calf, boot a mangled mess.

"Tie it off and keep riding," Ksenia said.

Neither warden protested the order. Honovi hit the gas pedal again and drove forward, the wardens again taking up position around them. Less than a minute later, Lore's modified racing carriage came roaring up beside theirs in the street. When Honovi glanced over at her, she looked washed out in the gas lamp light but still grimly determined and having not let go of the Zip gun.

The deeper they drove into Foxborough, the more detours they had to take after that first attempted pushback. The peacekeepers were coming out in force, as were Daijalan soldiers. The city wasn't under any formal occupation order, and no street barricades had yet been erected throughout the city to stall incoming forces. The velocycles and racing carriages Honovi's group drove could outrun the motor carriages used by peacekeepers.

They couldn't outrun an entrapment spell.

They were past another inner wall, barreling down a twisting sort of street, when Lore's racing carriage turned the corner and what looked like lightning crackled through the air, crawling all over the vehicle. Honovi slammed his foot on the brake pedal, the safety belt digging into his shoulder, but they'd been going too fast to stop in time.

Their racing carriage slid through the crackling demarcation of magic, and Honovi bit down on the scream that wanted to wrench itself from his lungs. He lost his grip on the steering wheel, but he never let up pressure on the brake.

Ksenia lunged across the gear shift, getting a hand on the steering wheel. The city map book slid off her lap and into the footwell, but at least it didn't go flying out of the racing carriage. They skidded to a stop, the racing carriage spinning around until they faced back the way they'd come. Honovi blinked colored spots out of his eyes, all the hair on his head and body standing on end. He lifted his chin off his chest, barely able to hear Ksenia's voice in his ear.

"*Drive*!" she snarled.

Honovi got his hands back on the wheel, shook his head hard, and focused on the road. He reversed the racing carriage, blinking away his double vision in time to see a warden magician point their clarion crystal–tipped wand at the cobblestones in the street to destroy the base of the entrapment spell.

Aether hissed like steam out of the fractured spellwork, the glow of magic fading from the spell shapes drawn on the cobblestones. Honovi's fingertips were numb as he turned the steering wheel to guide the racing carriage back around. The engine made a sound Blaine would tell him it shouldn't, but the wheels were still turning, and Honovi refused to stop now.

"The map?" he got out through gritted teeth.

Ksenia dragged it out of the footwell and opened it up again, flipping through the pages. She smacked her hand down on the neatly drawn lines, the clarion crystal twitching at the end of the leather cord when Honovi glanced down at it.

"He's moving. Whoever has him knows we're coming for him."

Honovi drew in a deep, centering breath, pressed his foot on the gas pedal, and drove.

Twelve

VANYA

Vanya burned his way to the family wing and left the palace uninhabitable behind him.

It was the only way to get past the revenants.

Historical portraits and artwork, statues that had been around for centuries, the history of the Houses that had held the Imperial throne—all of it went up in starfire if it got them through to the other side.

Vanya told himself he had no choice, that it was the only way to save himself, the people who'd come with him, and those they stumbled across on their way through. They'd passed bodies in rooms being ravaged by revenants, and Vanya had set those same rooms afire. Nothing survived. That was the point.

It was a kindness Vanya knew he would be judged on.

"Keep moving!" Javier shouted.

Vanya kept some of his attention on the starfire burning like a wall behind them, blocking the stairs they'd stumbled down. Several *praetoria* legionnaires were on the landing above—dead or nearly, judging by their ravaged state they'd been in before Vanya had called forth yet more starfire. Everyone was running low on bullets, and close quarters with a backup knife against revenants inevitably got people killed. But the *praetoria* legionnaires would not be swayed from their duty to protect the Imperial throne.

Even if it killed them.

Javier stayed by Vanya's side, always the first around any corner or down any hallway. The captain had run out of bullets well before they reached the private family wing and had fallen back on his wand and magic as a last resort against revenants.

When this is over, I'm promoting him.

Vanya tucked that thought away and focused on their current predicament of outrunning one horde straight into another. He had starfire burning at one end of the hallway and extended his arm in the other direction, calling up more. Flames erupted beyond them, catching the revenants crowded up against the far door in a miniature inferno.

The crowded group of survivors pressed ever closer, seeking safety that wasn't to be found there in the hall. The air grew hot and dry—thin in a way that made Vanya gasp for breath. He kept the starfire burning for several more seconds, sweat sliding down his face and throat, before banishing all of it. He breathed in deeply, smelling the scorched wood of the walls and floor and everything that had adorned it.

A single light cut through the darkness from the lone *praetoria* legionnaire who'd managed to secure a handheld gaslight from one of the dead they'd passed. Ash danced through the beam of light as Javier led the way forward to the closed and locked defensive doors.

Javier touched the knob before jerking his hand back, hissing at the heat of the metal. He shrugged out of his jacket and used it to get a better, safer grip on the knob and twist it, but the door wouldn't open. Javier looked over his shoulder at Vanya. "Locked."

"I'll handle it," a steady voice called out. "My magic is good with small things."

Yadvir was a young man who'd not yet reached his majority, heir to a minor House out of Oeiras. Vanya didn't know where Yadvir's father was or if the older man was still alive. But his son was a magician who hadn't lost his wand yet. He stepped closer to Vanya, robes dirty from ash and stained with things none of them liked to think about. His wand was made up entirely out of brass gears and pounded thin plates, the clarion crystal encased in sturdy metal wire to secure it at the tip.

He raised the wand and muttered something low under his breath, the aether flowing through the clarion crystal in a far gentler way than starfire. The doorknob twisted on its own, the unlocking spell moving what was too hot to touch. Javier grunted his thanks before using his foot to push the door open, leaving enough space to defend himself if necessary.

The *praetoria* legionnaire with the handheld gaslight moved forward, shining it into the dark. The door creaked open. Beneath the sound, Vanya heard the scrape of bone on the floor. He opened his mouth to shout a warning, but it was too late, and the *praetoria* legionnaire wasn't quick enough to dodge the revenant that darted through the space.

Javier shoved Vanya back, dragging Yadvir with them. Vanya threw starfire at the revenant whose bony fingers were now buried deep in the dying *praetoria* legionnaire's body, blood everywhere. Both burst into flames, blocking their way into the family wing. Vanya made a cutting gesture with his hand and put out the flames once he was sure the revenant wouldn't walk again. The *praetoria* legionnaire was nothing more than a mangled, burned body, flesh charred black and uniform nothing but ash.

Javier bent to pick up the handheld gaslight that had rolled off to the side, the device having escaped the heat of starfire. The light flickered but stabilized when he smacked his palm against the cylinder. Holding it and his wand in front of him, Javier entered the room on the other side, stepping over the bodies as he went. Yadvir went next, wand up as well, ready to call forth magic.

Vanya had been carrying the brunt of the defense within the halls they traversed, starfire the only weapon they had against the furious dead when they'd run out of nearly everything else. He spared a glance behind him to assure himself of Taisiya's presence. His *valide* was still held in the *praetoria* legionnaire's arms, the man having not let her feet touch the ground since the garden.

Facing forward again, Vanya stepped over the burned corpses and into the grand hallway that opened up the private wing he'd called home since he was born. He'd hoped—prayed—that the *praetoria* legionnaires on duty here had managed to barricade the wing, but he knew otherwise now.

The family wing was built to withstand a siege. That every door they passed was open, the windows broken in some of the rooms and bodies on the floor that hadn't risen yet, was proof the defenses hadn't been activated. Fear that Vanya had managed to push down and ignore threatened to strangle him just then. Letting it consume him wouldn't help, but it simmered in the back of his mind, the horrible knowledge of what he might find when he reached Raiah's suite of rooms.

His hand strayed to his pocket where the televox was, half tempted to try calling Alida again. But she hadn't answered—not once—and that worried him. Drawing in a breath, Vanya stayed on Javier's heels, tiny tongues of starfire flickering above their procession. It made them a target in the dark, revenants drawn to the light and the warmth of their bodies, but Vanya and the people with him couldn't survive in the dark.

They reached a portion of the hallway where marble pillars lined the section of it, stretching two stories high in an inner atrium. A set of stairs led to the second floor, where Raiah's rooms were located.

Huddled around the fallen figures of three *praetoria* legionnaires on the stairs themselves was a small horde of revenants. The glow of starfire caught the revenants' attention, skulls turning their way, dried-out holes staring at them without seeing anything.

Vanya clenched one hand into a fist and raised an arm, prepared to cast starfire. The revenants opened their mouths and let out an ugly, rasping sound that might have been a scream if they were alive.

But they weren't.

The ringing sound of metal against stone cracked through the air from above, drawing everyone's attention, even the dead's. Vanya's gaze jumped from the revenants to the figure standing at the landing, half-lit by Vanya's starfire and the handheld gaslight. That spiral of fear Vanya had been carrying suddenly dissipated, fading in the realization of who had arrived.

Soren didn't wait for the revenants to come to him.

Soren made himself the closer moving target, and the revenants went after him instead. He cut through them with brutal thoroughness, but there was a drag to his motions, a sluggishness that only Vanya might recognize. He knew how Soren fought, had watched the warden practice in the palace's salle over the years. Soren might be up and moving, but Vanya ached to get his hands on the other man to check for wounds.

When the last revenant had its head removed from its body, both parts thumping down to the stairs, Soren finally turned to face them. Vanya flicked his fingers at the starfire, casting it brighter, enough that he could see the shadows on Soren's face weren't all shadows but streaks of blood and bruises. The way Soren needed to use the railing on the way down made Vanya look for wounds he couldn't see.

The moment Soren got close, Vanya settled a hand on his hip to brace him, the other holding his jaw. Vanya tilted Soren's face up to better look at his bruised skin. Soren's gaze was steady enough despite the uneven pupils, an obvious sign of concussion.

"Soren," Vanya ground out.

The warden grimaced, angling his poison sword away from Vanya's knees. "It'll keep."

"Where were you?" Taisiya asked tartly, raspy voice louder than Vanya would have liked.

Soren's gaze flicked to his *valide* for a moment before returning to Vanya. He reached up to gently pry Vanya's hand from his face. "Knocked out and trapped in a coffin."

It was warm in the palace, air heated by starfire and the muggy night air flowing through broken windows. In that moment, all Vanya felt was cold. "*What?*"

"When I came back from the resupply station, I went looking for you at the star temple. I was told you might be praying. You weren't there, but Alida was. She wasn't alone."

Vanya went still at the mention of his majordomo's name and the burgeoning implications coming out of Soren's mouth. "Who was she with?"

Soren shoved a hand into his pocket and came up with a pendant on a necklace that Vanya didn't immediately recognize. Vanya took it from him, staring at the imprint of the House of Kimathi's crest in gold.

"Daijalan Blades and House of Kimathi allies." Soren swallowed, the sound loud in the silence that had settled over everyone. "She gave them the keys to the crypt."

When Vanya was a child, his mother had sat on his bed and woken him from sleep one night. Zakariya had smoothed back his hair and told him—dry-eyed but with a breaking voice—that she was sorry, but he was the heir now.

He'd known, even that young, what it meant when she'd slid the ranking necklace over his head, the one Iosiv had always proudly worn. It had felt like the worst of betrayals—that his brother was dead, that his mother had given him a road that shouldn't have been his to walk. It hurt back then, the same way it did now, when his world upended itself, ripped from its moorings like a damaged Tovanian ship-city left to drift amongst the waves.

"I sent her to Raiah," Vanya breathed hollowly, feeling as if someone were digging a knife into his gut and twisting it deeper over and over again.

"What crypt?" Cybele asked from behind them.

Soren blinked, a flicker of something passing across his face. An apology, perhaps, for giving voice to a secret every major House had kept for centuries. One which Joelle had ruined first with this play.

"The Dawn Star buried the first royals of Solaria at the beginning of our country. The Houses who have held the Imperial throne since then have followed her wishes regarding the royal dead," Vanya said after a long moment.

The major Houses knew their history. Cybele was from a minor

House, one who had never held the Imperial throne and who would not know of the dead that once slept beneath the Imperial palace. Cybele stepped closer, causing Javier to tense, but the captain didn't block her way.

"A crypt," she said in a low, furious voice. "We burn the dead. We don't *bury* them."

Vanya looked at her, at the betrayal and disgust in her face, and raised an eyebrow. "Do not tell me you would not adhere to the tradition Callisto demands for those who sit on the Imperial throne?"

"My House has never had the honor."

"And if it had, you would keep that tradition the same way every major House has since the founding of our nation." He didn't speak of the sanctions their country owed because of it, of the tithes they'd have to pay and which the wardens would need now more than ever. Eventually, they all would have to bear that cost.

Soren cleared his throat. "We can argue over the terrible decisions of your ancestors through the Ages later, but right now, we need to keep moving."

Cybele's gaze cut his way. "Are any more wardens coming?"

"No."

"Why not? Haven't they heard the warning siren? We need their aid."

"Daijal attacked the Warden's Island yesterday. From what we were told, the casualty toll was high," Vanya said.

The cries of shock from their group of survivors washed over Vanya. He'd meant to inform the Senate after the Conclave had ended, news which would then be disseminated to the general populace afterward. In delaying, he'd left an opening for Joelle to twist truth into a lie if he didn't survive.

"The warden manning the resupply station I went to was recalled to a city in Ashion. Their replacement isn't here yet." Soren swallowed thickly, blinking rapidly. "The governor is in Glencoe. I need to report back to her."

Vanya tightened his grip on Soren's hip, knowing that Soren would've been well within his right to have left without saying goodbye after hearing the news. But instead, he'd returned to the palace and stumbled upon a betrayal that targeted not just Vanya's own House but so many others.

Cybele's gaze dropped to the pendant cradled in Vanya's palm. She drew in a sharp breath. "That is the House of Kimathi crest."

Vanya curled his fingers over the pendant, clutching it tightly. "Yes."

"The House of Kimathi's *vezir* was not present for the Conclave tonight, and her heir left early. So did all their allies."

All true, Vanya knew. The Conclave was supposed to end tonight at a gathering where all the Houses were in one place. Glancing at Cybele, watching the way she went bloodless in her face, Vanya knew he wasn't the only one thinking that.

"Oh, the games she plays," Taisiya said from behind him, sounding impossibly, ridiculously impressed.

"*Valide*," Vanya ground out.

"Do you not see? We were all meant to die tonight."

Taisiya spoke a truth that could not be denied. Vanya looked over his shoulder at his *valide*, at the few remaining *praetoria* legionnaires who had fought to keep them all alive, and the scattered members of Houses, both major and minor, that he could not leave behind in their frantic push through the palace.

"Joelle has been trying to kill me since Nicca left to dance amongst the stars. I will not grant her that victory. Not tonight," Vanya swore.

"I passed rooms that revenants never made it to on the second floor. We can barricade everyone inside there before continuing to search for Raiah," Soren said.

The protestations were immediate, all aimed at securing starfire for their defense against the dead. While Taisiya could cast it, she was old and did not have Vanya's strength, and he would not put their survival on her shoulders, though she might take it up anyway. Vanya caught Javier's eye, and the captain nodded. He quelled the fearful uproar by virtue of being louder than everyone else.

"This plan is not negotiable. We'll move quicker with fewer numbers right now," Javier cut in. "We'll leave some *praetoria* legionnaires with you and come find you after we've rescued the Imperial princess."

"Leave us the warden!" someone cried out.

"I go where your emperor goes," Soren said before Vanya could deny them their request.

Javier headed for the stairs. "Then let's go."

Soren led the way, overtaking Javier, to bring them to a library Vanya's mother had always favored. Enough heavy furniture was inside for them to use as a barricade. The *praetoria* legionnaires wasted no time in corralling everyone inside. Yadvir and Cybele refused to enter the room, remaining in the hallway.

"My road is with you," Yadvir said, staring defiantly at Vanya, who could not refuse the request.

"There are those in the Conclave who will not believe a word you say, but they'll believe mine about what happens tonight," Cybele said.

Vanya looked over at Soren, who only shrugged. "She's right. You need someone impartial."

It went without saying that Soren was not, though it could be argued the same could be said of Cybele. But that was a problem for later. Cybele and Yadvir stayed out in the hallway with them.

Taisiya was the last one inside the library, finally being let down by the *praetoria* legionnaire who had carried her all this way. Her eyes reflected the starfire burning at the tips of Vanya's fingers, the light fading when she bowed her head.

"Good hunting," Taisiya said as the door closed between them.

Vanya turned away from the door and the sound of furniture being moved around within the room, finding Soren waiting for him a few feet away, *praetoria* legionnaires fanned out around them. Yadvir and Cybele stood pale-faced and determined nearby with Javier. Soren quirked an eyebrow at him. "Ready?"

Vanya nodded. "Lead the way."

Soren headed into the dark, starfire that Vanya commanded reflecting off his poison short sword like a beacon.

Thirteen

HONOVI

The crystal on the map moved through Foxborough, and Honovi never took his foot off the gas pedal of the racing carriage. "Are they still heading north?"

"Yes," Ksenia said, pitching her voice over the roar of the velocycles surrounding them.

"North is the rail station."

"It's no longer useable."

"It's still a way out."

Whoever had Blaine would have to be desperate to consider leaving a city at night. The only night travel anyone did was by airship or steam train. One never touched the earth, and the other was enclosed and moved at rapid speed, capable of outrunning revenants. Motor carriages and trucks traveled in convoys but only in daylight hours.

They were closer to Blaine than they had been—at least a mile out, according to Ksenia's map—and the Clockwork Brigade in Foxborough had been integral in keeping the peacekeepers and scattered Daijalan soldiers at bay. It helped that some of the peacekeepers sided with Ashion over Daijal, and internal strife was making it difficult for any real attempt to muster a solid pushback against the Ashion battalion.

The wardens were as good as any soldier—better, in some ways—and they had a few magicians in their ranks. When Ksenia gave the order for the wardens to split up, one of the magicians went with the group who were tasked with taking side streets to get ahead of the people who had Blaine. The one left behind came in handy when Honovi turned a corner and the racing carriage *finally* lined up with the crystal—

—and they came up against immediate defensive fire.

The bullets ricocheted off the hexagonal shield the other magician had erected, the miniature shapes snapping together to form a barrier. The pale blue glow of magic sparked where bullets hit, but the warden never slowed her velocycle down. She drove forward, and Honovi could only follow.

Lore's racing carriage overtook theirs, but she couldn't take any shot through the warden's shield. Honovi hit the brakes, steering their vehicle closer to the pavement. Some of the wardens had backtracked the way they'd come, disappearing down another street.

"Should I follow your people?" Honovi asked.

Ksenia snapped the map book closed. "No."

She undid the safety belt and hopped out of the seat, striding to the rear, where a small trunk was located. She popped it open and pulled out a weapon with an overlarge barrel and a spring-actuated revolving-cylinder magazine. Honovi craned his head around and watched with a distant sort of disbelief and horror as Ksenia calmly fed what looked like six grenades into the chambers of the cylinder one by one.

"We had *grenades* in our vehicle?" Honovi exclaimed. "What if we'd been hit?"

"I trusted you wouldn't let us" was Ksenia's calm response. "Besides, you fly with bombs."

He couldn't really argue that.

He did protest when Ksenia walked around the racing carriage and fit the stock against her shoulder, hands curled around the grip and base, finger resting against the trigger guard. "You can't shoot them if they have Blaine."

Ksenia never looked away from her target. "Your husband isn't my target."

Honovi swore as he scrambled out of the racing carriage, unholstering his pistol. "You don't know where he is in that group."

"This is how we find out."

She pulled the trigger before he could stop her, aiming high over the magician's shield. Honovi watched in horror as the launcher spat out a grenade with a clank of gears. The projectile arced over the magician's shield and landed between their defense and the cluster of Daijalan soldiers positioned around a makeshift barricade of motor carriages.

The ensuing explosion sent cobblestones flying into the air, shattered windows all along the street from the sound of the explosion, and swirled up dust and smoke. Gas lamps lost their casings as gaslights went out, plunging their area of the street into darkness. The only light came from the glow of the magician's shield, the interlocking shapes like tiny bricks floating in the air, and the bioluminescence poison that had been in the grenade.

"Ksenia."

She loaded another grenade into the barrel with a grind of gears. "It won't kill them. The poison is meant to incapacitate."

He could see several soldiers who had been closest to the blast lying on the ground, some of that strange bioluminescence spattered over their bodies. They weren't moving, but the soldiers behind them were shouting in Daijalan, looking to continue the fight. Their attention was split when Ksenia's advance team roared down the other end of the street, having managed to get ahead and trap the Daijalans in a pincer move.

The soldiers shouted in alarm, turning from Honovi's position to deal with the new threat. Gunfire echoed in the air, and Honovi flinched, trying to see through the shield that was taking on less fire at the moment. "You need to call off your wardens. I don't want to risk Blaine's life."

Ksenia was primed to fire again but held her position. "Those are Daijalans."

Wardens weren't known for revenge, though Honovi supposed, after everything that had occurred, they were owed a debt by that country. What Honovi forgot—what many people forgot—about wardens was that they may not be the typical soldier, but they still knew how to fight. Their enemy tended to be dead, and they had ways of handling the dead that no one else could safely duplicate. Wardens could survive many of the poisons found on Maricol, but the same could not be said for anyone else.

Screams rose above the sound of gunfire—one voice, then two, then more. The gunfire faded, but the shield didn't drop until a piercing whistle rent the air, the notes a frantic tone. Ksenia swore and pointed the grenade launcher at the ground, yanking her own wand free of its casing. "Move in!"

The remaining wardens drove toward the shield, which snapped apart in sections and let them through. Ksenia ran forward through the open spaces in the shield, Honovi matching her stride for stride. The magical barrier snapped back into place nearly on their heels.

"Honovi!" Lore shouted from behind them.

He didn't look back. "Be ready to cover us!"

"You'll want to be careful where you walk," Ksenia called over her shoulder.

The bioluminescent poison glowed faintly in the dark, marking out the explosion radius. The downed soldiers Honovi ran past never moved to attack, and he tried not to brush up against any of the poison on the vehicles. He couldn't avoid stepping on some of the poison spatters, hoping it wouldn't be able to penetrate the soles of his boots.

Gears clanked together, metal ringing against metal as a clockwork cat suddenly landed on the hood of a motor carriage to Honovi's right. He jerked back, bringing his pistol up automatically. Aether flickered like a heartbeat in the center of the large cage that made up the clockwork cat's chest.

It reminded him of the one on the Warden's Island, the beast having acted eerily alive in a way right before it tried to go for Ksenia's throat. This one was the same, lunging at Honovi as if it were a wild beast and not a device made up of gears and magic.

Honovi aimed for the cat's center mass, even as he stumbled backward, trying to get out of its reach. His bullets didn't find the clockwork heart, but Ksenia's magic did. Magic erupted from the tip of her wand like it had in the laboratory on the island, slamming into gears and plates that made up the clockwork cat's chest.

The clockwork cat slammed to the ground, the glow in its bottle-glass green eyes flickering like a candle about to go out. It struggled to get its legs beneath it, mechanical limbs jerking, but another hit of raw aether from Ksenia's wand shattered the spell framework animating it. The magic abruptly guttered out, and the clockwork cat collapsed to the ground, nothing more than lifeless metal and gears.

The clanking sound of gears from behind him had Honovi ducking, rocking on his heels as he tried not to touch the street and the hints of poison he could see glowing on the cobblestones. Ksenia twisted around, magic exploding from her wand like lightning to crash into the second clockwork cat hunting them.

"Maybe that warden of yours who made these contraptions isn't really dead," Honovi said.

Ksenia scowled at him, her white lock of hair falling over one eye. "Stay behind me."

Honovi scrambled to obey, knowing his pistol would be useless against the clockwork cats. It did well enough against Daijalan soldiers, a bullet finding a home inside one man's face when he lifted his head over the hood of a motor carriage. Honovi shoved aside the queasiness of the kill in favor of sticking close to Ksenia. The wardens had the area partially surrounded, and while the half dozen clockwork cats left were a problem, the biggest threat was a Blade.

She moved with the speed of someone well trained, dark hair twisted into a knot at the back of her head, teeth bared in a warning snarl. The Blade had a pistol in hand and was firing rapidly, forcing the wardens to take cover. The clockwork cats prowled the immediate area, darting between Daijalan soldiers to attack the wardens. In the mayhem that followed, one warden went down screaming with metal teeth in their forearm. Another took a swing with their battle axe at the clockwork cat coming for them and took several bullets to the chest.

Then the Blade unhooked something from her belt, ripped a pin out with her teeth, and tossed it into the middle of the street.

"Take cover!" Ksenia yelled.

Honovi dove behind a motor carriage, barely getting down in time before the grenade went off. His ears rang horrendously in the aftermath, and he frantically looked around for Ksenia. He saw her crouched on one knee, the grenade launcher braced against her shoulder and aimed at the rooftops, but she didn't pull the trigger. Honovi followed her aim and saw the Blade flinging herself onto the roof of the nearest building, having scaled it while everyone had tried to escape the explosion.

The blast had ripped apart two of the clockwork cats. The remaining four were still a problem, and it took precious long minutes for the wardens to neutralize the damned things while keeping the remaining Daijalan soldiers pinned down.

The firefight ended when the last Daijalan was taken out and the clockwork cats were ripped to pieces. Not all of the wardens got to their feet, and while some went to tend to their fallen brethren, the others approached the motor carriage barricade and started methodically ensuring the Daijalan soldiers were dead with brutal efficiency.

The smell of cordite and blood hung heavy on the air as the remaining wardens pressed forward, clearing the area. Honovi followed Ksenia, eyes darting from side to side as he searched for any sign of Blaine.

A flurry of movement around a motor carriage in the center of the barricade had him rushing forward, nearly stumbling over a body or two in his haste. The wardens had surrounded the vehicle in question, weapons drawn on a man illuminated by someone's handheld gaslight.

The last living soldier sat in the driver's seat of the motor carriage, facing down the ring of pistols aimed his way. Honovi froze when he saw who the soldier held on his lap in front of him like a living shield. Blaine didn't appear to be conscious, head lolling forward despite the muzzle of a pistol pressed against his throat.

He wasn't bound in any way, and the reason for that made Honovi choke on bile when he saw the ruined stump where his husband's left arm ended at past the elbow. The ugly black stitches there tied up inflamed flesh. For an agonizing moment, Honovi couldn't comprehend what he was seeing.

"You're going to let me go, or he dies," the Daijalan said.

"Nura?" Ksenia asked calmly.

"Deployed," a warden in the group said with a grim hint of satisfaction in her voice.

The pistol against Blaine's throat pressed harder, tilting Blaine's head at a sharper angle. "You really want to risk him dying?"

Ksenia snorted. "You Daijalans attacked our home and murdered our people and tithes. Your death is just the start of a never-ending payment for breaking the Poison Accords."

The man opened his mouth, but then he jerked. His free hand made to slap at the side of his own neck—only his arm froze halfway through the motion, eyes bulging in his face. Saliva bubbled at the corners of his mouth in seconds, drooling down his chin.

A warden darted forward on quick feet, leaning into the motor carriage to knock the pistol away from Blaine and haul him out. They left the soldier inside, but no one took a shot to put him out of his misery. Something tiny and mechanical flew out of the motor carriage with a buzz of wings. Honovi only got the glimpse of what looked like a mechanical wasp that could have doubled as a wind-up toy before all his attention was taken up by his husband.

The warden laid Blaine down on the ground, checking his pulse before swearing and looking up at Ksenia. "I need a kit. He's got needle marks in his arm. I can't tell if it's from what was done to him before or something that happened tonight."

Honovi jerked forward, wanting to be by Blaine's side, but Ksenia's hand shot out, grabbing him by the wrist in an iron grip. "Let them work."

"That's my *husband*," Honovi ground out.

"If you want to make sure you still have one come dawn, you will let them *work*."

One of the wardens still on their velocycle climbed off and ran forward, carrying a travel case in one hand. He crouched on the other side of Blaine while two more wardens pulled out their handheld gaslights to provide more light to see by. It did nothing to ease the horror done to Blaine, nor the guilt he felt for leaving his husband behind to this horror.

Honovi couldn't bring himself to look at the space where part of Blaine's left arm used to be, and so he focused on what the wardens were doing. The pair had vials and tins out, both of them passing items back and forth as they concocted something on the fly that Honovi wouldn't even begin to know how to mix.

"Broad-spectrum antidote," Ksenia said when Honovi made a sound as one of the wardens tipped a yellow substance down Blaine's throat. "We don't know what was given him and can't until we can test his blood, but we don't have time for that right now."

Honovi unholstered the flare gun from his hip and primed it, listening as the gears clicked together. "I'm calling Caoimhe in."

He raised his arm over his head, pointed the flare gun straight up, cocked back the hammer, and pulled the trigger. The crack of the flare releasing was loud in his ears, light flashing at the muzzle as the flare rose into the sky, a red-orange glow that flew upward like a comet. Moments later, it flashed brighter, a lingering glow in the dark that would hopefully provide enough time for Caoimhe's navigator to pinpoint their location with the astrolabe.

Honovi lowered his arm and reloaded the flare gun with another round from his belt. He'd need to shoot it off once the airship was on approach to better pinpoint their location. It hopefully wouldn't be long.

"Is Blaine all right?" Lore asked from behind him. "They didn't—"

She broke off with a horrible gasp as she came to stand by his side. Honovi knew she must have finally seen Blaine's partially amputated left arm. He never looked away from where Blaine lay so still and pale on the ground between the wardens working to stabilize him.

"He needs a doctor and a magician with an affiliation for healing magic," Honovi said.

"Is it safe to even move him?"

Honovi's lips curled. "I'm not letting him stay *here*."

He'd left him behind to suffer and would hate himself for that until he died. Right now, he had every intention of flying straight to Glencoe if the wardens thought Blaine would make it. Blaine would get the medical care he needed back home. He'd get—

Honovi swallowed, shoving aside all the fear and worry clamoring at the back of his thoughts. Falling apart now would do Blaine no favors.

The remaining wardens not tending to Blaine or lying dead on the street staggered their positions in the immediate area to better keep watch. Lore never moved from Honovi's side and didn't offer any platitudes for the situation at hand.

It was minutes later when the thrum of an airship's engine reached his ears, drowning out the distant sounds of bombs and gunfire at the outer wall of the city. The anti-airship guns had most likely been destroyed, which gave Caoimhe more maneuverability than she'd otherwise have.

Honovi aimed the flare gun at the sky again, shooting off another round to mark their position. Then he shoved it into his holster once the round was released and stepped past Ksenia to where Blaine lay.

"The airship is on the way. I'll need to carry him on board," Honovi said.

The warden who had administered the antidote looked up from the vial of blood she'd drawn from his husband's vein. "I'll need to go with you."

Honovi found it difficult to breathe suddenly. "Is the antidote not working?"

"He'll need more screening, and only a warden can provide that." Her attention focused behind him, on Ksenia, looking to the person she considered being in charge. "Ksenia?"

"The governor is in Glencoe. You can report back to her about what happened tonight. It'll be hours before we can get a report to her, and she needs to know," Ksenia said.

The warden nodded before starting to pack up her kit. She didn't look older than twenty, but the weight to her gaze spoke of surviving a road most others wouldn't. "I'm Banshari."

"Thank you" was all Honovi could think to say in return.

Pressure in the air had Honovi looking up, squinting as the *Celestial Sprite* descended nearly directly overhead. Someone had already flung a rope ladder overboard; he could see two crew members standing at the railing, ready to haul people up.

Honovi knelt and reached for Blaine, trying to ignore the stench of blood and urine that permeated his husband's clothes. He pulled Blaine over his shoulders in a fire brigade carry with gentle hands, hating the way Blaine was deadweight and never even reacted to Honovi's touch. Easing into a standing position, Honovi hunched over a little with a grunt.

"Someone toss me some rope," Banshari said.

A different warden pulled a loop of rope from their velocycle's storage compartment, and Banshari used it to deftly secure Blaine's leg and arm together where they draped over Honovi's shoulders. It wasn't a proper harness, but it would do for the climb up to the airship. He hefted Blaine higher onto his shoulders and turned toward where the airship was holding steady in the air above the rooftops, the keel on its hull lined up with the street. It dipped lower yet, the rope ladder there within climbing reach.

"You're staying?" Honovi asked Ksenia.

She nodded, still carrying the grenade launcher, though she'd put her wand away. "The Ashion battalion seeks to hold Foxborough. We want accountability from Daijal. It'll be a war of propaganda beginning tomorrow, but we'll stay as long as we can."

"Maybe Caris should have come after all."

"The duchess can send her when it's deemed safe if she feels the need to." Ksenia looked up at the sky, where the *Celestial Sprite* waited. "Best get going."

Honovi grunted a wordless goodbye and headed for the airship at a ground-eating jog. Lore joined him, reaching the rope ladder first. She got her hands on it to hold the ends steady while Honovi rocked up onto it with Blaine's weight hanging off his shoulders.

It was a precarious position to be in, but every E'ridian who served as crew on an airship was trained to haul up a fallen comrade the same way they trained with jump vests. Besides, there was no road in existence where Honovi would leave Blaine behind on the ground.

His shoulders burned with every ladder rung he reached for, Blaine's weight pulling him backward with the inescapable tug of gravity. He maintained his balance on the swaying ladder as Lore added her weight to it below, kept his head back, eyes on the crew members above him limned in gaslight from the decking.

It felt like an age before he reached the railing. Two pairs of hands reached for him and Blaine, hauling them both over. He fell to his knees on the decking, Blaine's weight lying across his shoulders and back, gasping for breath.

"*Jarl*, your husband—" one of the aeronauts said before swearing viciously.

Honovi fumbled at the rope securing Blaine. Someone batted his hands away, leaning down to cut away at the knots with a knife. "Haul Lore and the warden up and get us airborne. We're heading to Glencoe."

The rope came undone, and Blaine slid off his back, caught by more than a few willing hands. Honovi turned on his knees, reaching to pull Blaine into his arms. He bowed his head over Blaine's unconscious form, tears stinging his eyes as the stump of his arm pressed against Honovi's chest. Taking a breath, Honovi stood, bracing himself against the swaying of the ascending airship out of long habit.

By the time Lore and Banshari made it to the decking, Honovi was carrying Blaine below, the airship's assigned nurse right on his heels.

Fourteen

VANYA

They passed bodies of *praetoria* legionnaires who didn't appear to have died at the hands of revenants. Bullets to their heads and torsos were proof enough of betrayal. Vanya clenched his teeth, the heat of starfire as hot as his rage as they followed Soren through the familiar halls of the private family wing.

"What if they're not here?" Cybele asked softly, giving voice to Vanya's worst fears.

"If they've fled the wing and made it to the gates, the *praetoria* legionnaires there will not leave the Imperial princess' side. But I believe they must still be here. If they tried leaving, they would have put Raiah at risk. Alida would never allow that," Vanya said.

He wanted to believe that, despite her betrayal, Alida would never put Raiah in danger. If her loyalty truly lay with the House of Kimathi, if she was here to deliver his daughter to Joelle, Raiah needed to be alive for that to happen. There was no chance of surviving a horde of revenants that had them all cornered. Whatever escape plan Alida might have had, he doubted she had managed to fully implement it once the crypt was excavated.

"I'll clear the way through into the princess' rooms. You will *listen* to my warnings once inside, Your Imperial Majesty," Javier said fiercely.

"If Alida and the Blades are here, I think it's best I'm not the first one through any door they're hiding behind," Soren said quietly over his shoulder.

He was supposed to still be trapped in a coffin, hidden away for later taking. Vanya knew he'd never even thought to look in the crypt for Soren when he'd been missing during the day. How long until he would have succumbed to the lack of food and water, screaming for help in the dark? But he was here now, walking ahead of Vanya instead of returning to the wardens who surely needed him just as much as Vanya did.

"I'll cast you in shadow," Yadvir said to Soren, voice a mere whisper. "I'm not the best at spells of subterfuge, but it will hold for what we need, and you'll be able to enter before us when we reach them. I'll drop it when the emperor requests it of me."

Soren stood still as the magician channeled the aether through his wand. The spell wrapped Soren up in a darkness that made Vanya's eyes slide right off him, as if he weren't there—only a shadow to be ignored. Vanya didn't like not knowing where Soren was, but he knew the best way to get Raiah back was if Alida didn't know that Vanya knew the truth of where her loyalty lay.

Javier stood to the side and rapped his knuckles against the locked double doors that barricaded Raiah's suite of rooms from the rest of the palace. "Hail the Legion! Open the doors."

Vanya counted the seconds down in his head. When the minute mark hit, Javier gestured at Yadvir, who raised his wand and pointed it at the door handles. Magic twisted through the tumblers, tiny threads of aether pulling the gears out of position to unlock the doors. Javier nudged one of the doors open. No bullets met the motion, but that wasn't to say they'd find themselves on the receiving end of such an attack.

Javier used his foot to kick the door open wider, shining the handheld gaslight into the receiving room. The light fell on more overturned furniture and a revenant doing its level best to eat through the cavity of a dead *praetoria* legionnaire. Its head snapped around at their entrance, bloody mouth falling open.

Something dark flickered at the corner of Vanya's eyes; he felt the passage of air blow across the side of his face. He couldn't see Soren, gaze redirected from where he knew the warden to be. Whether or not the revenant could see him didn't matter. One moment, the revenant was crouched on the floor. The next, it lunged at them at the exact moment its head left its neck.

The desiccated corpse thumped to the floor along with its head. The cut from Soren's poison short sword was clean, and the poison ensured the revenant wouldn't rise again. But the fact it had been behind the barricade made Vanya want to tear through the suite of rooms in search of his daughter.

It took everything inside of him—and Javier gripping his arm—not to.

Javier went first with the few *praetoria* legionnaires left and Yadvir following, what weapons they had left drawn and wands up. Vanya entered after, starfire curling around his fingers, with Cybele on his heels. The receiving room was empty of any further threats but also of Alida and Raiah. It left Vanya's stomach knotted up with fear he couldn't give in to.

He licked his lips and crossed the room to the set of closed doors across the way. "Next room."

Javier forced that set of doors open, and they moved quietly into the next section of the inner suites. Vanya could hear the distant sounds of fighting on the palace grounds from those trying to hold back the revenants, but inside, the space was empty and quiet. They searched the entire second floor without finding signs of Raiah, but every door meant to barricade this area of the wing was closed and locked, barred from the inside.

"We'll try the first floor. There's a secured room on that level Alida might have brought Raiah to if they weren't able to escape," Vanya said.

Vanya doubled back to a set of stairs one hallway over, sending tongues of starfire drifting down into the dark like fading fireworks. No signs of revenants, but one could never be too careful.

Javier went first, *praetoria* legionnaires fanning out around Vanya. The shadow out of the corners of his eyes that stayed with him was Soren. Vanya gave quiet directions as they traversed the first floor in the dark. He noticed the metal shutters closed over the exterior windows, some with broken-off hands and arms lying on the inside floor, as if someone had chopped the revenants' bodies to pieces in a frantic effort to seal the area.

When they came to the closed doors of an interior parlor, Vanya directed Javier to open it. As before, Javier announced their presence with a knock and a raised voice calling out their presence, making sure to stand to the side. "Hail the Legion! Open the doors."

For a moment, everything was quiet.

Then bullets ripped through the door and would have cut down anyone who'd been standing in that area. Javier swore, gesturing at Yadvir. "Undo the locks!"

Yadvir knelt and leaned around the legs of a *praetoria* legionnaire, aiming his wand at the door. Vanya couldn't hear the lock being undone, but he saw the way the knob turned, guided by the aether. The door unlocked, and Javier kicked it open farther while a *praetoria* legionnaire used what precious bullets they had left to force whoever was on the other side back.

In the wavering light from the handheld gaslight, the shadows seemed to move. The door was pushed wider, all the way open, and Javier snapped his wrist, aether lashing out from the clarion crystal tip. It formed interlocking hexagonal shapes that clicked into place before them. The shield was wide enough to cover the doorway and allow them to enter behind it. The shield was curved to protect Vanya more than anyone else.

Vanya went through first despite the *praetoria* legionnaires' cries, forcing Javier to lunge forward and keep him in sight. Someone had lit lanterns he knew were kept in the secured room hidden behind the wall paneling. The parlor had no windows, built that way to protect the iron-sided room few knew about.

Inside were false star priests who carried Daijalan weapons in their hands.

Inside was Artyom.

Joelle's heir stood within an area of the palace he should never have stepped foot in, Vanya's daughter cradled in his arms. She looked asleep, lying limp against the bastard's shoulder, with the barrel of a pistol tucked dangerously close to her chest.

"A pity you're not dead," Artyom said.

Vanya was rooted to the floor, barely listening to the way Javier commanded the *praetoria* legionnaires to hold fire. All his attention was taken up by Raiah and the nightmare holding her. "Give me back my daughter."

Artyom's mouth twitched into a smile. "She's sleeping. When she wakes up next, she'll be with family."

"*I* am her family."

"Not for much longer." Artyom's gaze flicked around the room before settling on someone behind Vanya, eyes narrowing. "*Vezir* Cybele."

"Traitor," Cybele said with enough acid in her tone to burn.

"No traitor, merely a House intent on doing what is right for Solaria."

"Yes, by letting Daijal invade."

"There will be no invasion while my House holds the throne."

"You don't hold it," Vanya said.

Artyom's gaze snapped back to Vanya. "We will after tonight."

Vanya spared a glance for the Blades ranged through the room, pistols and a wand in hand, indicating at least one was a magician. Behind them, the bookcase had been swung open on hidden hinges, revealing the iron door behind it. That, too, was open, and the slim figure who stepped out from the space beyond made Vanya's rage burn hotter. He throttled it down, staring at Alida and the fear on her face and knowing it was all an act. That perhaps it always had been.

"Your Imperial Majesty," Alida said in a voice that trembled as if she were worried. As if she hadn't been the one to orchestrate this situation. "The *praetoria* legionnaires had gathered stragglers on the way here. I didn't know what Artyom had planned when he joined us."

Vanya stared at her, the lie she spun pretty enough that he might have believed it before Soren had found out the truth. He'd believed so many of them over the years, after all. "Just like you didn't know what would happen when you handed the key to the crypt over to Blades."

Alida jerked back as if she'd been slapped, eyes going wide. For a moment, she looked scared and uncertain, but it all disappeared beneath a calculating sort of hate that left no room for anything else. She gestured at the Blades, lips curling. "Handle it."

The room erupted in chaos and starfire all at once.

The *praetoria* legionnaires held their fire out of fear of harming Raiah, and it cost many their lives. One took a bullet in the back when he grabbed hold of Cybele and Yadvir and *shoved* them out of the room. The two wouldn't have anywhere to run, not with revenants on the loose, and Vanya knew he'd have to ensure the enemy never left this room alive.

That incandescent rage that had simmered beneath his skin since learning of Alida's betrayal exploded forth as a barely contained inferno. The nearest Blades combusted in flames, white-hot fire consuming them. The heat made Artyom stagger back as the dying Daijalans screamed for only seconds before starfire stole the oxygen from their lungs.

A shadow flickered amidst the brightness of starfire, and Vanya resolutely didn't look at it. He kept all his attention on his daughter being held in Artyom's arms. The pistol Artyom held was still perilously close to his daughter's sleeping—most likely drugged—form, and Vanya *knew* he couldn't risk harming Artyom if it would hurt Raiah.

It was why the bastard held her, after all, as if he had the right to keep her.

"Come any closer and you'll lose what you love most," Artyom snarled.

"If that happens, there is nothing in this world that will stop me from destroying your House and razing your *vasilyet* to the ground," Vanya promised.

His fingers curled around more starfire, the flames licking up his arms, reaching for the ceiling, the heat of it comforting in a way when nothing else was in that moment. Vanya stepped forward, jerking free of Javier's grip, the hexagonal shield glimmering in front of him. Starfire erupted around the remaining Blades, eating through flesh and bone with a ferocity that wouldn't be out of place in a prairie wildfire. Vanya sucked hot air through his teeth, never looking away from Raiah and the wild-eyed expression on Artyom's face.

"Stop!" Artyom yelled, a panicked edge to his voice, the pistol still too damn *close* to Raiah. "Stop or I *will* kill your daughter, just like you killed my niece."

Vanya stilled, the flailing, burning bodies of Blades staggering around the room the only movement around him. Vanya put out all but the smallest tongue of starfire, which he sent to the ceiling to give them light enough to see by since the lanterns had been destroyed by starfire. He ignored the way the savagely burned Blades collapsed to the floor, death minutes, if not seconds, away.

"Nicca died in childbirth. I didn't *murder* her."

Artyom bared his teeth, standing amidst the ashes of his treachery, and Vanya knew he had to be careful because there was nothing keeping Artyom from pulling that trigger. "Have your guard drop his shield."

"No" was Javier's instantaneous response.

"Do it," Vanya ordered, never taking his eyes off Artyom.

"Your Imperial Majesty—"

Vanya wondered if it might be the last time Javier ever used that title with him. "You have your orders, Captain. Obey them and leave."

It was, perhaps, a death sentence if Vanya hadn't known there was a shadow in the room. But if Artyom won this standoff and Vanya died, the Imperial throne would go to Raiah, and through her, the House of Kimathi. In which case, Javier and all the rest of the *praetoria* legionnaires would protect *them* because they held the Imperial throne.

The glittering hexagonal shapes faded slowly, Javier's distrust showing in his hesitation to quickly act. When the shield was fully gone, the tension in the room ratcheted up so thick Vanya felt it as a weight against his skin.

Vanya kept his eyes on Artyom, but his words were for Alida. "Why?"

"Because I had a family once, and you don't deserve to have what your mother stole from all of those in Rixham. What she stole from *me*," Alida spat.

Out of the corners of his eyes, he saw her arm move, the barrel of a gun glinting beneath starfire. Javier shouted and Vanya was shoved aside, the crack of a bullet loud in the room. Javier grunted, and Vanya staggered under the captain's sudden deadweight, reaching out blindly to catch him. When he chanced a glance down, blood was flowing from a bullet wound in Javier's shoulder, Vanya's fingers slick with it.

"Yadvir!" Vanya yelled. "The spell!"

Vanya looked up in time to watch the snarl on Alida's face change to a twist of agonized confusion, choking on a wet sort of gasp. She looked down at the blade sticking out of the center of her chest, the poison on it impossible to see through the blood. Alida raised a shaking hand but never managed to touch the edge of what had killed her before Soren yanked it out of her body. She collapsed to the floor in a heap, blood pooling on the floor beneath her lifeless body.

The shadows slipped away from Soren's body like water, dragging him back into focus beneath the flickering illumination of starfire above. Soren had his right arm outstretched, fingers hovering over the back of Artyom's neck. Vanya didn't know what to expect—poison or another secreted blade. Certainly not the starfire that curled around Artyom's head and face like a hungry beast.

Vanya froze, staring as Artyom jerked away from Soren, the starfire following his every move even as the warden dropped his sword and twisted around to yank the pistol from Artyom's hand. Then Soren wrenched Raiah from the other man's other arm as Artyom clawed at his burning face, and Vanya watched—

He stared—

—as starfire he hadn't cast cascaded over Artyom's body, consuming the man with a contained degree of heat and power no House other than Vanya's had been able to muster in several generations.

That's not possible.

The thought slid through Vanya's mind, disbelief and something worse leaving him kneeling there in shock, nausea heavy in his gut. Vanya wrenched his gaze from Joelle's burning, dying heir to where Soren stood, holding Raiah in his arms, bruised face pale and gray eyes haunted.

"Vanya," Soren rasped, stepping forward.

He didn't know what to say when faced with a betrayal that cut deeper than Alida's. Words died on his tongue, a strange roaring in his ears that Vanya couldn't hear past. There was an ache in his chest he couldn't comprehend in that moment—like the worst of grief settling in his bones.

If he could have found the words, he might have given voice to things he couldn't take back. But Yadvir pitched himself into the room just then, wild-eyed and panting, clutching his wand. "Your Imperial Majesty?"

Vanya packed up the tangle of emotions and shoved it all aside. He hauled Javier with him when he stood, the captain only half-conscious and needing his wound tended to, but they didn't have time for that. He pitched Javier into Yadvir's arms. "Take him. Wait for us in the hall."

Yadvir dragged Javier's good arm over his shoulder and left without a word. Then it was only Vanya, Soren, and Raiah left alive in the room, bodies between them, the walls scorched black. Vanya stared at Soren across a distance that felt as if it grew and grew with every breath he took and nothing in him was capable of bridging it.

"Give me my daughter," Vanya finally said, the order coming out hoarse. Soren didn't hesitate to hand Raiah over, her limp, sleeping form passed between them. Vanya clutched her close, listening to the soft sound of her breathing in the silence. He looked at where Soren stood so close, but it was as if Vanya didn't even know him. "You lied to me."

Soren's expression twisted as he raised one hand between them, dropping it when Vanya took a step back. "Vanya—"

"You will get us all out," he cut in, biting out the words. "You are the only warden in Calhames, and you will do your duty."

Soren pressed his lips into a hard line, clenching his hands into fists to hide the way they shook, but Vanya had seen the way they trembled. "Of course."

When they stepped out into the hallway, he found Cybele tending to Javier's shoulder, having ripped her gown at the hem to make padding with which to try to stop the blood flow. Of the *praetoria* legionnaires who'd gone with them after Raiah, only Javier had survived, and his continued survival was questionable.

"I don't think it hit an artery, but he needs a doctor," Cybele said shakily.

"Soren will coordinate with the Legion outside once we're back with the others," Vanya said, studiously not looking at the warden. "The revenants need to be contained and eradicated. Once it's safe to move, we'll evacuate everyone who secured themselves somewhere in the palace."

Their way to the palace gates needed to be cleared first. Vanya wasn't risking Raiah's life in a fight to leave the palace. If that meant Soren had to corral and trap whatever revenants remained in the palace, then so be it.

The dead were his duty, after all.

In the end, Vanya was grateful for whatever sedative Alida or Artyom had given Raiah, for she slept in his arms through the nightmare retreat back to that room where Taisiya was hidden, through the hours of waiting as a way out was cleared for them and everyone else who had sought safety in a palace that had become a grave and managed to survive.

Raiah slept and never knew just how tightly Vanya held her, dry-eyed in his anger and second-guessing all the moments in the past where he'd handed her over to Soren for safekeeping. She slept through every fraught step Vanya took on his way out of the palace when Soren finally came for them hours later with the Legion at his back.

When they reached the palace gates, their group surrounded on all sides by *praetoria* legionnaires, general-ranked legionnaires, and automatons, Vanya handed Raiah to Taisiya, studiously not looking at where Soren stood. His *valide*'s eyes flicked from him to the warden and back again, something curious in her gaze. But she asked no questions, only cradled Raiah close, and let the *praetoria* legionnaires sweep them to safety.

"Your Imperial Majesty, we have a motor carriage waiting," an officer said, practically vibrating with the need to get Vanya past the gates.

"In a moment." Vanya turned to face where Imperial General Chu Hua stood on the street, looking at him with such relief in her face. "Is everyone out?"

Chu Hua nodded grimly. "The survivors are clear."

"Did any revenants get past the palace gate and walls?"

"We're not sure, but right now, no one has sounded any alarms. We'll be initiating a search shortly."

Vanya turned away from her to face the forecourt and the wings of the Imperial palace. The stars above were fading, predawn light turning the world an eerie gray, all soft shadows as the sun waited to rise beyond the horizon. The Legion, with Soren's expert aid, had managed to seal many revenants inside the palace. The only warden left in Calhames couldn't help with their eradication without proving the wardens had broken the Poison Accords just as badly as Solaria had.

But Vanya could see to himself and his House.

He closed his eyes, thinking about the history that had lived and died in the walls of the Imperial palace. He thought about the dead that had been buried for so long, trapped in coffins the way they were trapped by the city walls in Rixham to the south.

Solaria had broken the Poison Accords in the Houses' need to please the Dawn Star. The hubris of ruling, of keeping to tradition, had ultimately become a debt every major House had carried in secret.

The dead were always supposed to be burned.

So Vanya burned them.

He cast starfire as wide as it would go, catching the palace up in flames, pushing it ever inward to eat through walls that had held up an empire for Ages. Vanya turned the palace into a pyre until not even the bones of its foundation remained.

All that was left as the sun rose was ash and memory dancing on the wind.

Revelations

936 A.O.P.

One

EIMARILLE

Two days after the attack on Foxborough found Eimarille taking a tour of the military production factories a two-hour steam train ride from New Haven. Located deep in the forest of Daijal, the military outpost housed numerous military personnel who oversaw hundreds of debt slaves who worked the production floors and the foundry.

It was where Terilyn found her, the Blade having redirected the airship she'd been traveling on. The outpost didn't have an airfield, but that didn't stop Terilyn from rappelling over the side and being lowered to the wall below. Eimarille met her on the ramparts, raking her gaze up and down her lover's body, searching for any hint of wounds Terilyn might have taken while away from her side.

Terilyn swiftly undid the harness and let the gear be hauled back up to the airship. The loud thrum of the airship's engine changed pitch as it ascended again. Eimarille didn't watch it leave, all her attention taken up by her Blade.

"Terilyn," she said, ignoring the military officers and her protective detail arrayed behind her who had escorted her to the outer wall.

Terilyn smiled tightly in the face of Eimarille's worry, the only hint of her exhaustion being a faint narrowing of her eyes. "I'm all right."

"I'll be the judge of that." Eimarille closed the distance between them, settling her hands on her lover's shoulders to study her. Then she leaned in and kissed her softly, sweetly. "I've read the reports of what transpired in Foxborough. I've been worried."

"I made it out of the city. Unfortunately, I could not bring the witness with me. The wardens and the Ashion army made everything difficult."

"Is the witness dead?" Terilyn shook her head, gaze flickering over Eimarille's shoulder. Eimarille hummed before half turning to address the officers. "We will meet you on the ground shortly."

The military officers saluted before leaving. Her personal guard were more hesitant to leave, but eventually, they followed her order. Less than a minute later found Eimarille and Terilyn standing alone on top of the wall.

Terilyn reached up and pulled Eimarille's hands off her shoulders, tangling their fingers together. "I couldn't get the witness out of Foxborough. We were ambushed by wardens in the city. I meant to bring him with me, but it proved impossible."

"Perhaps it would have been best if you had killed him."

Terilyn's gaze was steady when she looked at Eimarille, all grim determination that made Eimarille want to soothe away the furrow of her brow. "His true name is Blaine, and he is of the Westergard bloodline. You should know he was the one who brought Caris out of Amari during the Inferno. She *is* your sister. What's more, the prince might still be alive."

It was everything Eimarille didn't want, like a spanner thrown into gears to disrupt it all. "The Westergards were eradicated."

"Apparently, one was missed."

"And the prince?"

Terilyn grimaced. "Favored by the star gods as well. It's how he survived."

"If that is the case, did Blaine know where they took him?"

Terilyn shook her head. "I believe there is a strong possibility he might be a warden. No Ashion family has come forth with a man who can cast starfire, and there was the issue with the quarry."

"The wardens do not take any tithes who can cast starfire."

"True, but what if they didn't know?"

"Then we can only hope he died on the Warden's Island." Eimarille tugged her hands and turned to head for the stairs that led off the wall. Terilyn settled in beside her, keeping pace. "Kote informed me the Ashion army holds Foxborough for now. My spies tell me they've removed the mayor whose loyalty was to Daijal and appointed their own from the populace."

"There are plenty of people in Foxborough who are loyal to you."

"Yes, and I'm certain they'd be incredibly grateful to be liberated from a false government. Let me show you how we'll do it."

They returned to the knot of military officers and royal guards waiting on the ground near several motor carriages. Eimarille and Terilyn were then whisked away to the main production factory, the building towering over the others. They were given protective gear before allowed entry and guided up to the viewing catwalks. It was hot inside the factory, the noise almost deafening as debt slaves worked the production line of war machines.

These particular automatons were based off stolen Solarian designs for their sentinel class, standing three stories tall, the center mass filled in with gears rather than being empty for a driver to sit. Daijalan engineers had reworked everything from the framework out while magicians and alchemists following the *Klovod*'s teachings had created a clockwork metal heart that powered the automatons, giving life and otherworldly sentience to the creations.

Unlike other designs, no driver was needed to steer them; no orders would ever be disobeyed. These new infernal automatons were capable of reacting to problems and threats in the field without needing to be guided. Equipped with a range of weaponry, they would hold the front line of a war that would reach every border.

"We'll send them east and to the south to bolster our forces there," Eimarille said, pitching her voice loud enough to be heard over the noise of the factory.

The officer to her left nodded agreement. "We'll aim to retake Foxborough from the Clockwork Brigade. Of the options we have discussed with you, how do you wish to handle E'ridia?"

"I've expelled their ambassador after the attack they perpetuated on Foxborough and made it clear that any future aid given to the rebellion in Ashion will be seen as an act of war. For now, we can hold off on any outreach, good or bad. The Eastern Spine is a border that will need a particular plan to overcome, and the climbers aren't scheduled for production until later this year."

They needed to get Ashion under control first before she could focus on E'ridia, and that country was secondary to dealing with Solaria. The Legion was heading to their northern border, and Joelle had requested Daijalan support in defense of her *vasilyet,* support which Eimarille was more than happy to provide as a first test of her country's new war machines. The death-defying machine was still churning out the dead by the hundreds, and Kote knew best where the revenants would do the most damage.

Eimarille had a plan for Maricol's future, and she would be damned if some purported long-lost siblings ruined it for her.

Two

CARIS

Caris smoothed down the front of her lilac day jacket, the soft material and delicate embroidery catching on her roughened hands. She licked her lips, trying to ignore the uncomfortable twist in her stomach. Nerves, she knew, though she was doing her best to overcome them.

Pretend it's like a classroom presentation or a patent argument.

The mental cajoling did little to dampen the fast beating of her heart. It wasn't every day the national press descended on a small town, ready to report on the declaration of an Ashion queen. For so long, only Eimarille had ever claimed that mantle. Yet here Caris was, seeking to grasp headlines of her own, for a truth that still felt too much like a lie.

Staring at herself in the floor-length mirror in her borrowed bedroom in the Auclair bloodline's ancestral estate, she didn't *feel* like a Rourke. Caris couldn't say she looked like a Rourke despite the historical portraits Meleri had unearthed from somewhere that depicted the Rourke bloodlines through the years. Where she had kept them hidden was a secret not even Dureau knew, and Meleri had declined to share.

The portraits were being displayed at Veran's city hall, where Caris was expected in less than an hour's time, according to her pocket watch. Dureau had already rang the estate with the news the entire civic plaza was filled to bursting with reporters and spectators.

All that was missing was Caris.

She flattened her hand over her stomach and turned away from the mirror. No sense in trying to find the face of a dead woman in her reflection. Queen Ophelia might have been her birth mother, but everything that made Caris who she was today came from Portia and Emmitt. The thought of giving up the Dhemlan bloodline and name when her parents were essentially prisoners of war left her feeling ill. But being a Dhemlan wouldn't save them.

Being a Rourke might.

Someone knocked on her door, drawing Caris out of her swirling thoughts. She cleared her throat before answering. "Come in."

The door was pushed open, and Nathaniel stepped inside, dressed in a dark blue day jacket and trousers, a white button-down shirt, and a lilac waistcoat that matched the shade of her own clothes. His collar was done up to his throat, cravat neatly tied, no hint of skin or the vivisection scars he carried visible. His hair was tied back in a queue, boots polished to a shine. He looked every inch a respectable member of society and not a cog.

"The motor carriages are out front. Are you ready?" Nathaniel asked.

Caris nervously tugged on a curl, her own hair loose and nearly brushing her shoulders. She'd not bothered with any adornments, refusing the tiara Meleri had offered to let her borrow. "I suppose so."

Nathaniel let the door close gently behind him. It was terrible manners to be alone with him, out of sight of any chaperones, but propriety wasn't anyone's concern these days. The Daijal army was moving east with a relentlessness the broadsheets reported on with screaming headlines every morning.

It had been five days since the Ashion army had overtaken Foxborough with the help of E'ridia's air force and wardens. While casualties were low, people had still died from the bombs and bullets, and the Clockwork Brigade and wardens had carried much of that blame in the Daijalan press. Those broadsheets also refused to report on the attack which devastated the Warden's Island, but they *did* report on how the wardens had unilaterally pulled their support from Daijal.

Eimarille and her press had deftly spun a tale of wardens unable to do their duty, so was it any wonder their island had been attacked out of retribution for lost Daijalan lives?

E'ridia had fared no better in that regard, with the Daijalan press labeling their collaboration with the Clockwork Brigade as clear evidence of sovereign interference. E'ridia had yet to respond to the accusations, safe behind the Eastern Spine for now. Their reason for dropping bombs on Foxborough's outer-city wall was still in the hospital, from what Honovi had told Caris on a private call last night.

Blaine was alive. That had to count for something, despite everything that had happened. Meleri believed so, if only because Blaine was the only person who could stand as witness to Caris' claim to the Rourke bloodline. But he wasn't here, and she'd have to pretend she was queen on her own.

Fingers stroked down her cheek, startling her. Caris jerked her head back, blinking up at Nathaniel. He smiled at her, eyes a little sad. "What are you worrying about?"

"If I said everything, would you think less of me?"

"Never." Nathaniel reached for her hand and brought it to his lips to brush a kiss over her knuckles. The touch sent a shiver down her spine, and Caris tightened her fingers around his own. "That's a trait which will make you a good queen. It shows you care."

Caris smiled wanly at him, a twist to her lips he gently kissed away. She let him, parting her lips to accept the taste of him in her mouth. She knew those that were aware of Nathaniel's plight didn't view him as *alive* anymore, not with a clockwork metal heart beating in his chest. She'd seen the way Meleri had looked at him, all reserved politeness. She knew, too, how Meleri had excised him from the chains he'd held to save the Clockwork Brigade from further damage. Nathaniel walked beside Caris by the grace of magic and alchemy, a ticking time bomb no one could trust with sensitive information anymore.

Nathaniel was no longer a cog, and Caris was to be queen, and neither of them was what they'd meant to be in the end. But he cared for her, and she for him, and Caris wasn't walking this road without him.

He broke the kiss, and Caris licked her lips, opening her eyes. Nathaniel let go of her hand so he could offer her his elbow. "You'll do brilliantly. The duchess says you were born for this."

That's what frightened her—to become some ideal that everyone rested their hopes and dreams on and ruining them by not living up to the impossible. But if she didn't try, she'd leave the whole of Ashion to Daijal subjugation and the rest of the continent to invasion. She'd had a taste of such rulership growing up beneath a parliament beholden to the Daijal court and didn't much care for it.

Nathaniel escorted her out of the bedroom and to the first floor of the estate. Meleri waited for them in the foyer, her summer gown worthy of being seen for a promenade along the Serpentine River in Amari. She smiled at their arrival, gesturing at the front door a servant opened. "Shall we?"

Caris nodded, and they left the estate for a black motor carriage that carried two tiny flags over the front headlamps. The colors weren't the shades of the Auclair bloodline but of the Rourke bloodline, and Caris swallowed tightly. The trappings of royalty were slowly but subtly beginning to wrap themselves around her.

Nathaniel offered his hand to Meleri and helped her into the motor carriage, then did the same for Caris. Once they were in, he closed the door and went around the vehicle to take the front passenger seat. The motor carriages before and after theirs carried soldiers who wore a particular cut of uniform that Caris didn't recognize.

"Are they with the army?" she asked as their driver started the engine.

"Their regiment is the Royal Guard of the Ashion army. They haven't been active for twenty years. Eimarille has never had any need for them when she visited Amari. She tended to bring Daijalan soldiers for security and her own royal guards," Meleri replied.

Caris clasped her hands together over her lap and stared out the window, watching the buildings glide by as they drove toward city hall. Far more people were out on the street than she anticipated, and the knot in her stomach got worse. Eventually, the crowd of spectators grew thicker, and their motorcade became the center of attention. People waved and pointed at them, delighted smiles on many of the faces they passed.

Meleri leaned across the seat, catching Caris' attention. "Wave to them. Let them know you're receptive to their well-wishes. They've been waiting for you for a long time."

"They don't even know me."

"But they will. You'll show them who you are."

So Caris waved, and she smiled, trying to feel like less of a puppet. The motorcade wound its way through the city streets until it finally entered the plaza in front of Veran's city hall. The hands on the clock tower above the government building ticked their way to the top of the hour, the time when Caris was scheduled to give her speech.

A spectator stand had been erected in the plaza in front of a wooden stage. Five days was more than enough time for Meleri to find bunting in Rourke colors and have that bloodline's heraldic flag hung between the pillars of the city hall's entrance behind the stage. When she stood up there, Caris knew what she'd look like against that backdrop. Meleri was leaving nothing to chance. Cameras would capture Caris as she was meant to be seen.

A queen.

A pity she felt like a fraud.

The motorcade pulled up behind the stage, in a cordoned-off area guarded by soldiers and quite a few wardens, one of whom Caris recognized and was pleased to see.

"You made it back," Caris said as her motor carriage door was opened and a soldier offered her his hand to help her out.

Ksenia smiled crookedly, feet planted wide and arms crossed over her chest. "I wasn't ever going to stay in Foxborough. All our recalled wardens have been told to meet in Veran. It's my responsibility to get them sorted, and besides, the governor wants us to study the death-defying machine you were recreating."

"We're happy to have you," Meleri said as she came around the vehicle to stand by Caris' side.

"You'd be one of the few. We're not the most popular in Foxborough at the moment."

"That city will come around."

Ksenia grunted, offering no response to that statement. Nathaniel came to stand on Caris' other side, a familiar presence she wished she could lean on. Instead, she looked to Meleri, who took charge in the way of one used to issuing commands and expecting to be obeyed. It was a trait Caris could only hope to emulate.

"We have magicians and marksmen set up around the plaza. Every reporter and spectator went through security and was checked for weapons and vivisection scars," one of the Royal Guards said when Meleri turned toward him.

"Good. When the clock tower rings on the hour, I'll introduce Caris," Meleri said.

Until then, Caris and Nathaniel stayed behind the stage, out of sight of the cameras, and surrounded by soldiers and wardens. Caris made small talk with Ksenia, catching up with the master alchemist on what had transpired in Foxborough, getting a firsthand account of Blaine's rescue.

"Honovi said the doctors and healers in Glencoe are doing everything they can to heal him," Caris said in a low voice.

"I'm glad to hear that. His wound was severe but survivable," Ksenia said.

"He lost part of his arm."

"He's alive. Loss of a limb isn't a death sentence." Ksenia tilted her head in Caris' direction. "Perhaps you can help build him a new one."

"Perhaps."

Her dour thoughts were thrust aside as the clock tower chimed the hour. When the last note died away, Meleri's voice came through a voice amplifier, ringing through the air as she greeted the crowd. Caris only half listened to the introduction, fighting a losing battle with her nerves until Nathaniel caught her hand in his, giving it a gentle squeeze.

"Be yourself up there," he urged.

The only problem with that was Caris wasn't so sure she knew who she was anymore. But she'd run out of time to find out when one of the mayor's aides waved at her to head for the stage stairs. Caris uncurled her fingers from Nathaniel's and left to do a duty she still wasn't sure she had the right to carry.

But her feet took her up to the stage anyway, and Caris smiled the way Meleri had taught her, but her determination to do what was right? That came from Portia. From Emmitt. From those who had raised her to build things for others because Maricol wasn't often kind to her children, but Caris had learned to be kind anyway.

The popping sounds coming from a multitude of cameras as they took her picture were like fireworks in her ears. Caris smiled through the noise, through Meleri's words of encouragement, and found herself standing before a podium with a riser. The speech she had worked on for the past few days was all in her head, but as she looked out at the reporters and people seated in the spectator stand and filling in the rest of the plaza, the words momentarily left her.

She looked back the way she'd come, finding Nathaniel standing at the edge of the stage amidst a small group of politicians and wardens, his eyes on her. His lips shaped words she couldn't hear, but the fierce, prideful expression on his face was encouragement enough.

Caris turned to face the judgment of the crowd and the country they'd report back to. She took a deep breath and settled her hands on the riser, looking out across the sea of people, and found her voice.

"I want to thank the illustrious Duchess Meleri Auclair, both for her kind words and generosity but also for the support she has given me over the past few years," Caris said. She dug her fingers against the wood as the crowd quieted and tried not to squint beneath the sunlight. "I was in Amari during the riot where peacekeepers sent revenants against protestors exercising their right to be heard. I and my compatriots were some of the lucky ones during that horror. We escaped. Too many didn't."

She drew in a soft breath, the rapidness of her heartbeat evening out. "Too many of us are trapped beneath the rule of Daijal, coerced into offering up our lives as collateral to banks and losing them to debt bondage. Many of you remember what it was like before the Inferno, when the monarchy was held by the Rourke bloodline and not the Iverson one. When Ashion was a country to be proud of.

"I'm not proud of the road Queen Eimarille has set our country on. She calls herself Rourke, and perhaps that is true. Her name is still found in the royal genealogies. Mine isn't, and she'll say that gives me no right to the Rourke bloodline." Caris swallowed, the sharp click of her throat echoing through the voice amplifier. "But I was born during the Inferno. The Westergard bloodline kept their duty and smuggled me out of our burning capital to Cosian. I was given to the Dhemlan bloodline, and that name is all I knew until recently."

She dragged her nails over the riser before pulling her hands away, reaching deep to call forth starfire from the aether. It burst into existence against her palms like two miniature suns crackling there on earth. It dripped from her fingers like fiery rain, disappearing before it could hit the wooden stage. The crowd let out a collective gasp that broke into a flurry of voices as the cameras went off with countless flashes of lights that nearly blinded her.

Caris blinked spots out of her eyes, starfire cradled in both hands, facing a road she could not escape. "My name is Caris Rourke, and I say, Ashion is not for my sister to take."

SOREN

The House of Sa'Liandel's ancestral estate in Calhames wasn't anything like the Imperial palace, but it was home now for Vanya and Raiah. Soren hadn't set foot in it and wasn't sure he ever would after everything that had happened. The street leading to the estate was closed off to through traffic with a sentinel-class automaton standing guard at either end. He hadn't tried his luck to get past the *praetoria* legionnaires, uncertain of his welcome.

Solaria's government was reeling in the wake of what had occurred, but at least the ruling House had survived. He couldn't regret that, though the silence from Vanya was as devastating to Soren as he assumed the destruction of the Imperial palace and loss of House members was to the people of Solaria.

Soren licked his lips as he carefully made his way through the ashes of the palace. Of everything that had burned, some items of importance had survived by being located elsewhere. The throne room was gone, but there was still a throne in the Senate building for the emperor's use. A crown had been lost, but the Imperial jewelers had others on hand, kept secured in a building located off the palace grounds.

Some *vezirs* of Houses had survived while others had been reduced to ownership claimed by outlier families within the bloodlines to take up core responsibilities. Soren read the broadsheet every morning, heard the gossip on the streets as he drove between the unmanned resupply station he was staying at and the remnants of the palace. The Houses were going through an internal restructure, and he wondered about what that meant for Solaria.

No other wardens had answered the request for aid that night, recalled by the governor in the wake of what had transpired on the Warden's Island. Soren should, by all rights, be heading to Glencoe, but he remained in Calhames, tending to a broken border and his own broken heart.

The sun beat down on the ravaged remains of the palace, ash being displaced with almost every step he took. His brass goggles kept it from his eyes, the press of them warm against his skin in the sunlight. The headache from his concussion no longer lingered, dealt with by a magician skilled in healing the morning after the palace burned. They'd tended to his wounds, but he hadn't been around for follow-up care.

Some places the starfire had burned hot enough to slag the dirt and stone, turning sections into dark glass. The flagstones of the forecourt were streaked with such interruptions. The foundations of where the palace had once stood were outlined in scorch marks.

Some of the detached buildings still stood: the garage, the greenhouses, the bathhouse, and the star temple. The garden areas closest to the palace had burned to nothing, creating a demarcation between blooming desert bushes and ash. As Soren crossed that line on his way to the star temple, his steps kicked up a few rose petals that had drifted into the ash.

Praetoria legionnaires, peacekeepers, government inspectors, and engineers were scattered over the property as they all sought to secure the Imperial grounds. Soren had cleared the area days ago for safety purposes, finding no traces of spores in what was left behind. Not that he thought he would. Fire was cleansing, and starfire burned the hottest.

While engineers and others began the long but critical process of rebuilding, Soren's duty was to tend to the border he'd failed at securing. The high priestess of the Star Order in Calhames hadn't been present when Alida betrayed her country and the House she'd sworn to serve. The Blades and House of Kimathi supporters had murdered everyone within the star temple. Those bodies had long since been sent to a crematorium. Their names would be etched into the memory walls, as was tradition.

Soren wondered if all the names found below in the crypt would be transferred to marble on a memory wall somewhere else. The remaining bodies in the crypt would have to be excavated and cremated. Soren could not leave Calhames until he'd seen to that duty—a duty he should have handled months ago, years ago, when he'd first learned of the crypt. What had happened was as much his failure as it was Joelle's machinations. If he hadn't asked the governor to stay the sanctions, if he hadn't held off on confronting the Houses about the breaking of the Poison Accords, if he hadn't succumbed to Vanya's desires—if, if, *if*.

What was burned was ash, and he could not change that.

The *praetoria* legionnaires guarding the entrance to the star temple nodded gravely at him, allowing him to pass without a word. Once inside, Soren removed his goggles, the stinging ash not present in that sacred space.

He was surprised to see Taisiya was.

"*Valide*," Soren said, feet rooted to the floor as he stared at where she sat in one of the pews mere feet from the winched open entrance to the crypt. "What are you doing here?"

Taisiya didn't turn away from her perusal of the Dawn Star's statue with its eternal flame, but she did lift a hand to wave him forward. "Come sit with me. I was told I could find you here on the palace grounds."

Soren got himself moving, walking down the aisle to her. Star priests worked on record books at the altar while *praetoria* legionnaires kept their attention on Taisiya, pistols and wands close at hand. Soren took a seat in the pew ahead of hers, bending a knee and twisting his torso so he could look over the back of it at her.

Taisiya appeared tired, the droop of her mouth more pronounced. But her words were precise when she spoke, voice as ruined as ever. "You haven't been to the estate."

"I've been busy," Soren said.

"Raiah has asked for you."

He swallowed, thinking of the Imperial princess and missing her in a way he didn't have the right to. "She knows I come and go."

Taisiya's gaze was shrewd. "And are you leaving this time for good?"

"I'm a warden."

"That isn't an answer."

"Isn't it?" he asked sharply. "This whole mess lies at my feet. If I hadn't pushed for a stay of the sanctions, Joelle wouldn't have been able to use the revenants against the rest of the Houses."

To say nothing of the way Vanya had looked at him when he'd cast starfire in defense of the emperor and Raiah—as if Soren had turned out to be a worse enemy than Joelle with such betrayal.

"You were not the one who freed the dead and let them walk."

"My choices enabled hers."

"Perhaps, but you did so to protect my House. I cannot fault you for that."

His lips twisted bitterly. "Everyone else does."

Taisiya waved aside his words. "The major Houses obeyed the decree set by the Dawn Star Ages ago. The minor Houses will not argue that, no matter their losses."

"And the public?"

"Vanya ensured no revenants made it beyond the palace gates. He burned down his home rather than risk the lives of his citizens."

"Is that the story you're feeding the broadsheets?"

"It's the truth."

Soren snorted. "It's barely that."

"Truth is what you make of it, and right now, the truth keeps my House in power. The Conclave is set to gather in the Senate tomorrow to discuss Joelle's transgressions."

"I know."

"You will join me."

Soren reeled back, nearly falling off the pew. "I can't."

Taisiya arched an eyebrow. "Can't or won't?"

"It's not my place."

"My dear warden, it's too late to pretend otherwise. You are of the emperor's household. He beds no one else. This"—she leaned forward, sliding her fingers beneath the collar of his shirt to hook around the chain of the vow, pulling the medallion free—"is not given lightly."

Soren grasped the chain and gently tugged it out of her grasp. "I will not ask for payment."

"You will," Taisiya corrected with a knowing glint in her eyes. "Everyone always does."

He wished badly she wasn't right, but wishes were like prayers in his experience—useless and meaningless.

Taisiya pushed herself to her feet, smoothing down the line of her black robes. Calhames was in mourning, the House banners with the names of the deceased hanging from the walls of every estate who lost someone. It wasn't quite reminiscent of the pageantry that had accompanied Vanya's false death some years back, but the grief within the Houses was impossible to miss when he rode down streets for the palace grounds.

"The wardens will have a voice during the Conclave tomorrow. You will speak for them," Taisiya said.

Soren could do nothing but nod in the face of that order. He'd been the one to uncover Alida's treachery, after all, been the one to pull proof of Daijal interference from the throat of a Blade. "I'll meet you at the Senate tomorrow morning."

Taisiya patted him on the shoulder before leaving the pew, a squad of *praetoria* legionnaires swooping in to escort her out of the sanctuary. Soren got to his feet with a sigh, then approached the entrance to the crypt.

It was high time the dead were burned.

Four

VANYA

When Vanya alighted from the motor carriage, his attention was unerringly drawn to the figure waiting for them by the entrance to the Senate building. He tugged at the cuffs of his black robes, fingers catching on the delicate gold embroidery there.

"What is he doing here?" Vanya asked Taisiya in a low voice.

"You cannot hope to give your side of the events without the warden who uncovered your majordomo's betrayal and Joelle's treachery," came Taisiya's light and unaffected answer. "Come now, child. You've had your sulk. Rule as you should and do not linger."

His *valide* let the *praetoria* legionnaires escort her up the stairs to where Soren waited in front of the Senate entrance. Even from the distance that separated them, Vanya could feel Soren's gaze on him like a heavy weight. He had not seen Soren since he'd walked away from the warden with Raiah in his arms, passing through the ashes of a home he'd destroyed. He knew Soren had returned to the palace grounds every day since, working to handle the dead left behind in the crypt and coordinate the clean-up.

Soren had not come to the House of Sa'Liandel's estate, and Vanya hadn't asked him to.

Alida's betrayal was one thing, Soren's quite another. To know the warden who he cared for—who he wanted above all others—could cast starfire to a degree only found in royalty had Vanya rethinking everything he thought he knew of the warden. Everything he wanted to say was knotted up in his chest, a ball of iron where his heart beat, choking him with bitterness.

Vanya set aside the anger, swallowed the taste of fury on his tongue, and drew in a breath that smelled of summer and the incense used to mourn. Black banners hung from the Senate building's roof, prayers painted in gold over the fabric. Names, he knew, of those who'd been lost—either to revenants or starfire—were written out like prayers.

Squaring his shoulders, new crown heavy on his brow, Vanya climbed the steps to the Senate building, finding Taisiya and Soren waiting for him in the marble hallway inside. Soren wore his field uniform, the leathers clean, looking every inch a warden when he shouldn't be. He'd found a new gun belt and pistols, the hilt of his poison short sword protruding over one shoulder.

Vanya searched Soren's face, looking into gray eyes that had been so familiar once, and all he could think, in the quiet of his mind, was *who are you?*

But he kept his mouth closed, sweeping past the pair to lead the way to the Senate chambers. Taisiya left them at the stairs which led to the mezzanine, taking Soren's elbow to traverse the stairs. Vanya let them go and allowed the Senate chamberlain to announce him.

"His Imperial Majesty Vanya Sa'Liandel, of the House of Sa'Liandel."

Vanya walked through the doors amidst a burst of noise. The desks were full when they arrived, while the mezzanine above where the Houses sat was not. Seats were empty up there, bodies missing, and every last person wore black robes in mourning.

Of the Houses present, only the House of Kimathi had sent no one to bear witness to the end of the Conclave. Vanya rather thought Joelle had hoped he would die at the last gathering, but he hadn't. He was here, and she was not, and he would see her pay for all of their losses.

Vanya swept toward the only Imperial throne left in Calhames, taking his place on the grand, golden seat of power amidst the murmur of voices. He looked around the chambers, watching as senators took their seats and those in the mezzanine craned their heads to look at him. Quiet descended, a hush rarely heard in the walls that held the echoes of legislative arguments in every corner.

"We mourn the Houses," Vanya said into that quiet. "The ones who lost family through what transpired at the gathering and those through deceit from being turned into *rionetkas*. We mourn for the old ways we worshipped, as decreed by the Dawn Star, but that time has passed."

"The old ways put the capitol at risk," a senator cried out. "The Houses may play their games, but not at the risk of our city."

"I burned that risk to the ground. I burned our history to ash. But a palace is merely walls. They house us, keep us safe, like the city walls that encircle us. But when we outgrow them, when the city needs more room to grow, we build another wall. Make no mistake, we *will* rebuild the Imperial palace. While we can't replace the lives lost there, those responsible for the horror of that night shall not be left to their freedom."

A rustle of clothing had his gaze snapping to the mezzanine, where a woman stood, the crest before their area that of a minor House. "The dead were never meant to be buried. What say the wardens to that?"

Heads turned, everyone's attention directed to where Soren sat in the mezzanine behind the throne, out of sight, in the House of Sa'Liandel's seats. The rising murmur of the crowd abruptly cut off as Soren's voice rang through the air.

"The wardens' governor is aware of what the major Houses have done with their dead at the behest of a star god. The Poison Accords were broken. That is indisputable. There will be sanctions levied against Solaria because of it. Those sanctions were to be stayed, but I do not know how long that stay will last. The wardens are in need of tithes," Soren said in near-perfect Solarian.

Vanya could see the anger on people's faces, the furious desire for denial, and he cut the protests off before they could begin. "Solaria will pay with tithes as required."

"Pay from your Houses!" a senator shouted, causing a loud cry of agreement to rise up from the senators.

"I will ask the wardens' governor for mercy on behalf of the tithes owed. But our indiscretion is nothing to what Daijal will owe them," Vanya cut in. "Last week, Daijal attacked the Warden's Island on orders from their queen. Their actions destroyed the fort and murdered an untold number of tithes and wardens. Daijal would have you think they had nothing to do with it, but they did not kill everyone."

Senators stood in shock, many of the Houses leaning in to whisper furiously with each other as the news hit. The anger didn't leave anyone, but his words redirected to a different target.

"Good warden, is this true?" another senator asked.

"It's true," Soren said after a heavy pause. "I don't know how the Daijalan forces were pushed back, but I know E'ridia sent airships to give aid. The wounded were taken to Glencoe, and the wardens' governor went with them. She ordered all wardens to leave Daijal. We will not guard that country's borders. Your Houses' transgressions pale in what the Daijal queen has perpetuated. While that does not absolve you, wardens will still guard Solaria's borders."

The senator recoiled at his words, reaching back to grab hold of his chair for support. "What madness has possessed Queen Eimarille to order such an atrocity that risks her country's safety from the dead?"

"What madness indeed," Vanya drawled, his gaze sweeping the mezzanine until he found the House of Aetos, Vesper sitting straight-backed in her seat, their House whole. "Perhaps you would do well to enlighten us, Lady Vesper. You did make a show of leaving the Conclave early with the House of Kimathi heir before the attack, espousing your loyalty to them. Indeed, they are not here now."

"I do not speak for a House that is not mine," Vesper said, her voice ringing clearly through the chambers.

"Yet you and others threw support behind the House of Kimathi, a House who has turned their back on Solaria."

"A fine thing for you to say when they aren't here to defend themselves."

"Artyom never left the palace, did he?" Vesper's silence was as much an admission of truth as words would be. "He stayed and made his way to the family wing the night the crypt was opened."

"I know not what you speak of."

"Of course you don't. You weren't there when Artyom stood with Daijalan Blades and threatened the life of my daughter. You weren't there when I discovered the betrayal in my household. My majordomo stood with the House of Kimathi, the same House who sold our country out to Daijal."

The uproar was immediate, voices yelling over each other to be heard in the wake of Vanya's accusations. He kept his eyes on Vesper, watching as an older member of her House leaned in close to speak to her.

Vanya stood from the throne, drawing everyone's attention. The shouting eased as he stepped off the dais, standing in the space before the senators' desks. He pulled from his pocket the necklace Soren had ripped from someone's throat and set it on the desk belonging to the *magister* of the Senate, its most senior senator.

"The warden had his duty to guard the border that was the crypt. He discovered my majordomo colluding with Daijal Blades on orders from the House of Kimathi. Alida confessed as much to the warden and later to me when she stood with Artyom, threatening my daughter," Vanya said.

The *magister* picked up the necklace, studying the inlaid crest that had belonged to the House of Kimathi since its inception. She frowned, gaze flicking up to Vanya's face. "This belongs to the House of Kimathi."

"It was taken from a traitor's throat."

"There are Houses who will question this evidence."

Several of the surrounding senators murmured agreement with that observation. The senator for the House of Kimathi's *vasilyet* stood, gesturing furiously with one hand. "Such an accusation against the House of Kimathi is without merit. I will not stand here and listen as they are slandered."

"It's no slander if it's the truth," Cybele called out from the mezzanine. Vanya's attention snapped to the *vezir* of the House of Balaskas, watching as she stood, heads turning her way to see who had spoken. "I stayed with the emperor through our fight in the palace. His command of starfire ensured eradication of any revenants we came across. He ensured we survived while he searched for his daughter. I was there by his side when he confronted Artyom. I stand here as witness to the despicable actions of the House of Kimathi."

"Your House gave your loyalty to the House of Sa'Liandel. It is unsurprising you'd lie as such," Vesper shot back.

"As our emperor pointed out, you and your House left before the attack, along with others who gave allegiance to the House of Kimathi. You all would have gained much if our Houses were decimated worse than they were. One must wonder if your House had any dealings with Daijal. A forewarning at the very least, perhaps, to see you all safe beyond the palace gates when the revenants came."

Pointed looks and fierce mutterings grew in the wake of Cybele's sharp retort. Vesper didn't immediately reply, head bent toward her advisor. Vanya studied the expressions he could see, gauging the support the House of Kimathi might still have. The other Houses who had thrown their lot in with the House of Kimathi during the Conclave huddled together as well, cognizant of the growing displeasure from their peers.

Vanya stepped away from the *magister*'s desk and paced over to where the senator representing the House of Kimathi's *vasilyet* furiously argued with his neighbors. At his approach, the senator broke off midsentence to face him, mouth open to speak, but Vanya cut him off.

"*Vezir* Joelle is not fit for the title granted her, not fit to rule her *vasilyet*, and certainly not fit to claim a House when her loyalty stands with the queen of Daijal and not Solaria. *Rionetkas* attacked my daughter and I in Oeiras. They were sent after her and the warden I tasked with getting her to safety in Karnak. They've infiltrated our government and Houses, but none have ever been found in the House of Kimathi's *vasilyet*."

"We have suffered from more revenants than any other *vasilyet* in the last few years," the senator snapped.

"Because Joelle allowed Daijal to build a death-defying machine in her *vasilyet* and refused wardens access to her borders. The high count of revenants was perpetuated by her House. Joelle made agreements she and her House had no right to make. She does not sit on the Imperial throne. I do, and I say she is a traitor to Solaria, and traitors have no place in our country."

The senator reared back at his words, face going white, then red with anger. Before he could sputter out a protest, Vanya pitched his voice to carry through the chamber. "I call for a blood feud with the House of Kimathi on behalf of Solaria and the Houses she attempted to destroy. I call for retribution for a House that has allied itself with Daijal over their own people. The House of Kimathi has no right to be part of a government they've betrayed. What say the Conclave?"

Vanya had spent so long trying to keep Raiah safe. Joelle had not ever issued a blood feud in hopes she could gain the Imperial throne through his daughter. Despite all the deceit she'd cultivated since Nicca's death, he'd stayed his hand on issuing such a proclamation. But the Conclave had ended with his House holding the majority of support, and Joelle had reacted in a way that could not go unpunished.

His mother had eradicated a House once before and destroyed a city, breaking up a *vasilyet*. It seemed Vanya was set to do the same.

"The House of Balaskas stands with the House of Sa'Liandel," Cybele said before sitting down.

"The House of Vikandir stands with the House of Sa'Liandel," Malia called out, acting in the stead of her husband. The bite to her tone came from a banked fury and grief Vanya knew all too well.

What started as a trickle became a cascade of voices that threw their support behind Vanya's House that left no room for doubt as to Joelle's guilt. He'd been given Callisto's blessing, after all, and Joelle had committed the ultimate betrayal. It was one thing to scheme and murder to gain the Imperial throne; quite another to ally one's House with a foreign nation.

In the end, the Houses—passionately or reluctantly—gave their loyalty to the House of Sa'Liandel over the House of Kimathi. Even Vesper stood to bite out the thinnest of support, as did the other Houses that had sided with Joelle during the Conclave. Their vote for the blood feud on behalf of the nation was merely a way to save face and ensure their Houses continued to exist. Their agreement did not equate to support, and Vanya made note of the Houses he would need to keep an eye on.

When the last House finished voting to align themselves with his, Vanya focused his attention on the senator who represented the House of Kimathi's *vasilyet*. "Your services are no longer needed."

The man sputtered in outrage that turned to cries of protest as two *praetoria* legionnaires stepped forward to haul him away from the desk. "I have a right to represent our *vasilyet*'s people!"

"You have what rights I give you, which are none."

He watched as the former senator was hauled out of the chambers, decrying the manhandling and shouting for support that never came. The doors closed behind them with a heavy thud.

"All hail the Imperial emperor," Taisiya said from behind him in their House's section, her damaged voice easy enough to hear in the tense quiet.

Houses and senators alike echoed her words. Vanya raised his chin, gaze sweeping over those gathered as he addressed them once more. "I am formally closing the northern border and calling up the Legion to guard it. We'll take back the House of Kimathi's *vasilyet* to ensure our nation's security. Daijal is at war with Ashion and the wardens. If it's a war they want with Solaria, then it is a war their queen shall have."

Senators pounded their fists on their desks, a steady beat beneath the roar of approval that came from the Senate and most of the Houses. Vanya let the noise of it all wash over him as he turned to look up at where his *valide* sat alone in the mezzanine.

Soren was gone.

Five

BLAINE

He came to slowly, the world indistinct sound in his ears, as if he were hearing underwater. His body felt weighted down, a muffled sense of ownership making it difficult for Blaine to process anything. He let out a wordless sound, the vibrations shredding his dry throat.

"Blaine."

His name came from far away, pushing through the cottony feeling in his head that threatened to pull him back under. The haziness in his thoughts didn't make sense, but Blaine knew that voice. He'd dreamed of it through the feverish time spent as a prisoner of the Daijalans, wishing it were real. He flexed his toes, felt something warm slide over the fingers of his right hand. A gentle touch trailed down his cheek, resting against his jaw.

"Blaine, can you hear me?"

He wanted to fall back into that liquid sleep flowing through his veins, but that voice called to him in a way he didn't—couldn't—ignore. It took a great effort to remember he had eyes, that the Daijalans hadn't taken that, even if the magician and Blade had forcibly taken his memories. Blaine flinched against the hand resting against his skin, thoughts skittering away from his time in that dark, cold room, so far from the vastness of the sky.

It took a monumental effort to crack open his eyes, the world a blurry mess of shapes in dim lighting. He blinked slowly—once, twice—trying to resolve the shadows into something familiar.

"'Novi?" Blaine croaked out.

His husband didn't seem real, not even when Honovi bent over him and pressed their foreheads together, something warm dripping onto his cheeks. "You're awake."

Blaine closed his eyes, breathing slowly, trying to push through the fog of his mind. He could barely feel Honovi's fingers curled around his right hand and nothing at all of his left. He tried to lift his left hand to grab at Honovi's braid, but his arm didn't obey him. His shoulder moved, and a distant sort of pain snapped into his ribs, his spine, making him choke on a whimper, but he couldn't feel it in his fingertips.

Because he didn't have any.

The thought pierced through everything like a bullet. Blaine pressed the stump of his left arm against the bed and choked on the dull throbbing agony that he couldn't feel in the space where his arm used to be.

Honovi's hands framed his face, turning his head to the side so he couldn't look at what he'd lost. "Shh, it's all right. You're safe now. You're home."

Blaine forced his eyes open, staring up at Honovi's face, still blurry, but this time because of the tears he couldn't stop. They slid down his cheeks, and Honovi gently brushed them away. "My arm?"

It seemed like a dream, but Honovi nodded, lifting a hand to smooth Blaine's hair off his forehead. "We tracked you to Foxborough and fought to get you back. You'd...they'd already cut off your arm halfway up your forearm, but it became infected. The doctors here had to amputate more to stave off gangrene. But you're awake now, and that's good."

"What happened?" Because he had no memory after the magician had peeled open his mind like a tin of food, digging about in ways that made Blaine want to hyperventilate, but he couldn't find the wherewithal to do so.

"Later. I'll tell you later, when you're better."

"Can't be better with only one arm. Can't *fly*."

Honovi's smile became watery, but he didn't pull away. "You'll fly again, with one arm or two. How you are now doesn't make you any less of a person. Just because you lost part of your arm doesn't mean you lost who you are. You're still the man I love, with or without a mechanical prosthetic. You're clan and you're crew and you're *mine*."

Blaine closed his eyes, tears burning against his lashes, and tightened his hold on Honovi's hand, the only anchor he had in the drift of his damaged body and mind.

Six

HONOVI

Alrickson picked up Honovi's empty whiskey glass and set it out of reach. "This won't help you sleep."

Honovi looked up from the folios scattered across his desk in their clan home, blinking gritty eyes at his father. The hour was late, the clock hands pointing well after midnight. "I don't drink it to sleep."

"It won't help you forget either."

Honovi grimaced and leaned back in his chair, dragging a hand over his face. "I know."

"Don't fall into a habit of finding false comfort in the bottom of a glass. It's not worth it."

He knew it wasn't, but at a trying time like this, it was tempting. Honovi sighed, watching as his father deftly sorted out the folios into stacks for tomorrow—technically today—to deal with.

The *Comhairle nan Cinnidhean* had eventually issued an embargo for the whole of Daijal. The ripple effects were hitting their own company, and someone had to deal with the logistics of getting the Eastern Winds Trading Company back on track. That task fell to him, while the task of shielding Honovi from political fallout fell to his father.

The *Comhairle nan Cinnidhean* was going through a change of *cinn-chinnidh,* with some *jarls* taking over for their elders. The attack by Gregor, as a *rionetka,* had nearly shattered the peak of their country's government, and the new governing body was still finding their wings, so to speak, and learning to work together. What they all agreed on, however, was the threat Daijal and Queen Eimarille represented.

The threat wasn't enough to get the country to go to war. Honovi's actions in Foxborough aside, E'ridia was reluctant to commit any support to Ashion against Daijal at this time. Caris' claim of the Rourke bloodline couldn't be officially recorded, not until Blaine was there to stand witness for her, and right now, Blaine was not fit for travel.

It was his husband and the guilt he felt that drove Honovi to deplete his personal whiskey stores, but that sort of liquid bandage wasn't sustainable. Some part of him wished it was. "They took his arm."

Alrickson managed a wan smile. "They didn't take his life."

But his husband's livelihood was out of reach right now as the stump of Blaine's arm healed. He was *healing,* though, and Honovi kept that thought in the forefront of his mind. It'd been a week since Blaine had finally woken up, fever breaking, Banshari's intervention meaning he'd suffered no permanent damage from the poison administered to him. That didn't mean Blaine was healed. Far from it.

Honovi had brought Blaine to their clan home two days ago, his husband unable to stand being in the hospital any longer. Blaine was still recovering—would continue to recover for a long while—but he'd feel better at home. A nurse had been assigned to his care at home, and a doctor stopped by once a day to assess his body's recovery. Blaine's mental and emotional state was something else entirely.

"I don't know how to help him," Honovi confessed.

Alrickson stepped around the desk and rested his hand on Honovi's shoulder. "Adjustment takes time. Just be there for him."

Easier said than done at the moment. Glencoe's hospitals were overflowing with wounded wardens. Clans had opened their homes to take in those not critically wounded but still in need of care. Delani was governing out of one of his clan's homes, just down the street, the warden looking like she never slept every time he saw her.

Honovi knew the feeling.

A board creaked in the hallway, and Honovi's gaze cut to the doorway. Seconds later, a familiar figure stepped into view, making him tense with worry, half-rising out of his seat. "Should you be up?"

"Shouldn't you be in bed?" Blaine rasped, knuckling one eye. He was pale, the dark circles under his eyes prominent bruises, and he'd lost weight from his ordeal. He looked fragile in a way he never had, not even when he'd stepped off that airship as a child so long ago.

Alrickson gave Honovi a gentle shake. "Your husband has a point. It's late. All this will keep."

Honovi nodded and straightened up, leaving everything where it lay in favor of his husband. He couldn't stop himself from staring at how the sleeve of Blaine's nightshirt was tied up, showing off the empty space where his lower arm used to be. The sight of the missing limb was still jarring but becoming less so.

He still felt a deep, abiding sense of guilt for having not been able to rescue Blaine from the Warden's Island before the soldiers captured him. Honovi knew it was irrational, that if he hadn't been on the airship the battle might have gone differently, but he couldn't quite shake the feeling that his actions had caused Blaine such grievous harm.

He settled a hand on Blaine's hip, leaning in to press a soft kiss to his husband's mouth. "Did the pain wake you? Do you need more medicine?"

Fingers curled around the edge of the plaid he wore, worrying at the fabric. "No."

Honovi bit back a sigh. Blaine didn't like how the pain medicine made him lose time and feel confused. The doctors said it would help with his healing, but Blaine kept refusing it. It made Honovi ache to see his husband in pain, but if this was how Blaine regained control of his body, then he wouldn't argue.

He took Blaine's hand in his and gently guided him back into the hallway. "Come on. Let's get you back to bed."

Blaine didn't protest being led to their bedroom, a small gas lamp burning low on the nightstand. Since coming home, Blaine refused to sleep in the dark, and Honovi always made sure the gas lamp never went out. His own sleep had suffered a little, not used to constant illumination, but he was adjusting.

Honovi quicky stripped down to his underwear before joining Blaine on the bed. He dragged the covers over them both and rolled onto his side so he could sling an arm over Blaine's waist, drawing him close. They'd been forced to swap their usual sides of the bed to accommodate Blaine's still-healing left arm.

"What were you working on?" Blaine asked after a moment.

"Just some trade reports. Father was right, though. It can all keep until morning."

Blaine shifted against Honovi, his remaining hand settling over the arm Honovi had draped over his waist. "I can help you with that."

"You need to rest."

"I'm not an invalid."

The tension in Blaine's voice had Honovi shoving himself up on one elbow, leaning over his husband. He looked down into Blaine's face, wishing he could soothe away the distress and pain in those hazel eyes. He settled for smoothing back Blaine's hair.

"You're not," he agreed. "But you need to give yourself time to heal."

"I *am* healing."

Honovi rested his forehead against Blaine's, breathing slow and careful. "You are, but give yourself the grace you'd give others to learn how to live with a new normal. You have nothing to prove, not to me, not to anyone."

Blaine reached up to grip Honovi's braid where it spilled over his shoulder. "It feels like I do."

The quiet, agonizing confession drew a protesting sound out of Honovi. "You don't. You never will."

They stayed like that for a few minutes more before Blaine nodded jerkily, saying nothing. Honovi settled back onto the bed, pressing close. Losing an arm didn't make Blaine any less the man Honovi had grown up with and learned to love. He'd shown Blaine the sky once before, and he'd do it all over again if that's what his husband needed.

Seven

JOELLE

The smell of funeral incense that lingered in the air of the private star temple the House of Kimathi prayed in stung Joelle's eyes, but the *vezir* had cried all the tears she could afford. She folded her shaking hands together over her lap, staring blankly at the statue of Callisto and the eternal flame that burned there up at the altar.

The Dawn Star was not who she worshipped and hadn't for most of her life. Her prayers had never been answered by Solaria's guiding star but by another. Innes had promised her a road to power. Joelle had thought she'd paid enough for it, but apparently not.

Artyom had died in Calhames, branded a traitor rather than a victim in the broadsheets. Her only son was but a name on a memory wall now, his wife and children a wailing, grieving mess Joelle had sent to the family wing of the estate in the wake of the funeral rites.

Like with Nicca, her granddaughter, Artyom was another death she blamed the House of Sa'Liandel for. This time, there wasn't even a body to burn in Bellingham's crematorium. All they could do was pray and grieve while the rest of Solaria turned as one against her House.

The Legion marched to her *vasilyet* on order of the emperor. Scouts had sent back word of their approach, and it was only a matter of time before they attempted to lay siege to Bellingham how Vanya's mother had laid siege to Rixham.

She would not allow it.

Joelle reached for the pew in front of her and used it to brace herself as she stood. Her bones ached, her usual medication barely making a dent in the pain as she worked to shore up her House's position and power. Bellingham was a city beholden to her House, the surrounding *vasilyet* never one to welcome those who called Calhames home.

She stepped into the center aisle and turned to leave, nearly stumbling when she saw who stood in her way. For a moment, hatred washed through her so powerfully that Joelle swayed on her feet. "My lord."

"I hear your grief," Innes said.

Joelle swallowed thickly. "My son is dead."

"You still have a daughter here and a great-granddaughter in Calhames."

"Artyom made a better heir than Karima, and Raiah is beyond my reach. Vanya sends the Legion to take my *vasilyet*." Her lips trembled as she spoke, breath stuttering in her lungs from so much hurt and anger. "I am *owed*."

She'd been promised much when she'd allied herself with Eimarille at the behest of the star god in front of her. None of those promises had come to fruition for her, and Joelle had to wonder if they ever would. But it was too late to second-guess this road, to step off it. She'd made her choices years and years ago, given her loyalty to Innes in hope of claiming the Imperial throne. Joelle had sacrificed so much over the years, and she was tired of whittling down her House to prop up someone else.

"You are," Innes agreed, offering her his bent elbow. "Perhaps it will please you to know that a division of the Daijal army is less than half a day away and prepared to entrench themselves along your *vasilyet*'s borders. They will arrive before the Legion. You will have Daijal support to push back against any threat."

Joelle knew better than to ignore the offer of aid and so slipped her hand around the bend of the Twilight Star's elbow. "They have not fought against the Legion."

"Your country's Legion has not fought against the new war machines that have been designed and built specifically for the oncoming war." He smiled gently at her as he guided her toward the main temple doors. "I hear your prayers, and they will be answered. They are *being* answered."

"Did you hear Artyom's?" she asked harshly, unable to swallow back the words.

"I hear all who pray to me."

Hearing prayers was one thing; granting them was entirely different. She knew Artyom must have prayed when Vanya executed him—to Innes, and not Callisto. But there was no aid the star god had given him. If Innes had, then perhaps her son would have lived. If he'd granted her own, perhaps her House would have come out of the Conclave victorious. Too many forks in the road to be certain which path was the right one to take.

"Solaria needs new leadership," Joelle said as Innes led her out of the star temple into the warm night air. Her household had retreated back into the estate an hour ago, leaving her alone to pray.

"It does." Innes looked up at the dark sky above and all the stars strewn across it. "Your road is not over yet. The fight ahead will be a long one, but you are not yet destined to dance amongst the stars."

He pulled away from her, taking warmth with him, stepping out of her sight in the way only star gods could. Joelle swallowed her grief and headed down the stone pathway toward the estate, gaslights glowing through the windows. There was much to do, much to plan for, and she could not change the past.

She could only hope to change the future.

Eight

VANYA

Near the end of Eleventh Month, almost twenty days since the Imperial palace went up in flames, Vanya left his House's estate in the middle of the night. He refused a motorcade, allowing only a pair of velocycles to escort the motor carriage that drove him into the outer neighborhoods of Calhames.

In the hours after midnight, the city was quiet in a way it never was during the day. Gas lamps lined every street, lighting the way to the warden resupply station he knew Soren was staying at. Vanya hadn't seen the warden since that morning in the Senate, though his *praetoria* legionnaires dutifully reported back to him on Soren's movements. Soren hadn't yet left Calhames, even if it felt as if he'd left Vanya.

The motor carriage braked to a halt outside the resupply station, engine idling as Vanya opened the rear passenger door himself. He waved at the *praetoria* legionnaires to remain where they were on the street before stepping onto the pavement. Two strides brought him to the door, and he tested the knob, finding it locked. He pressed a finger to the doorbell without hesitation and impatiently waited.

He didn't have to wait long.

A quiet click indicated the lock being undone. The door was

opened, Soren's familiar face coming into view. The warden had hastily dressed, his shirt not even tucked in. His expression was impossible to read when once Vanya thought himself familiar with the range of Soren's emotions. Here, with everything between them hanging heavy like a shroud, Vanya found himself second-guessing everything.

"You haven't come by," Vanya said, breaking the silence between them.

"I didn't think I would be welcomed," Soren replied after a moment, voice quiet and careful. "I leave for Glencoe in the morning."

Vanya stared at him, words trapped in his throat like clarion crystal shards. Finally, he took a step back and gestured at the motor carriage. "Get in."

Soren hesitated before nodding. "Let me get my gear."

He disappeared, returning several minutes later looking far more put together. Vanya wouldn't begrudge him the weapons he carried, not when he'd seen firsthand Soren's skill with them. Soren closed the door behind him, the locks clicking into place, and joined Vanya in the motor carriage. The drive back was made in tense silence, the space between them in the rear seat mere inches, but it felt like a chasm Vanya couldn't begin to know how to bridge.

That searing sense of betrayal still burned inside him, but letting Soren go wasn't an option. It couldn't be, not with a vow hanging around the warden's throat—a broad promise of *anything* that, in hindsight, was so devastating considering what Vanya now knew. No matter what happened, they were tied together as long as Soren carried it.

The motor carriage drove past the sentinel-class automatons on duty at the end of the street before turning into the estate drive and pulling up to the front entrance. A servant waited on the porch to let them inside. Soren followed Vanya into the place his House now called home for the moment while the palace was rebuilt. And it would be rebuilt. Already architects were drawing out a new design, and engineers were gathering materials to use.

It was easy to rebuild the palace, far less easy to rebuild a home.

He watched as Soren paused in the foyer, looking up at the grand chandelier hanging from the ceiling. Light reflected off the blue mosaic tiles lining the walls and high ceiling, making it seem as if they were surrounded by the sky.

"This way," Vanya said, because while Soren had known the palace, he didn't know this estate.

Vanya wasn't sure he ever would.

He led the way through dimly lit hallways, rooms decorated by a different generation of his bloodline—none of it in a style he liked. Some part of him still ached for who he'd thought Alida had once been, for she would have taken charge and redone everything to match the tastes of his household.

Except all of her smiles, all of her aid, all of her quiet moments of friendship had been a lie.

Much how it was with Soren.

Vanya cut through a drawing room with an overwhelming amount of gold décor, but the arched glass doors on the other side opened up into a guest courtyard. The private one used for family was on the other side of the mansion, where Raiah slept with Taisiya down the hall.

No one followed them outside, leaving the two of them alone beneath the night sky with only distant stars to keep them company. The flowers and vines that hung from the surrounding balconies were only half in bloom, summer a season on its way out. The heady floral scent still lingered in the air, and Vanya thought he could taste it when he licked his lips as he turned to face Soren.

"Who are you?" Vanya demanded, voicing a question that had seeped through his thoughts like a poison for days on end.

"You know who I am," Soren said in a low voice.

Vanya closed the distance between them, hand snapping out to curl around the collar of Soren's shirt, tangling in the gold chain hidden there beneath the fabric. Soren balled his fists, rocking forward as Vanya yanked on the necklace, pulling out the vow, but he didn't try to break free.

"No, I *don't*. There were marks of starfire in the crypt when I went below to examine it, and you used starfire in the palace. You're a *warden*. They don't allow people who can cast starfire as tithes. It goes against the Poison Accords."

The hypocrisy made Vanya want to laugh, but it wouldn't have held any humor in it. He kept his teeth clenched together, glaring into Soren's eyes, their faces so close together their breath mingled.

Soren swallowed, the click of his throat loud between them. "The wardens don't know."

"I find that difficult to believe."

"It's the truth, princeling."

"It's *not.*" Vanya tightened his grip on the necklace, gold biting into his fingers. "Tell me who you really are."

Soren raised his chin, gray eyes dark like a storm. "No one of any worth, just like every other tithe sent as payment. The wardens never *knew* because the Dawn Star made it so."

Vanya jerked back at that confession, still keeping hold of the vow. He stared at Soren, the rush of blood in his ears sounding like drums as a thought formed, clarion crystal sharp, cutting through everything —how Callisto had said to keep the warden close. How their roads were always meant to cross.

Had they truly, when Soren had been keeping secret such a devastating ability?

Did they now, after he'd learned such truth?

Looking at Soren in the gaslight, standing there in the aftermath of everything they'd survived, Vanya realized he didn't know the warden.

He quite possibly never had.

And that *hurt*.

"I'm a warden, and that's all I'll ever be. Wherever I came from, I can't go back. I can never go home," Soren said, voice cracking, the gold chain still digging into his throat, held in place by Vanya's grip, but he never fought to get free. "I never lied about that."

"But you lied about the quarry. About escaping the crypt. You never used bombs to escape, did you? It was never some new-fangled warden weapon primed with alchemy, was it? Every time, it was starfire."

Soren said nothing for a long moment. When he finally spoke, his voice came out low and tight. "Would you rather I be dead?"

"I'd rather you had never lied to me at all." Vanya's fingers slid down the chain until he could wrap them around the vow, the face of the engraved lion pressing hard against his skin. "Ask me for what you want."

Soren's expression twisted, something pained and haunted crossing his face. "No."

"Ask me."

Soren planted his hands against Vanya's chest but didn't push him away, merely clenched his fingers around the soft summer weave of his robe. The chain of the vow was stretched taut between them, glinting in the gaslight. "I never wanted your vow, but you gave it to me anyway. I can do what I want with it."

"You've asked for nothing over the years."

"Because if I ever did, I'd have to *leave*." The words were snarled out, bitter and aching, and Vanya reflexively jerked on the vow, dragging Soren ever closer. "Is that what you want, princeling? Me banished from your road? Would that make you happy?"

It would fix so much, he knew, if he forced Soren to ask for something—*anything*—to let him fulfill a debt owed, to keep his vow. A life for a heart's desire. But it wasn't that simple. Vows like this never were. For Vanya knew an excruciating truth he'd learned as a child, when Iosiv had died.

The one thing you couldn't trade for your heart's desire was your heart.

"I never wanted you to betray me the way everyone else has," Vanya ground out.

Soren's expression *twisted*, devastation in his eyes that didn't comfort Vanya at all. The warden opened his mouth to speak, but Vanya was tired of whatever lies the warden might give voice to. Vanya leaned in to slot his mouth over Soren's, sliding his tongue past teeth to taste him, to breathe him in. He kept hold of the vow as he kissed him so hard their teeth scraped together, all fury and hurt in the motion. Soren raised a hand, hooking it over the back of Vanya's neck to tug him impossibly closer, to keep him there.

Because, despite everything, neither wanted to go but they couldn't stay.

Not as they once were.

And Vanya was so *tired* of the lies coming to light with the people he cared for.

The roots of that truth wrapped around the shattered pieces of his heart, holding it together, because he'd never had the luxury or the space to grieve what he couldn't have.

Vanya broke the kiss and let go of the vow to slide his fingers through Soren's hair and pull his head back. He stared down into blown-wide gray eyes and bit at kiss-swollen lips. "I'll have you tonight. The wardens can take you in the morning."

He was an emperor—he ruled a nation and commanded Maricol's strongest army—but he couldn't make a warden stay by his side.

"Vanya," Soren murmured, hand sliding over Vanya's neck to thumb at the hinge of his jaw. "You always had me."

"I wish I could believe that."

The ache of betrayal didn't stop Vanya from leading Soren back to his suite of rooms, to his well-guarded bedroom. The same spell-detecting security Chu Hua had set up in his old office had been set up here. Nothing reacted to Soren stepping inside and closing the door behind him, the lock clicking into place.

Vanya shoved him up against it, slotting his leg between Soren's and pressing up, pinning him to the door. Soren yanked him into a kiss even as he ground down against Vanya's thigh, shameless in a way Vanya had always appreciated. A small, vicious voice in the back of his mind wondered if that was a calculating move on the warden's part.

The thought made him bite at Soren's lips. "Strip and get on the bed."

It was familiar, the way they got rid of their clothes in between kisses, in between dragging, teasing touches. Soren's weapons were handled with far more care than Vanya's expensive robes, a trail of clothing leading from the door to the bed.

The windows were open to the night, the lone burning gas lamp on the dresser giving off a soft glow bright enough that Vanya could see the freckles scattered across Soren's skin. It reflected off the gold of the vow that hung from Soren's throat, a reminder of Vanya's foolishness when he was younger, when he thought a nameless, stateless warden couldn't ask for anything dangerous.

Only Soren never had, remaining stubbornly silent on any request, even now, as Vanya pushed him flat to the bed. He hooked his fingers around the chain, pressed his palm over the medallion, keeping Soren in place. He leaned over the warden, claiming his mouth for a kiss that had Soren bringing up a hand to cradle the back of Vanya's head, holding him close.

Vanya hooked his other hand around the bend of Soren's knee, pulling his leg up and out, giving him room to settle into the cradle of his hips. Soren's breath hitched in the back of his throat, the sound quiet between them as their half-hard cocks rubbed against each other. He opened his mouth, but whatever he was going to say, Vanya didn't want to hear it.

He let go of the vow to slide two fingers into Soren's mouth, pressing down against his tongue. Soren closed his lips around them, groaning when Vanya wrapped his free hand around both their cocks, stroking them. The dry friction was something Vanya teased them both with for a moment, Soren sucking on his fingers. He tipped his head back, and Vanya followed the motion, pushing his fingers deeper until Soren choked on them, words lost.

Hands settled on his shoulders, and Vanya shrugged them off as he straightened up. Soren's eyes were slits of gray between dark lashes as Vanya took his hands off the warm body beneath him. Soren pressed his knee against Vanya's ribs, lips spit-slicked. One hand darted out, fingers curling over Vanya's wrist, pressing into his pulse. "Whatever you need from me, I'll give it."

He wanted to believe that, but there was a vow between them that neither could give up. Vanya pulled free of his grip and twisted away from the cradle of his hips, reaching for the nightstand drawer and the oil kept there. Soren watched him with those stormy eyes of his, not bothering to hide the wealth of emotion in them, and Vanya—Vanya couldn't look at him like this.

Like he belonged, when he didn't, when he couldn't, no matter what Callisto had said.

"Turn over," Vanya said roughly.

Soren's abdominal muscles flexed as he sat up, stealing a gentle kiss that Vanya let him have before getting on his hands and knees, which wasn't quite what Vanya wanted. So he reached out with his left hand, pressing it between the wings of Soren's shoulder blades, and pushed him facedown onto the bed.

Soren grunted softly, elbows bending, not fighting in any way when Vanya knew he could. He stretched his arms over his head, fingers brushing against the wooden headboard as Vanya leaned his weight on Soren to keep him in place. His knees were bent, legs splayed wide, spine curved to put his ass on display.

Vanya bent over him, cock rubbing against his ass even as he pushed two fingers into Soren with no teasing, no warning, breath blowing hot over Soren's ear. "Did you ever even mean it?"

Soren's mouth parted on a rough groan, hips shifting against the intrusion, but he had no leverage like this, bent to Vanya's will, face turned to the side while he panted for breath. He swallowed loudly, voice sounding strangled when Vanya curled his fingers to press against that spot inside. Soren pushed back against the touch, arms flexing, and Vanya rested more of his weight on him, keeping him pinned.

Vanya skimmed his teeth over the curve of Soren's left shoulder, watching how Soren's hands pressed flat against the headboard, fingers tense. He added a third finger, too soon, he knew, but too angry—too hurt—to stop. The whine that escaped Soren's lips was a shattered bit of sound that made Vanya's cock twitch between them. "Answer me."

"Always," Soren ground out lowly, body rocking into his touch as much as he could, breath coming quick and rapid. "I never lied about that. I couldn't. I *wanted*—"

He broke off with a ragged, wordless sound. Vanya closed his eyes, pressed his forehead against the knobs of Soren's spine at the nape of his neck. He pulled his fingers out and thrust them back in hard, listening to the hitch in Soren's lungs. When he spoke, his lips brushed against warm skin, a gentle caress. "But you lied about everything else."

"Vanya—"

"I trusted you," Vanya ground out into the hot air between them, closing his eyes for a brief second against the light, feeling torn open and desperate. "I trusted you with Raiah. With my—"

He broke off, clenching his teeth together to hold back a confession he couldn't ever speak, not now. He removed his fingers and sat up, keeping his other hand pressed to Soren's back, refusing to let him up. Soren didn't move, breathing raggedly where Vanya had put him, always willing to submit to Vanya's desire.

Vanya stroked his hard cock with the remainder of oil on his fingers before digging his knees into the mattress, spreading Soren's legs wider. His ass tilted higher with the motion, and Vanya rocked his hips forward, just enough that his cock could slide against the crease of his ass. He stayed there for a moment, aching with the twin urges to stay or go. Then Soren moved his head, looking at him through damp lashes, gaze steady and warm.

"I know," he said, the words coming out soft like a secret prayer.

Vanya's hands spasmed against Soren's body. Taking a deep breath, he fit his cockhead against Soren's slick hole, pushing in slowly, relentless, Soren moaning beneath him, the warden's hands scratching at the headboard. He turned his face into the mattress, voice muffled against the sheets, but Vanya heard him anyway, quiet and begging.

"*Please.* Vanya, *please.*"

He sank into that tight, clenching warmth until he was pressed up flush against Soren, cock throbbing. Vanya curled over Soren, hips flexing with the motion as he drew in a harsh breath. Soren's moan sent a hard shiver jerking down his spine, and he pressed an open-mouthed kiss to the nearest stretch of sweat-slick skin. Then Vanya pulled out nearly all the way before thrusting forward hard enough to shove Soren a few inches up the bed.

Soren let out a strangled shout, hands scrabbling to better brace himself against the headboard. Vanya didn't give him time to get settled, to adjust, driving in with hard, punishing thrusts that Soren tried to meet, but the stretch of his body, the bend of his spine, didn't give him much leverage. He could only take whatever Vanya gave him, cock left untended no matter how much begging he did.

"Please, please touch me," Soren begged, face turned to the side, a flush to his cheeks that was spreading down his throat.

Vanya grunted, sinking in deep and grinding hard against Soren's ass, listening to the way the warden keened at the pressure against his prostate. "Do you think you deserve it?"

Soren moaned, shoulders curving up, elbows digging into the mattress, but Vanya's hand on his back kept him where he was. "I—"

Vanya hooked his other hand around Soren's hip, hauling him up just that little bit higher to keep him from gaining any friction from the sheets below. He pulled back, cock sliding almost all the way out, Soren's hole clenching desperately around the head. "Tell me."

The shout Soren let out when Vanya thrust back in with enough force to lift Soren's knees off the bed could probably be heard by all the *praetoria* legionnaires standing guard outside the bedroom. Vanya grunted, keeping to that same punishing pace as Soren writhed and wailed beneath him. He slid his hand up Soren's back, tangling in his hair to pull his head up at a sharp angle. Vanya licked a hot stripe up his neck, breath blowing hot over Soren's ear. "*Tell me.*"

"I don't deserve you," Soren gasped out wetly, the words stuttering in his mouth on every thrust from Vanya's cock. "But I wish I did."

Vanya groaned, removing his hand from Soren's back and hair, shifting so he could hook both beneath his shoulders and haul him up. Vanya rocked back onto his heels, bringing Soren with him. He wrapped an arm around Soren's torso, his other hand on Soren's hip to drag the warden down onto his cock where he belonged, split open and begging and crying out Vanya's name loud enough that everyone would know who he belonged to.

Soren turned his head, eyes closed, lashes damp, the sheen of tears on his cheeks. Vanya fucked up into him hard enough that he heard the clack of Soren's teeth when they came together, a gasp slipping past them.

"You had me," Vanya growled as he thrust up again and again, the sound of flesh slapping together a steady counterpoint to Soren's hitching gasps. "No one else ever did, but you *had* me."

Soren keened, high and broken as he came untouched on a particularly hard thrust, cock spurting his release over his stomach and the bed. Vanya tangled his fingers in Soren's hair, wrenching his head around for a biting, bruising kiss as he kept fucking into Soren, chasing something that might have been pleasure but only felt like loss, like grief.

When he came, the burn of it shook through him as he spilled into Soren's weakly clenching hole, grinding up and holding on and wishing tonight would never end. Breathing harshly, Vanya wrapped his arms around Soren's torso, hands splayed over warm skin as he sank fully down onto his heels, Soren in his lap, filled with his softening cock.

They breathed together for a moment, Soren shivering against him, tiny twitches of his body that Vanya gentled with careful touches of his hands. When Soren finally caught his breath, he reached up to slide his hand over Vanya's, interlacing their fingers together. Vanya bent his head and pressed a lingering kiss to Soren's shoulder. Eventually, he pulled his hand free and eased Soren up, sliding the warden off his cock. When Soren made to move away from him, Vanya snagged the warden's wrist without a second thought, holding on, wanting to be selfish one last time.

Soren stilled, turning to look over his shoulder at Vanya, the famed neutrality of wardens nowhere in his gaze. All Vanya could see in those familiar gray eyes was a fragile sort of longing that he couldn't soothe.

Not anymore.

"You had me," Vanya said again into the fraught silence between them, voice aching with so much he couldn't say.

Soren closed his eyes, expression crumbling, before he gently tugged himself free of Vanya's grip and crawled back over to him until they were almost—but not quite—touching. Soren's eyes were red-rimmed, hair sweaty and sticking to his forehead. He smelled like sweat and the sex they'd just had, naked and messy and everything Vanya had ever wanted over the years. But it had all been a lie, and Vanya couldn't risk his country any more than he already had.

He wouldn't—*couldn't*—make that mistake again.

Soren leaned in, bridging the distance, until his face was so close his features were blurred, the vow dangling from his throat like a noose that Vanya had placed there years ago. His lips brushed gently over Vanya's, breath ghosting across his skin, the words barely louder than a whisper. "I won't ask for myself."

Vanya let out a harsh breath, pressing his knuckles to Soren's collarbone before flattening his hand over warm skin. Soren leaned into the touch for a brief moment before he pulled away to get dressed with hands that shook only a little. Vanya stayed where he was, committing the sight of Soren to memory, because he wouldn't get tomorrow, and tonight felt like a fever dream of the worst kind.

Once Soren secured his weapons, they stared at each other in silence, and Vanya kept his teeth locked together, wishing the ache in his chest was something he could burn away. Then Soren returned to the bed only long enough to kiss Vanya one last time, a desperate, bruising thing that left them both gasping when Soren finally wrenched his mouth away.

"I'm sorry," Soren ground out raggedly, the words regretful, almost mournful, before turning toward the door. "I'm *sorry*."

He left, never looking back, and Vanya spent what remained of the night wishing Soren had.

Nine

SOREN

Soren didn't make it to Glencoe until the beginning of Twelfth Month, taking the long way east through back roads. He saw the Leviathan constellation spin low as the Eagle constellation arced high in the night sky, bringing with it the autumn season. He spent those days driving toward Seaville trying to settle his head and mend his heart, to no avail.

Everything just—ached.

By the time he boarded an E'ridian airship out of that city's airfield —the captain kindly offering free passage in deference to what had happened to his people—Soren was about ready to vibrate out of his skin, a mess in more ways than one. He spent the better part of the flight north to E'ridia hunkered down in the crew bunks belowdecks, staring at the wooden planks of the bunk over his and not seeing anything but Vanya's face.

The crew fed him, left him alone after the first few attempts at conversation in the trade tongue came to nothing. Soren stayed out of their way and kept to himself and tried not to feel as if his entire world hadn't been upended when it had.

Lying to himself had never been a game he was capable of winning.

When the airship finally landed in Glencoe, Soren thanked the captain and rolled his velocycle out of the cargo hold and onto the pier. He'd never been to E'ridia before, and the Sunrise Valley where Glencoe was located was a vast green space bracketed by the Eastern Spine to the west of them and rolling coastal hills to the east.

The elevation made his ears pop even when he had boots on the ground, and Soren sniffed hard to try to clear them. The air was colder here than it had been in Solaria. He missed the heat of that country already. He wished he had a heavier coat or one that was fur-lined like the aeronauts wore. Glencoe would have a resupply station he could get cold-weather gear from, but it would have to wait until he figured out just where the governor was.

Once he left the airfield behind, got inside the city gates, Soren became absolutely lost. He'd grown up speaking the trade tongue, was mostly fluent in Solarian, but he'd had no need to learn E'ridian. The flow and sound of the language was different from Solarian, and it buzzed in his ears, impossible to tune out. The street signs were unreadable to him. Soren huffed out a frustrated breath, grip tightening on his handlebars as he maneuvered the velocycle out of the way of the departure tunnel.

As a warden, he didn't need to go through customs, but the customs officers probably had a better idea of where the wardens evacuated from the Warden's Island had been sent. The maps in Soren's travel compartments were for Solaria, not E'ridia, and he'd need directions. He kicked the stand down and made his way to the building, searching out someone in uniform who might have some answers.

"The wounded are being cared for in a few different hospitals. The *Comhairle nan Cinnidhean* gave all the others use of several clan homes in the center of the city," the E'ridian said in the trade tongue. Her natural accent came through thick, and Soren had to concentrate to understand her.

He frowned. "You got a map I can see?"

She blinked at him in surprise. "You don't have one?"

"My borders are in Solaria."

At least, they were. He shoved down the ache at the thought of how he'd failed to do his duty and what that would mean when he reported to the governor. He wondered if she'd reassign him somewhere else in Maricol, some other country, where he'd never see Vanya and Raiah again.

The thought made him want to scream.

"Ah." The E'ridian waved him toward a door that had a sign nailed to it that read *Customs Only*. "Come with me, and I'll get you on your way."

They had some maps in the back that they couldn't give him, but Soren had no problem memorizing the route she showed him when it came to street names and wall gates. The main avenues and boulevards gave him the most direct route to the city center, and Soren thanked her before going on his way.

They'd landed in the afternoon, and the sun was skirting the mountain peaks when he finally pulled in front of a sprawling estate the E'ridians called a clan home. The gates were open, and a dozen velocycles were parked in the drive. Soren added his to the group, staring up at the building's façade as he mechanically withdrew what he needed from the travel compartments.

He'd left Calhames without that country's border reports. They'd been lost to starfire, for the Chief Minister's office had been within the palace. Caelum had survived, having been away from the palace, dealing with diplomatic issues at the time of the attack. The older records were stored offsite, but Soren knew they were transferred every decade. If the records on the island had been destroyed, recreating the data from the poison fields would be a huge undertaking.

Soren shouldered his rucksack and walked up the drive, boots crunching over gravel. The door was unlocked when he tried the knob. He pushed it open, stepping inside and looking around, seeing no signs of servants or anyone else.

"Hello?" he called out.

Someone shouted from down the hall, and a head poked itself out of a room. "What border did you come from?"

Soren headed toward them. "Solaria. I handled the one in Calhames."

Another voice called out a greeting as he drew close, Delani sounding as brusque as ever. "Is that you, Soren?"

He swallowed thickly, stomach hollowing out in relief at the sound of her voice. It was one thing to be told of her survival, quite another to witness it in person. The other warden slipped back inside the room once Soren made it to the doorway. It looked as if the space had been converted from a parlor into a meeting room.

The long table in the rectangular room dominated the area, all the chairs around it taken. Two desks were pushed into the far corners, the typewriter and telegraph machines there manned by two wardens who didn't look up at his entrance.

Delani sat at the far end of the table, surrounded by stacks of folios. The chairs closest to her were filled by wardens, while the ones closest to Soren were taken up by E'ridians. A map of Maricol was unrolled down the center of the table, with individual country maps layered over it. Voices chattering in a mix of trade tongue and E'ridian created a buzz of sound that abruptly cut off when Delani banged her hand on the table.

The wardens' governor stared at Soren with her one good eye, the glass one looking a little worse for wear. He didn't know what to make of the expression on her face—calculating and just a bit surprised, as if some puzzle piece had finally snapped into place.

Soren met Delani's gaze across the room. "Reporting back with news from Calhames and Solaria, governor."

"So you didn't die in that mess we've heard about," Delani said.

Soren tightened his grip on the strap of his rucksack. "Not for Daijal's lack of trying."

Delani's expression darkened, and she waved him into the room. "I haven't had a good report out of Calhames since we recalled the station wardens, but the broadsheets have reported about a revenant attack in the Imperial palace. Is that story true?"

"Yes. The House of Sa'Liandel remains in control of the Imperial throne, but the House of Kimathi allied itself with Daijal to try to gain it. My border was overrun in their effort."

Very few knew of the crypt beneath the Imperial palace. The governor had kept that knowledge retained by very few high-ranking wardens on the island at Soren's request, the stay still in effect. He wondered if that would no longer be the case after today.

"I see." Delani leaned back in her chair and crossed her arms over her chest. "Daijal's doing? Truly?"

"Blades were sent to infiltrate the grounds. They waited until the Conclave of Houses had everyone gathered under one roof to initiate the attack."

One of the wardens to Delani's right, an older man with dark skin and close-cropped hair, drummed his fingers against the table. "That would explain the Legion being on the move and the closing of the northern border."

"The emperor survived?" Delani asked.

Soren fought back a flinch. "He used starfire in defense of his people and burned down the palace with all the revenants inside."

"Royals are finally good for something," a warden muttered, eliciting an elbow to their ribs from their neighbor.

Delani was still looking at him as if she'd never seen him before, but her voice, when she spoke, was even and professional. "How certain are you a Solarian House is collaborating with the Daijal court?"

He thought of being trapped in an iron coffin, with a revenant scratching at the lid, trying to get *in* rather than out. He thought of the way Alida's face had twisted with hate so deep he'd wondered how she'd hidden it while in service to Vanya. He thought of Artyom's greed and the way he'd have gladly murdered Raiah in pursuit of power.

"Very," he said, voice gone momentarily hoarse. He cleared his throat, running his tongue over the back of his teeth. "The emperor confirmed it."

Delani lifted a hand to drag it over her mouth. "That's going to mean war between more than two countries."

Her words set off a round of furious discussion, most of which Soren barely understood the context of. He shifted on his feet, moving around the table to post himself up against the wall. There weren't any seats left, but he hadn't been dismissed, and he wasn't sure what other questions Delani had for him. He had his own, too, about the status of the island. The customs officer had mentioned wounded being held at the hospitals here, and he wanted to know how many had survived.

Soren slid his rucksack off his shoulder, lowering it to the floor. The back-and-forth going on was held mostly by the wardens, with the E'ridians present watching and growing increasingly concerned-looking. Soren didn't know what the different plaid or hair adornments meant, but he figured the colors and designs on the ones worn by the pair of men who arrived half an hour later meant they must be some sort of nobility.

The new arrivals both wore kilts and sturdy knee-high boots, the fitted day jacket favored by E'ridians on the ground hanging oddly off the blond's shoulders. Soren realized why when he saw the way the sleeve was pinned up, showcasing the stump of an arm that ended just below the elbow visible when he turned from addressing his companion. The blond looked pale, thin in the way of illness, with shadows bruised beneath his eyes.

The dark-haired man's black braid hanging over his shoulder held an assortment of metal adornments that put everyone else's to shame. The blond's hair was much shorter, though still styled like an E'ridian. Soren watched as both of them glanced around the room, clearly familiar with everyone present, but the second their attention landed on him, the two went absolutely still, color washing out of both their faces.

Delani hummed, the sound loud in the sudden silence. "I thought it was my imagination. Guess it's not. The resemblance is certainly uncanny."

People turned around in their seats to look at him, and something icy settled in the pit of Soren's stomach as he stared everyone down.

"Delani," the dark-haired man said, voice flat and hard and oh so angry. "He's a warden."

"I am aware of that, Honovi."

"I've always been a warden," Soren snapped, trying desperately not to think of the time before, because it didn't matter, couldn't matter, except for how it did.

How it always had.

"No," the blond said faintly, staring at him with wide, haunted eyes, giving voice to a truth Soren would give anything to stay buried. "You haven't, Alasandair."

I am actively writing the third and final book in the trilogy but have not yet settled on a release date. To stay updated on when a release date is announced, please join my newsletter.

If you like urban fantasy and mythology, check out Hailey Turner's Soulbound series, staring with *A Ferry of Bones & Gold.*

Short descriptions of words, acronyms, and phrases used in the story that weren't readily explained in text. Included as well are character names.

A.O.C.: Age of Constellations. A past Age on Maricol that occurred after A.O.S. and before A.O.P.

A.O.P.: Age of Progress. The current Age on Maricol, beginning in 0 A.O.P.

A.O.S.: Age of Starfall. The first Age on Maricol that encompassed landing and initial colonization of Maricol. This Age held the Dying Times and the Great Separation.

Aaralyn: Star god. Also known as the North Star, patron goddess of life. Apex star god of the Star Order. Her constellation is the Wolf, and her tattoo is located on her right arm.

Aeronaut: One who captains or crews on an airship.

Aether: The fifth element that powers magic and clarion crystals, located in an otherworldly plane.

Aetos, Vesper: Solarian. Listed in the nobility genealogies. Heir to the House of Aetos.

Age: Denotations of historical and current eras.

Airfield: A landing field located outside major cities and large towns for the anchorage of airships.

Airship: A lighter-than-air craft powered by steam engines and commercial flight balloons.

Akina, Kote: Daijalan. High General of the Daijal army.

Alida: Solarian. Majordomo to Vanya's household.

Alrickson: E'ridian. Listed in the royal genealogies. Current *ceann-cinnidh* of Clan Storm.

Amari: City. Capital of Ashion.

Ashion: Country. Debt bondage is outlawed within its borders. Its capital city is Amari. The country's patron guiding star is Aaralyn, the North Star. The country's affirmed constellation is the Wolf.

Ashionen: Denoting ties to or nationality of Ashion. Language descriptor.

Astrolabe: Astronomical instrument used for navigation.

Auclair, Brielle: Ashionen. Listed in the nobility genealogies. Named Whisper in the Clockwork Brigade. Oldest child of Meleri.

Auclair, Dureau: Ashionen. Listed in the nobility genealogies. Named Locke in the Clockwork Brigade. Youngest child of Meleri.

Auclair, Lore: Ashionen. Listed in the nobility genealogies. Named Mainspring in the Clockwork Brigade. Middle child of Meleri.

Auclair, Meleri: Ashionen. Listed in the nobility genealogies. Spymaster. Named Fulcrum in the Clockwork Brigade. Head of the Auclair bloodline.

Auron: Currency. Used in every country on Maricol.

Automaton: A clockwork machine that varies in size, shape, and use. Generally powered by steam engines but can also be powered by clarion crystals and the aether.

Balaskas, Cybele: Solarian. Listed in the nobility genealogies. *Vezir* to the House of Balaskas. Head of her House.

Bellingham: City. Located in Solaria.

Blade: Secretive Daijalan Star Order sect of assassins.

Blaine: E'ridian. Listed in the nobility genealogies. Clan Storm.

Married to Honovi. Last surviving member of the Westergard bloodline.

Bloodline: Those of noble and royal families who can trace their lineage back thousands of years through genealogies to prove genetics not damaged by poison.

Broadsheets: Daily printed publication containing news.

Caelum: Solarian. Chief Minister to the Imperial throne.

Calhames: City. Capital of Solaria.

Callisto: Star god. Also known as the Dawn Star, patron goddess of death. Her constellation is the Lion, and her tattoo is located on her neck and throat.

Caoimhe: E'ridian. Clan Sky. Air force aeronaut captain.

Catacombs: Ancient tunnels and passageways built beneath Amari with lost technology.

***Ceann-Cinnidh*:** (pl. *cinn-chinnidh*) Ruling rank in E'ridia. Position in the *Comhairle nan Cinnidhean*.

Chu Hua: Solarian. Imperial General of the Legion.

Civil War: The first war between bloodlines that ultimately cleaved Ashion into two countries, forming Daijal in the west and leaving Ashion in the east.

Clans: Distinctive groups within E'ridia. Currently number six in total.

Clarion crystal: Crystal mined from the earth that can transmute the aether into magic or energy, depending on the cut.

Clementine, Nathaniel: Ashionen. Merchant and heir to the Clementine Trading Company. Cog in the Clockwork Brigade.

Clockwork Brigade: Underground rebellion originating in Ashion that exists to free debt slaves in Daijal and smuggle them to freedom in other countries, as well as work against the Daijal court.

Cog: A rebel belonging to the Clockwork Brigade.

Collector's Guild: A powerful association formed in Daijal that helps companies and individuals find and retrieve escaped debt slaves.

***Comhairle nan Cinnidhean*:** Ruling body of E'ridia.

Conclave of Houses: Solarian political tradition wherein the

Houses gather to issue a public judgment on the ruling House and loyalties are bartered for support.

Constellation: Stars in the sky that represent a star god in a celestial map.

Cosian: City. Located in Ashion.

Daijal: Country. Debt bondage is sanctioned within its borders and an integral part of its economy. Its capital city is New Haven. The country's patron guiding star is Innes, the Twilight Star. The country's affirmed constellation is the Viper.

Daijalan: Denoting ties to or nationality of Daijal. Language descriptor.

Dávgon: Urovan. Listed in the royal genealogies. Ruler of Urova.

Death-defying machine: Machine that can turn the dead into revenants on a mass scale.

Debt bondage: Legalized slavery that results from citizens in Daijal putting up their lives as collateral on bank loans and being forced to pay it off with work when they cannot afford monetary payment. Bank loans with life collateral come with astronomically high interest rates, ensuring the people who are collected for bondage never escape it. The debt can be applied to families and rolled into generations.

Debt collector: A bounty hunter working for the Collector's Guild who hunts down and retrieves escaped debt slaves.

Debt slave: Someone who has sold themselves as collateral to a bank to pay off a loan. Their status is denoted by bank numbers tattooed onto their necks.

Delani: Warden. Current wardens' governor.

Dhemlan, Caris: Ashionen. Listed in the nobility genealogies. Magician. Engineer and heir to the Six Point Mechanics Company. Undocumented member of the Rourke bloodline and youngest child of Queen Ophelia.

Dhemlan, Emmitt: Ashionen. Listed in the nobility genealogies. Engineer and owner of the Six Point Mechanics Company. Caris' adoptive father.

Dhemlan, Portia: Ashionen. Listed in the nobility genealogies.

Engineer and owner of the Six Point Mechanics Company. Caris' adoptive mother.

Dying Times, the: A period of time during A.O.S. when the planet's ancient colonists struggled to adapt to Maricol's poison and deal with the threat of revenants.

E'ridia: Country. Debt bondage is outlawed within its borders. Its capital city is Glencoe. The country's patron guiding star is Nilsine, the Dusk Star. The country's affirmed constellation is the Eagle.

E'ridian: Denoting ties to or nationality of E'ridia. Language descriptor.

Emperor/Empress: Ruler of Solaria who has claim to the Imperial throne.

Emporium: A seller's market bridging the space between two inner defensive walls of Istal.

Farren: Star god. Also known as the Eclipse Star, dual patron god and goddess of the sea. Their constellation is the Leviathan, and their tattoo is located on their back.

Fletcher, Samuel: Daijalan. Listed in the nobility genealogies. Engineer and inventor. Creator of the death-defying machine.

Foxborough: City. Located in Ashion.

Genealogies: Identification records that track families from the earliest Age on Maricol. Created in the past to weed out genetic mutations caused by poison. Currently used as class markers.

Glencoe: City. Capital of E'ridia.

Great Separation, the: A period of time during A.O.S. when the people of Maricol split into different countries under the guidance of the star gods.

Gevorgyan, Suresh: Solarian. Listed in the nobility genealogies. *Vezir* to the House of Gevorgyan. Head of his House.

Haighmoor: City. Located in Ashion.

Helia: City. Located in Daijal.

Honovi: E'ridian. Listed in the royal genealogies. Clan Storm. Aeronaut captain, *jarl* to a *ceann-cinnidh,* and ambassador for his country.

Houses: Noble bloodlines in Solaria.

Imperial throne: Seat of power in Solaria.

Inferno: A coup by Daijal against Ashion, perpetuated by a star god, that resulted in the Rourke bloodline and all cadet branches being annihilated.

Innes: Star god. Also known as the Twilight Star, patron god of fire. His constellation is the Viper, and his tattoo is located on both shoulders and his pectorals.

Inventor's Guild: An engineering association with chapters in every country that helps members find mentors, jobs, teaching positions, and other work. It also provides networking opportunities to fund projects.

Isar: Ruler of Urova.

Istal: City. Located in Daijal.

Iverson, Aleesia: Daijalan. Listed in the royal genealogies. Queen of Daijal. Deceased.

Iverson, Bernard: Daijalan. Listed in the royal genealogies. King of Daijal. Deceased.

Iverson, Wesley: Daijalan. Listed in the royal genealogies. Prince of Daijal. Deceased.

***Jarl*:** Title of an heir to a *ceann-cinnidh* in E'ridia.

Karnak: City. Located in Solaria.

Khaur, Ezra: Daijalan. Listed in the nobility genealogies. Cog in the Clockwork Brigade.

Khaur, Melvin: Daijalan. Listed in the nobility genealogies. Magician. Named Marshal in the Clockwork Brigade, providing him with an officer-level position to guide cogs.

Kimathi, Artyom: Solarian. Listed in the nobility genealogies. Son of Joelle and Heir to the House of Kimathi.

Kimathi, Joelle: Solarian. Listed in the nobility genealogies. *Vezir* to the House of Kimathi. Head of her House.

Kimathi, Karima: Solarian. Listed in the nobility genealogies. Daughter of Joelle and mother to Nicca.

Kimathi, Nicca: Solarian. Listed in the nobility genealogies. Granddaughter to Joelle Kimathi. Wife to Vanya Sa'Liandel. Deceased.

***Klovod*, the:** Urovan word for *puppet master*. Ex-warden who is a magician and the creator of *rionetkas*.

Ksenia: Warden. Current master alchemist of the wardens.

Legion: Standing army of Solaria.

Legionnaire: Soldier in the Legion.

Lehan, Wyatt: Daijalan. Engineer and inventor.

Magic: The transmuted form of aether.

Magician: A person gifted with the ability to control the aether and transmute it into magic and control it with a wand.

Maksim: Urovan. Listed in the nobility genealogies. Urovan ambassador to Daijal.

Maricol: World. Named from a linguistic shift of the word *miracle*. The planet refugees from a galactic war drifted to after their generation ships were thrown off course. Its high levels of alkaline, alkaloids, spores, poisons, and toxins require continuous alchemist intervention for people to survive.

Matriskav: City. Capital of Urova.

Mind magic: A type of magic some magicians are skilled with that can interfere with a person's thoughts and memories. Can also be used to control people.

Molina, Javier: Solarian. Captain and magician in the Legion and in charge of the *praetoria* legionnaire.

Month: Part of the Fourteen Month calendar Maricol runs on.

Motor carriage: Four-wheel ground vehicle.

New Haven: City. Capital of Daijal.

Nilsine: Star god. Also known as the Dusk Star, patron goddess of wind. Her constellation is the Eagle, and her tattoo is located on her right thigh.

Northern Plains: Geographical area spanning much of Ashion and part of Daijal.

Oeiras: City. Located in Solaria.

Ornithopter: Flight machine with spinning blades powered by a steam engine.

Poison Accords: Binding agreement between all countries to tithe citizens to the wardens to ensure continued cleansing of the poison fields inside their borders and removal of revenants.

Port Avi: City. Capital of the Tovan Isles.

***Praetoria* legionnaire:** A soldier in a specialized unit who guards the Imperial throne and the House that controls it.

Provence: An administrative district in Ashion and Daijal. Generally overseen by a noble bloodline.

Raziel: Warden.

Revenant: (pl. revenants) Dead infected by spores that rise to walk again.

***Rionetka*:** (pl. *rionetkas*) Urovan word for *puppet*. People controlled through mechanical means, the aether, and mind magic.

Rixham: City. Located in Solaria. Permanently walled off and inhabited by revenants.

Rourke, Alasandair: (*see* Soren) Ashionen. Listed in the royal genealogies. Deceased prince of Ashion.

Rourke, Eimarille: Ashionen and Daijalan. Listed in the royal genealogies. Queen of Daijal. Heir to the Ashionen throne through blood.

Rourke, Lisandro: Ashionen and Daijalan. Listed in the royal genealogies. Prince and son of Eimarille and Wesley.

Rourke, Ophelia: Ashionen. Listed in the royal genealogies. Deceased queen of Ashion.

Sa'Liandel, Raiah: Solarian. Listed in the royal genealogies. Daughter of Vanya and Nicca. Heir to the Imperial throne and member of the House of Sa'Liandel.

Sa'Liandel, Taisiya: Solarian. Listed in the royal genealogies. *Valide* of Solaria and member of the House of Sa'Liandel.

Sa'Liandel, Taye: Solarian. Listed in the royal genealogies. Emperor Consort of Solaria and member of the House of Sa'Liandel. Deceased.

Sa'Liandel, Vanya: Solarian. Listed in the royal genealogies. Prince then Emperor of Solaria. Member of the House of Sa'Liandel.

Sa'Liandel, Zakariya: Solarian. Listed in the royal genealogies. Empress of Solaria and member of the House of Sa'Liandel. Deceased.

Scarlette: Daijalan. Cog in the Clockwork Brigade and freed debt slave.

Seaville: City. Located in Solaria.

Sextant: Double reflecting mirrored instrument used for navigation.

Ship-city: Mechanized Tovanian ships that traverse Maricol's oceans and seas.

Solaria: Country. Debt bondage is outlawed within its borders. Its capital city is Calhames. The country's patron guiding star is Callisto, the Dawn Star. The country's affirmed constellation is the Lion.

Solarian: Denoting ties to or nationality of Solaria. Language descriptor.

Soren: Warden who guards a Solarian border and secretly capable of casting starfire. Formerly known as Prince Alasandair Rourke, Queen Ophelia's only son and middle child.

Spores: The reproductive unit of a plant and fungus that reanimates the dead to ensure future continuous propagation.

Star god: One of six immortals who are the guiding stars for the citizens and countries of Maricol. Each star god was a refugee during the Age of Comets. Upon landing on Maricol thousands of years ago, they were poisoned by the planet and the aether to such a degree that they cannot die and became revered as gods.

Star Order: Continent-wide religion that worships the six star gods.

Starfire: The most powerful application of transmuting aether into magic and an extremely rare ability. Considered a mark of royalty or someone with connection to a royal bloodline.

Submersible: Underwater vehicle.

Telegraph: Point-to-point text messaging machine.

Televox: Handheld communication device. A newer invention.

Terilyn: Urovan. Blade.

Tithe: Citizen of any country given as payment under the Poison Accords to the wardens. Tithes are trained at the Warden's Island and turned into wardens through alchemy. Not all tithes survive the process.

Tovan Isles: Country. Debt bondage is outlawed within its borders. Its capital city is Port Avi. The country's patron guiding star is Farren, the Eclipse Star. The country's affirmed constellation is the Leviathan.

Tovanian: Denoting ties to or nationality of the Tovan Isles. Language descriptor.

Trade tongue: Language drawn from all others on Maricol into a pidgin form spoken for trade.

Urova: Country. Debt bondage is outlawed within its borders. Its capital city is Matriskav. The country's patron guiding star is Xaxis, the Midnight Star. The country's affirmed constellation is the Bear.

Urovan: Denoting ties to or nationality of Urova. Language descriptor.

***Valide*:** Title belonging to the matriarch of the ruling House that holds the Imperial throne in Solaria.

***Vasilyet*:** An administrative district in Solaria governed by a major House and overseen by a *vezir*.

Veil: A woven device created with thread magic that can alter a person's facial appearance.

Velocycle: Shortened from velocity cycle. Two-wheel ground vehicle.

Veran: Town. Located in Ashion.

***Vezir*:** Governing official of a *vasilyet*. Typically head of a major House.

Wand: A device used by magicians to focus the aether into magic, usually with the help of clarion crystal.

Warden: A person who is tithed from a country by order of the Poison Accords into the ranks of wardens. They become stateless and neutral. Alchemy is used to make them immune to most poisons and toxins found in the poison fields. Their sole job is to patrol the borders between countries and the ones between the living and dead, as well as map the poison fields for later alchemy intervention to cleanse the land.

Warden's Island, the: Island located in the middle of the Celestine

Lake, where wardens are trained and report back to. Considered a neutral administrative city under the Poison Accords.

Wastelands: Desert. Located in Solaria and rife with revenants and spores.

Xaxis: Star god. Also known as the Midnight Star, patron god of earth. His constellation is the Bear, and his tattoo is located on his hands and forearms.

Zip gun: A rapid-fire, multibarrel firearm.

Author's Notes

Sometimes roads go off the beaten path and you struggle to get to your final destination. That was definitely the case for me while writing this story. Real life tossed so many hurdles in my way, and while it took many months to overcome them, I did finally reach the end.

All my thanks to Lily Morton, May Archer, Lucy Lennox, and Aimee Nicole Walker, who saw me through all the ups and downs. Leslie Copeland is forever my right-hand overlord. Bear never fails to make my words look pretty on the page.

I would be thrilled and grateful if you would consider reviewing *The Emperor's Bone Palace*. I appreciate all honest reviews, positive or negative. Reviews definitely help my books get seen, so thank you!

Connect with Hailey

Keep up with book news by joining Hailey Turner's newsletter and get several free short stories.

Join the reader group on Facebook: Hailey's Hellions

Follow Hailey on Instagram.

Follow Hailey's author page on Facebook.

Follow Hailey on Facebook.

Follow Hailey on Goodreads.

Follow Hailey on Pinterest.

Follow Hailey on BookBub.

Visit Hailey's website.

Other Works By Hailey Turner

M/M Science Fiction Military Romance:

Captain Jamie Callahan, son of a wealthy senator and socialite mother, is a survivor.
Staff Sergeant Kyle Brannigan, a Special Forces operative, is a man with secrets.
Alpha Team, the Metahuman Defense Force's top-ranked field team, is where the two collide and their lives will never be the same.

Metahuman Files

In the Wreckage
In the Ruins
In the Shadows
In The Blood
In The Requiem
In the Solace

A Metahuman Files: Classified Novella

Out of the Ashes
New Horizons
Fire In The Heart

. . .

M/M Urban Fantasy:

Patrick Collins is a broken mage running from his past.
Jonothon de Vere is a god pack alpha werewolf searching for a home. In a world where magic is real, myths and legends exist, and gods walk the earth, Patrick and Jono are thrown together by the Fates themselves to fight against an enemy that threatens to consume the world. For if the gods fall and demons from every hell rise up, humanity won't stand a chance.

Soulbound

A Ferry of Bones & Gold
All Souls Near & Nigh
A Crown of Iron & Silver
A Vigil in the Mourning
On the Wings of War
An Echo in the Sorrow
A Veiled & Hallowed Eve

Soulbound Universe Standalones

Resurrection Reprise

LGBTQ+ Epic steampunk-inspired fantasy:

Welcome to Maricol, where the land will kill you, kinship turns the gears of war, and burning the dead lest they come back to life is the only way to survive.

Infernal War Saga
The Prince's Poisoned Vow
The Emperor's Bone Palace

Infernal War Saga Novella
An Emporium of Hearts

Contemporary gay romance

Short stories previously published in the Heart2Heart Charity Anthologies.

From the Heart: A Short Story Collection

Audible

All of Hailey Turner's books are available in audiobooks. Visit Audible to discover your next favorite listen.

Hailey Turner Audiobooks

Thanks for reading!

Ingram Content Group UK Ltd.
Milton Keynes UK
UKHW040626110423
419970UK00001B/3